WE'RE FROM THE GOVERNMENT—
WE'RE HERE TO HELP . . .

The senior sergeant and three other highway patrolmen herded the rest of the party toward the bus. Lor Lu confronted the leader. "Sergeant, I am Lor Lu, Mr. Aran's assistant. In his absence I'm responsible for these people. What exactly is this all about?"

"Mr. Lu, martial law has been declared in Arkansas. You folks are in danger of your lives, and Governor Cook isn't about to let Mr. Aran get killed here. Or any of the rest of you folks. Last night, a whole busload of folks were in another Celebrity Tours bus, on the I-40 bridge out of Memphis. Seems likely someone mistook it for yours. Slammed a bunch of rockets into it. Killed everyone on board. So you're under protective custody and one of my men is going to drive. He knows where we're going, and there's no need for any of you to worry."

Good God! Lee thought, *A whole busload killed!* She wondered if the police had anything to do with it.

The sergeant took a seat halfway back in the bus, and sent the remaining two of his men farther to the rear. The trooper driver seemed familiar with buses. After warming it up briefly, he drove from the lot, preceded by a patrol car and followed by others.

The bus TV hadn't been turned back on, so Duke Cochran booted up his laptop. *Protective custody*, he said to himself. *And the pope is Presbyterian.* He wondered where they were taking Dove, and if they'd be stupid enough to do anything to him. Jail him perhaps.

His thoughts were interrupted by a patrolman collecting laptops and cell phones.

Without them, Cochran felt naked.

THE
SECOND COMING

JOHN DALMAS

THE SECOND COMING

This is a work of fiction. All the characters and events por-
trayed in this book are fictional, and any resemblance to real
people or incidents is purely coincidental.

Copyright © 2004 by John Dalmas

A Baen Books Original

Baen Publishing Enterprises
P.O. Box 1403
Riverdale, NY 10471
www.baen.com

ISBN-13: 978-1-4165-0903-5
ISBN-10: 1-4165-0903-8

Cover art by Larry Elmore

First paperback printing, September 2005

Library of Congress Cataloging-in-Publication Number
2004000542

Distributed by Simon & Schuster
1230 Avenue of the Americas
New York, NY 10020

Production & design by Windhaven Press (www.windhaven.com)
Printed in the United States of America

dedicated to

Huston Smith
and
Chelsea Quinn Yarbro

Prolog

THE APARTMENT WAS SMALL, its furnishings expensive and conservative. As usual, its occupant ate alone—a TV supper in a plastic tray. Meat, mashed potatoes, mixed vegetables and a brownie, the portions meager for so tall a man, and there weren't even salt and pepper shakers on the table. His appearance had been likened to Lincoln's, before Lincoln grew the beard, but the resemblance was strictly skeletal. His mouth was nearly lipless, his hair disciplined and straight. Creases bracketed his mouth from nose to chin, curving sourly at the bottom, reflecting the absence of humor.

Just now he was eating to television, to the Authors Channel, waiting for a scheduled interview. An unauthorized biography of General Rodney Beauchamp had been published. Beauchamp had reoriented and reorganized the army for twenty-first-century needs, then been forced to retire for publicly criticizing foreign policy. The diner knew the general, and approved of him.

Meanwhile the coverage was for a book on someone of whom the diner did not approve at all. While he watched, his fork transferred small bites of food to his mouth. He chewed them thoroughly, as he'd been taught when a child.

On the screen, two men sat half facing each other, half facing the camera. "I've read a number of Ngunda Aran's columns," the host said, "and heard him lecture on TV. I find his viewpoints interesting."

"Actually," the author said, "I find them interesting too, but you need to consider them in context. Before Ngunda the writer and lecturer, there was Ngunda the philanthropist, whose good works brought him broad notoriety. Now he uses that base, that foundation of respect, as a public platform from which to expound his beliefs—if that's what they actually are."

The host interrupted. "But most columnists expound on their beliefs. And he hasn't proposed crimes, hasn't recommended civil disobedience, hasn't even been discourteous. What, exactly, is your complaint with him?"

"First let me point out that the bonds holding society together are stretched thin today, and fraying. And the ideas he expounds are foreign to the American social psyche. They add seriously to the strain. People admire him or they hate him, and polarization is something we don't need more of.

"Meanwhile, his Millennium Foundation has become a public relations organization for his self-image and metaphysical philosophy . . ."

The tall man pressed the mute switch. *Idiot,* he thought grimacing. *He's got something worthwhile to say, and dresses it in liberal-humanist babble.* His fork pierced a cut bean, some peas, and a fragment of diced carrot, raising them to his thin lips as the two men mouthed soundlessly on the screen. *Ngunda Aran.* Again he grimaced. *Satan smiling, garbed in good works.*

He would, he decided, explore some possibilities.

PART ONE

A TIME OF DISORDERS

1

> .... Ngunda Elija Aran is one of the more dangerous men in the world. He is far more dangerous than E. David Hilliard was, not because he appears more plausible—he doesn't—but because he has emerged in a much more dangerous time, when an increasingly large part of the population is susceptible to such fraud.
>
> Charles Heilemann, D.Sc.
> Emeritus Professor of Physics
> California State University, Northridge
> Letters page, *San Francisco Chronicle*

IT EVEN BEGAN ODDLY, the door chimes startling Lee, making her jump. Ben was downstairs doing laundry, so she put aside the *Times* business section, went to the door, and after a moment's hesitation, opened it.

A brown, brightly cheerful face confronted her, topping a small wiry body wearing jeans and a black T-shirt. The T-shirt was decorated with a running, space-suited figure pursued by a unicorn.

White teeth flashed. "Mrs. Shoreff, I've come to talk with you and Ben. My name is Lor Lu." The figure bowed, palms pressed together in front of him. "Holy man extraordinary," he added, eyes laughing. When she simply stared, he spoke again. "He's in the basement, doing laundry. Would you get him please?"

The strange introduction had deranged her usual poise. "Is—he expecting you?"

"No. We met in the WebWorld."

"Come in," she said uncertainly. "I'll get him."

Turning, she strode through the house, disturbed at her state of mind. It occurred to her she hadn't asked what he wanted to talk to them about. *He might,* she thought, *be a salesman. Or a collection agent!* The thought alarmed her.

At the head of the basement stairs, she closed the door behind her and called down. "Ben?"

"Yes?"

"There's someone to see you. Us."

Ben Shoreff came out of the laundry room, sleeves rolled to the elbows, forearms thick with dark curly hair. "Did he say who he is?"

Lee frowned. It was unlike her not to remember; she was good with names. "Lou someone." She lowered her voice. "And, Ben, he knew where you were: downstairs doing laundry!"

Frowning, Ben started up, rolling his sleeves down as he came. At the top he paused to button them. His attention was on who the visitor might be, rather than on Lee's odd comment. Lou was a common enough name; he must, he thought, know someone named Lou. Together they went to the living room, where he found an Asian he didn't recall seeing before. *Asian-American*, he corrected. *He stands like an American, holds himself like one*.

"I'm Ben Shoreff," Ben said. "Have we met?"

"On the WebWorld. I'm Lor Lu. From Millennium. We chatted."

Ben frowned, not recalling. "And you came here to . . . ?"

The grin reappeared. "I had asked to speak with Mrs. Shoreff. I'd read her business posting." He paused to grin at Lee, then turned back to Ben. "She wasn't at home, but you seemed interesting, so I asked you some questions. We need to expand our accounting office, and I like your skills and experience."

The Asian paused, turning again to Lee. "But it was your business posting I was actually following up on. I'd contacted the references you'd posted, and liked what they said about you."

Lee Shoreff stared, on the edge of being horrified, but interested in spite of herself. *From Millennium! A cult!* She had an automatic fear of cults, but economic depression had struck worldwide, and her young consulting business was clinically dead. Ben had posted résumés of his own, but meanwhile they were seriously in debt, and the mortgage company had sent a foreclosure notice.

"What—would I be expected to do?" she asked.

"Millennium is expanding rapidly, and our operations chart just sort of grew; we need something a lot better. We've tried adapting generic OCs, but they haven't been adequate, so Dove—that's what we call Ngunda—said to get someone who can come in and do the job right. I showed him your posting and the comments I'd gotten, and he told me to hire you."

Lee licked her lips. *What in the world did a cult need an operations chart for? And Millennium was out west somewhere: Oregon or Colorado. Why hadn't they talked to her by Web, instead of sending someone all the way across the country?*

"I suppose I can handle that," she heard herself saying. "The principles apply to anything. If you saw my posting, you know my fees. I'll give you a questionnaire, so you'll know what information to fax."

Lor Lu shook his head. "That's not how we want it done. We want you on site. Our operations and services are unlike any you've had experience with, and you'll need to be personally familiar with them to handle the job. Get to know the people."

She cast a quick glance at Ben. She was, she realized, afraid of this job. "I—how long on site? I have a husband and two school-age daughters."

Lor Lu gestured. "No problem. Bring them. We'll provide a three-bedroom house, furnished, and we have a state-licensed school on the premises. Our employees consider the school better than average, and you can take your meals in our dining room if you'd like. The cost is nominal." He laughed. "Cheaper than buying groceries, and the kitchen staff takes care of the cooking and cleanup."

Inwardly Lee squirmed, feeling somehow trapped, vaguely desperate. "But—how long?"

"I can write the contract for two months, with extensions as necessary. And we pay transportation, of course, including freight for belongings up to fifteen hundred pounds."

"Two months? I'm sure it won't take that long. One at most."

"Two months. We'll want you there to debug it, and groove our people in on it. And we are, after all, an international operation, so there will be some travel. Two months, with extensions as necessary. Then, if you like us and we like you, we may want your expertise on other things.

"Your rates are reasonable enough for short-term jobs of the sort you usually do, but because of the length of the contract, we'll want to pay you by the month. We were thinking in terms of sixty-five hundred dollars, with credit transfers on the fifteenth and thirtieth."

He stopped, arms folded now, but the grin was still there. Again she looked at Ben, interested in spite of herself. At Mertens, Loftus, and Hurst, her salary had reached $7,500 a month, but in the fourteen months since she'd quit, she hadn't come close to that. She'd topped $3,000 only three times. In the month previous she'd grossed just $375, and that by cutting her rate drastically. She was good at what she did, the best, but in times like these, businesses weren't hiring consultants or anyone else. And effective promotion would cost more than she could borrow. Especially now, with their credit rating down the drain.

Ben spoke then, his tone diffident, but the words

to the point. "You said you were interested in hiring me, too. What would I be doing?"

"You'll be in our accounting office, helping set up procedures that will work efficiently in your wife's new system."

Ben gestured. "Have a seat, Mr. Lu."

They sat. *My God,* Lee thought, *I never asked him to sit down! He's offering us jobs, and I never asked him to sit down!*

"What would my job pay?" Ben asked.

"It would start at thirty-five hundred dollars."

"On the basis of my posting and a WebWorld chat?"

"I did other research. On both of you." The Asian gestured casually. "And of course there are your auras."

Our auras?! Lee thought. *Our auras?!*

Ben glanced at his wife, then turned to Lor Lu again. "How soon do you need a commitment?"

"My plane leaves tomorrow morning at 8:57."

"When would we have to be there?"

"There's a degree of urgency. We need a new OC in place as soon as reasonably possible. We want both of you there by the first of next month."

"Have you got a number we could call today? This evening? My wife and I need to talk about this."

The man was grinning again. *Like a cat with a mouse under its paw,* Lee thought. "I'm at the Veldrome Hotel, at the airport. The number is 614-555-7100, Room 312." He spelled his name for them. "Call me any time before eleven."

He left copies of Millennium's standard employment contract for them to read, then shook their hands and left. It seemed to Lee his grip had some sort of electrical charge.

She stared after him. What had he said when he'd introduced himself to her? *Holy man extraordinary.* Good God! And he'd known that Ben was in the basement doing laundry.

"Ben," she said, "I don't want to go out there."

He looked at her. "Why not?"

"Honey, it's a cult! And you know what happened to Laura."

He did know. Laura had suicided. Her favorite cousin. "That was the Church of Universal Truth," he said, "not Millennium."

"They're both cults."

"And because the Truthees screwed some people over, broke up some families, Millennium is dangerous?"

Her lips thinned. "And I'm afraid of that man!"

"Of Lor Lu? Why?"

"He's—strange!"

Ben smiled. "Strange is what your parents call me. Why they don't like me. That and because nominally my mother's Catholic and my father's a Jew. With a touch of Falasha at that, though they don't know it. But you married me."

"And he knew you were in the basement! Doing laundry!"

Ben nodded, a completely inadequate response.

"And Ngunda Aran is a *guru,*" she went on. "He writes a syndicated new age column. You read it every day."

"Sweetheart, the term for people who write columns

is *columnist*, not *guru*. And I don't read it every day. He only does two a week."

"That's beside the point! He *is* a guru! And this Lor Lu introduced himself to me as a 'holy man extraordinary'! Ye gods, Ben! And he knew you were in the basement . . ."

"Doing laundry. Right."

"How could he have known that?"

He laughed. "Maybe it's the kind of thing holy men know."

"Dammit, Ben, it's not funny!"

He nodded. "You're right, it's not. It's about you making sixty-five hundred, and me another thirty-five hundred, which total ten thousand. A month. With the possibility of employment that could last us through the depression."

"He wants us to move out west!"

"We have to move at the end of the month anyway. We're being evicted, remember? Without enough money to move our stuff or store it. And you've already told me you couldn't stand to move in with your folks. Especially with the girls."

Lee cringed at the thought of Becca and Raquel exposed to the judgements and sarcasms of her parents. "But—there's a mob of hippies there, probably smoking dope and screwing one another all over the place."

"I'm sure we won't have to join in."

She glared.

"He didn't invite them, he doesn't cater to them. And their camp is miles from Millennium headquarters. The ranch is a big place." He shifted the conversation. "You've read about *Iiúoo*, the Ladder. It was featured in the Sunday *Times* a few years ago. Among other places."

She did remember, vaguely. Ladder was a program providing free counseling on Indian reservations, and supposedly had had impressive success. She'd never put much stock in psychological counseling, or in free anything.

"Then you know who started it," he said.

"Ngunda Aran. Your goo-roo." She exaggerated the syllables.

"He's not my guru, sweetheart," Ben answered gently. "I simply read his columns. He's a licensed psychotherapist who had a highly successful clinical practice and did pro bono Life Healing in the Colorado penitentiary. Then he spent two summers on the Crow Reservation in Montana, dealing with alcoholism, drugs, and futility."

Her husband, she thought, was sounding like a Millennium flack. "What's that got to do with hippies flocking to him?" she asked.

"I suspect they're like a lot of other people; they've lost faith in a system that screws over certain groups and then punishes them for not fitting in. But the hippies' main interest isn't therapy. They're looking for a spiritual fix, and they like what he says in his columns and talks."

For a minute she didn't say anything. She was thinking of $10,000 a month. Finally she gazed thoughtfully at her husband. "Is that why you're attracted to him? Because you're looking for a spiritual fix?"

"I'm attracted to Ngunda because he's been effective. And because to me he makes sense." He paused. "Let me ask a question now. It's my turn."

She nodded.

"How much faith do you have in the system?"

She examined the question. "It's never worked terribly well. Socioeconomic systems are composed of human beings, and we know what they're like."

"What are they like?"

"Let's say we're—imperfect. Irrational and perverse, not to mention greedy and dishonest." She paused. "Not everyone, but enough. What was your original question again?"

"Have you lost faith in the system? Do you think it will get us out of the current depression? Heal the pessimism? Reverse the fifteen percent unemployment? Workers getting by on twenty-hour workweeks so executives and stockholders can make bigger profits by avoiding worker benefits? Professionals working twelve-hour days to keep their jobs, like you did? The anger and cynicism? The violence and vandalism? Mortar shells dropping on gated enclaves for the wealthy?"

Lee had wilted at his listing, especially the mortar attacks. "I'm—not sure," she answered softly. "I really hope it can. Times have been bad before and the country's come out of it."

Ben thought of saying that people often survived a first major heart attack, sometimes a second, even a third. But if they kept having them . . . Instead he put an arm around her. "I hope it can too. But people will have to change in the process. More greed and more government won't work." He smiled, barely. "End of sermon."

Lee's sigh was gusty. "What'll we tell—what's his name again?"

"Lor Lu. How about yes?"

She looked at her husband. At five-feet-eight, she was fairly tall for a woman, but he was considerably taller. And looked Levantine: swarthy and hairy. Not a handsome, exotic-looking Levantine, but virile. Sexy in spite of his calm, his flexible disposition, his mild good nature. It was his sexiness that had first attracted her. Then she found they could actually talk out their disagreements without either of them getting angry the way she and her first husband, Mark, had. She hated it when she got shrill.

Sighing again, she nodded. "Okay, I'll go." She made a face at him. "If you promise not to sit around on a pillow with your feet in your lap, saying Ommmm."

He laughed. "I promise, absolutely." Then turning, he drew her to him, kissing her.

Her response was distracted. She was worried about her daughters now. She'd check the WebWorld. See what she could learn about the Millennium school that what's-his-name had mentioned. Lor Lu. Maybe they could register them in a private school, in some town near the Millennium ranch.

2

> Physicists recognize four basic forces in
> the physical universe: the strong force, the
> electromagnetic force, the weak force, and
> gravity. Actually those are derivative, not basic.
> The basic force is love, and the principal
> secondary force is fear.
>
> From *The Collected Public*
> *Lectures of Ngunda Aran*

THE TRIP HAD NOT begun well. There was an
ongoing gun battle at Kennedy Airport between a Port
of New York security force and militants of some sort.
Thus their commuter flight from Bridgeport had been
diverted all the way to Dulles, the air traffic overload
at LaGuardia and Newark being extreme. At Dulles

they'd lucked out. Their tickets were business class, so they'd gotten on the second flight to Denver, a little more than two hours later than their scheduled flight from Kennedy.

On the Denver flight, and the commuter flight to Pueblo, there'd been no complications. American Airlines had rearranged their reservations, and informed the charter plane that would take them from Pueblo to Henrys Hat.

Henrys Hat. A strange name for a town, Lee told herself.

She stared. In all her thirty-six years, Lee Shoreff had never been west of the Mississippi. And while she'd seen mountains—the Adirondacks, Greens and Catskills—she'd never seen anything remotely like the chain of snow peaks some twenty miles ahead. They stretched as far north and south as she could see from the small plane, their upper slopes white with late-September snow.

"Ben!" she murmured. "They're beautiful! I wonder how high they are."

It was Lor Lu who answered, looking back from his seat beside the pilot. "In that range, the Sangre de Cristo, there are probably ten peaks higher than fourteen thousand feet. See those three over there?" He pointed southwestward. "The tallest is Blanca Peak, the highest in the range."

"Will we fly over them?"

"No, we're almost to Henrys Hat."

Scanning she asked, "Where?"

"See that creek ahead to our right? Where the trees are? That's Henrys Creek. Henrys Hat is the village, those buildings you can see up ahead, where the road crosses the creek."

She stared. "That's—it?" She was surprised that so small a place would have a name. As they approached, she decided it might have a dozen houses, all of frame construction, all weatherbeaten. Plus what she recognized as garages, barns and sheds. And what had to be a store, with a low porch and fuel pumps in front, and a flagpole and flag at one corner. There was nothing resembling a school. A half mile past it was a small airfield, with two parked planes and a large metal machine shed. The only thing she found aesthetic about any of it was the cottonwoods along the creek, their leaves golden, with dark spires of spruce scattered among them.

The eight-place Beechcraft landed smoothly on the grass runway, and they disembarked. She, Ben, and the two girls stood by while Lor Lu settled things with the pilot, whose belt computer first scanned Lor Lu's plastic, then his thumb print. An ungainly looking vehicle had been waiting for them, its front half an eight-seat carryall, its rear a long pickup bed. Now it rolled to the plane, and a lanky man got out. He began to transfer their luggage, Ben helping him. Each piece, before loading, he put in a large plastic yardbag, which he then tied. When Lor Lu finished with the pilot, he joined them.

"Hello, Bar Stool," he said, "how's the Mescalero?"

"If it was flyin', I wouldn't have come in the eight-pack." He gestured at the dust-coated vehicle, which had four doors, and bench seats. *Bar Stool,* Lee thought, *looked sixty or so, his hair white, his face seamed. But he seemed strong and agile*. He fit Lee's concept of a cowboy.

Lor Lu turned to his wards. "Bar Stool," he said gesturing, "meet Ben and Lee and Becca and Raquel."

"Glad to know you," said Bar Stool.

They shook hands with him, the girls included. Bar Stool's was large and callused.

"Do you, ah, have another name besides Bar Stool?" Lee asked.

"Yep." Bar Stool opened one of the back doors. "If you folks will climb aboard, we'll get to the Ranch in time, you can shower down and settle in before supper."

They boarded, dust flying as they slammed the doors. Then Bar Stool took off with as much of a jackrabbit start as the eight-pack provided, the truck bouncing along the rough road, trailing a plume of tawny dust. He drove too fast for the conditions, it seemed to Lee, fifty miles an hour on ill-graded gravel, slowing and speeding according to the bends, curves, and holes. "How far is it?" she asked—loudly; the ride was noisy.

"Twelve miles."

She'd already given up on the girls attending a private school. There wasn't even a public school in Henrys Hat.

"Mr. Bar Stool," Becca asked, "how did you get your name?"

Bar Stool looked at her via the rearview mirror. "Ask Muong Soui Louie here." He thumbed toward Lor Lu beside him. "He tells it better than me." Lor Lu glanced back, grinning. "It was at the Raven hootch at Long Tieng," he said. "The Ravens were a secret

U.S. operation. Not secret from the Pathet Lao or the North Vietnamese. Secret from America. And the hootch was the house we lived in, with a cage outside, and two Himalayan black bears we fed beer to. We had a little club nearby, where we drank, and the club had bar stools. Bar Stool got his name because he got so attached to one of the stools, sometimes when he left he'd take it with him."

Becca looked uncertainly at Lor Lu, getting no notion at all of what he'd been describing. Neither did her mother—no clear notion. It was Lee who spoke. Cautiously. "Where was that?"

"Laos. Long Tieng was the center of Hmong resistance to the Pathet Lao. The Hmong were a mountain people, and the Pathet Lao were communists."

"Then this must have been . . ."

"Bar Stool was there from '69 to '72."

Lee stared at the small Asian. The truck hit an exposed culvert and jounced, hard, her seat harness holding her in place. "Was that—in the Vietnam War?" she asked.

"In a manner of speaking. Peripherally."

She stared. He'd said "we" as if he'd been there. And the Vietnam War had ended—what? Forty years ago? Yet Lor Lu couldn't be much over thirty, if that.

The strangeness killed the conversation while stimulating Lee's fears. She sat, unable to think coherently, as if some small but dangerous beast crouched in ambush, watching for weakness. Grassy hills flowed past, with occasional small groups of grazing cattle. The grass wasn't even green; it was dead. Dun-colored. To the west the foothills rose higher, patches of dark pine marking them, coalescing into distant forest. After twenty minutes or so she saw a large camp ahead, with tents of different kinds. Hippies! Tents enough for a hundred people or more, even now at the beginning of October, with cold weather coming. Here and there were structures she assumed were sanitation facilities—latrines perhaps, and bathhouses. On a nearby knoll stood a large water tank.

And a barbed wire fence, with a sign reading CHILDREN AT PLAY, SPEED LIMIT 15. Bar Stool had slowed way down. A uniformed entry guard waved them through a gate without stopping them. *Why barbed wire?* Lee wondered. *And the guard wore a pistol! Good God!*

The truck tires had thrummed momentarily as they passed through, a sound they'd heard several times since leaving Henrys Hat.

"Mr. Bar Stool, what was that sound?" Raquel asked.

"That was a cattle guard, honey. Made out of railroad rails. Cows won't cross them; afraid they'd get their feet caught. Which they would. It's all range land around here. Pasture. That's why the place is fenced: to keep the cattle out."

The adults Lee saw in the camp stood or squatted or sat in openings among the tents. Children ran and played. They should, she told herself, be in school somewhere.

Then the camp was behind them. Bar Stool's mundane comments had relieved and emboldened Lee. "I noticed the guard had a gun," she said.

"Yep. There's been murder threats. On Dove. Ngunda."

She supposed there had been. Another worry. There were crazies running around.

A knoll ahead had a watchtower on top, like those at prisons. The road curled around it, and a mile or so ahead she could see—not exactly a town, but with a lot more buildings than Henrys Hat, if with less character. As they neared it, she began to see details. The central and largest building was long and three-storied, of dark brick. An office building, she decided, its ridged tile roof bright red in the autumn sunlight. Near it on one side were several long, two-story frame buildings suggesting small motels or dormitories. Their siding appeared to be one of the new synthetics, cream colored. Their roofs were bright red, green, or blue. The rest, fifty or more, seemed to be small ranch-style homes. They looked much alike, but again with red, green, or blue roofs. Their sidings were various pastels or white. Everything was landscaped, the trees small. Two or three hundred yards beyond the "village" were several large machine sheds.

The last half mile was blacktopped, and the village streets had traffic stripes. Bar Stool pulled up before one of the houses. "This is it," he said. "You're home. The water should be hot by now, so you can shower if you want." He paused. "Sorry for all the dust. Ordinarily I'd have flown you here in the Mescalero."

Lor Lu got out and went around to the rear of the ungainly vehicle, while Ben held the door for Lee and the girls. Becca popped out quickly, Raquel close behind. Lee got out almost reluctantly, as if not wanting to see what the house was like inside. Ben and Lor Lu began taking luggage out of the yardbags, which were gray with dust. Bar Stool led Lee and the girls onto the front porch, unlocked and opened the door, and handed the key ring to Lee.

"There's four keys," he said, "all the same. Far as I know, no one here locks their doors, but I suppose some do at first. Force of habit."

Then he turned back to the eight-pack to help carry up the luggage. Lee went inside more slowly than her curious daughters, and scanned the living room. Even with all the basic furniture, the place felt empty. Foreign. There was no dining room; the living room had an extendable drop-leaf table. The kitchen was well equipped, and had not only a breakfast nook, but a pantry and freezer. *It should have,* she told herself grimly, *as far as it is to the nearest supermarket.* Henrys Hat barely had a general store.

She'd never been good with maps, but she'd put a highway map of Colorado in her shoulder bag. Before looking through the rest of the house, she took it out and spread it on the dining table. Ben had drawn a thick red circle around Henrys Hat, whose population wasn't listed. The next nearest town was Lauenbruck, population 567, fifteen miles the other side of Henrys Hat. Even Lauenbruck wouldn't have a mall, she told herself, and wondered how people lived there. The school couldn't be much either, and it was twenty-seven miles away.

Looking for the basement stairway, she found instead a small utility room with washer, dryer, and water heater. There was no basement, she realized.

She was aware now that Ben was behind her. "Not bad, eh?" he said. "It's even been dusted."

Not bad? she thought. She found a three-quarter bath—with only a single washbowl. Something was building inside her, something between dismay and anger. Ben was leading now. They peered into one of the three bedrooms, not very big, with two narrow beds. *The girls',* she wondered, *or are we supposed to sleep separately?* A second bedroom was even smaller, and unfurnished. She wondered what possible good it could be without furniture. Then, from behind her, Ben said, "Ah! Our computer room!"

Their own bedroom was somewhat larger, with a queen-sized bed. It had two doors besides the hall door: one a sliding door to a small patio; the other was to another three-quarter bath, this one with double washbowls, in a vanity with a false marble top.

"Tell me what you're thinking," Ben murmured.

She answered without turning. "I'm thinking . . . I'm thinking it's for just a couple of months. Maybe three. At ten thou a month for the two of us. Then we can leave. Go home."

He smiled, realizing she wasn't up to being grinned at. "We don't have a home, sweetheart. Remember? We got foreclosed on. Sold the furniture and appliances to pay on our debts."

She nodded. "I miss our things," she said stiffly. "The things we shipped."

"They'll be here in a few days."

"I know." She gathered herself, but when she spoke, there was no fire in it. "We don't have a thing in the house to eat. Or a car. How will we get to a store? We should have driven here."

"We talked about that." His words still were soft. "By road it's more than thirty miles to Walsenburg, population 3,100, and part of the road is unpaved. Pueblo's twice as far, population 78,000, a steel mill town. And we're higher here than Henrys Hat, which is 7,500 feet above sea level, so there'll probably be quite a bit of snow, and it probably won't melt very fast. So we decided . . ."

"Right." She nodded curtly. "Where are the girls?"

"In their room, probably. Or outdoors."

She turned to him and put her hands on his shoulders, her eyes on his. "Ben, this isn't easy for me. I'll try not to take it out on you, but be patient with me. Okay?"

He smiled softly. "Sure."

She took a deep breath and let it out slowly. "This isn't really that bad," she said. "This house I mean. I just wish Millennium wasn't a cult. And there's the school to worry about . . ."

The doorbell rang, and Ben strode from the room, Lee following. While he headed for the front door, she went into the kitchen, where she could hear the girls' voices. "Mom," Becca said, "there's a little building in the backyard, probably to store stuff in. But it's empty, and we don't have anything to store in it, so Raquel and I want to fix it up for a playhouse. And there's a girl's bike on the patio next door, so we'll have someone to play with! Do you know when our bikes will get here?"

"Not exactly. In a few days."

"Lee?" It was Ben, looking in from the living room. "There's a man here. He'd like to take us to meet Ngunda."

"Now?"

He nodded. "If we're ready. Or we can make it later."

I need to shower, she thought, *and do something with my hair. Maybe change . . . Oh to hell with it!* "All right. Let's meet him." *If he doesn't like the way we look, let him fire us.*

The man in their living room was young, perhaps thirty she thought. And personable, his smile convincing. She didn't trust him a bit. "Mrs. Shoreff," he said, "I'm Larry Rocco. Ngunda would like to meet you two today. He'll be leaving on tour in the morning."

Lee nodded curtly. "Fine," she said brusquely. After instructing the girls not to leave the house, she and Ben left with Rocco. As they stepped off the porch, Rocco gestured with his right hand. "I'm your neighbor," he said, "three houses down."

There was no car in front; they were expected to walk. *Of course,* she realized. *Everything here is so close. Everything but a town, a real town.*

As they walked, she noticed the landscaping was quite good. Give the trees and shrubs a few more years to grow . . . There were even sidewalks and curbs. Whoever bankrolled Millennium had deep pockets, and she wondered about that, not for the first time. It occurred to her to ask where the school was. "Actually I'm really more interested in seeing the school than in meeting Mr. Aran just now."

"Why don't we go there after you've met him. I'm sure he won't keep you long. We're quite proud of our school, incidentally. Six teachers and six aides for—the last I heard, it was ninety-eight kids. Their coursework and visual aids come via computer link. What our people do, mainly, is guide and elaborate. Expand on the coursework, and handle any problems the children might have with it."

The school might, she thought, *be rather good in some respects*. She'd be surprised, though, if there weren't some cultist ideas thrown in. *I'll deal with that when we come to it*, she told herself. *If need be, we can send them to boarding school. Surely there's a decent one in Pueblo.*

Like their house, the brick administration building was utilitarian. Even Ngunda's office, on the third floor, was utilitarian, as was his desk. At least he wasn't into extravagant display. Three file cabinets seemed excessive though, given his cutting-edge computer. She'd take care of that, she told herself, when she reorganized their operations. Smiling, Ngunda had stood as they entered. He was taller than Ben, rather lanky and quite dark. She found herself surprised at his appearance. She'd seen him on TV, and pictures of him on Millennium's web site, and in magazines. But the image she'd carried with her had been influenced by editorial cartoonists.

She'd heard he had charisma. Now she felt it, before he'd even spoken. She'd read up on him since they'd contracted to come here. He was 43 years old and an only child, born in Malawi of an African mother. His father was a New Zealander—Maori, Irish, and English.

"Dove," their guide said, "I'd like you to meet Ben and Lee Shoreff."

Ngunda grinned, a flash of white teeth. "It's a pleasure." His deep, resonant voice reminded her of the actor, James Earl Jones, in his prime. "Lor Lu tells me you're just what we need here."

"I trust we won't disappoint him," Lee answered. "Or you." She was in her professional persona now, confident, businesslike.

"And you've brought two daughters. How old are they?"

"Rebecca is eleven and Raquel is nine. They love the idea of a ranch. They've imagined riding horseback here."

"Ah! The possibility has been raised before. Perhaps it's time to lease some horses. Larry, talk to Bar Stool about it. He'll know what the possibilities are, and what's necessary." He turned back to Lee and Ben. "Tomorrow noon I'd like you both to check in at reception. Lor Lu will have you introduced to our organization, and to your jobs. If that is not too soon?"

"That will be fine. It gives us time to take the girls to school and meet their teachers."

"Good. Will noon be all right with you, too, Mr. Shoreff?"

"Me? Yes. That will be fine."

Color rose in Lee's cheeks. She'd ignored Ben, as if he hadn't been there. She'd done that before, and hated herself for it. It was the sort of thing husbands did to wives, a thing that had always annoyed her.

"Well then," Ngunda said, "I hope you two will have supper with me."

"I'm afraid I'll need to press some things first," Lee answered, "and my iron and ironing board are still on their way from Connecticut."

"Ah! As far as I'm concerned, you look fine as you are. We're quite informal here. Most people wear jeans at work. We'll eat in an alcove off the staff dining room. The menu is the same for everyone. Do you think your daughters would care to eat with us?"

He raised an eyebrow at Rocco, who grinned and

turned to the Shoreffs. "They can eat at our table if they'd like," he said. "My girls are eight and six. Or someone with older kids may invite them to theirs when they see them."

It seemed workable to Lee, and Ben agreed, so they thanked Ngunda and left. She'd decided tomorrow would be soon enough to visit the school, so Rocco walked them home. The front door was open, and from the front walk, Lee could hear the voices of more than their two girls inside. They found two others with them: Lori and Kari Klein, ten-year-old twins. Minutes later the twins' mother stopped by, identifying herself as the welcome lady. Before she left, she'd invited Becca and Raquel to eat at the Kleins' table that evening.

From Susan Klein, who was a teacher, they also learned that school started at 9 A.M. Lee should bring the girls at 8:30, to register and get a quick tour. Registration would take about ten minutes.

There was also a storage building with surplus furniture and appliances, and a small commissary with a limited selection of basic household supplies, and groceries. The commissary had the use of the Ranch's helicopter, and twice a week made a shopping run for residents, to City Market in Walsenburg. It was about thirty miles by air.

Susan also told them the name "Ranch" didn't apply to the "village," strictly speaking. A newsman had learned that in Malawi, Ngunda meant "dove," so he'd dubbed this place "the Dove Cote" before it had even been moved into. That was quickly shortened to "the Cote," and "the Ranch" came to mean the entire, sixteen-square-mile property.

After Susan Klein had left, it occurred to Lee she might adjust to this place pretty decently. The day had gone well, and no one had seemed at all like a fanatic. If only the school was okay. Susan Klein's personality—pleasant and intelligent—had been reassuring. *Cross your fingers, Lee,* she said inwardly.

Supper with Dove also went well. The food was rather simple, mostly low fat, and well prepared. And instead of talking religion or philosophy, the great guru had talked about the school, about the Rockies' late season skid that had lost them a place in the National League playoffs, and about the Broncos' rookie quarterback, their first-round draft pick out of BYU. As far as she could tell, he wasn't putting it on for her benefit. He seemed as knowledgeable and interested as any casual fan might be. Despite his magnetism, though, she couldn't see why so many people made such a big deal of him. In letters to the editor, he'd even been referred to as the new messiah. Ben said Millennium made no such claim, but it wouldn't. Bad PR. Let others make it for them.

Obviously a lot of money had been pumped into Millennium, which meant someone hoped to make big money out of it. Perhaps it was his PR image that drew people. He might be nothing more than a magnetic but amiable puppet, mouthing someone else's scripts. Or the scripts could be his own. Big Money might see him as a resource. Might have moved in on him, providing financing and promotion.

Walking back to the house, Becca and Raquel did most of the talking. Actually, Raquel did seventy percent of it. They "really really liked" the Klein twins.

Their eagerness to start school the next day bemused Lee. When she'd been a girl, the prospect of changing schools had given her an upset stomach.

If cult values and ideas were taught, she wasn't sure she could deal with it.

3

 . . . . Many people accept only physical phenomena as real. To them we are born, live awhile, then die, and with death cease to exist. To them, the prospect of death can be especially frightening. But you are, in fact, an undying soul, and your loved ones are undying souls. Death ends neither your existence nor theirs. Each of us survives as a soul, despite war, murder and plague. We would survive collision with a 5-gigaton asteroid that killed every human body on our planet.

While incarnate on Earth, we are a soul united with a primate, in a very close relationship, and the primate has its own reactions to dangers. Because the body *does* die, and regardless of Church doctrine, is not resurrected. Thus being convinced of

one's soulhood, one's immortality, does not
automatically exempt us from fear.

From *The Collected Public
Lectures of Ngunda Aran*

THE ROOM WAS DARK, except for flickering light
from an aged television. Near one side of the room
stood a stove made of a 35-gallon oil drum standing
horizontally on four legs. Its draft was closed, its
damper nearly so. An occasional muted *pop* sounded
from its interior, and around its door a red line
glowed, thin and dull. To one side lay a small pile
of split pine, on the other a shaggy cattle dog, head
on forepaws. In the weak light, it might easily be
overlooked. Its eyes were not on the screen, but on
two men, seated. Footsteps sounded on the front
porch. The door opened and closed, a brief chill wind
blowing in. There was a smell of barn boots. The two
men did not turn.

"What ya watching?"

The younger of them, large in the darkness, answered
from the sofa. "The son of God."

"Shit!"

"Careful now, Carl," the third man said. "God'll
get ya."

Carl grunted, stepped to the set, and squinted far-
sightedly at the digital display on the satellite tuner.
Then he sat down on an easy chair and watched. Now
and again he cursed. The program had been two-thirds
over when he'd entered. When it finished, he got up
and turned the sound off.

"Goddamn jigaboo!"

The large, younger man grinned. "That's giga*ton*. *Five* gigatons."

"What the hell you talking about?"

"That five-gigaton rock he's going to call down to land on your roof. Drive you clear down to hell if you're not careful."

Carl swore again. "Lute, you listen to that Un-gunda enough, your brain'll rot. It's like smoking dope."

Lute laughed outright. "Like that snoose'll rot out your jaw? When dope comes in a bottle, I may get interested." He got to his feet. "Right now, though, I'm going to freshen up my coffee and listen to you tell me why it's worth my time and somebody's money to kill the guru."

He went to the kitchen. It was lit by a Coleman lamp, despite the generator humming in an add-on behind the house. The firebox in a hybrid wood and propane stove kept the coffee pot hot on the back-burner. Luther Koskela poured from it into a mug, and sat down at the table. His uncles followed, the eldest hunched and limping, and sat down across from him.

"When he's dead," Carl answered, "people won't have to listen to him anymore."

"That's it? Jesus Christ, Carl, it's a hell of a lot cheaper and easier to change the channel."

Carl's voice was implacable. "It's reason enough. The man's an abomination to God. God'll be glad when the sonofabitch is dead."

"Huh! When he's dead, people will declare him the second coming of Christ, and he'll be on television from then on. They'll replay every word he ever said!

Every Sunday! That's what makes someone a messiah. Leave him alive. After a while, people'll get tired of him. Then he'll die out on his own." Lute paused, grinning hugely. "Leave be, Carl, and listen to him. Maybe he'll save your soul."

Carl swore at greater length, this time more angry than surly. Lute laughed. "Well, never let it be said I turned down fifty thousand."

The swearing stopped. Carl stared. *"Fifty thousand?!"*

"A hundred maybe. I'll have to pick my team and pitch it to them. Fifty might not be enough."

"Why goddamn it, that's robbery! I'd rather do it myself!"

Lute snapped his fingers. "Sounds like a winner. Go down there, knock on his door, and when he answers, shoot him. Come on, Carl, get real! This is a job for trained professionals."

The third man spoke now. "Where do you recommend we get that much money?"

"The last time, if I recall the newspaper story, it came from SeaFirst Bank in Spokane."

"That wasn't us. You ought to know that."

"Not you personally, I don't suppose. And then there was that armored car heist down in Denver. A million something."

Carl couldn't restrain himself. "We don't even *know* who did that one! Probably the Mexican Mafia."

Lute laughed again. "And you want to kill him just because some stupid shits say he's the second coming. What makes you so sure there was ever a first coming?"

"Don't talk like that, Lute! You're our nephew. Don't

embarrass your mother's soul. She cringes when you say things like that."

Lute stopped laughing, and the grin disappeared. His eyes gleamed in the lamplight. "When's the last time you were in church?"

"Damn churches don't know a thing. They're all nigger lovers. Either that or they want to tell you what to do."

Again Lute laughed. "That's what really gripes your ass, isn't it, Carl? Ngunda's a nigger, a sharp brainy nigger with lots of money." He paused. "I'm not Aryan, you know."

Carl's answer snapped. "Watch your mouth! Your mother's our big sister!"

"And my dad's a Finn."

"Finns are Aryans!"

"You ever hear Finnish? It's kin to Mongol. Finns are Asiatic."

"I don't give a *shit* about the language! I've *seen* Finns. Used to work in the woods with 'em. Worked with your dad. He was blond, blonder than Anna, and when you were little, you had hair the color of cotton. That's Aryan!"

He paused, waiting for Lute's comeback. When all he got was another grin, he asked, "How come fifty thousand?"

"How many people do you think would like to kill Ngunda Aran?"

"God! There's got to be millions! I know a hundred myself."

"And he's still running around breathing and talking. Why do you suppose that is?" When neither of his uncles replied, Lute answered his own question.

"To him, fifty thousand is nothing. He wipes his ass with hundred-dollar bills. He's living on a big ranch in Colorado, farther out in nowhere than you are, and you can bet your ass he's got protection. High-powered, expensive, professional protection."

He paused for effect. "I'll tell you what. You give me—three thousand ought to cover it—and I'll drive down to Colorado. Go to the Soil Conservation Service and buy the aerial photos for Huerfano County. Then I'll rent a plane and fly over the place. Learn the terrain. There's a squatters' camp full of hippies on the property; I'll go there and see what I can learn. Snoop around in the dark with night binoculars, sketch out a map. If it looks doable, I'll talk to some guys I know. Old buddies from my merc days; best pros you can find. Then come back and talk business. If it doesn't look doable, you're out three big ones, and I've wasted three, four weeks of my time."

He raised the mug and sipped boiled coffee. There was a long silence before Carl spoke again. "Three thousand's a lot of money for no guarantee."

Lute grunted. "You ought to be used to that. You put in a crop every spring without knowing if you'll get diddly out of it. And I drove nine hundred miles from Portland with no guarantee, because you asked me to."

"Shit. Three thousand dollars." This time Carl's voice was pensive. "Well—" He turned to his older brother. "What do you say, Axel?"

It was Lute that Axel spoke to. "You'll have to stay around a day or two. Carl will talk to some folks. Get the three thousand. You can help me with the chores."

Lute's eyes gleamed as he studied his uncles. He wondered what they'd say if they knew who he planned to pitch to. Sarge was bigger than he was, and tougher, maybe even smarter. And black. The grin reappeared, grew. "Sounds good," he said cheerfully. Abruptly his face turned hard. "But be goddamn careful who you talk to about this, and what you tell them, 'cause with that Anti-Terrorism Act, I'll be putting my life on the line."

That touch of reality sobered Carl into silence. He left the kitchen, going to his bedroom early, as usual. He was strong as a grizzly, but because of Axel's damaged back and hip, Carl did all the heavy work. Someone had asked him once if he didn't resent that. He'd answered he'd rather do the heavy work than go through what Axel had, and anyway Axel was his brother.

Axel's back and hip also interfered with sleep, and he spent long hours on his recliner, reading by the light of a Coleman lamp, sipping a little whiskey from time to time to ease the discomfort. Lute sat on the other side of the lamp, also reading. Axel laid his open book facedown on his lap, then took his glasses off and rubbed the bridge of his nose. "D'you still read all the time, like when you were a boy?" he asked.

Lute snorted. "I never read all the time. I spent too much time cutting wood, chopping and heaving out frozen cow shit, and fixing fence. And doing sports. The only way I got through all those books was, I read fast."

"Well maybe you can tell me what the hell a *jiggerton* is. Or is jiggerton like saying whatchamacallit, means whatever you want it to?"

Lute laughed. "You thinking about what Ngunda said?"

"No, I'm just curious."

"It's not *jiggerton*. It's *gigaton*, without any *r*. You got a dictionary?"

Axel gestured. "On the shelf. Next to the Bible."

Lute got it and opened to the *G*s. "*G*—Giga. Here we are. *Giga*—one billion—ten to the ninth power. So a five-gigaton asteroid is a five-billion-ton rock—we're talking a rock that's miles thick—clipping along at maybe twenty or thirty thousand miles an hour. That's *way* faster than a bullet." He returned the dictionary to the shelf. "It'd drive more than this house down to hell," he added. "More than Blaine County or Montana. If it hit here, it'd pulverize North America and wreck the whole damn planet. Like an aught-six soft-point hitting a punkin."

"Is there such a thing? As a five-billion-ton asteroid?"

"You bet. Various of them."

Axel said nothing for a minute, just sat looking at the stove. "You know," he said at last, "the way the world's getting, God might take a notion to do just that. Show us who's boss."

Lute's smile was lopsided. "Five gigatons would wipe us out so quick, it'd be a waste of time. We'd be dead before we knew it hit us." Again he laughed. "There's satellites watch all the big asteroids that might hit us someday. Give us plenty of warning, so we can all convert to Catholic—confess our sins and be saved. Although there's some of us with so many sins, we might run out of time." He laughed again. "Can you imagine the lines of people waiting to confess? And the priests would be all tied up confessing to each other what they did to the altar boys."

Axel shook his head. "Lute, I can't always tell when you're kidding."

"That's all right. Neither can I."

"How old is it they say the Earth is?"

"Four billion years, they say. That's four thousand million."

"Huh! And it's still here. I won't spend much time worrying about it then." Axel put his glasses back on and picked up his book.

Lute watched him for a minute. *Carl and Axel,* he thought, *two old farts so soured on the world, they'd hire someone killed for no more reason than somebody else said he was the messiah.*

He shook his head, both amused and fond, and turned to his own book, failing to wonder about somebody who'd kill someone for them.

4

The questioner asked what the point is of all this living, dying, and being reborn, and the lessons learned in the process. In other words, why, ultimately, was the Earth School created? And why did we choose to matriculate in it? I don't know the answers to those questions. Much about the Tao—God, if you will—is beyond human comprehension.

First Human Forum speech by
Ngunda Aran, at the National Press
Club in Washington, D.C.

ON THEIR FIRST MORNING at the Cote, all four Shoreffs ate breakfast at their own table in the dining hall. Then Ben left to report at the finance office and meet his new boss, while Lee walked to school with her daughters. Susan Klein was Becca's teacher. Lee stayed awhile to observe, and left encouraged. She couldn't dismiss the possibility of cult indoctrination, but at least the classroom was well-equipped, and the people seemed rational and competent.

She'd discovered that her new home had utilitarian tableware and linens, adequate till her own arrived. But while everything seemed clean, she went from school to the commissary, and bought cleaning supplies. The rest of the morning she spent doing laundry and dishes, washing down kitchen surfaces, and writing a list of groceries and supplies for the commissary to pick up for her.

As Lee cleaned already clean shelves, and put things away, she wondered why the Cote was so large. What sort of operation was this that took so many people to operate? Why was it located in the middle of nowhere? And who had paid for it?

All those things, she supposed, would start to clarify during her orientation that afternoon.

The girls arrived home at twelve, and walked with their mother to the dining hall to eat lunch with Ben. Again the food was excellent. The main course was a vegetable-pasta casserole, and fried chicken. There was also sandwich material, salad makings, a limited fruit buffet, cider, and hot water for one's choice of instant hot drinks. After lunch, the girls walked themselves back to school, about which they'd spent much of lunchtime chattering.

Rather than pleasing her, their enthusiasm troubled Lee. If they liked school *that* much, they'd be more susceptible to any cult material they were exposed to.

At one o'clock she reported to the receptionist, who walked her to the office of Anne Whistler, the operations chief. Whistler was a graying, 50-ish woman, four inches shorter and thirty pounds heavier than Lee. "Call me Anne," Whistler said when they were introduced. After buzzing her immediate staff, the woman led Lee to a conference room to meet with them. Each department head had brought not only her current departmental organization chart, but had prepared a detailed flow chart to acquaint Lee with their operations.

"Just getting ready for you has helped," one of them told her. Anne Whistler, in turn, had prepared a master flow chart that pretty much tied all the others together. She described how the situation had developed: as the operation had expanded, things initially done off the cuff came to require differentiation and organization.

Meanwhile, Millennium had continued to expand, and experience had grown. New procedures had evolved and old ones changed. At first the changes had simply been superposed on the original OC, then computerized generic systems had been adapted and tried, but hadn't worked well.

Service delivery, accounting, and quality control were the best-organized areas in the operation.

Lee asked basic questions, starting with what the services were that they delivered. Their answers were concise. They had a good grasp of what they did, and how, which was going to make her job easier than it might have been.

She'd anticipated resentment at her being brought in to change how they did things. In her experience, that had been invariable. Her job was to horn in on people's bailiwicks and make them do things differently than they were used to. It usually ended up with divisions and departments changed, some personnel demoted, moved, or lopped off like deadwood. Resentment was expected. But surprisingly, these people showed none of it.

They would though, in time, she had no doubt. Because she'd have to make a *lot* of changes. She was surprised the organization functioned as well as it did, presumably a result of individual good sense and good will.

Their system of quality control was remarkable, both in the delivery of seemingly sensitive services, and in employee performance. Besides dealing with the usual quality problems, their program undertook to identify and correct personality difficulties, learning difficulties—anything that might cause operation and delivery problems.

Whistler concluded the meeting at 4:30. When the others had returned to their separate offices, she told Lee she was to recommend any changes she felt necessary, regardless of whom they affected. She was not to feel constrained in any way by the status quo. "I'll want to review your progress each Friday," she added. "Meanwhile, feel free to talk with me whenever necessary."

The woman paused, but Lee sensed she wasn't done yet. "It will help," Whistler said, "if you become personally familiar with our services. Some of them, certainly. I suggest the basic Abilities Release series—what we call Life Healing."

Aha! Lee knew a bit about Life Healing: it was the

hook, the beginning of Millennium brainwashing. She never blinked. "I don't know," she said. "I'll talk about it with my husband this evening. But to be honest with you, I probably won't try it. I'm uncomfortable with psychotherapies."

"I understand," Whistler replied.

Lee hoped the woman didn't. She also wondered, as she left Whistler's office, whether this would cause difficulties. She'd discovered she really wanted to do this job. She wanted the money—they needed it—but she also wanted to *do the job*. It looked really interesting. Challenging and interesting.

As she walked home, it occurred to her that Ben was probably somewhere in the admin building, working, and no one had been at home for the girls after school. She should, she told herself, have instructed them about that. So she hurried, but found no one there, and assumed they were playing with new friends. After using the bathroom, she'd go to the Kleins and check. But Ben arrived before she left, and moments later the girls came in.

"Where have you been?" she asked them.

"At school, Mom," Becca answered matter of factly. "Children whose parents both work have to stay. You work on your homework first, and then, if there's time, you can play on the playground or in the gym, or read if you want. Some of the other kids stay too, because there are teachers to help if you need it."

Then both girls sat with their parents in the breakfast nook, describing their afternoon and their classes, and talking about new friends, till it was time to go to the dining hall.

That evening the commissary truck came by and delivered Lee's order. When she'd put it away, she sat down by herself in the nook, to relax, and review her day over a cup of tea. She felt good about it, stimulated, unworried about Whistler's suggestion. And the bill the commissary had given her, for her order from Walsenburg, hadn't been as steep as she'd anticipated. But most especially, the girls had really liked their new school, and apparently there'd been no breath of cultism there. Perhaps there was a system of home teaching for that.

5

THE FRAME HOUSE WAS a century old, but well maintained. Its raised front porch was as wide as the house, and shaded by maples that lined the street. Set back only a dozen feet from the sidewalk, it gave an elevated view of passersby. Just now, however, the residents were inside at supper.

Mrs. Edmund Buckels looked across the table at her daughter. "I don't approve of that university anymore, letting that Ngunda Aran speak there. Your father and I have decided you should go somewhere else. Bethel. It's a good Baptist school."

Jenny Buckels shrugged slightly. "My scholarship's at Chapel Hill, and I've paid for my room for this semester."

Her mother's lips pinched. "I don't want you going to that school any longer. It's run by atheists."

Let it lie, Jen, her brother prayed.

She tried. It didn't work.

"Speak to me when I talk to you!"

Jen's voice was quiet. "Mother, I'm trying not to argue."

"I suppose you went to hear him."

She could have lied, but wouldn't. "I did. It was an assignment in Journalism 201. Otherwise I wouldn't have."

"What did you think of him?"

"He was interesting."

"That's no answer!"

Jenny's response was quiet but firm. "Mother, it *is* my answer. The man was interesting."

"How long did he talk? An hour? It had to be more than just interesting."

"My report's in my course folder, back in the dorm. I'll mail it when I get back." She tried to smile. "I write better than I talk. I got an 'A' on it."

So far her father had stayed out of the discussion. Now he stepped in. "Jennifer, don't evade. Answer your mother."

She straightened, turning her gaze to his, clenched fists on her hips, the softness gone from her voice. "All right. Just remember, you insisted. I found Ngunda Aran . . . thoughtful, tolerant . . . and compassionate." She paused, shifting her eyes to her mother's. "More than some Christians I know."

Even as she said it, Jen knew she'd made a mistake. With a sharp cry of exasperation, Mary Lou Buckels grabbed her mashed potatoes and chicken gravy with a bare hand and tried to throw it at her daughter. Her multiple sclerosis and the consistency of the potatoes and gravy made the attempt largely unsuccessful. A bit of it reached Jenny's blouse, but most of it squeezed out of her mother's hand, or stuck to it.

"You insolent *slut*! Tolerance? Contempt is more like it! Contempt for God and His Truth! The Truth of His Words, written down in the Bible!"

A retort screamed in Jen's mind. Like *"you hypocrite?" "Love your enemy?" "Judge not?"* But all she said, and softly, was, "I'm sorry I made you angry, Mother. I'll pack and leave."

She got up from the table, but her father moved between her and the dining room door. "You will go nowhere!" he said. "You're grounded! Give me the keys to your car!"

She stopped, stared, then barked a disbelieving laugh. "Grounded? Keys to my car?" Her voice hardened. "I'm twenty-four years old, Father. A *grown woman!* I worked for five years saving money for college. *I* bought that car, such as it is, and earned the scholarship, such as *it* is."

He answered hoarsely, emotion burning his throat. "Then get out of this house! Right now! We never want to see you again!"

"I'll get my things and . . ."

Her father took a step toward her. "You will *not* get your things. You will leave this house *now.*"

"*My things are mine!*" She shouted it in his face. "*Bought with my money!*"

Edmund Buckels raised a fist. His son, already on his feet and moving, wrapped his arms around the older man, pinning him from behind. "Dad! Dad, don't do it. You'll regret it forever."

The word "forever" took the starch out of his father. His mother, on the other hand, had gotten up without help and attacked her son feebly, succeeding mainly in getting mashed potatoes and gravy on his back. He turned, gripped her shoulders, and firmly but gently seated her back on her chair, where she burst into tears and disconcerting howls. Jenny, deeply shaken, hurried from the room.

A couple of minutes later, Steven Buckels followed. Her suitcase was open on her bed, but she was shaking too badly to pack it. "Hi, Sis," he said quietly. "Can I help?"

She turned, her expression more bitter than grieving. "And they claim to be Christians! They read the Beatitudes with that—oily righteousness of theirs, and then—" She swallowed, choked, then threw herself facedown on the bed beside her suitcase and wept, fighting the sobs. When she was able to, she sat up and looked at her brother. "How can they be so—two-faced?"

"They don't know what to do, Jen. They're afraid. Afraid of the world, of how it's getting. And afraid for your soul. You've always been something of a rebel, you know. To them that's the great treason, sinful in itself." He shook his head. "Don't look for logic in it. There isn't any."

Somehow his words dissolved her anger; her pulse even slowed. "Are you afraid for my soul?" she asked quietly.

He chuckled; that helped too. "I know you too well for that. God made this world . . . difficult, and he made us. And he's a loving God.

"Mom and Dad are the way they are. I have some like them in my congregation. I don't understand them—I leave that to God—but I'm used to them. I feel for them, and love them. It's much easier for me. They're not so uptight about me. I'm male, and a Baptist minister."

White-faced, she looked at him, seeming to consider what he'd said.

"Why don't you stop at Barlow on your way to Chapel Hill," he went on. "It's not far out of your way, and it's a pleasant drive if you pay attention to the countryside, instead of . . . this. Spend the night there. Tell Dorothy I sent you, that there was a row here. I'll drive back in the morning. I need to be here with Mom and Dad this evening."

Jen looked at him with something like wonder. "You love them, don't you?"

He nodded. "I do. I'm thirteen years older than you, and have memories of them that you don't. From when they weren't so—troubled." He smiled softly, surprising her. "And thirteen years more practice at living. Getting older can have its good points."

He carried her suitcase to her car for her, and she drove away thinking of her brother instead of the fight. He'd spend the evening dealing with their parents, and probably come through it without upset. *He's the only real Christian in the family*, she told herself. *Too bad we can't clone him.*

6

**Excerpt from "An Interview with
Ngunda Elija Aran,"
in American Scene Magazine, by Duke Cochran.**

ASM: As I understand it, you had a very good job as vice president of AAIS, Inc.

NEA: But not *the* vice president. One of three. I was in charge of theoretical explorations.

ASM: Perhaps we should establish what AAIS stands for.

NEA: Advanced Artificial Intelligence Systems. The acronym, incidentally, is pronounced *ace*. It's a major firm in its field.

ASM: After graduating from the University of Toronto in computer science, what came next?

NEA: I went to work with AAIS as a research assistant on an adjusted workweek, while going to grad school part-time. AAIS encourages continuing education. At age twenty I was promoted to research associate, and worked up from there. I became a vice president at age twenty-five. [Chuckles.] I'm afraid I was a workaholic.

ASM: And you resigned at age thirty. Why?

NEA: The job itself was no longer enough. I was experiencing spiritual changes, though at the time I didn't think of it that way. I simply knew that I very much wanted time to do other things. But I still wanted a reliable income, so I continued with AAIS as a consultant, with the understanding that I wouldn't put in more than twenty hours a week.

ASM: Didn't that mean quite a reduction in pay?

NEA: Sixty percent. But forty percent left a comfortable paycheck. I'd been living well below my means since age twenty, developing an investment portfolio.

ASM: So how did you invest your newly won free time?

NEA: [Laughs.] I joined a zen group, and for some while practiced meditation from 6 to 8 o'clock at the zendo each morning. I still meditate regularly. For a time I belonged to an evening group that practiced dance as worship. And I read: biographies, history, philosophy, and a broad spectrum of sciences. And religion, especially eastern religions and new-age spiritual philosophies.

On an impulse, at age thirty-two I took a week-long workshop in NLP—neuro-linguistic programming. Which has nothing to do with computers. And things began to—let me repeat *began to*—come together for me. On how I wanted to invest the rest of my life. NLP is a psychotherapy, and I found it exciting. After that I spent two evenings a week providing free NLP treatments for street people, at bowery missions in Rochester, New York. I lived only fifteen miles from downtown Rochester.

The next summer I flew to Seattle, and took an intensive five-week course in an early form of Life Healing, another psychotherapy, from psychiatrist Dr. Peter Verbeek, who'd developed it.

ASM: And then?

NEA: If you passed the course, and a four- to eight-week internship, you were certified to practice.

ASM: And apparently you did.

NEA: Not right away. First I went home and did some work I'd promised AAIS. Then I turned in my consultant hat, and drove back to Seattle to do the internship.

ASM: Which left you unemployed. Even if you could afford it, you must have felt at least a little uneasy.

NEA: Not really. I'd learned to trust the voice of my essence, my inner self. A few months earlier, while driving through the Finger Lakes region, I'd experienced a powerful epiphany. Powerful enough, I pulled off onto the shoulder. For several minutes, everything looked different. Trees and cows had auras. The grass and flowers glowed along the roadside. Auras weren't all of it, not even the major part of it, but they're something we have language for. I was seeing energy fields not normally visible to human eyes.

ASM: Do you still see them?

NEA: [Laughs.] You look quite nice in your pastel glow, Mr. Cochran.

ASM: Had you been on any—uh, medication at the time?

NEA: [Grinning.] Not then, not now. I've enjoyed excellent health all my life, and I've never been interested in mood-altering substances. After that experience, I realized I no longer wanted to continue in artificial intelligence research, useful and remunerative though it is.

ASM: So that's effectively when you decided—what? To be a spiritual teacher?

NEA: No, I wasn't ready to know that yet. But it was then I knew—really knew—I needed to invest my life in people.

ASM: Could you live on your investment income? Until you developed a psychotherapy practice?

NEA: Adequately, yes. And I intended to practice *pro bono*, or largely *pro bono*. Many of the people who most need Life Healing have little or nothing to pay with. And as I practiced, I became more and more excited by the potentials. That's when I conceived of the Hand Foundation.

ASM: You know, of course, that some people say you're a charlatan, a con man. But what do you think of the ones who say you're a messiah?

NEA: That's almost inevitable, when someone teaches as I do.

ASM: And that is?

NEA: As one who knows, Mr. Cochran. As one who knows.

7

DUKE COCHRAN SHUFFLED nude and blurry-eyed into the bathroom. He was a fairly large, strongly built man, with curly, blond-brown hair on head and chest. Peering into the mirror, he decided he could skip shaving, if he didn't go out. After a shower and shampoo, he shaved after all, then pulled on bikini shorts, went into his office, and called up his mail.

With one exception, it didn't require action. The frozen-frame face that appeared on the screen was one he didn't know: a young Asian male. The Web-World address meant nothing to Cochran, but the geoaddress did: Henrys Hat, Colorado. He wondered if Millennium was going to complain about something in the published interview. All he'd done was tidy up the language a bit.

"Roll and record, now," he said. The mouth began to move, a voice issuing from the speakers in precise American English, the written words crawling quickly across the bottom of the screen.

"Mr. Cochran, my name is Lor Lu. I am Mr. Aran's administrative assistant. Millennium has a business proposal you may be interested in. If you'd care to know more about it, please call me before 1150 or after 1310 Mountain Daylight Time, before October 6th. Thank you."

"Hmm." Cochran looked at his wall clock, then went into his bedroom and wakened Adrielle. Her nubile body caused a pulse of desire, but he tuned it down. He had business to take care of. "Time to greet the day," he said. "You told me you had classes this afternoon. Cereal and sugar are on the table; juice, milk, jam and margarine are in the fridge. Bread's in the bread drawer. Put your dishes on the counter. I'll be on the Web. On visual part of the time, so don't come in before you leave."

She mustured a sleepy affirmative. He took her chin in a hand. "I'll try to call you this evening," he added, his voice soft now. He kissed her lingeringly, almost changing his mind about calling Ngunda's administrative assistant that day. "Or you can call me," he added. He watched her round firm rear sway through the door of the bedroom bath. Normally he discouraged women from phoning, but Adrielle was the best he'd bedded in a year. Enthusiastic, talented, creative, and not into power games like a lot of college girls.

In the kitchen he skinned a banana, poking the peel into the "Tasmanian Eats-All." Then he dialed a tall coffee with fat-free creamer and three spoonfuls of honey—his default setting—and ate a mini-breakfast over the comics in the morning paper. He'd never found the comics as entertaining on the WebWorld or fax.

You're a fogey, he told himself.

He left the kitchen, taking his electrothermal coffee mug with him, and at the computer, dialed Lor Lu. A receptionist cleared the call, and the brown face appeared again on Cochran's screen, an unfocused fragment of office in the background.

"Mr. Cochran! I'm Lor Lu. Thank you for calling."

"You said you had a business proposal to discuss."

"Right. Mr. Aran liked both your interview and your style. And of course you have an established reputation. He'd like to have you cover his activities in a Millennium context. Regularly that is. You would accompany him on his tours, and spend part of the non-tour time here at the Ranch, learning and writing about Millennium."

"If you're offering me a job, I already have one."

"Not a job. Access. We're offering you access that other journalists don't have, for columns and articles. And for a book, should you decide to write one."

Cochran felt an electric jolt of excitement: Ngunda was becoming a very major figure, a superstar in the American public eye. "I might be interested," he said, "if I'd be free to write as I please. No censorship, no sweetheart treatment. And I'll still be with *American Scene.*"

"Of course. If you were an actual employee of Millennium, your public acceptance would be seriously compromised, no matter how much freedom we gave you. No, a fair-minded, independent skeptic is what we're looking for. Anything less would be recognized and devalued. Shall we discuss it further? Or do you want to talk to your editor first?"

"My initial reaction is guardedly favorable, Mr. Lu, but I need to think about it, and talk it over with Mr. Nidringham. He may want to put limits on my involvement. May I call you back about four your time?"

"Four Mountain Time. Good. Are we done for now, Mr. Cochran?"

"So far as I'm concerned."

"Well then, I look forward to your next call."

"Fine. And thank you very much for your proposal."

Cochran broke the connection and stood up, feeling pumped. Fred would definitely go for it, and it would probably double the column inches he got. Quadruple his name recognition. The challenge would be to keep Millennium content with what he wrote; he did not intend to be their PR flack.

He went to the kitchen again. Adrielle stood with her back to him, wearing one of his flannel shirts as a robe, its tails down well toward her knees. He stepped over to her, put his arms around her and murmured in her ear.

"When did you say that first class is? Something good just happened to me, and I feel like celebrating." Chuckling, she reached back and groped him.

"Nothing till two. I can leave here as late as 12:30."

Before supper, he and Lor Lu had come to an agreement. He'd fly to Pueblo that Thursday. It seemed to him his future was made. Especially if he could learn what—or who—lay behind Ngunda and Millennium. He'd already read what he could find in the WebWorld—including a ferret search—before he'd done the interview. And found little more than the public faces of Ngunda Aran and his organization.

There'd be more though. There always was.

He almost phoned Adrielle again, but resisted. *Don't get addicted,* he told himself. *Call Ginny instead.* Director of marketing research for Latscher and Kearney, Ginny had a salary two or three times his. She was mature and independent, and shared his attitude toward affairs. Which he classified into three main kinds: (1) strictly physical but good—extremely good in Adrielle's case; (2) brief and passionate, hot, generally with someone's guilt-troubled wife; and (3) good, comfortable, and convenient, between peers.

Ginny couldn't screw like Adrielle, but she was good in bed, and she could carry on a mature conversation. They could do dinner, followed by a show or concert, then make love, and enjoy all of it.

He wondered if he really was turning into a fogey.

8

Headline News Fax, Oct. 7, 9:30 A.M.

In Rome today, at 3:07 P.M.—that's 9:07 this morning, Eastern Time—the traditional plume of smoke issued from a chimney on the roof of the Vatican palace, signalling the election of a new pope. He is Irish-born Joseph Cardinal Flannery, ex-Archbishop of Toronto. For more than twenty years he has served in administrative posts in the Vatican. He also served as mediator in developing the Ottawa Accords that ended a resurgence of religious terrorism in Northern Ireland. His major acclaim, however, was for helping engineer the Irish Republican Army's denunciation of its own unregenerate terrorists. This effectively defused a terrorist campaign that threatened to undo the good work done in Ottawa and earlier.

The new pope is seventy-six years old. Though said

to be somewhat liberal, he is not expected to initiate changes in the Church. He is seen as a compromise between conservative and liberal factions.

A congressional bill to withdraw the United States from the International Ecosystem Accord was vetoed this morning by President Metzger. She had earlier recognized the need for revisions in the Accord, and will make a speech this afternoon at 12:30 Eastern Time, outlining her approach to the problems.

By a vote of 52 to 50, the Senate this morning passed the so-called "Anti-Militia" Bill. This allows the government to use military force against anyone resisting lawful arrest by means of armed groups, or with military weapons. All nine America Party senators voted against the bill, along with thirty-three Republicans, four Centrists, and four Democrats.

Eighteen senators who rejected essentially the same bill a year ago, this time voted in favor. When asked what caused them to change their votes, most specified the so-called "Walpai War"—the Arizona Militia's raid and takeover of the Walpai County courthouse and jail last September. In that affair, eight county employees were killed, including the sheriff, four deputies, a county prosecuter, a judge, and the judge's fifty-year-old female secretary. Four Bureau of Land Management employees also were killed in execution-style murders. All nine jail inmates were released, recruited, and armed. . . .

The hunger for a savior has surfaced again. In Esfahan, Iran, yesterday, forty-year-old Mohammed Ahmed was proclaimed by a Shiite faction as "the

Mahdi," the long-awaited Islamic Messiah. This brings the count of proclaimed messiahs to eight since the year 2005. Seven have acknowledged the honor. They include one other Mahdi, in Syria; one Buddhist Maitreya, in Burma; and five Christians, two of them in Russia, one in Bolivia and one in Brazil. Another, in the United States, has not accepted the nomination. So far no Jewish or Hindu messiah has been proclaimed.

The death toll from last night's gang-related shootout at St. Stephen's Church in Brooklyn has risen to eight. The most recent to die was one of the gunmen, of injuries received while being kicked and stamped by parishioners at the scene. Another gunman has reportedly told police the intended target was thought to be attending vesper services at St. Stephen's.

Twenty-seven people were wounded. Six are in serious or critical condition.

9

. . . . In times of major social stress, political power tends to gravitate to the ruthless, and ruthlessness is dangerous to democracy, especially when government is ineffective, as ours has become. The American trilateral system—the executive, the legislative, and the judicial—was reasonably functional in a two-party political environment. Initially the two parties were the Federalists and the Democratic-Republicans. Over time the country changed, and with it, the issues and party labels. Third and even fourth parties appeared from time to time, but they were minor. When one became major, it became one of the two, replacing a predecessor.

Now we have four major parties, with two minor parties snapping on the fringes. Our system and our constitution were not intended for four parties—particularly the Senate, with only a third of its members exposed to replacement at any election.

Thus Florence Metzger was voted into the White House with far less than a majority, and her Centrist Party into dominance in the House of Representatives. But a Republican-Americist coalition controlled the Senate until this year. It still controls important budget legislation, because the Balanced Budget Amendment requires a two-thirds majority for emergency deficit spending. And in our new Great Depression, that shortcoming could prove deadly. Especially with the most extreme social stresses the nation has experienced since the War Between the States.

Scene from a Tall Soapbox
Henry Clay Johnson
the Cleveland Plain-Dealer Syndicate

The people around the long table were the President's specialists on civil order, a term that sounded better than civil *dis*order. "Madam President," said one, "this might be the time to reconsider declaring martial law."

"I have considered it. And the time may come, but it's not here yet."

"It might be better to do it before it's necessary. To preclude its becoming necessary."

"William, I can see why you'd feel that way. But if you think we have problems now . . . I'm tempted to have you sit down and write a list of probable side effects. If I declare it at all, it'll be when it won't result in a revolt by Congress, and an insurrection by a sizeable part of the public."

The man subsided, blushing faintly. *A lawyer who blushes,* thought Florence Metzger. She looked around the table at the vice president, attorney general, FBI director, her now embarrassed anti-terrorism advisor, the chairman of the joint chiefs . . . *The blind leading the blind,* she told herself.

"Everett, update us on your anti-terrorist platoons."

General Stearns grunted, his broad mouth turning down at the corners. "All but one platoon is trained, drilled, and installed. Obviously they haven't been tested yet, and I hope they never are, but they're as good as training can make them. The men were chosen from ranger battalions on the basis of their personnel files. Most are married, exemplary family men, and none has a history of extremist sympathies or bigotry. We did our best, and we've trained them very carefully for their new roles."

He glanced around at the others before returning his focus to Florence Metzger. "We now have a platoon at each of four military posts." He took discs from a briefcase and passed them around the table. "I'm trusting everyone here not to mention these platoons. Their existence hasn't leaked yet, and I trust it won't. To explain their special training, we've called them a Delta Force, but that wouldn't hold up under close examination." He spread his hands, palms out. "That's all I have."

The other council members were called on in turn. When they were done, they discussed, briefly, the overall scene, then the President dismissed them. No one had commented on the problem the anti-terrorist platoons might cause with Congress, when it learned of them. But Heinie Brock and the attorney general were well aware of the worrisome potential.

It was nearly noon, and most of them went to lunch. The President, however, headed for her massage room, adjacent to the indoor swimming pool built during the Franklin Roosevelt administration. Her back was already tightening up on her.

A noon massage was standard procedure. She could and, when necessary, did take medication for her back, but she worried that it might affect her mental sharpness, so she relied very largely on skilled massage. When traveling, even on unofficial trips, her physical therapist, Andrea Jackson, ordinarily traveled with her.

The natatorium smelled of chlorine. When she entered the massage room, Andrea was waiting, and putting aside a tabloid, got to her feet.

"Hi, Andy! Am I glad to see you!" the President said, and closed the door behind her.

"Thank you, Madam President. I hope your morning went all right."

Florence Metzger's reply was a grunt. She peeled off her blouse. "Back," she said, "say hello to Andy. She's the best friend you'll ever have." Andrea unhooked her bra for her, and hung blouse and bra on a hanger while the President positioned herself against the tilt-top rubbing table. Then Andrea lowered it to horizontal, the President on board.

President Metzger provided a lot of back. She was commonly referred to as "Big Mama," not around the White House, and not generally by the print and broadcast media, but around the country and on the Web. She'd never been married or had a child; the term "Mama" was rooted in the black slang for woman. At six-feet-one and 255 pounds, the President was larger than her therapist, who was almost as tall but 60 pounds lighter. The President's father, Carl "Muscles" Metzger, had played defensive tackle at the Naval Academy— eventually he'd made rear admiral—and her mother had been Samoan, though raised on Oahu. Both had given their youngest daughter genes for large and strong. She'd attended Cornell on a swimming scholarship, majored in government, and at age twenty-two, at 170 pounds, had won an Olympic bronze in the 200-meter freestyle, and a silver in the 400-meter freestyle relay.

The kinks began to slacken almost at the therapist's first touch. "What were you reading?" asked the President.

"The *National Express.*"

"Huh! Anything interesting?"

Andrea laughed. "The lead story starts out, 'French crowd witnesses winged Ngunda hovering with the Virgin Mary over Lourdes shrine.' Can you believe they printed that?"

"Hon, they'd print anything."

"Last week they had 'hundred-foot angel halts Kansas bus, tells driver and passengers Ngunda is the antichrist.'"

The President said nothing for a few seconds, then asked, "Do you believe in God, Andy?"

"I thought you knew I did."

"I always supposed you did, but I didn't actually know. What do you think of all the different messiahs turning up around the world?"

"We already had one; that ought to be enough. If we can't make it with him, maybe we're not worth the trouble. No, if I was God, I'd tell people to straighten up, get together, and solve their problems."

"I don't know. I remember a book I read in college, *The Religions of Man*. By a Harvard professor, Huston Smith. That was, huh!—thirty years ago. I hardly remember anything specific in the whole book, except for one sentence, but it struck me so, I can just about quote it."

She stopped there until Andrea prompted her. "What was it?"

"He was discussing Hindu theology. And what he wrote was: 'Whenever the world falls too far into disorder, and the slow ascent of humankind toward divinity is seriously endangered, God descends to Earth as an avatar, to unblock the jammed wheels of history.' I don't suppose that's an exact quote, but it's close." She paused. "Are you familiar with the word 'avatar?'"

The therapist nodded. "It's like Jesus: it's God incarnate. Do you think the wheels of history are jammed?"

"Feels like it." The President paused. "And we could use a little divine help. Maybe he could come down and kick butt."

The therapist didn't reply, just worked on the president's broad back.

"I know," the President went on. "It's not likely to happen. That's what you were thinking, wasn't it?"

"No, ma'am. I was thinking about all those supposed-to-be messiahs. If they make a difference, a good difference, I don't much care if they're a real messiah or not."

10

California's Riverside County has another new incorporated city, Hefa. It is named for Haifa, one of the Israeli cities devastated by nuclear attack in the One-Day War. The new Hefa lists a population of 7,583, of which 99 percent are said to be Jewish, and 85 percent recent Israeli refugees or their children.

Hefa is the seventh new Jewish settlement to be incorporated in Riverside County since the war. Numerous other refugee housing developments are springing up in the county's dry hills, greatly straining county services and water resources. This has already resulted in new action on the proposed seawater desalinization plant near Laguna Beach.

The establishment of Hefa is expected to increase the pressure for a new county to be carved out of eastern Riverside County, which now has a refugee population listed at

321,718. The proposed new county would be named Khadash Yisra'el, New Israel.

Most non-Jewish residents object strenuously to the proposed Khadash Yisra'el, the laws and government of which would inevitably reflect Israeli and Hebrew culture and values. (And there is essentially no prospect at all of a new county being formed in which any substantial number of residents object to the proposal.)

Most of the refugees have settled in already-established cities, or in unincorporated areas with substantial non-refugee populations. This has drastically changed their ethno-religious mix, and incidentally stimulated a surge of neo-Nazism.

One Khadash Yisra'el proposal would establish the new county in the form of eight geographically separated rural and urban townships, an administrative and service nightmare which, however, could probably be gotten to work. Unofficially, Riverside County itself is said to be open to the proposal. Especially since, in those eight areas, non-Jewish, along with numerous long-time Jewish-American residents, are rapidly selling out to newcomers, speculators, and their agents. Booming real estate prices will no doubt entice many other owners to sell.

Numerous refugees packed into rental housing, in cities such as Riverside, Elsinore, and nearby towns in Orange and San Bernardino Counties, say they would eagerly move into the proposed Khadash Yisra'el if they could afford

to. And the recently formed Fund for a New
Israel is accruing and expending funds for their
resettlement. If the proposed eight-part Khadash
Yisra'el is formed, it seems quite possible that
subsequent land purchases will result in its
enlargement, and perhaps amalgamation into
fewer parts, or even a single unit.

U.S.A. Today
Arlington, VA
October 11

THE PARKING LOT and warehouse were surrounded
by a corroded eight-foot chain link fence topped with
accordion wire. The gate, however, had been left open
as if no one cared; as if there was little inside worth
looting. It was night, and only four cars and a step
van were parked there, all more or less old, possibly
even abandoned. A single, aged delivery truck stood
beside the loading dock, like a tramp steamer tied
to a wharf. On its side was painted *Shefner's Used
Furniture.*

Rafi Glickman parked his ten-year-old, soot-grimed
Honda, locking the door before leaving it. He'd have
preferred it washed and waxed, but dirty, it didn't
draw the wrong sort of attention.

Beyond his choice of loyalties, personal preference
played little part in Rafi's life. He was a veteran of
the proud Israeli intelligence service, the Mossad,
defunct since the Exodus. Recently he'd become an
operative in the New Mossad, named in honor of
the old. Rafi considered this no honor, but an insult
to the original.

Unknown to the New Mossad, he was also a member of a New Israel anti-terrorist conspiracy so secret, it had no name. A conspiracy that undertook to reduce terrorism in any form in the Americas, Israeli as well as anti-Israeli. A conspiracy whose special weapon was the quiet phone call, normally to the FBI's public informant number. They wanted no credit—anonymity was security—and so far the FBI seemed not to have uncovered them.

Rafi crossed the graveled lot, climbed concrete steps to the loading dock, and pressed a button by a door. Inside, he knew, someone was examining him on a screen. There was a brief buzz; he turned the knob and pushed the door open. Inside, the place was poorly lit. He deliberately did not look around, simply walked down an aisle between stacks of furniture, turned right, entered a hallway, stopped at a door and knocked.

Someone opened it, and Rafi stepped into a room with an eight-foot-long table and straight-backed wooden chairs. There were two metal desks, battered but large, each with a computer. There was also a pair of old, mismatched file cabinets. A man sat leaning back in a swivel chair, his jacket open, exposing a white shirt, and a shoulder holster with pistol. Facing him, five men and two women sat at the table. No one greeted or questioned Rafi. He too took a place at the table. Rafi was the newest member, but like the others, sat looking semicomatose, saying nothing—a function of institutional paranoia, giving the impression of profound boredom.

The New Mossad lacked not only the mission, focus, and sense of limits of the old, it lacked its camaraderie, sometime enthusiasm, and any trace of humor. What it had in abundance was ruthlessness, dedication to violence, and broad-spectrum hatred, the ugly products of defeat, frustration, bitterness, and psychosis.

They sat like that for several gray motionless minutes, waiting. Then a buzzer buzzed, and reaching, the man in the swivel chair pressed a button on an ancient intercom. "What is it?" he asked in Hebrew. The answer was cryptic, two initials. "B and B," the voice said.

The man reached again, and pressed a switch that unlocked the office door. A minute later another man entered, tall, powerfully built, wearing a sweatshirt and jeans. He might have been thirty-five years old; perhaps forty. He looked to be, and was, the joint product of a martial arts academy and a military academy. Radiating charismatic ruthlessness, he performed as well as lived his role. Being conspicuous was his primary weakness; he stood out in any crowd as dangerous. Rafi feared and hated him for things the man had done in the last weeks of their homeland: Moishe Baran had been in charge of interrogations.

By contrast, the man who'd come in with him was more *in*conspicuous than any of them—and more dangerous than even Moishe Baran. In the New Mossad, he was the leader, "the first among equals" in the ruling threesome calling itself "the Wrath of God." Another borrowing from the true Mossad that offended Rafi deeply in this new context.

He despised all three leaders, but hid it well. On the day it showed, he would die.

The meeting was businesslike. Local projects were summarized, their problems enumerated. Assignments were made or changed, new projects proposed and discussed. No action decisions were made. Decisions were a function of the Wrath, and made in private.

Nothing was said of teams elsewhere in the country. Rafi knew nothing specific about them. But appropriately, Riverside held the central command—the Wrath.

Near the end, it was proposed that all reputed "messiahs" be assassinated, as an affront to God. There could be only one messiah, and he could only be Jewish.

My God, thought Rafi. *These people have graduated to murdering the deluded.*

It was decided that the Mahdis and Maitreya did not pretend to be the actual, true Messiah. Only "messiahs" in the Jewish and Christian traditions qualified for execution, and the only one with a meaningful following was Ngunda Aran. To Rafi it seemed likely that a project would be set up to kill the man.

Finally, miscellaneous observations were called for and shared.

Rafi would remember all of it, nearly verbatim and in detail: that was his unique talent. He'd write it down in the privacy of his small apartment, then leave his report in the "letter box" of the week.

When all the rest had finished, Moishe Baran made a final announcement. "I have succeeded in obtaining a Ninja Junior, a highly accurate, ground-to-ground cruise missile with a five hundred-pound warhead, a speed of zero point eight mach, and a range of nine hundred and fifty kilometers. At our next meeting, we will discuss possible uses for it."

The meeting was then adjourned.

11

PEOPLE WERE STILL FILING into Sacramento's Arco Arena and seating themselves. There'd been a bomb threat, not the first for an Ngunda appearance, and the search had delayed the opening for more than an hour. The arena was not more than half full, and the inflow had already thinned notably.

Even half full impressed Duke Cochran. *If I were one of Ngunda's public,* he told himself, *I'd have gone home—or stayed home—and watched it on TV.* But obviously ten or twelve thousand hadn't felt that way.

The great majority of bomb threats were fakes. Most were examples of the so-called "two-bit sabotage" that had become common, producing gross confusion and delay for no more than the cost of a pay-phone call. And if enough people went home, an arena wouldn't earn out the cost of putting on the event and cleaning up afterward. Enough of that, and arenas thought twice about handling events offensive to activists or even political parties.

Like most people, Cochran was in favor of the new law making terrorism and armed insurrection capital offenses, but they didn't apply to two-bit terrorism. So now most public phones required identity cards. Anonymous telephone and Web threats were harder and harder to get away with.

Shortly the flow of people thinned to a trickle. He wondered if any had managed to smuggle in a weapon of some sort. Security scanners were manned at every entrance, capable of picking up anything including fiber glass pens. Their computers analyzed all of it, instantly and unobtrusively. A plastic grenade might look like a pocket flask; a ceramic, one-shot pistol could resemble a key case; a bag of explosive could be swallowed, and detonated by what appeared to be a hearing aid. Anything that suggested the size, shape, or composition of a large catalog of unacceptable objects brought a quick followup by guards with drawn guns.

But human beings were resourceful. One never knew.

Now the program participants entered, and took their seats on the speakers' platform. There were four of them—four plus a pianist and her instrument. Cochran assumed the piano, too, had been thoroughly scanned.

Among the four speakers, Ngunda Aran stood out. And not, it seemed to Cochran, because he was black. He radiated charisma—a charisma boosted, Cochran suspected, by the energy of the thousands of admirers in the arena.

Cochran himself sat in the second row, in the press section. In a section of the first row were about a dozen young people: college students with a role in the program. A microphone stood on the floor in front of them.

On the platform, a woman got to her feet and approached the podium—Sacramento's mayor. Adjusting the microphone to her height, she cleared her throat softly to alert the crowd, then spoke. As introductions went, it was brief and intelligent. She introduced herself, then Ngunda, then the guest singer, and finally the chairman of the Philosophy Department at Cal State Sacramento. *Probably*, Cochran thought, *the professor considered himself an Ngunda scholar.*

He kept his comments short, too. Then Ngunda himself stepped to the podium.

"Good evening," he said. "I am Ngunda Aran. Thank you for your patience during the bomb search." He turned, acknowledged the mayor and professor, then continued: "This evening I will focus on karma."

The voice is part of it, Cochran thought. *Deep and rich.*

"Karma is neither punishment nor retribution, though it can be perceived as such. It is a force that helps us learn. And one of the lessons—just one of them—that humans learn from karma is that acts balance out over time."

Cochran wasn't impressed with Ngunda's opening. He glanced around at the crowd. Most seemed to be paying close attention. But then, if they weren't interested, they wouldn't be there.

"The term *karma* is often applied to two different,

though similar, sorts of phenomena. The most important is the *karmic nexus,* formed by killing someone, crippling or wrongly imprisoning them, brainwashing them, or in some way effectively blocking their chosen course of life.

"But even rudeness is sometimes spoken of as karmic, and this can be confusing. The sorts of unpleasant acts we perform many times in every life do not create a karmic nexus. If they did, each life would be a complex maze of between-life agreements with hundreds of people, for prearranged opportunities to balance and extinguish karma. The scheduling problems and compliances would be impossible. So I do not use the term karma for anything that does not create a nexus, a specific karmic note payable to the bearer sooner or later."

He paused, scanning around, seeming to register each person his eyes touched.

"Then, you might ask, what becomes of the negative energy created by lesser acts? As our lives roll by, we find ourselves doing innumerable good acts, large and small, not because of any karmic nexus to be canceled, but because it seems appropriate. Often these are simply random acts of kindness. But at other times we are making amends for old wrongs of lesser sorts than those which create a karmic nexus. In either case, these good acts serve to clean up the environment, so to speak. We do not graduate from the cycle of lives and deaths without having approximately extinguished the negative energy we've created. Including, of course, extinguishing all our karmic nexuses . . ."

Cochran glanced again at his watch; the talk was

barely under way. Then he looked around at the audience. Their attentiveness was nearly total, so far as he could tell.

Ngunda continued for fifteen minutes more, then sat down again, and the mayor stepped to the podium to introduce the singer: Jenny Tallhorse. "The Dakota Nightingale," someone had dubbed her. She wore what appeared to be doeskin, bleached white, and ornate with beads and fringe. The "tall" in Tallhorse was appropriate. According to the critics, the nightingale part was too. She was a contralto, comparable, it was claimed, to Marian Anderson.

She sang two numbers. Then the crowd stood and applauded until, smiling, she stepped again to the microphone. Her encore was in what he supposed was the Sioux language. Somewhere he'd read or heard that her family was from the Devils Lake Reservation, though she'd grown up in Minneapolis. It occurred to him that when he was done with this Ngunda gig, he might approach her about co-authoring her autobiography. It ought to be interesting, and it ought to sell well. And she was a great-looking woman, worth getting close to.

When she'd finished to another standing ovation, the professor moved to the podium, Ngunda with him. "In the front row," the professor announced, "are twelve undergraduate students from Cal State Sacramento, volunteers from the University Discussion Club, that meets weekly to discuss current issues, events, and personalities. Students, if you will please stand up . . ."

They stood to mild applause, most of them looking self-conscious as the professor named them. Then they sat again. "They will," he explained, "ask Mr. Aran questions related to the subject of karma. Ms. Guzman, you are first."

A student from one end of the row stood up and approached the microphone. "Mr. Aran," she said, "I don't believe in karma, and I don't see how you can. I can't see any legitimate evidence for it."

"It's your choice to believe or not," the guru replied. "Karma operates regardless of disbelief. And it's all right not to believe. There is no punishment for not believing."

The student sat down, a little perplexed at the answer. Another was recognized and answered, then a third arose to ask his question.

"Should you even be teaching karma?" he asked. "If people believe in karma, they'll use it as an excuse to do harm. In India, the Brahmins have used karma for thousands of years, as an excuse to dominate and abuse the lower castes."

Ngunda looked mildly at the young man. "The key term there is 'excuse.' The word 'karma' is sometimes evoked to justify doing harm. In general, however, the harm would be done regardless."

The young man looked somehow annoyed as he returned to his seat. A young woman took his place at the microphone.

"What about professional abortionists?" she asked, her voice accusatorial. "They've killed millions of babies! Innocents! That's worse than any other kind of murder!"

Ngunda's reply was calm and mild. "The soul—that which makes a person human—does not unite with the body until the first breath is taken after birth.

Karma-wise, to abort a fetus is equivalent to aborting a puppy."

"That's not what the Bible says!"

"The Bible says nothing about when the soul assumes the body. But even if it had, the people who recited and wrote the Bible were limited in both their knowledge and their understanding. And some had agendums beyond what they may or may not have thought were the intentions of God or the words of Jesus."

Ooooh! Touché! Cochran thought. He decided Ngunda had more to recommend him than he'd realized.

The journalist became aware, then, of a new quality in the silence of the crowd. As if most had been unprepared for such blunt iconoclasm. It affected the professor, too. He paused for a troubled moment before introducing the next student.

The young woman got up and stepped to the microphone. "Mr. Ngunda— Excuse me, Mr. Aran, I mean. What—what *good* is karma? Why would a god ever invent it in the first place, except as punishment? And I've read some of your stuff in the New Age Wonks' Club House. You say the Tao doesn't punish. You said it here tonight."

Her initial diffidence had fallen away, replaced by a tone of challenge.

"Karma," Ngunda answered, "uses the positive and negative energies of the games people play to make sure each of us learns certain lessons. In order eventually to cycle out of the Earth School, and into what you might think of as the graduate curriculum. Which, I might add, is much less traumatic."

The girl still stood at the microphone, and spoke again, upset now. "You said 'inevitably.' But you've also said and written that 'all is choice.' How does *choice* go with *inevitable*? Suppose I don't choose to balance off some karma? And anyway, saying 'all is choice' is bullshit! My older sister was hit by a car last year, and killed! She certainly didn't choose that! She was happily married, with two neat kids!"

The girl was glaring now. Cochran's gaze shifted to the professor in charge, who sat looking as if he didn't know what to do.

"Ah," Ngunda said, "from some viewpoints it can certainly seem like bullshit. But suppose that in the year 1606, you were galloping on a horse recklessly and ran someone down, killing them. Without ill intent. Unless it was a karmic payoff, that incident would create a karmic nexus. One which sooner or later you would deal with, for it was your decision, your choice to ride as you had. Thus at some future time, often centuries later, you would either be killed by your earlier victim, or in some manner *save* a later incarnation of that victim. In either case extinguishing the nexus.

"Each of us, between lives, decides what karmic nexuses, if any, we'll undertake to cancel in our next life. Then we make between-life agreements with other parties to cooperate. Between lives, the troubles that often go with living as humans—the griefs and fears, the anxieties and pains—seem rather academic. So we plan boldly.

"But reborn again, things seem quite different, and in addition we rarely remember, consciously, the karmic act or the agreement. Our Essence, our core self remembers—our offstage prompter so to speak—but Essence does not compel. Or explain, for that matter. It nudges, sometimes lightly, sometimes more forcefully, but *it does not compel*. One or both persons may avoid the connection, perhaps choosing to be elsewhere, or simply rejecting the act. Or other events may intervene; that is common. But over subsequent lifetimes, the pull of the nexus will strengthen. Sooner or later, the principals *will* choose to extinguish the nexus."

Cochran watched, frowning. He didn't feel well, and wondered if he was coming down with the flu. Still unhappy, the girl returned to her seat. One by one, the other students rose and spoke. The eleventh abandoned karma as a topic. "Mr. Aran," she said, "if you died tomorrow, what one effect would you want to have had on the world?"

Ngunda's grin was wide and electric, startling Cochran. "I would wish to see materialism and gain replaced as the focus and orientation—*the focus and orientation*—of human beings and human society. Replaced by compassion, and awareness of our oneness of spirit. For we all are part of the Tao—of God, if you will—and the Tao is present in each of us, as our Essence."

Again there was a moment's silence. Then applause began, building, spreading through the arena, people rising to their feet till most were standing. Cochran too found himself on his feet, without knowing why. The guru's words hadn't impressed him.

The hairs prickled on his forearms, his nape. *He's powerful,* Cochran told himself, and wondered again what this man was really after. Perhaps Aran himself controlled Millennium after all, rather than some behind-the-scenes manipulators.

But as he worked his way through aisles and corridors, Cochran dismissed the notion. Because in his mental universe, money and know-how outweighed charisma.

In his room that night, Duke Cochran slept restlessly, dreaming strange dreams that slipped away on wakening.

12

EDGAR YARNELL LOOKED up from his Mexican omelet at the man who'd stopped at his small table.

"Hi, Bar Stool," the man said. "I'm Ben Shoreff. You picked up my family and me at Henrys Hat earlier this month. May I sit with you?"

"Sure. Sit."

Ben still stood. "I had in mind asking some questions. You may not feel like questions at lunch."

"Give 'er a try."

Ben put down his tray and sat. "You and Lor Lu talked as if you knew one another, forty years ago in Southeast Asia. Is that right?"

"That's right."

Ben looked bemused. "I'd have guessed your age at fifty-five or sixty, and his at thirty."

"I'm sixty-eight."

"And still working!"

"Nope. About all I do is fly, maintain the aircraft and take naps."

Bar Stool was not, Ben thought, *a voluble man.* "Ah," he said, "but what about Lor Lu?"

Bar Stool surprised him; an unexpected smile wreathed his face. "Lor Lu. He's something. Want to hear a story?"

Ben grinned. "I'd love to."

"You got a while?"

"Sure."

"This'd be confusing without some background. During the war I was a Forward Air Controller in northern Laos. On paper I'd been discharged from the Air Force, to fly for a company called 'Air America,' a CIA cover. There was a whole army of Hmong guerrillas, under their own general, Vang Pao. A hell of a lot better general than that chickenshit Westmoreland the Pentagon sent us. The Hmong were a stone-age tribe that'd been fighting the Pathet Lao, the communists, since about 1950. Armed first by the French. We—the U.S.A.—started supplying them in about '65.

"Anyway I got sent to Long Tieng in '69. After 20 years of fighting, the Hmong had lost so many men, a lot of their fighters were kids 13, 14 years old. And it'd get worse. Before I left, some were 11 or 12, looked more like 9 or 10.

"Mostly we were flying O-1 Bird Dogs, looked kind of like Piper Cubs. Top speed supposed to be 115 knots, but loaded, more like 60. We'd fly over the jungle looking for enemy, and when we'd find some—troops, a truck park, whatever—we'd radio in the location. Maybe fire marking rockets. Let the Air Force or Hmong take it from there. We got shot at a lot, of course, and the

O-1s were as innocent of armor as a young girl's heart. The gas tanks weren't even self-sealing. So they were kind of dangerous, but great for finding enemy on the ground."

Bar Stool took a bite of omelet, chewed and swallowed, then continued. "The O-1 was a fore-and-aft two-seater, and we'd take a Hmong with us, in back, to help spot the enemy. And while the Hmong weren't short on guts, getting shot at in aircraft was a lot different to them than fighting in the jungle, where they felt at home. Some of them didn't do too good up there, and when you got a really good backseater, you liked to keep him.

"That's what happened with me and Yang, Lor Lu's dad. His eyes never missed a thing. So whenever I went up, I tried to get Yang as my backseater. Sometimes he'd be out with someone else. Al Lewis used to grab him whenever he could, until Al got killed. Al seemed to attract ground fire more than most. Killed in '72, but got shot down twice before that, once near Muong Soui. Which is when he got the nickname Muong Soui Louie. Lots of times he got back with bullet holes in the aircraft."

Muong Soui Louie! Bar Stool had called Lor Lu that, driving out in the eight-pack! Ben was almost sure of it.

The flyer raised his coffee cup for a thoughtful drink, then put more hot sauce on his omelet and took another bite. "I got shot down right after Al got killed, and after I got out of the hospital, I got sent home. So I went to work for the Roth Brothers out of Lauenbruck, cowboying and mechanicking. Never heard how things were going with the Hmong. The newspapers and television never paid any attention to them, which was just as well. Over there they generally got things screwed up anyway.

"After we pulled out of Southeast Asia, the CIA busted their ass for the Hmong. They'd got to know and admire them, and hated to leave them in the lurch. But they were way short on resources and way long on restrictions. Then, somewhere around '90, I read that some Hmong refugees had been settled on the Arkansas River, working for farmers there. That's a big irrigation district in the southeast part of the state. So I took a notion to go see how they were doing.

"Not too well, it turned out. The country there's a lot different than the Laotian jungle. It's even flat, and so far east, you can't see mountains. I asked around, and they told me the people to check with about the Hmong were preachers, so I went to one and told him I'd like to find an old Hmong friend of mine. All the name I had for him was Yang. He told me thousands, probably tens of thousands of Hmong had been flown to the States to keep from getting massacred by the Communists. They were scattered all over the country. But he did know a Yang, and told me how I could find him.

"So I went, and by God it was him! One chance in thousands, like playing the lottery. It was him. He'd already known a certain amount of English, and gotten a lot better at it since, so he'd been made foreman of the Hmong working on this big produce farm. I'm not ashamed to say we cried all over each other. It was minutes before we could even talk."

At the memory, the flyer's eyes had welled up. He paused to take another bite of omelet and another swig of coffee while he recovered himself. When he spoke again, it was with a grin. "Yang had kids by then, one of 'em being Lor Lu. Maybe six or eight years old, about the size of a healthy flea, born in a refugee camp in Thailand. And he came up to me and called me Bar Stool! Not even *Mister* Bar Stool. And I asked Yang how he knew that name, because Yang'd been calling me Lieutenant Yarnell.

"Yang was kind of apologetic. Said that here, the kids didn't always use proper manners. They'd got American habits from the kids they went to school and played with." Bar Stool paused to eat the last bite of omelet. "The Hmong, some of 'em anyway, believe in past lives. From Buddhism, I suppose. And Yang explained that Lor Lu had been American his last life. That he'd been Lieutenant Lewis."

Bar Stool peered thoughtfully at Ben. "I guess that answers your question." He gestured with his fork. "Your lunch is getting cold."

Ben ate. He had a whole new appreciation of the man across the table from him.

"And that," Ben said to Lee, "is how he explained Lor Lu's being Muong Soui Louie."

Lee Shoreff looked dismayed. "And he believes this?"

Ben smiled. "There doesn't seem to be any other explanation available."

"But—it makes no sense! None at all!"

He shrugged, still smiling.

"And you believe it," she said accusingly.

"Seems fine to me. I've always felt comfortable

with the idea of past lives. I believed in them the first time I heard of them."

She looked at the girls, who'd been listening with great interest, ignoring the television. Then she turned again to her husband. "I wonder if it's true that Abilities Release gets into past lives . . . what purport to be past lives."

"Among other things."

"I suppose you'd like to try it out."

"My dear," he said, "I took Life Healing shortly before I met you. At the first east coast Millennium center, on Long Island."

Lee's jaw dropped. "You didn't!"

"Sure did. You weren't there to tell me I couldn't, so . . ."

"Ben, that's not funny!"

"It's not dreadful, either."

She frowned thoughtfully. This man she loved, this good and gentle man . . . "What ever happened to your life that needed healing?" she asked.

"This life? Nothing much. But some earlier lives . . ." He cocked and waggled an eyebrow comically. The girls giggled.

"Ben, please! You're not making this any easier for me. Why didn't you tell me before?"

"It never came up till we met Lor Lu. And after that I knew it would upset you. Probably more than it does now."

"Mom," Becca piped up, "I'm old enough to take Life Healing. And Raquel will be when she's ten. Can we? Please?"

Lee took a deep breath and let it out slowly. "No, you may not."

Their response to that worried her. They didn't

plead, they didn't fuss. They didn't even say, "But dad did, and it didn't do anything bad to him." They simply turned their eyes to the television, though she had no illusions about their ears.

In bed, two hours later, she asked Ben what Life Healing was like. "You sit in front of an aural field enhancer," he answered. "It looks a bit like a desk computer with a small antenna. Your guide reads from a list of short questions till he gets a meaningful aural response. Then he asks other questions until you see the event that caused the response. See it for yourself. That's when it gets hairy. You revisit things that were done to you, or things you did to others, or saw done to others—traumatic incidents that left scars on your psyche. Once you get grooved in, most of them are of past lives, or deaths, because there've been so many of them."

Lee said nothing for half a minute. "On your psyche," she said at last, her voice brittle. "What does that mean? What good does it do?"

Ben's answer was soft. "It makes life easier. Among other things, it makes you less vulnerable to things that happen in this life."

"It's a cult thing!"

"Not really. It's a psychotherapy suitable for ordinary people, developed by a licensed psychiatrist, Dr. Peter Verbeek. Synthesized from elements of earlier practices, actually."

A *licensed psychiatrist*, she thought. *As if that's reassuring.*

"You might try reading some of Dove's columns and talks," Ben added.

She tightened inwardly. *Not likely.* She'd felt Ngunda's magnetism, probably more effective for being casual. It was easy for some people to be hooked by him. "You'd like the girls to have Life Healing, wouldn't you?" she said.

"It would be good for them, but it's nothing I'd lobby for. They're doing great as they are."

He peered at his wife in the darkness, knowing she'd lie awake stewing. "Tell you what," he said. "Why don't you and I get up and watch TV awhile. *The African Queen* is playing on seventy-four about now. I'll mix you a Hungarian screwdriver."

Lee sighed. "We might as well. Or I might as well. There's no need for you to lose sleep."

He chuckled. "You'll need someone to help you through the more exciting parts."

She snorted. "What parts are those?"

He laughed. "Parts is parts. Whatever parts excite you."

She hit him with her pillow, then rolled out of bed before he could grab her. "All right," she said. "But make the drink weak. I'll want more than one."

13

LEE WAS THOROUGHLY in love with her office, and for a lot stronger reasons than the Dial-a-Mug beverage station, or the view of the Sangre de Cristo Mountains. As much as she enjoyed those, it was the design and equipment that really made it, especially the 5x8-foot wall screen. Ngunda himself had ordered it for her. On it, a command to her computer called up her rough-draft operations chart, as far as she'd gotten on it. Either in standard form, or as interlocking flow charts with call-up overlays. She used it as an easy-to-read working tool, as well as for conferences.

She'd decided to like Ngunda for now, despite his being a guru.

Most people at Millennium headquarters left their office doors open. She preferred hers closed. Thus Larry Rocco knocked and identified himself. When she called, "Come in," he brought with him a man she'd never seen before.

"Hi, Lee," Larry said. "This is Duke Cochran, a writer for *American Scene*. Duke, this is Lee Shoreff, our resident organizational genius." He turned back to Lee. "You've probably read Duke's articles. He'll be with us for a while, writing about Millennium and Dove, and I'm introducing him around. He did a great piece on Dove's Sacramento appearance in the new issue. He may ask you for an interview between tours."

Involuntarily she'd gotten to her feet. Here was another kind of magnetism; this was a *sexy* man. He grinned. "Hi, Lee. I've never met a genuine organizational genius before. Do you do personal consulting? My life could use some organizing."

"I only do personal consulting for my husband and daughters. We have an agreement: I don't charge them, and they don't take my advice."

Both men laughed. "Sounds like a workable system," Cochran said. "And I *will* call you sometime for an interview."

The two men left then, and after a few seconds she realized she was still standing, looking at the closed door. *Lee*, she told herself, *can you spell trouble? That's a man to avoid.*

In his room, Duke Cochran sipped coffee and reviewed the day. This continued to be an interesting assignment. He was already satisfied that nearly all the people he'd met here were for real, doing their best for a cause. *True believers*, he thought, *but not idiots. None of them are likely to do something stupid to embarrass Ngunda or the Foundation.* Lor Lu probably did all the executive hiring, he decided. The little Asian was more than smart. He could read people.

But the controlling brain, or brains, Cochran told himself, *are high up, out of sight. Ngunda's the necessary gimmick and figurehead, someone that people, lots of people, believe in and admire automatically.* Equally important, his charisma came across on television, despite his speaking style. Or maybe that style worked for a guru. Maybe he'd even cultivated it.

Basically, though, Cochran told himself, *he's a megalomaniac brilliant enough to be plausible.* "I teach as one who knows!" *Good God!* The words had rung a bell, so he'd checked a concordance of the Bible, on the Web. It was a paraphrase of statements in the Gospels of Matthew and Luke, describing how Jesus taught. Yet Ngunda mostly came across as casual, matter of fact. As Harriet Wilson had described him in a column: clean, likeable, and straightforward. But it seemed to Cochran she'd left something out. She should have added, "with personality and style that lets him say the things he says and get away with them."

All in all, Ngunda Elija Aran was a man you might buy a used car from without troubling to raise the hood. A figure to turn to if you wanted a safe and stable anchor point in a world increasingly chaotic and threatening. Someone you'd give your support to, your loyalty—maybe your pension fund. It seemed to Cochran that before this scam was over, Ngunda *would* declare himself messiah. The tabloids already had, along with more than a few fanatics.

Meanwhile this place—the Ranch, the Cote, its staff—had cost lots of money. Up-front costs for establishment, and ongoing costs for operations. No way were Millennium's psychotherapies paying for even a fifth of it. Several investigative reporters had shown that. Outside interests had to be financing it big-league, especially given the Hard Times, and they'd require some kind of payoff. The membership of its board of trustees was public knowledge; anyone could check it out on the Web. All were big-league rich. But what their actual roles were . . . For that matter, the number one Mister Big might not be a trustee. Probably wasn't.

Lee Shoreff's probably as well informed as anyone short of Lor Lu and Whistler. And she's different than the others here; she doesn't feel like a true believer. If she comes across something, she might even spill it.

He looked at the possibilities thoughtfully. "Maybe I need to get her in bed," he murmured, and mentally backed off, evaluating. She was taller than he usually went for, but good looking, athletic looking; and beneath that professional demeanor, sexy—though she covered it well, with more than her horn-rimmed glasses and no-fuss hairstyle. She'd be passionate, once he got her started, especially if she got into a guilt trip. *And she was capable of multiple orgasms,* he told himself; he had a sense for things like that.

He pictured her naked, examining her from all angles. *Let her think you're passionately in love with her,* he told himself. *Get her in a hotel room, screw her out of her skull, and unless you really louse it up, you'll find out what she knows—or not. There are worse ways to spend a weekend.*

14

THE TEMPERATURE WAS 65 degrees, and late afternoon sun shone mellow between the trees, but there'd been three light frosts on the Chapel Hill campus, and the leaves were turning. The sweetgums were fiery red. Jenny Buckels noticed none of it. She trotted up the few steps and into the Charles B. Aycock Library. Her last class of the afternoon was over, and she wanted to check her mail before reporting to work at her dormitory dining hall. There was more anonymity in the library than in the computer room in her fourth-floor dorm wing, and the computer in her room was likely to be tied up by her roommate.

She chose a carrel in a back corner of the stacks, logged on, inserted her voice card and put on the headset. All she found in her box was an electronic notice of what she'd already been told. Then, on an impulse, she spoke the address of her brother's office. He answered, looking tired.

"Hi, Sis. What's new?"

"Nothing good." It occurred to her then that Steven had to listen to the complaints not only of their parents, but his parishioners. And now here *she* was, about to recite her problems. "But it's not really bad," she added. "The U is like the rest of us; it needs to cut costs. Starting next week my pay's being cut, but I'll still get my meals."

"Cut to what?"

"No cash, but I'll get my meals. And I've already paid for my room through fall term, and my scholarship covers tuition and fees. And I don't need new clothes. I just won't have the money to drive home for Thanksgiving or Christmas, but I wouldn't be doing that anyway."

He nodded, which relieved her. She thought he might try to talk her into it.

"Dad wants to drive here for Thanksgiving," he said, "but Mom's gotten worse. You saw what she was like a month ago; she's gotten more irrational since then. So Dorothy and I will drive there. With the kids," he added, then paused. "Tell you what. Why don't I send some money for gas, and you can drive here to Barlow the day after. We'll have a sort of Second Thanksgiving at our house. Not fancy, but Thanksgiving."

Jenny almost declined. Cash would be tight for Steve, too. But she accepted, because there was something to be thankful for, an important something: Steven and Dorothy, and the kids. Just now it seemed to her they were all that gave life meaning.

"How's Dad doing?"

"Not well. Besides the stress of mom's condition, he's become . . . He hates the world. Fortunately he hasn't become critical of me, and even more fortunately he remains really patient with Mom. There's genuine love there. What's unfortunate is, he denies to himself that she could be in the wrong, so he blames you for the upset."

Jenny nodded thoughtfully. "How much blame *does* belong to me?"

He peered at her image on his screen. "Don't think in terms of blame, Jen. Mom was looking for a fight with you. It's the way she is now. We just have to accept that she's not sane anymore."

"And you're carrying the whole load, while I carry none of it."

"Hon, they wouldn't *let* you carry any of it. That's the way they are now, and it's no fault of yours. They have every reason to be proud of you, but they can't see it. It's best for all of us if you keep clear of them."

She didn't say anything for a moment, then asked, "What's going to become of them?"

He shook his head. "I suspect Mom will have to be institutionalized soon. When Dad can't handle her any longer. Then—I don't know what'll become of him. He's still functioning, but he's emotionally unstable. He may slip into severe depression, even try to take his own life." He pursed his lips, sighing. "I never imagined they'd come to this. It's a matter of our times, of what the world's become. And along with Mom's MS, they're not able to deal with it." He paused. "I can't help wondering if it's not the time that John wrote of, actually coming to pass. The Biblical millennium."

They talked for a minute or two longer, then disconnected. As she left the library, it occurred to her it might be best for all of them if both their parents were institutionalized. As for "the time that John wrote of"—that was no more real to her now than it had ever been. *It's humanity's mess, and humanity's job to clean it up, if we can,* she told herself. *Till then we'll have to live with it.*

15

This just in! At 10:42 A.M.—moments ago—an explosion shook the New York Stock Exchange, doing extensive damage, and killing an undetermined but presumably large number of people.

Headline News
Atlanta, GA, Oct. 21

—————————

WHEN LUTHER KOSKELA arrived in Montana, his face had worn a week's growth of reddish stubble. When he arrived at the Ranch, it had had ten days more growing time. Lank, sandy-brown hair showed beneath his rolled stocking cap, and he wore a crucifix outside his shirt. He knew he didn't come across like a hippie, but neither did he fit the crewcut or skinhead image people had of mercenaries and militia.

He drove the newly bought but well-aged Ford across a cattle guard, and stopped for one of the uniformed entry guards: an Indian, who walked up to the driver's window as Lute lowered it. "This is a private road," the guard said. "Do you have a permit to drive on the Ranch?"

"Nope."

"How long do you plan to be here?"

"I don't know. A day. A couple weeks. Does the Dove come out here sometimes?"

"Not since I started work here in July. Park over there." The man pointed to a large area, leveled and gravelled. Twenty or so cars and pickups were already parked there. "That's as far as you're allowed to drive without a permit. Do you have camping gear?"

"A sleeping bag." Frowning, Lute gestured at the tent camp. "What about those? Can I use one of them?"

"They belong to people that brought them. Ask around. Maybe someone will let you stay with them. And please use the latrines. It's unsanitary to relieve yourself on the ground, and disrespectful to other people."

Koskela nodded, rolled up his window and turned into the lot. The cars already there tended to be in scattered small clusters. He parked behind one of the clusters, well away from the guards. Then he got his day pack from the back seat, slipped into the shoulder straps, and walked toward the tents, wondering what the people were like here. "Hippies" was an old term resurrected, and applied to a range of types. *Those camped up here at 7,800 feet in October,* he told himself, *couldn't be too tender.*

His watch read 11:17 A.M., and in the thin, high-elevation air, the sun was bright and warming. The temperature, he guessed, was in the fifties. He wondered what it had been at daybreak. Maybe twenty.

A few of the tents were canvas tepees, with smoke rising barely visible from their vents. He knelt outside the door of one. There was a smell of burning manure. Someone there knew the old Plains Indian practice of burning dry buffalo chips, or in these times cow chips.

"Helloo," he said. "Anybody home?"

No one answered, and he peered in. A young woman in a Navaho-style blue velvet skirt sat crosslegged like a yogi, hands loose in her lap, cupped palms upward. Her eyes were closed, her face relaxed. Meditating, he realized, and went to another, where two small children played outside. They were digging in the dirt, one with a spoon, the other with a screwdriver.

"Hi!" he said to them, and they raised dirty faces to look alertly at him. "Is your dad at home?"

The elder got up and scurried to the tepee's entrance. "Dad," he called, "it's a stranger!"

A man ducked out through the opening. He was big and thick-waisted, with a pirate mustache beneath a broken nose. His forehead had encroached halfway back across his skull, but behind that his hair was long, black streaked with gray, and gathered in a ponytail.

"What can I do for you?" The man's voice was rough, and vaguely Hispanic.

"I just got here," Koskela said. "I've been hearing

about this place, and the Dove, and thought I'd check it out. Just now I'm looking for someone who can tell me stuff."

"Stuff?" The tone was guarded.

"Yeah. Like what's the attraction here? Does Dove come out and talk to you guys? Does it seem like he might really be the Second Coming?"

The man grunted, then looked at the children. They were playing again. "Thurl," he called, "don' lose my screwdriver. If you do, you don' eat till you find it." He turned back to Lute. "The Dove came out once when we first come here, last June. Circulated aroun' and talked with people, then left. There was a lot more of us then. And the attraction? Depends on the person, I suppose. To me the place feels clean. Plen'y of dirt, living like this, but the vibes are clean. And Dove? I don' worry whether he's the Second Coming or the Fifth. Or just somebody spiritual, with a line to God. 'Cause he's got one; read what he says. And man, his vibes are unbelieveable! Those Indian guards have clean vibes, too. We talked to one of them, from the Yakima Nation up in Washington. Invited him to supper." The man laughed. "Kind of a hoot, white eyes like us inviting an Indian into our wigwam. He had that Ladder treatment, Life Healing, back on the reservation, and tol' us a little about it. Cindy says she'd like to try it, and I guess I would too. Maybe we will someday, when we get a little ahead on things."

He tilted his head back, and looked at the empty blue sky. "We're gonna leave this week. It's closing in on November, and up here it can snow any day now.

"I got my knee all shot to hell in the Lagos Rescue,

and we lived on my partial disability money, till it got cut way back a couple years ago. Gotta cut those taxes, you know. Keep up those stock prices and executive bonuses."

He said it without heat, then shrugged. "Up here we can still live on it. We'll go back to Phoenix for the winter, and I'll work for my uncle again, cutting up scrap. It ain't much for pay, but it don' take a lot of walking around, and my uncle's a good guy to work for. He's got a mobile home he lets us use cheap, and his wife presses juice from their orange trees. Gives us all of it we want, for nothing." He shrugged again. "It ain' very exciting, but it suits us okay."

He half-turned to the tent. "Come in and meet Cindy. She ain' feeling too good today. You know how it is. But maybe she'll invite you to lunch."

Later, Koskela visited another tepee, then an ordinary walled tent and an old camper rig, killing time till nightfall. Giving his name as Lloyd Krause. Most of what he learned, he got from his lunch hosts, Al and Cindy Espinosa. What the others had to say wasn't much different. His questioning had been cautious and casual; it wouldn't do to arouse suspicion. Mostly he let the conversations take their own course, only now and then bringing up a subject.

Little of what he heard was useful, except about the guards. Apparently three were on duty at any given time—two on the gate, one on the tower, day and night. They worked three-hour shifts, alternating with six hours on standby at the guard house, for one long day and night. Then they were off for twenty-one hours. They lived at the Cote with their families.

The tower stood like a forest lookout tower without a forest, on a knob a mile inside the gate. He'd seen it on his overflights, two days earlier, and again while driving.

Koskela was uncomfortable with what he'd learned. It was no doubt honest, as far as it went, but something was missing. The Ranch was said to be four miles on a side—sixteen miles of perimeter. And with all the threats against Ngunda's life . . . Uh uh. The place was too unprotected. There was something more, something these hippies didn't know about.

Koskela had never, of course, intended to stay with anyone that night. He'd been blowing smoke, to mislead the guard. At dusk he went back to the Espinosas' tepee. He'd been invited back for supper, and intended to leave off a five-dollar bill, significant money these days. The temperature had already dropped sharply, and he stayed to talk for more than an hour after supper. The Espinosas had grown up in Phoenix, and Al's military service had been with the 5th Ranger Battalion. Koskela didn't mention his own. He told them a bit about an imaginary childhood in northern Minnesota, drawing details from time spent there as a boy, with an uncle and aunt.

After returning to his car, he sat considering for a while, the radio tuned to a country western station. He needed to walk the perimeter fence, and this was the night for it. The moon was like a fat lamp in the clear sky, only one night past full. But a major part of the perimeter would be visible from the tower. What did they have up there for night surveillance?

Hell, even he had night goggles and night glasses in his pack.

By nature and training, he preferred more data before acting, but saw no prospect of getting it except by sticking his neck out. So after a few minutes, he switched his dome light to the *off* setting, got out of his car, and closed the door without slamming it. After putting on his recreational day pack, he crossed the road, walking through the camp and a hundred feet beyond it before donning his night goggles. Then, for two hours he hiked within sight of the fence, west two miles to a fence corner, then four miles south to the next, then east, fast and steady. After the first hour he gave little attention to the tower.

He found nothing interesting, except that the fence showed no sign at all of being electronically rigged. It was ordinary stock fence—barbed wire fastened to steel T-posts driven into the earth. No doubt by a sweating cowboy wielding a heavy post driver. He'd done enough of that himself as a teenager, on his dad's ranch, and his uncles', and for hire by neighbors. Crossing that fence would take no effort at all: spread the top two strands of wire and duck through, or flatten yourself and crawl under.

At a point opposite the encampment, he saw little reason to continue his perimeter inspection. He'd seen all of it he needed to. So he left the fence and started north.

All in all, the ground sloped gradually downward toward the east, but superposed on that tendency, it was undulant to rolling. He knew his next objective—a low bluff overlooking the Cote on the southeast—and he went to it. There he spent an hour on his belly, studying the place house by house through his 6X night glasses. A few windows were still lit, along with occasional streetlamps, but he saw not a single headlight. So, no patrol cars. And nothing that looked like surveillance equipment. Only the community's satellite dish, on the roof of the three-story brick building he assumed was Millennium headquarters. Any surveillance equipment would be on the tower a mile north.

Hell, he thought, *maybe Carl could have done it; knocked on the door and stepped in shooting.* But he didn't believe it; not for a minute.

The major question left was where, down there, Ngunda lived. The Cote hadn't been there when the aerial photography was flown, and he'd kept his own overflights as innocuous and incidental-seeming as possible. Once across at a slow eighty knots—an orientation pass—and once back, a quarter-hour later, both at 2,000 feet local reference.

Now he felt more confident of what he'd seen. One house, one of the smaller, was a little separated from the rest. The trees and shrubs around it were larger, as if bigger stock had been planted, and it was one of the nearest to the big brick building. Ngunda's house, he felt sure.

There was no point in freezing on the ground any longer. Stowing the night glasses in his pack, he put his goggles back on. Then, at a jog, he started back to his car, swinging well east, to keep distance between himself and the tower.

16

AT THE SAME TIME Luther Koskela was drinking tea from a mug in the Espinosas' wigwam, the Shoreff family had been sitting around their dining table, two miles away. They'd begun eating supper at home, instead of in the staff dining room. Lee wanted to get away from Millennium in the evenings, and just be with family.

Ben had not only agreed, as the family's best cook, he'd volunteered to prepare the suppers. Meals that could be reheated—casseroles, meat loaf, pastas—and things that were quick, like omelettes and frozen pizza. They'd "eat out" at the staff dining room twice a week, for variety and to give him a break.

Over dessert, Becca and Raquel began to argue about a friend. "It's natural for her to act like that," Becca said. "She's a mature artisan in the caution mode."

"She's not either! She's an artisan-cast scholar in the observation mode, with an attitude of skeptic. She spends half her time reading the encyclopedia!"

Lee frowned, half afraid to ask. "What are you girls talking about?"

"We're sorry, Mom," Becca said. "It's nothing."

Lee shot a glance at Ben, who pretended not to have heard. Inexplicable fear and anger rose in her. "Nothing or not," she said, "I expect you to tell me, young lady!"

Becca looked at her stepfather apologetically, then back at her mother. "It's about overleaves. Basic personality traits, that is. Each month, each study group is given a book we're supposed to read and discuss. This month's is *The Michael Primer*. That's all."

"Yeah!" said Raquel. "It's neat! Between lives you decide the kinds of lessons you want to learn in your next life, so you pick overleaves that will help. They give you personality tendencies"—she said the words as easily as an adult might have—"to help you experience those lessons. Each set of—"

With a stricken expression Lee jerked to her feet, bumping the table and knocking over two water glasses, then turned and fled to her bedroom. Becca gave Raquel a dirty look. "And you're a young sage with a mode of big mouth and an attitude of stupid," she muttered.

"Okay, girls," Ben said, getting up, "enough of that. Help me take things to the kitchen. Then you can finish the cleanup."

"Yes, Dad."

"Sorry, Dad."

With the table cleared and the girls wiping up the

spillage, Ben went into the bedroom. Lee lay on her back with a forearm across her eyes.

"Hi, kiddo," he said. "Want to talk?"

"Oh, Ben, talk is useless. I just want to *leave* this place. The girls! They're being turned into *cultists!*"

"Because they talked about overleaves?"

She nodded. After a moment she spoke again, coldly, with a tinge of a sneer. "I suppose that's part of Life Healing."

"No, it's part of the Michael teaching."

"Michael who?"

He didn't answer at once. She wondered if he was trying to compose a reply or avoid one.

"I think of Michael as—possibly the source of stories of an Archangel Michael, but that's just a notion that occurred to me."

"*Archangel!?* Are you serious!?"

He nodded. "Yep. I was then anyway, more or less."

"Good grief!" She paused. "Where did you run into that?"

"The Michael teachings? I heard about the books maybe twenty years ago. Read them and reread them. They were one of my New Age interests."

Lee sighed—perhaps in resignation—and sitting up, turned on her reading lamp. "I need to be alone awhile," she said, "to read something; clear my RAM. I can't deal with this stuff right now."

Ben nodded. "You produced a marvelous pair of daughters," he replied. "As you know. I'll check the mail, and maybe browse the Web a while—let the girls work things out on their own. They're good at that."

❖   ❖   ❖

The suds had risen well above the rim of the sink before Raquel turned off the water. Then, with her small bare hand and forearm, she swept the topmost layer off into the other half of the sink. Her older sister watched. "You know," Becca said, "it wouldn't foam up so much if you didn't set the head to spray. Or at all if you waited till near the end to add detergent."

"I know."

"Then why do you do it?"

"Because I like to watch it foam up. It's fun."

Becca shrugged. "That's why you like to wash by hand, too, instead of using the dishwasher."

Raquel nodded. "Uh huh. I'm an old sage with a goal of acceptance and a mode of passion, only I think of it as enthusiasm. In the intellectual part of moving center, so usually I act first and think later. You're an old scholar in moving part of intellectual center, with a mode of observation and a goal of dominance. The only overleaf we have in common is a soul age of old, and strictly speaking, soul age isn't an overleaf."

Becca regarded her thoughtfully. "You know, we really have to avoid upsetting Mom like this. It's mean and thoughtless."

"I know."

Raquel got down from the sink stool and dried her arms and hands, then pushed the stool to the refrigerator. Opening the freezer door, she got out a carton of ice cream and put it on the kitchen table, Becca watching critically.

"We already had dessert," she pointed out.

"Mom didn't." Raquel took the ice cream scoop from a drawer, then a dessert plate from the cabinet, hoisting herself onto the counter to reach it. Finally she put a slice of peach pie on the plate, for a fifteen-second shot in the microwave before adding abundant ice cream.

"That's Neopolitan," Becca said.

"I know."

"Neopolitan doesn't go with peach pie."

"I like it okay. And Mom will. She'll like it because we took it to her. She'll like it better than if we used vanilla. To her that'll make it more loveable, and she could use feelings like that just now."

Becca's eyes widened a bit, dispelling her frown. "You're right," she said. *Sages,* she told herself, *could not only get really good ideas sometime, they could be really insightful. Especially old sages like her sister.*

Ben had seen the girls go to their room some time earlier. Now he stood with an ear to their bedroom door. Quiet. He went to the living room, turned on the night light and turned off the reading lamp. Then he went into the bedroom and closed the door behind him. There, too, only the night light was on. Very quietly he went to the open closet door, undressed, hung up his clothes and took out his pajamas.

Lee's voice took him by surprise. "What the girls did, that was sweet. Did you suggest it?"

"Nope. It was their idea all the way." He pulled his pajamas on. "I thought you were asleep."

"I was thinking. Wondering how they got so— wise."

He got into bed. "Wise. That's the word, that's what they are. I don't think I ever knew children quite like them before. Good genes. From their mom."

"What happened to Mark's genes? That asshole."

"Uh-oh! Maybe I'd better sleep on the sofa tonight."

She grabbed his arm. "Don't you dare. I need a friend by me tonight." She paused. "You three are awfully good to me. I'm afraid I get overwrought sometimes."

"Mature warriors in the passion mode can be like that now and then," he said playfully, expecting a swat with her pillow.

She didn't take the bait, simply lay staring at the ceiling. "Is that what I am?"

"That's how it seems to me."

"That's more Michael, I suppose."

"Yep."

"And you've known this—stuff for years. Pretty well, apparently."

"Yep."

"Apparently it hasn't hurt you. That's what helped me get over my upset. I won't ask you to explain it though. My head hurts just thinking about it."

Again she lay silent. Ben too said nothing, not wanting to interrupt her thoughts. "What did happen to Mark's genes?" she asked finally.

"They did what they were supposed to do. They helped produce two lovely children. Picture Mark, then look at Becca, and you'll see what I mean. Coloring, the chin . . ."

"Mark *is* an asshole though."

"Inarguably. Spoiled. Totally self-centered, overbearing and intolerant." He avoided adding *a young warrior in aggression mode, with a goal of rejection and a chief feature of greed, with a secondary feature of self-destruction.* "That's why you divorced him and married me. But those things aren't genetic."

"You don't think so?" she said thoughtfully.

"Consider the girls. And he's their dad."

"I'm glad Mark paid so little attention to them when they were little." She sighed, and snuggled up to Ben. "I did a much better job on my second try. You're more the reason than anyone else for what they're like."

"I'll accept a little of that. A supporting role. But each and both of them started out superior. I'd say both you and I are learning from them."

Lee raised herself on an elbow and kissed him softly. He returned the kiss with interest. After a moment she laid a hand on his belly, sliding it under his waistband.

Later they lay quietly, letting sleep gather. "Why do we always make love after I've been upset?" she murmured.

"Because it feels so good. And because with people who love one another, it's almost the human ultimate in closeness. That's what makes it healing."

"Healing. I seem to need that at times."

He chuckled. "Happy to oblige, ma'am. Just call me Dr. Ben. My motto is, 'I make house calls.'"

She elbowed him softly. "Husbands!" she murmured, then turned onto her sleeping side and closed her eyes.

17

Rev. S: Mr. Aran, perhaps you are aware of Jesus's words in Matthew, Chapter 16, verses 24 and 25: "If any want to become my followers, let them deny themselves and take up their cross and follow me. For those who want to save their life will lose it." And in Luke, Chapter 12, verse 25: "Can any of you by worrying add a single day to your span of life?"

Yet you have security specialists with you all the time. How do you justify that?

NA: Hour.

Rev. S: Sir?

NA: The word is "hour." You misquoted Luke. He wrote: "add a single hour to your span of life."

But to answer your question: First, in the

immortal words of Mad Magazine's Alfred E. Newman, "What? Me worry?" I do not worry. I trust. And secondly— Let me tell you a story not from the Bible, but one I read years ago in a magazine. It went something like this: A river was in flood, and with the water above the first-floor windows, a man sat watching from his roof. A skiff came along, and the paddler invited him to get in.

"No," the man answered, "God will save me if it's necessary."

The water had covered the porch roof when a power boat came along. The people on board urged him to join them, but he refused, giving the same reason. Still later, with water to the upstairs windows, a helicopter came along, and he waved it off.

Shortly afterward, the house was washed off its foundation, and he drowned. Received in heaven, he went to God and complained. "The Bible says you'd take care of me, yet you let me drown!"

"Dear Soul," God answered with ineffable love, "I tried to save you. First I sent a skiff, then a power boat, and finally a helicopter. You refused them all."

Now my answer to you, good Reverend, is that Art Knowles came to me as a security expert, and offered his services. I accepted with gratitude.

> From: *Ecumenical Encounters*,
> Ngunda Elija Aran as guest.

LOR LU'S INTERCOM buzzed, and he pressed a key. "What is it, Carla?"

"Mr. Knowles would like to speak with you."

"Send him in."

The square-built security chief entered, and, ignoring the visitor chairs, remained on his feet. "Lor Lu," he said, "we may have a security problem. I got a call from Tommy Yellow Bear. He thinks we had a prowler last night, and asked me to come out to the camp. So I did."

"A prowler?"

"A guy driving an old car. He seemed okay when he drove in. Afterward he visited several tents, asking questions. Ate lunch and supper with a family named Espinosa. Later they discovered a pen they thought was his, so Espinosa went to the guy's car to give it to him. He wasn't there. Thinking maybe he'd gone to the latrine or shower house, Espinosa hung around for a few minutes. When the guy didn't come back, Espinosa returned to his tepee. Later, before going to bed, he went to the car again, and the guy still wasn't there.

"Before breakfast, about 7 o'clock, he tried again— Espinosa, that is. The car was gone. Aside from some chewing gum wrappers, all he found was this. So he went to Tommy with it, and Tommy called me." Knowles laid his attaché case on Lor Lu's desk and took out a metal disk the size of a fat nickel.

"What is it?"

"That's what I asked Espinosa." Knowles held up the small metal disk again. "He was in a ranger battalion.

He said it's the kind of battery they used in their night goggles. And it made him suspicious, because some of Krause's conversation had seemed a little strange. Krause is the name the guy gave. Tommy verified it. They use similar goggles on the tower. I suppose they're used in other things, too, but it's suggestive." Knowles laid the battery on the desk.

"It got Tommy interested, so they went over and looked in the parking lot trash barrel." He took another object from his attaché case, a clear plastic envelope about a foot square, marked with black grease pencil. "The barrel was emptied yesterday evening, and this morning, except for a garbage bag, this is all he found in it. Tommy worked for the Yakima tribal forester. They used envelopes like this to carry aerial photos in, when they made forest examinations." He handed it to Lor Lu.

"According to Espinoza, this cast some light on Krause's conversation. When Espinoza mentioned getting shot in the knee during the Lagos Rescue, Krause's eyes had lit up for a moment, as if he was really interested. Espinoza thought he was going to ask something about it, but he didn't. He never mentioned the military in the two hours they were together.

"Espinoza said that by hindsight, the guy sounded almost as if he was establishing an identity. And he asked questions about the guards; said maybe he'd apply for a job.

"When he came back for supper, Krause mentioned talking with other people camped out there. One was in a camper rig, and there's only one out there now. I talked to the owner, a fellow named Johnston, and asked him what they'd talked about. He mentioned

Krause asking about the guards, too, telling the same story. Johnston's an ex-Marine, an older guy dating from the Gulf War. He said he took for granted that Krause was ex-military, not too long out. That he'd just seemed that way. Some elite outfit, he thought. Rangers or airborne, because he didn't know a marine term Johnston used, though otherwise he had no trouble with military terms. But when Johnston asked him if he'd been in, he said no.

"Another person Krause talked to was a single guy in a tent, and Krause asked him about the guards."

"But the men on the tower didn't spot anyone?"

"Right. But at that distance from the tower, a guy alone might not be detected. The grass is crotch-high out there, and to the west and south, he'd have been covered by terrain part of the time.

"I realize the evidence is thin, but it seems to me Lloyd Krause was casing the place. He probably hiked the fence during the night, and maybe snooped the Cote, then left. Jimmy Ramirez came on gate duty at 6 A.M., and he knew what the plastic envelope is too. He'd used them in land-suitability mapping on the Jicarilla Reservation."

Lor Lu picked up the envelope and examined it. Then holding it to his forehead, he closed his eyes. "A big man," he said. "Blue eyes. Sandy brown hair. Unshaven but not bearded. A late-level young warrior of mild disposition, not intrinsically violent." He paused. "But impaired in recognizing others as being persons like himself."

He opened his eyes, looking up at Knowles. "You'd like this man. I would. But he intends us harm. What do you have in mind?"

"I'm going to phone Major Ennerby at Fort Carson. He's my contact there. He called a couple of weeks ago and told me the new anti-terrorist platoon was in place, ready to go. It hasn't been used yet—hadn't then anyway. I'll get in touch with him right now, and tell him what we've learned—and surmised. We'll see what he says."

18

Today the Vatican announced that next July, Pope John XXIV will convene the Third Vatican Council, to be titled "Transition to a New Era of Human Spirituality."

Headline News
Oct. 19

IN CERTAIN CIRCLES, Jack Russell was a man of importance. Until a few years earlier, he'd been a "captain" in the Irish Republican Army's long-disowned terrorist wing. He'd been responsible for planning and overseeing a number of bombings and assassinations, notably in England. Finally he'd left Ireland, partly because of the good work of Joseph Cardinal Flannery, now John XXIV.

For despite the Cardinal's hard-won amnesty for such as Jack Russell, the captain refused to live in an Ireland containing an autonomous Ulster, even under the constitution of Eire. Each night in his prayers, he cursed Joseph Stephen Flannery for his interference, and Gerry Adams for his perfidy.

In Canada, Russell had found a new cause and a new group—the (at most) loosely organized Catholic Soldiers in America. Most, like himself, were from Ireland, while of the rest, most were Canadians and Americans of Irish descent. (Poles, Italians, etc, need not apply, though a few token Québecois had been accepted.) Their cause was the salvation of Catholicism as they considered it should be, a Catholicism partly of the past, and partly of their various imaginings.

They had no real working plan. They brooded darkly in apartments and flats in Montreal, where the RCMP could not molest them, and plotted to murder "enemies" whose prominence would gain them publicity. So far they'd bagged two liberal bishops and a senator, as well as less prominent Catholics who'd offended them. None of the murders had taken place in Quebec, of course.

In his physical habits, Jack Russell was an orderly man, and believed everyone should be. It was that, he considered, which made him a superior planner and superior person. Thus he looked around Thomas Corkery's Boston efficiency apartment with evident distaste.

Disgraceful! he thought. It was nearly noon, and the bed was scarcely made, a lumpy quilt simply thrown across it. Books were stacked on a window sill, most with library labels on their spines. Probably overdue.

Newspaper sections and separate pages lay on sofa and table as if scattered by the wind. A banana peel lay black and curling on the kitchenette counter, making Russell's nose wrinkle, while on the table sat a saucer with a dozen cigarette butts. He could see three different coffee cups sitting about the room, all undoubtedly dirty and perhaps half full. For all that Russell knew, still others could be hiding beneath newspapers, all no doubt used by Corkery himself. The man would hardly be having guests, for who would come here, short of necessity?

At least there was no sign he'd taken to drink again. Russell himself, of course, was a conspicuously sober man, and hated working with drinkers. Unreliable! The habit was especially incompatible with one of Corkery's strongest points, his marksmanship with handguns. It was said he could shoot the spade out of the ace of spades at 10 feet without sighting.

"What brings you down from the frozen north?" Corkery asked. "Is it a job you have for me? Some little task—some wetwork you'd rather hire out than do yourself?"

Except for "wetwork," he said it in Gaelic, which he spoke fluently by the standards of the time. Spoke it deliberately here, to put his guest at a disadvantage, for Russell had barely learned it in school. Used carefully, allowing for his limitations, he could understand it, but he spoke it miserably, his tongue clumsy as a peat spade. Even as Corkery spoke, a great burly tomcat entered through an open window, probably from a fire escape, Russell thought. It jumped from the sill and stalked over to Corkery, followed by Russell's exasperated glare.

Leaning, Corkery began to scratch the scarred, nearly earless head, and a deep thrumming rose from the beast's throat. Russell's thin lips compressed. He was allergic to cats, as Corkery undoubtedly recalled, and the petting would make it worse.

Corkery's blue eyes peered across at him mockingly. "I used to call him Cuchulain, but recently I renamed him Pius XIV, in honor of the late lamented. God rest his soul. Would you care to pet him?"

Russell refused to honor the offer by replying. Corkery stood, and Pius XIV, after briefly rubbing at his human's shins, stalked to a bowl in a corner, to lap milk no doubt souring.

"So," Corkery said, "what is it you'd have me do?"

"I've an execution I'd like you to carry out." Russell answered in English, hating Corkery for his one-upmanship. The Gaelic was no proper measure of a man's Irishness, nor any sign of virtue in Corkery. It was circumstance, nothing more. Corkery had grown up in rural Kerry, apparently in a family that still used it at home. As for himself, he'd grown up in Dublin, where one seldom heard it except in school.

"A killing is it?" Corkery sounded interested, speaking English now. "And who would it be?"

"Ngunda Elija Aran, who has presumed the title Messiah. An affront to the Holy Church and to God himself."

"Aran? I've followed him in the papers, and heard him on the telly. I wasn't aware he'd claimed the mantle of Christ."

"Others claim it for him, and he's never rejected it. He'll say it in time, if he lives."

"Ah! A terrible crime." Corkery's tone was mocking. "Well, let's talk about it. After all, messiahs are supposed to die at the hands of the wicked. Why not mine?" He chuckled, then added, "No doubt you've had thoughts on how it might be done?"

The man is cold, Russell thought. *Cold. He kills for money and pleasure; the Cause means nothing to him.* "He'll be here in Boston. In January, speaking at the Bentham Avenue Unitarian Church. And Thomas, the man's security people are the best. We want no shootout, nor anything that could lead to our identification. Use a bomb, not a pistol. If it sends some Unitarians to hell with him, there's little lost."

"It won't be cheap," Corkery said. "Planting bombs of suitable size, bombs that won't be found, takes arranging and care. Also, I'll need information on the church and its services, and we're unlikely to have an insider to work with. I do know someone who custom-makes bombs, excellent bombs, but he has a cause of his own, and always needs money. Then there are costs I can't foresee till I've a plan sketched out." He paused, grinning, rubbing thumb and forefinger together in Jack Russell's face. "And of course there are my own small needs."

Russell's lips twisted sourly. It always came down to that: his specialty, getting the money. "Times are hard," he answered. "I'm prepared to give you three thousand cash today, Canadian. For a rough plan in ten days, by mail, and a detailed plan in four weeks. Then we'll see how much more is needed."

Corkery shrugged. "Indeed. And meanwhile, what derring-do will you be up to?"

The question was further mockery, another annoyance

atop the others. Russell knew what was said of him—
that when it came to killing, he lacked the stomach for
it. "I'll be in Rome by December," he answered drily,
"disposing of the antichrist with my own hand."

Corkery's eyebrows rose. "With your own hand, you
say? I'll believe that when I hear of the old man's
murder on the telly." He paused. "And you named
as the triggerman."

When Russell had left, Corkery filled a coffee cup
with the dregs from three, and put it in the microwave.
*To let a contract on a man because others call him
Messiah!* he thought, and shook his head. *Russell's
crazier than I am. He has no cause now, only hatred
looking for targets.*

"Well," he murmured aloud, "it helps pay the
bills."

19

The great Millennium scam is back in the news today. Several of its apostles are visiting foreign countries in Europe and Asia, while another is favoring South America with his holy presence. Last night a Russian-speaking disciple spoke to an estimated fifteen million viewers on Russian television.

Meanwhile Millennium's great guru has been on a flying trip to Australia and New Zealand, hoping to cash in on his father's down-under origins. . . .

The Heartland Superstation
Rock Island, IL
Oct. 22

DUKE COCHRAN HAD FALLEN asleep with the plane still on the ground in L.A. Now the pilot's voice tugged him reluctantly awake.

They'd been on the move for eleven days, days that with the help of jet lag had blurred together in Cochran's mind. They'd crossed the Pacific to Sydney by Superjet, then by charter plane had crossed and recrossed Australia. Ngunda had spoken in the continent's five major cities, then crossed the Tasman Sea to New Zealand, where he'd spoken in three more. After that they'd returned to Sydney, and another trans-Pacific jet.

The crowds had totaled 145,000, and in addition, Dove had been watched by an estimated 7.5 million on Australian and New Zealand television. Impressive, considering that the two countries combined had less than two-thirds the population of California, in an area the size of the lower forty-eight states.

They'd land in Pueblo in fifteen minutes, the pilot said. The weather there was sunny and breezy, the temperature 53 degrees, and a crowd was waiting to greet them. The Pueblo County sheriff's department estimated it at six to eight hundred. Deputies were on hand to escort Mr. Aran and his party to their helicopter. Their luggage would follow.

How many deputies? Cochran wondered, *Six? Ten? A dozen at most, and in a crowd of several hundred, there were bound to be nut cases.* He took several deep breaths to activate his groggy system, but succeeded mainly in hyperventilating.

Margaret Colletti waited in her wheelchair, unaware that her hands were twisting the rosary beneath the blanket on her lap. Or that her guts were churning. Her attention was on the chartered turboprop settling in toward the end of an east-west runway. Screened by the crowd in front of her, she lost sight of it before it touched down.

She'd planned to be on the tarmac earlier, up front, among the first, but her guts had been so nervous, she'd needed to use the restroom. The process had taken considerable time. Her sister-in-law, Elyse, at only 115 pounds, had needed to support her out of her wheelchair, and afterward back onto it. When finally they got outside, the crowd was already packed against the rope set out to help control them.

Almost without volition, Margaret began her prayer. She was a modern Catholic—one more traditional wouldn't be there—and ordinarily she'd have prayed directly to God. But somehow this time she prayed to the Virgin, the words audible to her brother holding the handles of her wheelchair.

Initially the plan had been for Fred to run interference if necessary, but Elyse had insisted on doing it. People would, she told him, get out of the way more willingly for a determined 115-pound woman than for a 180-pound man.

Margaret wished she could see more than jacketed backs. It seemed to be taking an impossibly long time. "Hail Mary, full of grace . . ." she prayed.

Her brother watched the aircraft taxi toward them from the runway. It came to a stop some two hundred feet from the crowd. A wheeled ramp was waiting, and men positioned it. A door opened in the plane's side. After a minute, people began to disembark, led by a husky white man followed closely by a tall black: Ngunda Aran.

Fred Colletti wondered sourly what had given his sister the crazy idea that this goddamned guru could do anything for her. Anything at all, let alone heal advanced, cancerous degeneration of her knees and hips. All he could see growing out of this was disappointment. He hadn't voiced his skepticism—Elyse would kill him—but he wished to hell they weren't there. *Maybe disappointment was what they needed,* he told himself, but he didn't like it. Maggie'd had more than enough grief.

He watched Ngunda say something to the husky man, then both turned and began walking toward the crowd and the police. The rest of the Millennium people started toward a nearby helicopter.

Fred Colletti watched the guru coming, a pink-palmed black hand raised in greeting. *Well hell,* he told himself, *here goes nothing,* and opened his mouth. "Make way!" he bellowed. "Make way for the wheelchair!" Elyse took it up at once, forging ahead. "Make way for the wheelchair!" she yelled. "There's someone to be healed!"

Like the Red Sea supposedly had for Moses, the crowd began to part, pressing to the sides, and Fred pushed the wheelchair through the gap. Startled deputies moved to close it off, as if a bomb or gun might lurk beneath Margaret's blanket and coat, despite the electronic screening and search she'd passed through. But Ngunda called something, and the deputies stopped.

Waiting, Margaret Colletti had been sick with an anxiety that had nearly suffocated her hope. But with Fred propelling the wheelchair at a near trot through the opening aisle, hope flared suddenly bright. Reaching the front of the crowd, she saw Ngunda not a hundred feet away, and joy surged. She heard her own voice crying out: "Heal me, Master! Heal me!" Almost shrieking it, she missed entirely Fred's muttered, "Jesus Christ!" Her brother and her wheelchair were stopped by a deputy, just short of the rope barricade.

The deputy, and the sound of her own cry, had jolted Margaret out of her ecstasy, and she stared, fearful again as she waited. Ngunda's grin softened to a smile, and reaching the rope, he stepped over it. Her eyes were fixed on him; she could feel herself trembling, vibrating. A long black hand reached toward her as if in blessing.

His words did not seem loud, but they were firm, and somehow they carried. "Stand up and walk," he said.

Again she was swept with rapture; her body almost burning with it. Unwrapping the blanket from her wasted legs, she threw it off with such strength that Elyse, who'd bent to help, backed away. Then, with hands on the arms of the chair, Margaret Colletti raised herself to her feet for the first time in half a year. For just an instant she wavered, but before Elyse could help her, she took a tottering step, then another and another toward Ngunda Aran, each step stronger. He was backing away, pushing the rope back, not retreating but encouraging, making her walk. At the same time holding out his hands, inviting her to follow. She kept coming, then screaming clutched his wrists, and he embraced her.

"It was you and God who did it," he said quietly. "I was simply the instrument."

After a moment she found herself turning, and no longer tottering, walked back to her wheelchair, lowering herself onto it unaided. *I can walk!* she told herself, *I can walk! But I won't overdo it. My legs are still weak.*

It was Elyse who pushed the wheelchair back to the terminal. Her husband was weeping too hard to steer. Meanwhile the crowd, which had watched silently, began to cheer.

A TV camera followed, recording it all: the woman, the wheelchair, the guru, and her brother's face, tears streaming. It would be on the news all over the country, the world.

The Mescalero's crowded cabin was loud with the sound of engine and rotors. Thoughts, images, memories filled Cochran's mind. Briefly he'd felt certain that the wheelchair was an assassin's ploy. When it became clear that it wasn't, he'd jumped to another assumption, that the healing was faked, a Millennium setup.

Either that or a phenomenon he'd learned about in elementary psychology—hysterical "healing," in which a disabled person, gripped by religious fervor, could sometimes briefly rise above their condition.

Cochran watched it again later, on the television in his room, while stripping off his clothes. After a shower, he collapsed for an unbroken twelve hours of sleep.

20

Arlie Ross: You spoke of loving our enemies. That's a lot easier said than done. How would you propose we go about it?

Aran: First let me say that the Tao does not insist on anyone's concept of perfection. It is infinitely understanding, infinitely accepting, infinitely loving.

As for your question . . . By the word "loving," I refer to a spectrum of emotions, a gradient scale of relating to things. At the upper end is what the ancient Greeks called agapé: loving without imposing conditions of eligibility, and without expecting anything in return. Hope, yes, but not expectations. Requiring performance of any sort falls well short of agapé.

At the lower end is violent hostility, and

equally low, the hypocrisy of saying, "I love them, I love them," while despising them or treating them as inferior, usually accompanied by demands that they change. Some clergy have been at that end.

And how can we get from the lower end to the upper? The first step, should you choose to take it, is to abstain from physically assaulting people you disagree with. The next is to abstain from assaulting them verbally. Then putting up with them grudgingly, though perhaps avoiding them so far as possible. Then learning to tolerate them philosophically. And next, respecting and even admiring them, except perhaps for some who are just too much, and whom, for the time being, you can at best tolerate. That is a major accomplishment, one you can be proud of.

Loving, truly loving one's enemies is the final step. Don't think of yourself as evil if you fall short of it. But you might want to choose agapé as an eventual goal and make progress toward it.

From Collected Conversations
with Ngunda Elija Aran

Headline News *Oct. 25, 6:00* P.M.

Today the Senate voted 57 to 44 against withdrawing from the United Nations. The withdrawal bill was not expected to pass, but the vote was expected to be closer. This was the largest Republican crossover vote during the Metzger administration.

The House Rules Committee declined to pass on to the full House an America Party proposal to establish a guiding principle for all legislation. This would be: "God's injunction to man to be fruitful and multiply, and fill the earth and subdue it; and have dominion over the fish of the sea and over the birds of the air and over every living thing that moves upon the earth."

Rules Committee Chairman Bill Staszik, Centrist from Ohio, commented afterward that while Hebrew folklore contained much valuable wisdom and inspiration, twenty-first-century Americans needed to evaluate it in the light of twenty-first-century conditions. He also pointed out that the proposal was wildly unconstitutional.

In a particularly bizarre incident, another executive of a major corporation was targeted by terrorist assassins today. Roy C. Wallace, the leading star of mergerdom, was attacked moments after leaving his midtown Manhattan offices. Wallace is the founder and CEO of Carley Jane Management Enterprises. Explosives and firebombs were thrown at his armored limousine, stopping it and engulfing it in flame. At the same time, automatic weapons fire was directed at it from windows. Despite wearing flak jackets, Wallace's chauffeur and both his bodyguards died at the scene. Eight bystanders were killed. Seventeen others were injured and taken to hospitals, eleven in serious or critical condition. Wallace was rushed by helicopter to the Cornell University Medical Center, where he was pronounced dead on arrival.

He had been released from Merlyndale Hospital less

than two weeks ago, after recuperating from bullet
wounds received in August.

A CNN News Feature Summary, *November 1*

Five years ago this month, the Newcastle Four were
convicted of felony computer sabotage. That they were
uncovered and a compelling case made must have
shocked crackers. While the severity of their sentences,
and the Supreme Court's refusal to review the case,
were sobering on the one hand, they were assuring
on the other.

That and technological innovations in computer security
shrank computer sabotage virtually out of existence.
The almost invariable requirement of reparations can,
in severe instances, strip the computer criminal of
everything he owns, while appropriate amends to society
can require productive servitude for years, even life.

Computer security specialists, however, have insisted
all along that it was only a respite. Yesterday's so-
called "Black Plague" virus proved them right. The
virus crashed ICL, the International Computerized
Library, whose opening, early last year, was heralded
as the greatest single advance in the communication
of knowledge since invention of the transistor. The
ICL stored and gave access to virtually every existing
public document except the most confidential. It was
heavily used by researchers and students of every kind,
as well as the simply curious.

So far the FBI is saying nothing about the investigation.
However, library personnel believe the virus was written

and inserted by someone with intimate knowledge, presumably inside knowledge, of the ICL programs. Because the backup cubes made were also infected, during the last months, the amount of retrieveable data is expected to be a small fraction of the total.

The direct damages are expected to be in the hundreds of millions. Indirect costs, due to postponed and cancelled library services, the increased costs of doing research, and the development and installation of new security measures, will be much greater. And more seriously, to reenter the billions of documents will take years.

21

Breuer: You've said that hypersensitivity is a major weakness in society, but it seems to me that *lack* of sensitivity is a much greater weakness.

Aran: [laughing] Lack of sensitivity *is* a weakness. But consider how many people are afraid of learning, of doing, of expressing their opinions, because they're afraid of criticism, and especially of scorn. This is particularly true of children. And how much criticism results from hypersensitivity to imperfections—and *perceived* imperfections—in other people! And in public and private agencies! I'm talking about intolerance now—often chronic intolerance—of modest flaws. That's a major weakness in society all by itself.

Breuer: But isn't the alternative a fatal

permissiveness of poor performance and malfeasance?

Aran: If carried to extremes. But what levels of performance can we appropriately require? From the viewpoints of tidiness, of efficiency, of communication, of loving each other—from those viewpoints—we're an imperfect species in an imperfect world. Let me repeat: an imperfect species in an imperfect world. Our most precise and perfect science—tool, field of learning—is mathematics. But when applied to the real world, even math has a wealth of imperfections. How much more true that is of such imprecise activities as parenting, teaching, business, government—and evaluating people!

This doesn't mean you shouldn't try to improve things. What it does mean is not being *hyper*critical. It means being compassionate, instead of attacking or ridiculing people for perceived flaws, which may, after all, exist largely or entirely in the eye of the beholder. And when pointing out demonstrable shortcomings, it means being mild, factual, and constructive, not scathing or scornful.

Compassion, incidentally, is not the same thing as pity, though they sometimes resemble each other superficially.

Breuer: Okay, I see what you're getting at. But surely you don't imagine people will stop scathing and ridiculing others.

Aran: Not entirely, and not all at once. But I do imagine scathing and ridiculing becoming

much less, as people become aware of them
as harmful. And especially as they grow in
love—in love of themselves and one another.
　　　　　　　From the first appearance of
　　　　　　　　　　Ngunda Elija Aran on
　　　　　　　　Conversations with Warren Breuer

───────────

THE WORD HAD BEEN passed two days earlier:
A team from CNN would arrive at the Cote to tape
a special on Millennium. A chartered shuttle-copter
from Pueblo landed shortly before 9 A.M., and a CNN
production van pulled in minutes later.

The crew scattered almost on arrival, different
people looking at different aspects of Millennium's
headquarters' operations. At noon, cameras even
recorded families eating in the staff dining room.

At lunch, Lee's daughters, especially Raquel, were
full of a camera team's late morning visit at school.
It had recorded classes in operation, and interviewed
several children. One team had recorded an exchange
of questions and answers between Raquel and a teacher,
Mrs. Lundgren. Then it had visited with Raquel alone,
which Becca said demonstrated the attraction sages
had for public exposure.

A Ms. Thomas visited Lee's office at 2:10, accompanied by two cameramen. Meryl Thomas was darker
than many African-Americans. Perhaps forty years old,
she was tall, slender, stylish, and sure of herself. She
suggested that Lee call her Meryl, and asked intelligent
questions without being confrontational.

To Lee it was obvious that Thomas had been well
briefed in advance. By Anne Whistler, she supposed.

She herself had been given several areas to avoid discussing, but beyond that was constrained only by professional ethics.

The experience wasn't bad at all, but when Thomas and her camera team left at 2:50, Lee was glad to see them go.

At 4:20, Lor Lu stopped by. "How was it?" he asked.

"Better than I'd expected."

"Ah. And what did you think of Meryl Thomas?"

"Intelligent. Able. Courteous! I liked her as well as I would anyone under the circumstances."

"Good. She's asked to interview some staff families in their homes, and I agreed to let her pick two, one each evening. Subject to their agreement, of course. She wants to do yours: you, Ben, and the girls."

Lee's face registered her dislike of the idea.

"You don't have to do it," he went on. His easy gaze never let her go. "It's your choice. I've asked Ben, and he said fine if you're willing. I presume the girls are willing." He laughed. "Raquel could occupy a team by herself."

When he left, Lee couldn't quite remember how it had happened, but she'd said yes. They were to expect a camera team at 7:30. She looked forward to it uneasily, and called Ben to let him know. They decided to eat supper in the staff dining room.

Lee didn't eat much. She felt somehow threatened, though how and by what she didn't know.

The team arrived at 7:30, and by 7:35 all four Shoreffs were seated in the living room with Meryl

Thomas. She addressed them one at a time, beginning with Becca.

"I understand you just arrived here a month ago. How do you like school on the Ranch?"

"A lot," Becca answered. "I like my teachers a lot, and the other kids, and my classes. I've always liked school, but I like this one best."

"What do you especially like about it?"

"You really learn things here. Where we came from, I was in a class for gifted kids"—Lee noticed she didn't name her old school, and Meryl Thomas didn't ask—"and the ordinary classes here are at least as . . . tough's not the word, or demanding. Maybe *requiring*. I'd just started trigonometry there, but here, lots of kids take it in fifth grade, some in the fourth. I'm in the sixth. I don't think anyone here gets through the sixth without it."

Thomas turned to Raquel. "What do you like about it here, Raquel? Or dislike?"

"I don't dislike anything about it. It's fun! One of the things I'm taking is human geography, that they didn't even have in grade school, back—where we came from. And the teachers know how to help by asking questions that make you realize stuff.

"And I really *really* like book discussion class. We've just started on the Life of Socrates. He's *really* interesting! And after school, the older kids can get Life Healing. Becca's old enough now, and we're working on Mom for permission. In January, when I'm ten, I'll be old enough, too, and if Becca gets to, then I will. And . . ." She paused. "I better stop and let other people talk. I forget to sometimes. I'm an old sage in passion mode, with a goal of growth. We tend to talk too much."

Thomas laughed. "I think you're neat, Raquel, and you really helped me feel what it's like."

After that, Meryl Thomas talked mainly with Lee and Ben, until 8:30, when the hour was up. Before she left, she told Lee she'd like to talk with her privately, off camera. "I have questions not appropriate for this interview, second thoughts that developed after our talk this afternoon. There's a small coffee shop in the visitors' lodge. We can have a degree of privacy there. Our conversation will be off the record." She grinned. "You can ask *me* questions, if you'd like."

Lee usually had good presence, even when she was disturbed, and she knew it. Also, she almost always handled herself well one-on-one, though the realization never seemed to protect her much from advance nervousness. But this invitation felt somehow dangerous—and it was with surprise tinged with dismay that she found herself agreeing again.

She rode in the production van with Thomas. It dropped them off at the visitors' lodge, and before they went in, Thomas paused, looking upward. "The sky here is unbelievable," she said quietly. "I've never seen so many stars. It's the lack of city lights, I guess, and the elevation. The thin air."

They went inside. Lee had never been in the visitors' lodge before. A single employee was tending the softly-lit coffee shop. "Our team is most of the visitors they have in this building just now," Thomas said.

She led Lee to a window table. A minute later the waitress came over and took their orders. Thomas asked for low-fat lemon cheesecake and an herb tea,

Lee a dinner salad and decaf. For a moment they disagreed over who would pay, but Thomas prevailed. "You're here as a courtesy to me," she said, "and I'm on an expense account."

She paused. "You're wondering why I asked you. After our interview this afternoon, I talked with Lor Lu about my interviews, and told him you were different than the others. I couldn't put my finger on what it was though, so I asked him. Do you know what he said?"

Lee smiled slightly. "He probably told you to ask me."

Thomas laughed. "Exactly." Her face became suddenly intent. "What is the difference? Between you and the others."

"I suppose it's that they're true believers, most of them at least. They believe in Mr. Aran, in what he says, and they probably believe he's . . . whatever it is he's supposed to be. I've never heard it said here."

"Interesting. Are you uncomfortable with that?"

"A little. Sometimes. The people are remarkably easy to work with. Smart, and with very good attitudes. I like all of them I've met, without exception, including Mr. Aran. But the things they seem to believe . . ." She shrugged.

The waiter arrived, set their orders on the table, then left. Both women began to eat, Lee poking fitfully at her salad, afraid she'd said something she shouldn't have. By contrast, Thomas ate with evident enjoyment, taking small bites and savoring them.

After a couple of minutes she asked, "Why did you come here if you have misgivings? Clearly you do."

Lee nodded. "I like the job and the challenge.

And my office. And in these times I especially like the money; they pay me well."

"I suppose they do. Lor Lu says your job is quite important, and that you're very good at it."

"He's right."

"What does your husband think of all this?"

"He likes it unreservedly. I think he believes. Or maybe it's more that he doesn't actually disbelieve. He's been interested in New Age philosophies since before we met. We've been together nearly five years."

"And your daughters believe?"

Instead of answering aloud, Lee simply nodded.

"It's that bad, is it?"

"Meryl—if it weren't for the girls, I'd love working here. But they're children. I'd never have brought them into a cult environment if my consulting business hadn't basically died. We were seriously in debt, our home was being foreclosed on, and neither Ben nor I were having any luck finding work. So when this opportunity found us, it seemed we had no choice. I mean, they wanted both of us! Ben and me!"

Thomas frowned. "So the problem seems to be that your daughters believe. How bad is that, actually?"

"It's a cult, Meryl, and my children are becoming part of it. They may grow out of it, but for now . . ."

"What makes it a cult?"

For a moment the question stalled Lee's mental processes. "It's—the things they say. That they believe."

"And what are those?"

"Oh, past lives. And things like Raquel was talking about to you this evening—that she's an old sage in passion mode. *Passion mode,* for god's sake! She's only a child!"

Meryl Thomas's dark eyes were intent now, seeming to gleam. "What does that mean: old sage? And passion mode?"

Lee looked blankly at her. "I . . . don't know. Some cultist thing."

"Wait a minute. Let's see if I've got this straight. Things like 'old sage' and 'passion mode' make it a cultist thing. But how can you know that if you don't know what 'old sage' and 'passion mode' mean? And as for past lives, two of the world's oldest and largest religions believe in them—as well as a lot of mainstream Americans. 'Try this out, see how it feels.' Instead of 'true believers,' think of the Millennium people as dedicated to what they consider as helping."

She paused, waiting. When Lee didn't respond, she continued. "What church did you grow up in?"

"Evangelical Reformed. It's pretty strict, I'm afraid."

"And they taught you . . . ?"

"About heaven and hell, and Jesus . . . The usual."

"Those are pretty far out, aren't they? And what does Ngunda teach?"

Lee sank inwardly. "I don't know," she answered, realizing that her WebWorld search had avoided that part of it. She'd told herself it was irrelevant. She realized now she'd been afraid to know.

"Maybe your fears are worse than the reality."

Lee didn't answer. It occurred to her she should be angry at this black woman who was exposing her to herself.

Thomas reached, and lay a hand on one of Lee's. "My dear, I've horned in where I have no business being, and I apologize. It's a characteristic of mine, I'm afraid. I'm a mature scholar in aggression mode. Now it's time for you to ask me questions."

Lee sat unspeaking. *Mature scholar. Aggression mode.* Ordinarily she'd feel betrayed by this woman. Angry. Instead she felt somehow defeated. Defeated beyond redemption.

"Well then," Thomas went on, "I'll volunteer some things. I grew up in Arlensville, Maryland, in one of the projects. I never knew my father. But we weren't as bad off as lots were, because my mom had a decent job, and my grandparents lived in the same building. They looked after me when Mom was at work. I grew up in the Methodist Church, and learned some strange things there that all in all did me more good than harm. A lot more, I think; I've never tried to sort it out. I've got an older brother who's a career Marine NCO, a gunnery sergeant. After the third grade, my granddad home-schooled me. He'd been a teacher, but he quit to look after me, and worked nights at the post office. I took journalism at William and Mary, on a scholarship. I was married once, a disaster, and haven't cared to try again. And I'm in aggression mode, as I mentioned. Overall it's stood me in good stead, but it's a considerably mixed blessing.

"And actually I arrived here knowing quite a bit about Millennium, in a tangential sort of way—more than routine preproduction research would tell me. I did a piece on Ladder, two years ago, at White River, Arizona, on the Fort Apache Reservation. The piece got a lot of favorable attention, and impressed my bosses. That's why they were so ready to approve this one.

"And Ladder really impressed me. Enough that afterward I got Millennium's Abilities Release processing in Atlanta, the whole procedure."

She paused, squeezed Lee's hand. "I'm sorry, but I seem to have totally blown this conversation. I betrayed your trust, which I shouldn't have. It was arrogant; arrogance is my chief negative feature. It's a lot weaker than it used to be, but right when I least expect it, snap! It grabs and runs with me."

Lee's mouth was a thin and bitter line, and she didn't meet Thomas's eyes. "I need to go home now," she said stiffly. "Ben will be wondering about me."

"Of course. I'll be right back, with keys to the van."

She returned within three minutes. Neither talked on the short drive back to the Shoreff home, but Thomas walked Lee to her porch, then stood with her hands on the white woman's arms. "Lee," she said, "just know that I respect and admire you, as a mother, wife, professional, and person. You're quality, a class act."

Then she turned and left.

Lee said little to Ben, except that she was getting a headache, a fiction she'd never resorted to before. Then she disappeared into the bedroom, leaving him to put the girls to bed. When he came in, an hour later, she was still awake, memory loops old and recent cycling sluggishly, fruitlessly through her mind. She did not turn to sex for consolation, as she commonly did when troubled. She was sunken in apathy, that lowest and darkest of moods, where it seems that nothing will help. Consolation felt out of reach, and Ben seemed to know it, for when he lay down, he simply murmured, "Healing dreams, sweetheart," and very lightly kissed her cheek. Then he closed his own eyes, and soon slept. As eventually she would, a healing sleep deeper than her apathy, and busy with dreams that would not be remembered even vaguely. When she got up in the morning, a scalding shower and scalding coffee soon had her fit for work, though she was more indrawn than usual.

22

WORK BROUGHT LEE the rest of the way out of herself—a morning of aligning job descriptions with their flow charts, then running them through various trial sequences in her computer. At lunch she was somewhat uncommunicative, but her mind was on the tests, not on the night before. The television crew was still at the Cote, doing interviews, but they weren't impinging upon her.

Shortly after returning to her office, there was a knock at her door. "Yes?" she called.

"It is I. Dove."

The voice itself, and the grammar, would have been enough. "Come in," she said. He had, she supposed, seen rough cuts of yesterday's TV coverage, and was stopping by to comment.

She was mistaken. "Lor Lu went over your progress with me," Ngunda said. "He is unreservedly pleased, and I agree with him. He'd expected excellent results, but hadn't realized how excellent. I thought you'd like to know."

She did. "Thank you," she said. "At the beginning, I was surprised at how positive he was that I was the person for the job. I knew my recommendations were good, but . . ."

"Your references were a relatively small factor in Lor Lu's expectations. He is a *bodhisatva,* and thus without many of the perceptual barriers typical of humankind. So meeting you and Ben sharpened the vectors for him—his sense of the—let us say the probabilistic spray of results which might transpire should we hire you."

For a moment, Lee felt light-headed. In a general way she'd understood what Ngunda was telling her, but all she found to say was, "Actually he rattled me. He could easily have left with a poor impression, or worse."

Ngunda laughed. "Different beholders, different conclusions."

Different beholders. "What," she asked, "is a *bodhisatva?* Is that what he meant by 'holy man extraordinary'?"

Ngunda's eyebrows jumped. "Ah! Probably, in a humorous vein. A *bodhisatva,* as we use the term, is a soul which has graduated from the Earth School, so to speak. It has completed a full curriculum of lessons, of lives and deaths, and of course the between-lives reviews. But it chooses to be reborn anyway, to carry out some task, some project. And having no further karma to deal with, and no necessary lessons still to learn, is more perceptive than other humans. Thus

Lor Lu gained a sense of you, simply by putting his attention on you from a distance. Then, by meeting you, his perceptions of the vectors were both strengthened and expanded."

The words washed over her without sticking. She should, she thought, be perturbed by all this weird, New Age credulity, but somehow it didn't seem that terrible. Crazy, yes, but she could deal with it—as long as it didn't seriously infect her daughters. That was the bottom line.

"When he returned from Bridgeport," Ngunda continued, "he told me you would be able to examine a complex of situations, see potential problems, and intuitively recognize approaches to their solution."

Lee nodded. She'd never looked at it that way, but it fitted. "Thank you for your courtesy," she said, almost as if dismissing him. "I'm happy things are working out that well."

"You are quite welcome," Ngunda answered, and turning, left.

Bodhisatva! she thought as the door closed behind him. *The first time I hear that word from Becca or Raquel, I'll blow my top.*

23

What does the Tao intend us to do? Why, to choose, make our own choices. Which we can't help doing, even when we *choose* to follow someone else's orders or advice. Or when we choose not to *choose*, for that too is a choice, with effects on ourselves and on others. The Tao intends us to navigate our own way among the shoals and whirlpools of life, learning as we go.

Hopefully keeping an eye on our life task as we steer. Not some goal or task that someone else—our parents, our peers, society—has selected for us, but the goal and the task that each of us chose for this life before we were born into it.

Such remembering is easier said than done. Our Essence knows, and undertakes to remind us; but given the pressures and distractions of life—perhaps what others think we should do—too often we don't notice or heed those nudges and impulses. So it can be useful to sort out for ourselves what our life goal and life task might be.

But if we go astray, we are not damned. The Tao damns no one. We don't even damn ourselves. We simply experience results, and take responsibility for our actions. There are lessons and growth in every choice we make. No choice is wasted, and the Tao continues to love us unconditionally.

From *The Collected Public Dialogs of Ngunda Elija Aran*

————————

THE OLD DODGE all-wheel-drive carryall looked like a lot of vehicles used by backcountry types—large mud tires, a front-mounted winch, and camouflage paint, recamouflaged by dried mud and road dust. A spotlight, cleaned of mud, was mounted in front of the driver's door, available for poaching at night. The Colorado license plates were not those it normally wore, back home in Albuquerque. They'd come from a junk vehicle.

It was Lute Koskela who drove, though the rig was not his. They'd set up this operation on a tight timetable, and he was the one who'd scouted the area. He drove slowly, without lights, till the ill-graded gravel road took him into pine forest. There, dimmed headlights would not be visible from a distance, and in the

forest they were necessary; trees drastically reduced
the natural twilight. Now he watched for the faded
pink surveyor's ribbon he'd tied round a tree more
than two weeks earlier. An old inconspicuous ribbon,
taken from a roadside tree miles away, a meaningless
leftover from some years-old survey job. Which was
exactly how he'd wanted it to look.

He was perhaps an hour behind schedule, the
result of slow service at a restaurant, and a flat tire.
But they'd continued. Sarge wanted to get it over
with, and the delay didn't seem serious. And Lute
wasn't much given to reading omens into things. By
nature, he was alert and observant, and by training
and experience doubly so. Spotting the ribbon, he
turned off the graveled road onto a primitive truck
trail, which wound half a mile to the forest's edge.
There he parked, the carryall screened by a fringe of
saplings. Then he and the others climbed out.

Sarge, the large black man who owned the carryall,
removed a panel in a false deck in back, exposing a
shallow compartment. By flashlight he took from it five
M-16s, five web harnesses with appended gear, and
an Uzi. Then he replaced the panel and the carpeting
that covered it. From a pocket on their harnesses, five
men took night goggles. They'd traveled light. They
didn't expect a serious fight, or any fight at all, and
should be back before dawn.

A sixth man stood by, scar-faced from a broken
bottle in a bar fight, and with one leg surgically shortened after an ugly wound in Nigeria. He was taciturn
in almost any circumstance, and at a time like this
said nothing at all. When the five were ready to go,
Koskela spoke to him, quietly and needlessly. They'd

been over it before, but under the circumstances, redundancy was advisable. Excusable at least.

"We should be back by daylight," he said. "If we're not, hang out here till nine, then drive to Big Spring Campground. You know the drill."

The scarred face jerked a curt nod, clearly visible by night goggles. The five then walked out into the rangeland, and Lute took a compass shot; after that he'd guide mainly on stars. Then they set off across the grassland, and were swallowed by night.

When Lute had scouted the area, he hadn't expected to carry out the operation till the following May. Typically, Carl hadn't considered the problems, including snow cover, when he'd called Lute in Portland. Lute had half expected snow by now, which would preclude the operation. He'd made that clear before leaving Montana, and later on the phone. Carl hadn't been happy. He wanted Ngunda dead long before spring. He'd actually sounded worried that someone else might kill the guru first, denying him involvement.

So Lute had rented computer time at Kinko's in Pueblo. On the Web, he checked out the thirty-day weather outlook for the region. A dry autumn was expected.

On that basis, he'd gotten hold of Sarge, who'd agreed to the proposal. Sarge had always been reckless, and had so far gotten away with it. Sarge in turn had gotten in touch with others in the Southwest, from as far as Phoenix and El Paso. Four had signed on, including Romero, who'd stay with the vehicle.

There'd been a couple of worrisome days when a Pacific storm moved northwest across Baja, but it had dumped most of its moisture on the Arizona plateau and the San Juans—forty inches of snow on Wolf Creek Pass, and twenty-one at Conejos, wherever the hell Conejos was. But that ate up most of the storm, and it ran out of juice on the west slope of the Sangre de Cristos. At Lauenbruck, according to the Web, all they'd gotten was a trace, not enough to settle the dust.

The ground was drier than a popcorn fart. For his purposes, conditions were definitely better now than they'd be after the spring thaw.

A slender moon stood about forty degrees above the western horizon, with maybe three hours to go before it set. With night goggles they didn't need it. Two more miles and Lute called a break. None of them were in prime shape, nothing like when they were in active service, but they never let themselves get soft. Their endurance just wasn't what it had been. While they rested on the lumpy bunchgrass slope, he stargazed. *This might,* he thought, *be my last gig.* He'd never planned to make it a lifetime profession. Too many of the oldtimers, if they survived and stuck with it, got eccentric beyond belief. *Which is all right, if that's what you get off on,* he'd told himself, *but for me?* And some of the people you worked for were assholes through and through, no more trustworthy than a skunk in a henhouse. Others were more or less trustworthy, but ignorant. Like Carl. Carl had no idea what a job like this took.

A meteor streaked across the sky, disappearing in mid flight. Burned up, Lute supposed. He wondered if a big one would hit in his lifetime. Maybe like the one that had made Meteor Crater near Winslow. He'd visited it once, 4,000 feet across and 600 deep, made some—he couldn't remember its supposed age—twenty thousand years came to him. Someone had estimated the meteor at 85 feet across, probably breaking up just before it hit, traveling yea-many thousand miles an hour. It was hard to imagine something so small making such a big hole, but at that speed . . . He wished he could have watched it happen, maybe from the high peak north of Flagstaff, fifty miles distant.

He looked at the glowing face of his watch, and grunting, rolled to his feet. *Five years ago*, he told himself, *you didn't grunt like that.*

Lieutenant Jerry Marovitch led his two squads in ranks to the Bell Commando, the "whisper craft" that waited, warmed up and ready on the short-takeoff strip. It could make a miles-long glide approach, drop troops from under a thousand feet, and not have to draw on engine power for another mile and a half, even given the elevation of this drop zone. Great for inserting people undetected.

He and his men had all jumped many times— qualifying jumps, training jumps, and recreational sky-diving—but none had seen combat. Tonight they just might. Not a full-fledged military encounter, but a firefight. Quite possibly with casualties, depending on the weaponry, quality and attitude of the people they'd confront.

Whatever, he told himself. *What we won't do is embarrass ourselves.*

He had no doubt of the outcome. He had all the advantages: surprise, and satellite info hardly short of real-time. The terrorists would be either captured or shot, depending on whether they surrendered. The OH-6G would be on hand immediately after the jump, with high-resolution night viewers. And if it came down to it, a sponson-mounted 7.62 Thrasher, and variable-proximity, anti-personnel Bummers. From a bit farther away, the noisier Blackhawk could arrive within minutes to pick up prisoners and casualties.

And if somehow the satellite data were in error, and they needed more muscle, there was a 6HD standing by on a ready pad at Carson. It could deliver the rest of the platoon within half an hour, and haul plenty of prisoners and casualties.

What he really had on his mind, though, was not casualties or prisoners or the outcome of the fighting. He was worried about any and all of the unforeseeable goofs that might occur in a maiden action. For this was the baptismal mission of the president's new, secret, anti-terrorist platoons, and he was in charge. He remembered the World War Two stories his grandfather had told, about the snafus in upper echelon planning and aerial delivery that *his* old unit, the 509th Parachute Infantry Battalion, had had to overcome by dint of blood and sweat, from North Africa to Germany. The cost of doing things for the first time, things no one had done before.

This couldn't be that bad. The risks were less military than political. But if something went wrong, and the story leaked, the president's enemies would be on it like a Rottweiler on a pet rabbit, and his own career would be in deep shit.

❖   ❖   ❖

Lute realized they were in the soup shortly after they'd crossed the fence onto the Ranch. A voice called for them to stop where they were and throw down their weapons. It sounded electronic, a hand-held loud-hailer. Lute hit the ground instantly, knowing intuitively the voice was backed by firepower.

"We have you in our sights," the voice continued, "and will not hesitate to shoot. Either comply or be killed."

Lute scanned the ground. Whoever they were, they had to be pros, and well trained. Airborne rangers, probably. They'd taken advantage of a topographic undulation about eighty yards ahead; had probably been watching through a periscope. Now, through his goggles, he could see where they were, but not any targets. They'd have instructions to bring in prisoners if possible, otherwise corpses.

The question was, what would it take to start the shooting? They hadn't fired when their quarry hit the dirt. That was hopeful. What was less hopeful were the penalties provided for in the Anti-Terrorism Act, a minimum of twenty years in a federal penitentiary, with no time off for good behavior.

"What now, Koskela?" Sarge murmured.

"That little draw off to our left," Lute answered quietly. "It'll give cover. Whoever wants to can stay here." It was only forty yards or so. Just near enough to be tempting.

He counted softly to three, then all but he broke for it. It took a second or two before gunfire erupted. Lute stayed for perhaps three seconds more—hopefully the ambushers had their full attention on the others—then crawled off in the opposite direction, expecting to draw fire momentarily. After the first twenty seconds he began to hope. A minute later he came to another shallow draw, and rolled into it.

He could hardly believe he was alive.

This draw was smaller, perhaps four feet wide and twenty inches deep, and its soil had stayed moist longer. And inside the fence there'd been no grazing; thus, in the draw, the grass stood some thirty inches high, hiding him from ready notice by troops on the ground. But if they searched, they'd find him. From the air, the most casual instrument scan would find him.

Koskela didn't think those things, he simply knew them. For the moment he lay gathering himself. Then he heard something that brought a muttered oath from him, the sound of a chopper approaching.

He hugged the ground more tightly, and for the first time he could remember, began to pray.

Koskela heard the little OH-6G land, heard the rotors stop, heard distant voices, and realized that if he had a chance at all, this was it. He began crawling down the shallow draw as rapidly as he could, which, given infantry and ranger training, was fast. Meanwhile the draw deepened a bit, and rising to a crouch, he began to trot.

A quarter mile later, his night goggles showed him possible salvation ahead, in the form of a windmill and a large round livestock tank. He arrived at about the time he heard the OH-6G in the air again. Peering into the tank, he saw a few inches of smelly water; not nearly enough to submerge in and hide his heat signature.

Anxiety gripped him, and he started around its

perimeter. If he lay close against it on the side away from the chopper . . .

That's when he found the burrow, apparently excavated by a coyote to shelter an expected litter. At this time of year, no one should be home. Taking off his gear, he pushed it into the hole, wriggled after it feetfirst, and pulled his M-16 in with him. Then he lay with his head inside the entrance, listening to the chopper fly a search pattern.

He prayed that the warmth of his body, where he'd lain sweating in the draw, had dissipated enough from the dry ground surface that the chopper wouldn't spot the signature. If it did, they'd trail him sure as hell. It occurred to him to wonder if his prayer had helped, but he rejected the thought even as it arose. Things like that didn't happen. In following the draw, he had inevitably come to the tank, and circling the tank, could hardly have missed finding the burrow.

His mind went to his buddies, and his abandonment of them. Rationalizing, he could have told them to surrender, but he couldn't imagine Sarge doing that, any more than he would. The others conceivably, but not Sarge. With all the shooting, he had little doubt they'd been cut down. He could only hope they hadn't all been killed.

About an hour after he'd heard the last of the chopper, Luther Koskela crawled from the burrow. He felt dangerously exposed, out in the open, and had no doubt at all he'd need to be well away from there before daylight. Meanwhile he was on foot, and a long way from safety.

24

Q: Well, suppose someone breaks into my house, and I'm afraid he'll kill me. So I shoot him, and he dies. Am I guilty of karma?

A: You may or may not be guilty of manslaughter, but you're never *guilty* of karma. Karma is a mechanism provided by the Tao to help learning take place. And when we choose certain actions, we create or extinguish karmic nexuses.

Let's suppose you do kill him, and that prior to that moment, you shared no karmic nexus with him. Now you've created one, even though you may have felt compelled to it by a perceived danger to your life. And someday you'll have to cancel that nexus with him, with both of you learning lessons in the process.

On the other hand, if you choose not to kill him, and he kills you, then he creates a karmic nexus. And if neither of you chooses to shoot—if he flees, or if you let him rob you—normally no karmic nexus is created. But lessons result nonetheless.

Q: What about a soldier in wartime, that kills a lot of people? What about the crew of the bomber that dropped the Hiroshima bomb? How in the world would they ever cancel—extinguish—so many karmic nexuses?

A: War is a special case. A soldier does not create karmic nexuses with those he is required to kill in battle. He does learn powerful lessons, but the process and the lessons are not karmic.

Q: That's the most outrageous crap I've ever heard! It treats killing as nothing more than—than some kind of legalistic *game!* Jesus would never have said anything like that!

A: To create a karmic nexus requires depriving someone of choice in some major area of their life. If someone chooses to treat it as a game, that is their prerogative, but they will, of course, deal with the consequences sooner or later. As for the teachings of Jesus, they were the teachings most needed by the people of his time, phrased in terms meaningful to them. They established a new platform for the further social and spiritual evolution of the human species. Put another way, Jesus's teachings produced an important turn in the flow of human history. Which was all the Tao intended.

From The Collected Public Dialogs
of Ngunda Elija Aran

THE LIGHTS WERE STILL on in Art Knowles' office. He had a secure telecom line with Major Ennerby at Fort Carson, and he'd be informed if there was anything he needed to know. Anything necessary for the safety of Millennium's people. Still, he wished he had the platoon's confidential radio frequency, and the necessary descrambler, to hear what was going on. He hadn't heard the whisper craft pass over the Cote, though it had powered up its quiet engines by then. But later he'd heard automatic weapons in the distance, continuing for about five seconds.

He hoped no one had been killed. He hoped no terrorists had gotten through. He hoped . . . *Hell,* he told himself, *why don't you just go to bed and leave it to the Tao?* What was that line in Luke again? He'd enjoyed it in the exchange between Dove and some pharisee: Who, by worrying, could add an hour to his life? That was the gist of it.

Instead of going to bed, he went to his beverage station and drew a cup of decaf. It was too late at night for real coffee. Then sitting down with a long-unread volume from his Raymond Chandler collection, Knowles leaned back and began to read. He'd stay up awhile and see if Ennerby . . .

His phone rang. *Ah ha!* he thought, and reaching, switched it on. There were two or three seconds of strange sound, suggesting an ultra-condensed violin concerto, followed by a beep—the descrambler disposing of residual data, and reprogramming itself. "This is Art Knowles," he said.

"Art, this is Major Royce Ennerby, at Carson. All's clear. We've rounded them up."

"What are the stats? I'm curious."

"If I could tell you, I would. And maybe I can, in a day or two. I'll make a point of asking. We'll see."

"Thanks, Major. Remember, I put in a good word for you."

It was their little joke. The major had asked him to put in a word for him "upstairs," and he'd said he would. He hadn't, of course. He considered his sense of spiritual dynamics quite limited, but such as it was, it didn't accommodate prayer of that sort.

The White House chief of staff didn't like to bother the President at breakfast, even when she ate it in the Oval Office, which more and more she did. But she had asked to be informed as soon as he'd heard. It was, after all, a sort of pet project.

So he was there an hour earlier than her receptionist, rapping firmly on the President's office door. "It's Heinie," he said.

"Come in," she called, and he entered. "Pour some coffee if you want."

"I had some." He paused. "The Fort Carson platoon saw action last night."

She straightened, her eyes sharpening. "Really! What's the story?"

"Millennium had evidence that someone had snooped the Ranch, so they informed Major Ennerby. He then had the Mid-America geosynchronous satellite instructed to provide a focus on any apparently human activity within a ten-mile radius of the Cote, except for the immediate vicinity of roads, and the hippie camp. Anything outside certain parameters, it would relay to him with visuals.

"Last evening about dark, it showed five humans start out of the woods, eight miles away, on what appeared to be a compass course for the Cote. He sent out a squad in a whisper craft, and they took a terrain position to intercept. When ordered to stop, the intruders broke for nearby cover. The rangers opened fire, killing three and wounding one. The fifth was captured. I can't imagine they have a clue to how they'd been found out. The two prisoners have been kept apart, so they can't compare notes. They're being, or will be, interrogated by the Bureau, but I haven't been informed of any results."

"What about evidence? What did they find?"

"Contraband M-16s, fragmentation and concussion grenades, and shriekers. Each man had a sketch map of the Cote, sketched on aerial photo blowups, with Ngunda's cottage circled. Their van contained assorted other military contraband, including electronics."

"I suppose the squad had an advocate along?"

"One jumped with them; I've talked to him. He assured me that everything was done by the book."

"And none of our people were hurt?"

"None. I asked."

"A success then."

"A success."

The President sat frowning. "Then why don't I feel good about it? This project is my baby, or one of them, and its very first operation has been a success."

"Maybe because the AT platoon concept—the whole Anti-Terrorism Act—crowds the Bill of Rights pretty hard. Now if you were to declare martial law . . ." He shrugged.

"That again. You know where I stand on that. Martial law is like morphine; it requires larger and larger doses. Use it for anything short of a deadly emergency, and you're asking for addiction."

"Agreed."

"That's it then?"

"There's one thing I haven't gotten to yet. There was a CNN news team at the Cote—they'd just completed a special there—and they heard the gunfire, obviously automatic weapons. They don't know what the situation was, but they heard the racket. Millennium declined to comment on what it might have been, but carrying honesty to an extreme, they didn't deny knowing. They only said it wasn't them. And the army isn't commenting.

"However, there's nothing in law to prevent CNN's reporting the gunfire, and speculating about it."

The President shook her head in annoyance. *God damn Murphy's law!* "Keep informed of the interrogation results," she said, "and let me know anything interesting."

Andy was working on the President's back before supper, when there was a knock at the massage room door. "Madam President, it's me. Heinie."

"Just a minute." Andy threw a large towel over the president's bare back—standard procedure—then disappeared out another door. "Okay, c'mon in."

Her chief of staff entered, closed the door behind him, and came over to the rubdown table. "Ennerby just called. There are developments in the Millennium firefight. The fifth man they got wasn't with the other four. He hadn't made that clear to me before. A man had been left at the intruders' carryall, and a different squad captured him. Now it seems *he* was actually a sixth man, and there'd been a different one with the four they shot. A man that got away."

The President frowned. "How the hell did that happen? If the satellite reported five? Did the troops see five out there, or didn't they?"

"They thought they had. The casualties were scattered somewhat in the tall grass, and at first no one realized they'd only bagged four. When they gathered them up, the lieutenant in charge sent men looking around for a fifth, assuming he'd been hit too, and crawled off. By hindsight, what he should have done was send the chopper back up right away, but he didn't. He'd called it down right after the shooting, to load prisoners and casualties, and held it on the ground to load the additional casualty he expected his people to find. Which actually was sound thinking, but this time . . ." He shrugged.

The President lay there trying to keep the story elements straight in her mind.

"When they didn't find anyone," Heinie continued, "he sent it up wounded and all, to hunt for him. And radioed the larger copter, the one with the backup squad, calling it in. Earlier he'd had it backtrack the intruders and see if it could find the vehicle they'd come in. For evidence. It backtracked them to the forest and a truck trail, spotted their carryall through gaps in the trees, and put its men down. No one was there; there had been, but he'd heard the chopper and run. Walked, actually; he's got a bad leg, presumably from some old mercenary contract.

"Anyway, the squad leader left three men there to watch the carryall, and took off again. They spotted the guy hiking along the edge of the woods, and picked him up. He'd been armed; carried an Uzi. Illegal of course. Fortunately he'd thrown it away—trying to dispose of the evidence—but they saw him get rid of it, and found it." Heinie realized how bad it might sound to her, but he continued. "When the big chopper picked the guy up, they'd radioed the lieutenant and told him. So when the small chopper didn't find anyone, he decided his men hadn't really seen five out there. They'd *expected* five, because that's what the satellite reported. And he decided the fifth was the man with the carryall. That he'd probably stood with the others outside the edge of the woods, and been reported by the satellite as one of them."

"He hadn't trusted his own eyes? Or his men's?" The President sounded as much disbelieving as exasperated.

Heinie blew through pursed lips. "Not after the small chopper didn't find anyone. It should have, you know, if there was one."

The President frowned again. "So how do we really know there was? Maybe the lieutenant's right."

"No, he's not. Because the data cube shows five intruders, all the way from their carryall to the Ranch."

"Wouldn't the satellite have seen anyone running away?"

"I'm afraid not. Ennerby had cancelled the program

as soon as the lieutenant called in that they'd bagged the targets. Cancellation's required when a special program's not needed anymore. Programs like that tie up onboard computer capacity, which runs all the orders and feedback, and has a lot of routine demands on it, typically complex as hell. It gets lots of special jobs requested by everyone from sheriff's departments, Forest Service, BLM, DTF, INS . . . Hundreds of requests, for the DTF and INS especially, each requiring a customized and complex program. It gets backlogged sometimes, and can't handle all the approved requests."

Heinie Brock brought himself back to their problem. "*Everything* received by the data analysis mainframe at Carson is on cubes, of course. Not just our project. And they've reviewed the one from last night. But enhanced cubeage like they need, the satellite doesn't transmit in real-time. Ordinary cubeage is, but when the data require massaging, it gets transmitted in pulses, scheduled by the onboard computer to accommodate overall demands. There can even be backlogs for transmission.

"Anyway, the sequence they needed didn't get transmitted before Ennerby disengaged the program. The satellite doesn't store 'unwanted' material."

Brock looked unhappily at his boss. "The unenhanced material is available, but it won't show the detail we need. It's just not there. There's a program that can enhance raw cubeage after the fact, and they're working with it, but it's not very promising."

The President scowled. "But the satellite transmissions show they did have a fifth man. Huh! And there's no chance that's a mistake?"

"None at all. The cube shows five intruders all the way to where the shootout took place. What's lacking is cubeage that showed what happened to the fifth."

"Did anyone think to go back out on the ground and see if they could track him?"

The thought startled Brock. It hadn't occurred to him. "I don't know. They didn't mention it. I'll check."

"Do that. Now. *Muy pronto*." She fixed him with a flinty eye. "I need to do some creative swearing, and I don't want to shock you."

He turned and went to the door, then looked back, trying for humor. "Not in front of Andy, I hope. She's a lady, after all."

"So am I, but there are things you don't know about ladies. Now git!"

She watched him leave. Hopefully the missing fifth man wouldn't be heard of again. *If he keeps his mouth shut*, she thought, *then God bless him*.

In a log farmhouse in Blair County, Montana, two men drank coffee and watched *Headline News*. Watched a brief report on, and speculation about, automatic weapons fire on the Millennium Ranch. When it was over, Carl turned to Axel.

"You suppose it was Luther?"

"I expect so."

"What do you suppose happened?"

"How would I know? Maybe one of the guys he recruited for it said something to someone, and the army or someone was waiting for them. That's all it would take. Or maybe Luther said something and didn't realize it, or one of us. Or one of the guys that kicked in money. Sure they didn't know much, but there's always fools that like to seem important. And if one of them let something slip, someone else could have heard it and notified the feds. The feds aren't all damn fools, you know. They can put two and two together."

Carl stared worriedly, unseeingly at the set. "The government had something to do with this, some way or other."

"Probably."

"What ought we to do?"

Axel grunted. "I'm staying right here. They won't likely trace it this far anyway."

Carl nodded slowly. "I suppose you're right." He paused. "I'm too old for this kind of shit." He paused again. "It's getting so's you can't trust people anymore."

Neither said anything for a long minute. Axel looked at Carl, who sat slumped on the old sofa, seeming mesmerized. *What happened to Mr. 'Rouse the People Down With Government!'* Axel wondered. *Maybe you are getting old, Carl. Maybe even smart.*

After a moment, Carl spoke again. "I sure as hell hope they didn't shoot Luther. I'd feel like I had his blood on my hands if they did."

Axel looked calmly at his brother. "No way to know. But considering the stuff Luther got into and out of all his life, if he was at a gunfight and anyone came out of it whole, it'd be him."

25

The history of humankind is a valuable study, even with the holes in the knowledge, and the prejudices and assumptions of the people who write it. It provides important information, insights, and understandings.

The history of the individual soul can also be a valuable study. It provides insights and understandings into the dynamics, current condition, and possible futures of that soul. The work of early psychotherapists provided some limited insights, but these were distorted by their prejudices and procedural carelessness. (And more severely by their misconception that one's personal history begins with birth, or possibly conception.)

(Which is equivalent to a working assumption that the history of humankind, or of a culture, began with the birth of its oldest living person.)

Why is Aunt Ida a favorite of yours? Why do you fear horses? Why does your boss have such remarkable antipathy for Poles? One can imagine various, entirely mundane reasons: Aunt Ida may be invariably friendly. Horses are large and potentially dangerous. And your boss may have been bullied by Tommy Sobleski in third grade.

But rather often, such phenomena result from experiences in past lives, and simply being aware of that can simplify life, while to revisit those experiences in Life Healing can provide powerful insights, as well as dealing with major or minor phobias and psychosomatics.

From *The Collected Public Lectures
of Ngunda Aran*

"BEN!" LEE half wailed the name.

"What's the matter?" Her husband called his answer from the bathroom.

"Oh, Ben! Oh, God! It's too much!"

What now? he wondered, and reached for the roll.

When he emerged, a minute later, she was slumped in her reading chair, a sheaf of papers on her lap.

"Would you care to elaborate?" he asked.

She picked up the sheets and held them out. "Ellen, in Communications, just came to the door and hand-delivered these."

He took them, and looked them over, frowning. This *was* a crisis! "Okay if I call Lor Lu about it?"

"Lor Lu?" She'd seen this as a family emergency. "Why Lor Lu? What can he do about it?"

"Sweetie, consider that beautiful operations chart you're developing. Lor Lu will show this crap to Legal, and if necessary, Mike Shuster will call Conroy, Morgenstern, and Blasingame in New York. They're as good a legal firm as you'll find, and Millennium pays them a sizeable retainer each month." He grinned. "I do work in Accounting, you know."

Her gaze turned thoughtful, though fear still lay beneath it. "Do you think they can beat this?"

"I have no doubt they can." Mentally he crossed his fingers. He expected they could, but courts were something of a mystery to him. "You're an important part of this organization, you know. Lor Lu won't let this go through."

"Mark is such . . ." She looked around as if for her daughters, then remembered they were at the Kleins, playing with Lori and Kari. "Mark is such a damned *asshole!*"

"You have my whole-hearted agreement on that. Why don't we call Lor Lu now?"

"It's 5:30."

Ben laughed. "He's a bachelor; he lives in his office. And he'll want to know." Ben stepped to the living room phone. "I'll call him, if that's all right."

She nodded, and his fingers pecked out a number. "Lor Lu, this is Ben Shoreff. Lee just got a very disturbing registered fax from"—he looked again at the first page—"from the Monroe County District Court, Rochester, New York. Her ex-husband has initiated a suit to get custody of Becca and Raquel. On the basis that Lee is an unfit mother, a member of a cult, and the children are growing up in the cult. He probably watched the CNN special, saw the family interview, and got visions of revenge."

He stood listening for a moment, then spoke again. "Lee divorced him on the basis of his cocaine addiction, and got custody of the girls. Mark didn't even contest it, and Lee had gone to work with a high-powered consulting firm, so supporting them wasn't a problem. Meanwhile, Mark's dad had cut him off, no doubt for the same reason Lee had. But apparently Mark got clean. And I suppose that dad, the source of money and all good things, took him back into the family and the family law firm."

Again Ben listened. "Sure. Just a moment." He switched off the transmitter. "How about eating with staff this evening?" Lee nodded, and he touched the transmitter switch again. "We'll eat at staff this evening, and give you the papers after supper."

Lee's gaze had taken on increasing life as he'd talked. Now he disconnected, and dialed another number. "Hi, Betty," he said. "Lee and I have decided to eat at staff this evening. Would you send the girls home, please? . . . Thanks."

Again he disconnected, then grinned at his wife. "There you go, sweetheart. It's as good as handled."

He really had no doubt it would be handled, but he also didn't doubt that the unpleasantness had only begun.

The next morning there was a knock on Lee's office door. When she called, "Come in," it was Ngunda Aran who entered.

He smiled. "Lor Lu has told me of the unpleasantness with your ex-husband. It may take some time to settle, but I want you to know it *will* be handled, and as smoothly as possible."

He left, Lee staring after him. She'd felt a lot better after talking with Lor Lu the previous evening, and this visit, brief as it had been, had added to her assurance level.

She would though, she told herself, prefer quickly to smoothly. She also told herself that if she was still with Mertens, Loftus, and Hurst, she'd be on her own in this, dangling in the wind.

26

From the second appearance of Ngunda Elija Aran, on Conversations with Warren Breuer

Breuer: I suppose you have thoughts on Congressman Weigner's proposed Public Works Employment Bill.

Aran: The bill would provide economic first aid. It would undertake to slow the bleeding, ease the pain, and keep the patient alive. And it reflects an institutional compassion, which is a lower grade phenomenon than personal compassion, but has the virtue of reach.

Breuer: Both the Centrists and Republicans insist the Depression will blow over; that it's just a matter of time till things straighten out. What's your take on that?

Aran: I am optimistic. [Pauses thoughtfully.] Usually I bypass questions on economics or politics. They are not where my attention lies, or my insights. But for you I'll make an exception. [Grins.] You may wish I hadn't.

The American economic and social body has various systems that tend to produce recovery. Among others, these include politics, education, science and technology. Therefore there _is_ a chance that the disease will run its course, and that American democracy has a healthy vigorous future.

Notice I said _disease_. The disease is materialism, a distortion of basic human physical needs.

The fact is, we live in a physical universe. We occupy physical bodies. We have physical needs and wants, with varying degrees of importance. And so far, the most effective way to support those needs and wants is free enterprise.

Free enterprise is a sort of organic system, continually evolving, continually adjusting, to fit, provide for, and profit from human needs and wants. However—[long pause]—to increase profits, it has undertaken, very successfully, to increase those wants by advertising. By permeating our lives, overtly and covertly, with images and sounds to make us want. Want more than we have, and again more than we have, continually expanding the limits.

One result has been much of what makes life comfortable, convenient, even efficient. Another has been a society that continually wants more. More "stuff." A society whose most powerful drives are material, whose basic values are material. Many of us _can't_ be satisfied. What we have is never enough. The result has been the strongest competitors getting rich at the expense of the weaker competitors. And aggressively manipulating the financial and political systems to their own advantage. Often without regard to the environment, or to the welfare of the public as a whole.

Thus in the free enterprise system, the key virtue—if we can call it that—the key virtue has come to be *aggressiveness*. Power and ruthlessness are secondary "virtues," and also quite useful in the struggle. Good intelligence is helpful but not necessary. It is quite possible to succeed greatly in business with quite ordinary intelligence—if one is sufficiently aggressive.

Fortunately, money can be used for many things besides yachts, mansions, summer homes in two hemispheres, and conspicuous consumption in general.

And high intelligence sometimes recognizes the problems, and the vectors that might lead to solutions. That is the current thrust of the Millennium Foundation, and of some other entities.

27

The world, especially the world's Catholics, were surprised this morning by a Vatican announcement that Pope John XXIV met privately yesterday with the controversial New Age guru, Ngunda Elija Aran. The two men talked for an hour.

What they talked about was not reported, but a Vatican spokesman quoted the pope as saying: "Mr. Aran is a devout man with a deep love of God and humanity. We enjoyed an interesting conversation, and agreed to agree where we agree, and to disagree where we disagree."

Headline News
Atlanta, GA, Nov. 16

THIS TIME JACK RUSSELL had insisted on meeting somewhere other than Corkery's apartment. They'd settled on a church in Corkery's heavily Irish, South Boston parish.

It was early afternoon, and except for Russell, the nave was empty of humans. Quiet, peaceful. Shafts of winter sunlight slanted in, tinted blue, red and amber by stained glass. He'd deliberately arrived early by half an hour, and gone directly to a rear pew without approaching the tabernacle. Sitting there, an inner calm settled on him, an elevation he never felt except when alone and quiet in God's House.

Corkery, on the other hand, arrived twenty minutes late. Perhaps also deliberately, thinking to irritate his countryman. Sliding in beside Russell, he greeted him in Gaelic, then turned to English, speaking quietly for privacy.

"I suppose you have questions."

Russell spoke in a soft murmur. "I'd like to know what progress you've made toward disposing of Ngunda Aran."

"Ah! The black Jesus! I know the layout of the church, and where the bomb will be placed below the floor, directly under the speaker. The explosion will be more than adequate. There's a utility panel in the ceiling of the hallway below. I've seen it, examined the wiring in fact, and made a bid for some work I'd arranged to be needed. There's room between ceiling and floor to accommodate the bomb. I'll enter at night, put it above the ceiling, and slide it into position with a telescoping rod I've had made.

"And when the day arrives, I'll sit in the back of the church and detonate it myself, without ever taking my hand from my pocket. You see, the target walks about when he talks, and it's best to blow it when he's behind the pulpit. To make sure it kills him."

Russell stared, eyes wide. He'd already forgotten his irritation with Corkery's offensive "black Jesus" comment. How had he learned and arranged all that without an inside confederate? Corkery was good, that he knew, and ingratiating when he wanted to be. But all that? Or could the man be putting him on?

"As for the bomb—" Corkery's smile was smug. He knew he'd impressed Russell. "The maker's as good as his reputation. He demonstrated the detonator for me, without explosives, of course. You'd love his work."

He paused. "But now let's see more money. I need it. The arrangements have not been made without risk and cost."

"You've kept records of expenses, of course," Russell said. "With receipts."

"Receipts?" The pseudo-friendly voice had turned sharp, fierce, hissing the word. "It's murder we're talking here, not commerce."

Corkery's sudden ferocity threw Russell off stride, but after a moment he answered, stiffly. "The people financing this are not ours. They do things differently. They want receipts."

Corkery's voice softened, but an edge remained. "Tell me, Jackie boy, which do they prefer? Receipts, or Ngunda Aran dead?" As he spoke, a large hard finger, an Irish farmboy's finger, poked Russell's shoulder hard enough to leave a bruise. "Because I will not give them both. The murdered guru is receipt enough." He paused, then finished. "Tell me now, and let me see the next five thousand. See and take!"

Jack Russell's lips were always thin. Now they'd disappeared entirely. Reaching into his inside breast pocket, he removed a thick wallet, and spreading it, exposed the money. Corkery's fingers snapped sharply, demanding. Grimly, reluctantly, Russell removed the money and handed it over. In the shelter of the pew in front of them, Corkery counted the bills, then put them inside his own jacket.

"And now, Mr. Russell," he murmured, "I'm curious about your plans for the Holy Father. I suppose you've seen the news about his meeting with your dear friend, Mr. Aran . . . Ah, I see you have. And while assassinating a pope hardly compares to assassinating a messiah, it's important in its way."

Russell managed to stiffen even more. "The plan is progressing nicely. Beyond that, I cannot talk about it."

"Have you considered a bomb? Bombs can be nice, if properly built and used. I could introduce you to my friend. He designs according to need. Besides, I like the concept: hiring a Shia Muslim to kill the Holy Father, in order to rescue the integrity of the Church. A lovely irony!"

Russell could stand the man no longer. Rising, he sidled to the aisle and left the building, his stomach burning. It would be the next day before he could keep food down.

PART TWO

DISORDERS BUILD

28

The Labor Department this morning reported November's unemployment at 20 percent, up 3 percent in the last month. Despite being braced for the expected bad news, Wall Street showed signs of panic. By midday, consumer product shares, already seriously depressed, had fallen an average of 15 points on the New York Exchange, while major industrials dropped an average of 17.

At 2:30, heavy selling pressures brought an abrupt plunge, and the floor was closed to trading. It was the worst day on Wall Street since 1933.

Headline News
Atlanta GA, Dec. 11

LEE SHOREFF WAS TENSER than anyone else at the Millennium all-hands staff meeting, the first in her two-and-a-half months at the Cote. She was afraid of losing her job. She knew that what she did was valuable to the organization. It was an awareness abundantly validated by her marvelous office, robust paychecks, and personal treatment by everyone involved.

But she'd never allowed herself to be fully convinced.

Now Wall Street was foundering, and surely she'd been adjudged a luxury they could postpone. There was going to be a reduction in force, and she'd be the first to go. Ben would probably be RIF'd too—last hired, first fired—and they'd get hauled off to Pueblo to a cheap motel. There they'd buy a used car and go—where?

On top of that, the weather was in tune with the economy, an ill omen, if you were into omens. Dry snow fell thickly, had been since early evening of the day before, and the temperature stood at −4 degrees Fahrenheit, with a windchill of −18.

She overlooked entirely that they'd been blessed with one of the warmest, driest autumns of record there. And that truck farmers along the Arkansas River, not too many miles east, had been praying for snow, to fill the reservoirs when the thaws arrived in April—and May, June and July, depending on slope direction, elevation, and weather.

Now she sat in the auditorium with virtually the entire staff. At 8:20 A.M., Lor Lu entered and walked to the lectern, brisk and cheerful. She did not allow herself to be encouraged.

"Good morning," he said. "None of you will be

surprised at the reason for this meeting. It's financial. We are among the more financially secure organizations in the world, but we are not immune to the worldwide Depression."

Lee's gut tightened.

"As you know, we are not self-supporting. We depend heavily on financial support from a small number of dedicated major contributors—'financial angels,' so to speak. None of them are in imminent danger of going under, but they are all strongly impacted by the worsening Depression, and are unable to continue supporting us at the level to which we're accustomed.

"Our financial operations are monitored, of course, by a review board within the Foundation, all of them graduates of the Millennium Procedures. It is they who provided Rudi and me with the basic data we used in reviewing our financial situation. He and I worked out our adjustments yesterday, and checked them with Dove before he left this morning."

It seemed to Lee his eyes paused on her.

"No one is being RIF'd, but like most workers in the world who still have jobs, each of us will have his pay reduced, a few as much as fifty percent, some only twenty. Those at the top of the scale will receive the largest cuts. When you return to your desk, you'll find an envelope with your name on it."

He grinned then, taking Lee by surprise. "And that's it. If you have questions, buzz me. I'll be in my office till 10:30 A.M. Then I'm taking off for New Orleans."

He left, and the staff followed, flowing out the door. *Without any of the eddies and muted babble there'd have been at Mertens, Loftus, and Hurst,* Lee thought.

There, human vortices would have formed, carried slowly along by the current, murmuring speculations on who got what cuts, and whether in fact top management had been cut at all, or whether they'd voted themselves a bonus for trimming expenses.

Lee went quickly to her office, wondering if she'd been an exception, with a pink slip in her envelope. Intellectually she knew there wouldn't be, but her guts did not believe her.

There was, she discovered, no pink slip. Her salary had been cut forty-five percent. She breathed a sigh of relief.

The girls came home from school in down coats, thick mittens, and furry earlapper caps—gear recommended by the school. Arriving pink-cheeked and happy, Raquel was exuberant in fact, full of the day. At afternoon recess, the supply room had issued red fiberglass snowshoes, and everyone who'd wanted to—which meant everyone—had gone outside and put them on. It wasn't that fourteen inches of snow required snowshoes, but it had been *fun!* Mostly they'd played fox and geese on them, galloping and falling, and afternoon recess had lasted an hour, instead of the usual thirty minutes. Raquel, despite excellent coordination, had fallen "almost more than anyone," she claimed, and enjoyed the experience hugely. "Mom, Dad," she said, "I'm really glad we came here! You're the best mom and dad in the world!" She distributed hugs. Becca had stood mostly observing, smiling indulgently. Now she too hugged her parents before shedding her boots.

❖   ❖   ❖

After the girls' nine o'clock bedtime, Lee and Ben talked about their day. Christmas was almost upon them, and she'd just had a pay cut of forty-five percent, he of thirty. But they had more money in Millennium's credit union than they'd ever owned in their lives, and for the moment at least, Lee was not worried. Not even about Mark's court action, which had been stalled by Millennium's attorneys.

For Lee, that night, sex was a celebration, not therapy. When she and Ben were spent, they lay talking. "I'm surprised," Lee said, "that I got cut almost the maximum. I can't be that near the top of the pay scale."

"Ah, but you are! Just ask your friendly family representative in Accounting. There is one level above you. That's all."

Her eyes widened in the darkness. "Ngunda and Lor Lu?"

"I can't give out particulars like that."

"Why in the world would I be in the next to top bracket?"

"You'd have to ask Lor Lu, but I presume it's because what you do is very important, and requires highly unusual skills. After all, Millennium has operations in fourteen countries, with nineteen centers in the U.S. alone. Which doesn't include Ladder and Hand, of course, or Bailout."

She lay contemplating what he'd said. "I'm not—I wasn't—really that well paid after all, was I? Considering my abilities."

"Well enough, I'd think. Millennium isn't here to get rich."

She examined that, too. "What is it here for?"

"Sweetheart," he said, "you'll have to find that out for yourself."

Altruism, she thought. A cult could be altruistic, she had no doubt. But one set up like this one? So sophisticated, in important respects so *slick,* with money appearing out of nowhere? Altruism wasn't the answer.

So then. What was it there for? Or for whom?

29

RAFI GLICKMAN TOOK a small round table for two, near the back. From there he could see anyone entering. Moishe Baran's call had given him a case of nerves, but it wouldn't be apparent to a casual observer. That the deli-cafe was American Jewish was not reassuring. If Baran intended to have him executed, this would be a good location. To the Wrath of God, the execution of a Jew in a place like this did double service. It disposed of an undesirable, and presumably intimidated American Jews who were insufficiently chauvinistic. "False Jews," Baran called them. Unpatriotic Jews.

Executions were almost always scripted to do double service. According to Baran, to murder someone unobtrusively was wasteful.

Rafi did not suppose that Baran himself would meet him. It would be some "soldier," someone inconspicuous, whom witnesses would have trouble describing usefully. Someone would either pass him a note beneath the table, or draw a pistol and shoot him through the brain.

He knew the procedure well, though he himself hadn't killed anyone under those circumstances.

When the person came in, she surprised Rafi; women were seldom assigned to carry out executions. But his trained eye knew she was the one, plain and unmemorable. And an agent, not an operative, because he'd never seen her before.

He did not react. It was as if he'd abandoned himself to death.

She walked over, and with a slight smile, sat down. "Hello, Rafi," she said quietly. "I have a message for you. They were pleased with your professionalism on Monday."

A bomb, exploded by a remote triggering device when the place was crowded. It had destroyed a home in the Antelope Valley, the main hangout of the most violent gang of anti-Semitic skinheads in southern California. Eight persons had died; six others had been hospitalized. At one time he'd have felt satisfaction in such an act. A few long years ago.

God forgive me. His thought was a prayer. Rafi wondered if God factored in that he was an anti-terrorist mole, who carried out terrorism only to maintain his cover.

"And they sent me to give you this." She handed him a piece of paper. *Not* under the table. He unfolded it and read. It had been typed in Hebrew, on a type-writer, not a computer, which suggested Yeshua Ben David himself as the author.

It began: "Because of your excellent performance of duties, in particular that of last Monday, and your intelligence, training, experience and good judgement, you are hereby promoted."

There was no signature. It did not say promoted to what. (Nothing in it identified anything or anyone.) He looked at the young woman who'd given it to him. "Thank you," he said gravely. She nodded, got up and left.

Promotion would be to senior operative, which meant his stipend would be doubled. He'd be expected to leave the job he had—eighteen hours a week as a computer technologist for a Hebrew newspaper—and serve the Mossad full time. His promotion would associate him more closely with the Wrath. He might then get a line on the teams upstate, and in the east and midwest.

And commit more offenses before God.

He put coins on his saucer to pay for his coffee, then left as gray and expressionless as he'd walked in. Like the gray and expressionless Yeshua Ben David, first among equals, whom Rafi feared most of all.

Walking to his car, he didn't notice the sunshine.

30

Today President Metzger issued an executive order to all government departments responsible for entitlement payments, reducing each payment from 20 to 40 percent, as authorized by the Balanced Budget Amendment. But reduced entitlement payments were not the only income reversals for the elderly. Negative profits and heavy mutual fund losses have severely impacted pension plans and retirement incomes, in general.

Also today, the president once more requested authorization to override the balanced budget requirements.

The recent epidemic of executive suicides claimed its twentieth victim yesterday. Arnold Tarnbrook, president and CEO of HydroTech

Industries, jumped to his death from the sunroof of the Panorama Restaurant, fifty-five stories above Miami's Jasmine Place. He left two adult children and a grandchild.

Headline News
Atlanta, GA, Dec. 17

On the eve of his death, Jesus is quoted as saying: "You always have the poor with you." And ever since, people have used this partial quote to justify their greed, their lack of compassion, their callousness to poverty.

But according to the Gospels, Jesus also told a rich man, "Go, sell your possessions, and give the money to the poor, and you will have treasure in heaven."

Would the poor be less poor if there were no rich men? Money fuels civilization, and provides material needs. Wealth permits one to help those in need, often needs which government is ill-suited to deal with.

What would you advise a rich person to do, here in the twenty-first century? Convert his possessions to money, then walk through the skid rows of the world, giving it to derelicts? Or give it to scholarships, foundations, shelters for the homeless, and research toward solutions to the world's problems? Or some to each?

Even if used to buy wine or drugs, it is appropriate to give money to someone destitute on the street, because he thereby experiences human compassion. But broad good can be accomplished by investing in strategically selected organizations.

There is a difference in valuing wealth solely for material gratification, and in valuing wealth for the good you can do with it. Increasingly we have the means to make poverty obsolete. What is needed is the will.

As for the person who dies while wallowing in material pleasures, he too, in time, will dwell in the richness of the spirit. Meanwhile, for now, "richness of the spirit" may seem unreal to him, unbelievable. And how can he value it when he doesn't believe in it?

Rich or poor, let him believe what he believes, disbelieve what he disbelieves, value what he values—without being assaulted for it, physically or verbally. In time he will learn the lessons of materialism, and pass on to new lessons.

What we can do now, within limits, is inhibit him from harming others. But it is well not to restrain him too closely, for in his actions lie his lessons and our own. We interact, and through those interactions we grow. All of us, evolving together in the spirit.

> From *The Collected Public Lectures of Ngunda Aran*

THE WAS A KNOCK on the door to the Oval Office. "Madam President, it's me. Hank."

"Come in."

He entered, and she fixed him with a cocked eye. "What in hell are you doing up at this hour, Groenveldt? It's after one in the morning."

"Checking on you, Madam President. You should be in bed."

"The hell you say! Who assigned you as my nanny? I read awhile to clear my register of the bullshit I deal with all day long. Otherwise I dream the damn job all night, and the dreams are worse than the real thing. Frigging nightmares!"

"Maybe you should read in bed, and fall asleep reading."

"I'm like the five hunded pound gorilla, Enrico me lad. I read where I want to." She paused. "Don't look at that statement too closely; it won't bear scrutiny. And don't tell people I weigh five hundred pounds; I'm down to two forty five. Even that damned nag Beliveau only wants me down to two ten, so two forty five isn't half bad. Big frame, big bones, big muscles, big—never mind."

She'd ranged from mock truculent to mock humor, but he sensed a tautness beneath the surface, a tension, something that could snap under added stress. The job, the constant crises, the frustration of trying to work with a hostile Senate were getting to her. She held the book up, the cover toward him: *"The Turbulent Mirror,"* she said, "by Briggs and Peat. On chaos theory, appropriately enough."

Hank stood uncomfortable and worried.

Her expression changed to grimness. "What would you think if I declared martial law tomorrow?" she asked.

He voiced his syllables carefully, the words spaced, speeding a bit as he got tracked. "It seems to me you were right when you said it shouldn't be done hastily. And to me, tomorrow seems too soon. At least politically."

Face hard, eyes hard, she looked at him, then nodded curtly. "Thanks for your viewpoint, Groenveldt. Go home and get some sleep, and tomorrow don't stay so late. Perfecta deserves to see more of her husband." He turned to leave, but her voice stopped him at the door. "And, Hank, I agree with you. About martial law. But I might do it anyway. I need to be *effective, for chrissake!*"

She snapped the final three words, her voice rising in pitch and volume.

He paled and nodded. "Yes, ma'am, you do," he answered quietly. Then he went home and had his own bad dreams.

Senate Republican leader Riley Woodrow was large and rumpled. He looked like a long-ago Crimson Tide offensive guard gone to seed. Which he was. The press liked him. Many of them didn't care for his politics, but they liked *him.* From a rural community and farm roots, he had the homespun and somehow courtly style of an earlier generation. His language was colorful, and he enjoyed political confrontation. Sometimes he even went out of his way to inspire it, which kept things lively; interesting. Yet he was seldom truly insulting, and almost never truculent.

Riley Woodrow had always been staunchly conservative, but not far enough to the right to join the breakaways who'd formed the America Party. Initially he'd even lampooned them, but when they'd proved they could be a force in Congress, at least for a while, he'd made peace with them.

And with that, he steered his cohorts rightward in an effort at damage control, because several seemed a threat to switch parties.

That rightward tack had cost him two seats, moderate Republicans who joined earlier breakaways to the Center Party. But there'd been no avoiding it, and they'd tended to vote with the Centrists anyway. So he held that rightward course, making common cause with the Americists whenever his scruples allowed.

He didn't actually dislike Florence Metzger—she was about as good as he could reasonably hope for, given the times—but as a matter of politics, he undercut her whenever practical. She was, after all, an opponent.

And a woman. He had no qualms about women in the Senate, but as the nation's chief executive? Metzger had a woman's genes, a woman's glands, and "a woman's inability to make good decisions under pressure," as he'd put it privately.

Furthermore, it had been a bad day. At least three of his borderline votes against balanced budget override authority were wavering. Lose two of them without picking up others, and he'd lose the floor vote. And these people pushing microphones at him, usually an agreeable experience, were going to ask questions he couldn't answer frankly, because his reasons would hurt his cause.

"Senator Woodrow, what do you think the president's prospects are tomorrow?"

"What prospects? She's too old to snag herself a boyfriend."

No one laughed. *Not a good time for jokes, Riley,* he told himself, *and not a very good joke. You ought to know better.*

"Senator, could the depression ever become serious enough that you'd relent and pass her request?"

He fixed the man with one of his better glowers. "Son," he said, "basic principles of governing have been bent or discarded too often in the past. The White House calls it expediency, but it's really panic. Do it often enough, like the liberals have, and you end up with no principles at all.

"That's where they are in the White House today. No principles at all. No integrity. Florence Metzger wasn't too bad as a senator, but since she's been in the Oval Office, she's become morally corrupt."

He realized as soon as he'd said "morally corrupt" that he'd overstepped, but barged on. "The crisis we find ourselves in today is the fault of a Democrat-Centrist coalition, and electing Florence Metzger president. And when the American people correct those mistakes, we can get the country back on track again."

He pushed his way through the reporters then, thinking he'd have done much better with a "no comment."

"Madam President, how do you respond to Senator Woodrow's comments?"

Normally Florence Metzger enjoyed dealing with the press, but today she was in no mood for bullshit. "Usually," she said, "I don't respond to comments like those, but in Senator Woodrow's case, I'll make an exception. A person's principles are their own. Someone else's will be different, often a lot different. Woodrow needs to look around and see the world as it is. Not through some distorted nineteenth century lens that wasn't worth much then and has been getting more and more out of focus ever since."

She knew that was a good place to stop, but she too charged on. "Woodrow's main problem is, he was born scared and brought up scared. Scared to look at the world. So he looks at a small weaselly mental picture of it—two-dimensional line drawings in black and white. Not even any grays, just stick figures in black and white. Without faces. And he clings to it in spite of hell, where I do not doubt the proprietor is waiting for him with gleefully shining eyes."

The rest of the questions were throw-aways. She didn't even remember them afterward. She was too busy wishing she could withdraw at least that one last sentence.

"Senator, the President had some pretty strong things to say about you this morning. Would you like to respond to them?"

It had been a bad afternoon session, and Riley Woodrow felt testy. He'd have liked to shove the man's microphone down his throat; or better yet . . .

"Well," he drawled, "she talked about how hell was waiting for me. I expect she knows quite a bit about hell. She's got close ties there. You've heard of guardian angels? Hers have leather wings. Her problem is, she's a big, frustrated old maid who never had a date. What she needs is a man, but I wonder if she's not more interested in that masseuse she hauls around everywhere with her, at taxpayer expense."

He felt good about his comeback for perhaps eight

seconds. But by the time he reached his office, he felt sure his mouth had gotten him in major trouble. *To hell with it, Riley*, he told himself. *You've been mealy-mouthed too often. A man's got to let her rip from time to time.*

But he didn't feel convinced. Not at all.

Before Woodrow left for the night, the e-mail was piling up. His staff would give him the for-and-against counts after the flow slowed, but of the messages themselves, they showed him only approvals. Which were numerous, for his jabs had been as widely broadcast as the president's.

The message that counted, though, was by phone. It was from long-time congressman and sometime GOP House Speaker Carl McGrath, six years retired. McGrath had been a senior congressman when Riley Woodrow first came to Washington, had taken a liking to the loquacious rookie and become his mentor and sponsor; had advised him, and gotten him favorable committee assignments. They'd developed a strong personal fondness and closeness, and despite occasional political differences, Woodrow's respect for McGrath approached reverence. They'd remained close even after Woodrow moved to the Senate, until at age seventy-four, McGrath retired with a heart condition.

Woodrow felt a twinge of discomfort when his secretary told him who was on the line, but he took the call. The face on the screen was pale, and puffy from medication. Woodrow realized with embarrassment how long it had been since he'd called McGrath, and determined to do better.

"Hello, Carl," he said genially. "I've been meaning to call. How's the world treating you?"

"Not too badly, Riley. I keep taking my medications, and reading. I always used to complain I didn't have time to read a lot of things I'd have liked to. Now all I've got is time." He chuckled. "Sounds strange, coming from someone eighty years old with a bad heart. But it's true. I recommend retirement to anyone interested. When they feel ready."

He paused. Riley Woodrow knew without question why Carl McGrath had phoned him.

"I saw you on television this evening, Riley. At supper." He paused, inviting response.

"Yeah, I suppose you did. That wasn't too good, was it."

"I did feel pretty bad to hear it. I suppose you've been having second thoughts."

"Well, she didn't talk too nice about me yesterday."

"No, no she didn't. But, Riley, it might be well to make peace with her, instead of war. She's trying to steer the country through one of the most dangerous times in our history, and while I wouldn't urge you to vote one way or another, she needs all the moral support she can get. And what you did was, you basically implied she's a homosexual. You see."

Riley Woodrow exhaled audibly through pursed lips. He did see.

"But I suppose you've already thought about all that, and decided whatever it is you want to do."

"Well, not entirely. I'm still thinking on it."

There was another lag, and he thought of asking McGrath how he'd vote on the Balanced Budget override, but he already knew.

The older man filled the vacuum. "How's Addie these days?"

"Addie? She's fine. Like always. Busy with the library board and the DAR—that sort of thing. Makes herself useful in the world. Goes to the Senate wives' club three times a week, and cavorts with the bouncing ladies, to keep her figure."

"Good for her. Wish I'd taken better care of myself . . . Well, I didn't intend to make this a long call. You've got more important things to do than spend the evening talking to someone who doesn't. Give Addie my kindest regards, and next time you get to south Florida, it'd be nice to see you."

With that, McGrath cut the connection, leaving Riley Woodrow looking at the blank screen for several long sober seconds. Then the senator called his bodyguard and chauffeur, gathered his coat and briefcase, and headed for the subterranean parking garage.

When she arrived at the White House next morning, Andrea Jackson's face was puffy, her eyes red.

Florence Metzger didn't ask why. She simply said, "Andy, you could use a drink." Without waiting for a reply, she pressed keys on her intercom, signaling the second butler. "Romney, bring two whiskeys and water to the Oval Office. I've got a friend in need, and I could use one myself. Make them weak though."

She touched the key again, the light blinking out, and turned to Andrea. "I don't keep a bottle in my desk. Temptation.

"So. You look like you need a friend. Besides Franklin. You want to talk?"

Andrea's voice was barely audible. "Madam President, here's my resignation." She held out an envelope, and when the president didn't take it, laid it on the desk. "I—can't work here any longer. I just can't."

The tears began to flow then. *It's a wonder she's got any left,* the President thought, and getting to her feet, went around the desk and gripped her friend's arms. A hug might not be welcome under the circumstances. "Honey," she said, "you've done nothing wrong and said nothing wrong. There's no reason on God's green Earth for you to leave."

"There is. It looks bad for you, for me to be here."

"The hell you say. Tell you what. I'll ask Woodrow over, and when he gets here, I'll butter his necktie and shove it, um, down his throat. You can watch. How's that?"

Andrea smiled in spite of herself. "No, ma'am," she said, "no need to do that. There's other jobs; I'll be all right. We can live on Franklin's pay."

Well, shit! "Tell you what. I won't accept this right away. Maybe later. But first I want you to take a two-week vacation, with Franklin. You've both got annual leave coming. I'll buy you plane tickets to Miami, and a cruise."

Andrea shook her head, but her eyes were uncertain.

"Think about it. Talk to him. Here, I'll buzz him. You can talk in Sheri's office. She's off today."

Before she got to her intercom though, it buzzed for her. She answered. "What is it, Marge?"

"A call for you on three, ma'am. Senator Woodrow."

Metzger moved quickly to her chair, thunder on her brows, and faced the screen. "Put him through," she said grimly.

And there he was, a study in remorse. It did not touch her. Her voice was as hard as her face. "What do you want, Senator?"

"Madam President, I have an apology to make."

"To whom?"

"Well, you to start with, you being right there on the phone. For the hateful, unconscionable things I said yesterday to the press. And another one to your masseuse, when I can get hold of her.

"I guess you know I'm not used to saying I'm sorry. I wouldn't even admit to myself that I ought to, till last evening I got a call from Carl McGrath, down in Port Charlotte. You know old Carl. He didn't chew me out or even criticize, but he caused me to look at what I'd said.

"Then, when I got home, Addie met me at the door and said 'Honey, we've got to talk.' She's the one made me look at how your masseuse—hell, I don't even know the lady's name—how she had to feel. Anyway, by the time Addie was done, I was ready to call you right then, but she said, 'No, wait till morning; she's prob'ly in bed.' So here it is morning, and here I am, hat in hand."

He looked as if he were peering out of the screen at her. "Whether you're willing to accept this or not, I'm going to apologize publicly, to the press. Eat me some well-earned crow.

"And something else. Carl said something like, 'That woman is trying to steer the country through its worst internal dangers since the War Between the States.

She doesn't need insults just now.' Those weren't his exact words, but that's what they amounted to.

"Anyway, I didn't sleep a whole lot last night, but I did a lot of thinking. And I'm going to suggest to my Republican colleagues that they vote yes on your Balanced Budget override. Because I am. It's a dangerous precedent, and it troubles me deeply. But the times are dangerous too, and it seems to me the risk is justified."

Florence Metzger stared. "Senator, I'm glad I don't have a weak heart, or they'd be swearing Charles DeSales in as president this morning. Now I have something to tell you, but first I want to introduce you to someone." She beckoned to Andrea, who'd been listening wide-eyed. The therapist came around the desk, and the president angled the pickup to show her.

"Senator Woodrow, I want you to meet my therapist, Andrea Jackson. She came in early today and tendered her resignation. I haven't accepted it, but if she insists, there's not much I can do about it."

Riley Woodrow peered earnestly from the screen. "Miz Jackson, I would consider it a favor, to me and my conscience, if you would withdraw your resignation and accept my abject apologies."

Her voice was even quieter than usual. "Senator, I will do both. And I thank you for—for being the sort of person who can do what you're doing."

The president turned to her. "Anything else, Andy?"

"No, ma'am."

Metzger readjusted the pickup. "Senator," she said, "You have just saved me not only a good therapist, but someone who's not afraid to disagree with me when I ask her opinion.

"Now, what else I need to say is, I owe you an apology, too. So I suggest we meet the press together, and apologize mutually. It will do the whole damned country good to see and hear it. We can set a good example, maybe even start a civility trend."

31

THICK DRIZZLE FILLED Jenny Buckel's headlight beams as she swung her elderly Toyota into the parsonage driveway. *Six or eight degrees colder,* she told herself, *and North Carolina would be having a white Christmas.* At least a white December 23rd. According to the radio, the Smokies were already white. By morning Barlow might be too.

She pushed her door open, then poked her umbrella out and opened it before getting out herself. She'd leave her suitcase in the luggage compartment with the rest of her stuff. She hadn't told Steven she was coming. He'd have wanted to know why, and she didn't want to talk about it via a computer or telephone.

The porchlight flicked on—someone had seen her drive in—and as she trotted up the steps, the door opened. Dorothy stood looking out at her. "Hi, Jen! It's so good to see you! You took me by surprise."

Jenny closed her umbrella and stepped inside,

putting it in the umbrella rack as she answered. "I
know. Maybe I shouldn't have, but . . ." They hugged,
then Jenny went on. "It wasn't something I wanted to
talk about on the Web. Even if I *could* see and hear
you." She looked around. "Where's Steve?"

"Upstairs changing into lay-abouts." She gestured
toward the church next door. "He just got in from a
meeting. Find yourself a chair in the living room. I'll
tell him you're here. I'd call up the stairs to him, but
the children are in bed. Sleeping I think."

While Dorothy hurried upstairs, Jenny went into
the living room and sat down on the sofa. The coffee
table held several issues of a Baptist magazine, and
a theological journal featuring something new on the
Essenes. Normally Jenny would have begun browsing
the latter, but just now her mind was on hold. A
minute later Steven and Dorothy come in.

"Hi, Jen," Steven said. "It's been a while."

Jenny got to her feet, and they hugged.

"What brought you here?"

"I'm leaving school."

Steven's eyebrows rose. "Anything wrong?"

"Nothing in particular. My scholarship seemed safe,
and my job in the dining room, as long as I kept my
grades up. But I didn't have enough money to pay
for spring quarter, let alone next year." She shrugged.
"So I lined up a job in Atlanta."

"Umm! That far away. Doing what?"

Jenny looked long at her brother before answering.
"The training is in Atlanta, but the job itself will be
in North Carolina." She paused before continuing.
"It's with the Millennium Foundation. They plan to
open a center in Raleigh or Durham."

Steven's expression could be described as stricken. It was Dorothy who spoke. "What will you be doing?"

"Public relations."

"How well does it pay? Can you make a living?"

"The pay," Jenny recited, "will be not less than one hundred and fifty percent of the federal minimum wage."

"They must have had a lot of applicants."

"You'd think so, in times like these. But they didn't advertize their jobs. They're interviewing people who've been recommended to them. I'd told my journalism adviser I was going to leave for money reasons, and he told me about this opening. And provided Millennium with my transcript and a recommendation."

Steven still looked worried. "It could work out all right, as a job," he said. "But, Jen, I feel very uncomfortable about it. I'm afraid of Millennium. It's a cult. And their theology's at odds with Christianity."

Dorothy intervened. "Make me a promise, okay?" she said. "If it turns out to be—unsavory in any way, promise me you'll quit."

Jenny nodded solemnly. "That's a promise."

Dorothy changed the subject then, and Jenny agreed to stay over Christmas day. There'd be enough turkey and with-its, and they'd bought no Christmas gifts this year except for the children. Jenny already had presents for them, in the car. They got through the rest of the evening without anything more being said about Millennium, beyond Steven's agreement that their father shouldn't hear of it.

Jenny was especially glad there were no more questions. Strictly speaking, she hadn't lied, but she hadn't come close to the real truth.

32

A Brian Boulet Closing Commentary, on
The News Hour, *with Margaret Warner*

Lately I've noticed a media trend toward publicizing "good acts." As if good could possibly be worth our attention.

Even in the best of times, acts of goodness tend to be lost, ignored in the journalistic eagerness to display and describe—often in infinite and intimate detail—the shocking, the threatening, the disillusioning, and the merely disgusting. And certainly it would be dishonest not to show the blemishes and flaws, the cruelties and insanities. Especially in times like these, such things need to be exposed, for like it or not, they mirror the worst impulses in all of us.

But acts of human compassion are also important. They also mirror humankind. And recently, in both print journalism—my primary venue—and on television, acts of compassion are moving toward . . . not equal attention, but substantial attention. One can think of several instances that received major nationwide media attention in the last month. . . .

Acts of compassion, and now acts of honesty! It is two of the latter, intertwined, as it happens, that inspired me to write this. I speak of the joint public appearance of President Florence Metzger and Senator Riley Woodrow, in which they unreservedly apologized for their earlier, ugly, unforgiveable blowups at each other. Which proved forgiveable after all, and by the persons most offended—each other.

Acts of political honesty, of course, are subject to more skepticism than acts of ordinary honesty. But this one seems genuine. Particularly given Senator Woodrow's description of his awakening to the moral implications of his attacks, under the gentle prodding of his old political mentor, Carl McGrath. And a—scolding is probably not the word—perhaps a gentle chiding by Woodrow's unassuming wife, Addie.

The long-term effects remain to be seen. Presumably the philosophical differences between these two national leaders continue in force. But the apologies all by themselves are heartening, and a benefit to the nation and its people. And having once made peace as they have, I find it difficult to suppose they will reach such depths of animosity again. At least not openly, and not toward each other.

So here's to the trend! The good news trend! May it not end when the Christmas ornaments are back in their boxes, and the trees put away. The publicizing of compassion, honesty, courage, love—all serve as reminders, as models and food for thought, as we continue our uncertain way through this young century.

A century in which people of good will and intentions must create a decent and functional world despite powerful philosophical and historical differences.

The alternative is terrible to contemplate.

Headline News
Atlanta, GA, Dec. 23

Police in San Jose, California, today found a body which had been crudely tortured and mutilated before death, apparently over a period of days. A note at the site identified the victim as Eduardo DeCampos Gomes, a free-lance computer programmer who was a resident of San Jose. It stated that the victim had boasted of writing and introducing the Black Plague virus which tragically destroyed the International Computerized Library.

The note also told where the bodies of his parents, sister, estranged wife and small daughter could be found.

Police are investigating.

33

To me, an outsider living in the midst of Millennium, its people are more interesting than its philosophy. They are calm, friendly, and as far as I can tell, very competent at what they do. Yet even in the midst of what some call a "cult environment," they are very much individuals with their own personalities. The sketches I give you in these weekly articles are less than the people deserve. . . .

"In the Midst of Millennium"
American Scene Magazine
Duke Cochran

DURING HIS DOVE assignment, Duke Cochran found his sex life nearly nonexistent, and sex was extremely important to him. On tour he was constantly on the move. The rest of the time he was stuck at the Ranch, where the women seemed unlikely candidates, the facilities not conducive to seduction, and the nearest singles bar too far away. Lee Shoreff was the woman here he found most stimulating. She was both sexually attractive and married. The first was essential. The latter intensified his interest.

Twice he'd approached her, asking for an interview, and twice she'd claimed to be too busy. He knew better. She was afraid of him—afraid of his magnetism and sexuality, afraid to be alone with him.

He was newly returned from another long tour, what Lor Lu had termed the "Mississippi Tour"—New Orleans, Memphis, St. Louis, Davenport, and Minneapolis, with a side trip to Louisville and Cincinnati. Desperate in Memphis, he'd had a call girl up. She'd been reasonably talented and eventually enthusiastic, but the encounter had been—dissatisfying.

He'd examined the prospects of getting Lee Shoreff in bed. Besides sexual gratification, there was the hope of information that would lead to the real *who* behind Millennium. But she'd have to go with him to the guest lodge, to his room. Unseen. And if any trouble came of it, it would kill the whole setup. So he'd decided to forget about seduction. Instead, he'd interview her in depth—feed her the right questions and see how she responded. Surely he'd get at least a hint of what to look into next. She might even surprise him, and cooperate actively on an exposé. Might even lay him in her office.

It was 4:20 P.M. when he knocked at her office door. "Yes?" she called.

"It's Duke Cochran." He opened the door as he said it. "You still haven't given me that interview."

She looked at him. *Get it over with, Lee,* she told herself. "I suspect, Mr. Cochran, that you won't find it much of an interview. Much of what I do is confidential."

His gaze had turned to her wall screen, where she'd been playing with the chart. Reaching to her keyboard, she turned it off. "Sorry," she said, "that's part of what's confidential. And the most interesting part of what I do."

He grinned. *"Part* of what's interesting," he answered. "You're the other part, the major part: How you came to be here, what your life is like here, what you like and dislike about this place, and why. What you did before you got involved with Millennium. That sort of thing."

He pulled a chair to him and sat down on it backward, facing her. "So when can we get together? I want to very much, and I wouldn't be surprised if you ended up enjoying it too."

Her look and tone of voice were businesslike, as he'd expected. "I can give you one hour this evening, 7:30 to 8:30. I'll be coming back anyway, to finish off some things."

He got to his feet. "Thanks, Lee. I'll be here at 7:30 on the dot. I'm looking forward to it."

When he'd gone, she stared at the closed door for a long moment, then shook her head and turned the wall screen back on. She had trouble concentrating though, and left a few minutes early.

It seemed to her he must have been watching through the window in the elevator alcove, and seen her coming down the sidewalk. She herself used the stairs. Her office was on the third floor, and she believed in taking advantage of exercise opportunities. She'd hardly hung up her coat before he knocked. "Come in," she said cordially; she'd make the best of this.

He was grinning again as he entered, reminding her of a college jock, a Big Man On Campus. He was definitely attractive and very sexy, and unquestionably he knew it. Thought of himself as God's Gift to Women, she had no doubt. He hung up his jacket. Beneath it he wore a knit polo shirt well out of season. His arms were large and muscular, as if he worked out. His belt fitted snugly, with no fatty bulge. A hard body.

She pulled her gaze away, wondering if she'd stared. Two of her visitor chairs had desk arms, like a school desk, and he positioned one to face her from no more than five feet away. Closer than she preferred. Then he put a recorder on her work table, its pickup facing them, and smiling, sat down with an electronic notebook. *He was*, she thought, *more attractive when he simply smiled*. His grin had seemed aggressive.

She glanced at her wall clock. "It's almost 7:30. We might as well start. The ball's in your court, Mr. Cochran."

"Fine. I'll do a better job of this if we start at the beginning and move toward present time. Where were you born?"

"Good. I was afraid you'd ask when. I was born in Rochester, New York. Grew up there, went to school there, and went to college at Syracuse, only an hour and a half away."

"Whoa!" he said. "From the cradle to the university in what? Four sentences? I need more than that."

He took the interview over then, completely, and she discovered he was very good at what he did. When it occurred to her to look at the clock, it was 9:05, and he knew more about her early years than almost anyone. About her best friends in childhood, early boyfriends, stories of living in the Delta House . . . She hadn't told him everything, of course.

"My god!" she said, "It's after nine! And we never got close to Millennium! I really have to go home."

His smile was warm and reassuring. "But it's gone well," he said. "The early years are the most important, and I feel as if I really know you now. Next time we'll talk about your career before you came here. After that we'll talk about Millennium."

She felt a moment's uncertainty. "I really shouldn't spend more than one more evening on this."

"Two more should do it, or possibly one long one." He paused. "May I walk you home?"

"I . . . Yes, that would be all right."

Without speaking, he helped her on with her coat, then pulled on his own and they left. The hall and stairwell were somehow dreamlike, pregnant with— something. The place seemed deserted except for them, their footsteps surprisingly loud, the solitude subtly electric. He couldn't help thinking about sex on a desk with her. Her physical attraction went beyond explanation.

Neither spoke till they were outside walking. The night was mild, for the season and elevation—perhaps 15 degrees Fahrenheit, and still. The sky was clear and deep, the stars incredible. Duke put a gentle, gloved hand on her arm, stopping her. "Look," he said, pointing upward. "In a sky like that, you can see why it's called the Milky Way."

She nodded. "It's beautiful."

"My Norwegian grandmother called it *Vintergata*, said it meant the winter road. I thought of the Norse gods traveling it on sleighs across the sky." He paused. "Did you ever watch the northern lights when you were a girl?"

"Oh yes! From our summer place on Lake Ontario. There wasn't any city glow there, and we'd see them fairly often. I'd stand outside till I was shivering uncontrollably, it was so hard to stop watching."

He nodded. "My parents had a summer cottage on a small lake in northern Wisconsin. When there were northern lights, I'd row alone out to the middle and watch. It was magical."

When they started walking again, he took her gloved hand in his for a moment, then let go, as if realizing what he'd done. They were in front of her house within three or four minutes.

"I really enjoyed our evening," he said. "You're a—very nice person, Lee. It was a privilege to get to know you so well. I'll tell you what: You call me when you see an opportunity for our next talk."

He did grin then, and this time she found it not aggressive at all. "If I don't hear within a couple of weeks, I'll check with you at your office."

"Of course," she said.

He stepped away from her, backwards, gave a small salute, then turned and strode off down the sidewalk, Lee staring after him. Duke Cochran was a *very* attractive man, and nice after all. Slowly she turned and walked to the house.

It was the first time since she'd known Ben that she'd even for a moment thought of sex with anyone else.

34

THOMAS CORKERY ARRIVED at the Bentham
Avenue Unitarian Church early enough for a seat
in a pew very near the rear. While the congregation
gradually filled the seats, the organ played music
unfamiliar to him. Before long the place was packed,
with people standing in the outer aisles. The fire
warden, Corkery told himself, would be unhappy
when he learned of it. As he soon would; the climax
assured it.

Television cameramen stood in a back corner and at
both sides in front, as well as in a balcony overlooking
the pulpit. *They have no idea,* he told himself, *what
a spectacle they're in for.*

He looked forward to the service with curiosity. The pastor wore black jeans and a thick baggy
sweater, and there were no kneelers for the praying.
If, in fact, these people prayed. When the service

began, there was little he identified with. No altar boys, nor any other celebrants than the pastor, the choir in its loft, and the organist at her keyboard. When the congregation stood to sing, he stood too, his hymnal open to the indicated page, but no sound issued from his lips.

Ngunda Aran sat a bit to the pastor's right, standing when the congregation stood, but otherwise taking no part in the service, such as it was. There was a prayer, a reading and a unison reading—neither from Scripture—and announcements. Then, accompanied by organ music, the ushers passed the plates; that part Corkery found familiar. Afterward another unfamiliar hymn was sung, and the pastor introduced Ngunda Aran.

"As most of you know," the pastor said, "Roberta Gunnel of our congregation suggested last June that we invite Mr. Aran to speak to us. After several discussions and a certain amount of heat, it was decided we would, and we got in touch with him."

Corkery wondered amusedly what they'd think of that decision-making procedure back in Ireland. Or for that matter, what they thought of the Holy Father meeting with the guru. At least Aran's last name was Irish. He put a hand in the right pocket of the warm jacket he wore, briefly fondling the detonator, the size of a pack of cigarettes.

The pastor continued. "Mr. Aran graciously agreed, and suggested we compile a list of written questions, to be presented to him on his arrival. A number of you suggested questions, from which the senior deacons and myself selected fifteen that we felt covered a suitable spectrum."

He turned. "Mr. Aran," he said, "the pulpit is yours."

A sheet of paper in one hand, Ngunda Aran stepped to the pulpit and stood beside it. Not behind it. *To explode the bomb now*, Corkery thought, *might not kill him*. Quite likely cripple him, but the man might well survive.

"Thank you for inviting me to speak," Ngunda said. His deep rich voice filled the sanctuary without need of a microphone. "The first question asks my view of God. God is the universal creative power, which is all there is. I generally prefer the word 'Tao'; it carries far less extraneous baggage. But those are labels. The reality behind them I perceive only vaguely. Incarnate souls, like you and me, comprehend only limited aspects of the Tao, and those imperfectly."

To Corkery it didn't seem like much of an answer. *I wonder*, he thought, *how much they're paying him? Maybe they'll be satisfied with the voice.*

"The next question is, 'Will humankind ever become spiritually enlightened?'" He scanned the crowd. "It will, but step by step. We evolve as individuals, and in the process our species evolves collectively. That is as true spiritually as it is biologically. From time to time, however, our spiritual evolution bogs down. Then that aspect of the Tao which you might think of as the Infinite Soul, comes among us in human form, resulting in a new level of awareness, a new point of view, a new social and religious paradigm. Jump-starting us, so to speak.

"But God does not coerce. We make our own choices, and evolve our own enlightenment."

The answer bemused Corkery. The language was unfamiliar, but some Jesuits would be comfortable with it. Near the front, he saw a hand stabbing the air. Aran pointed.

"The lady in the indigo coat," he said. "Speak loudly, please, so the congregation can hear you."

"Are you talking about a messiah?"

"The question is, am I talking about a messiah. Yes, I am. But let me clarify. A messiah, in the way we usually use the term, is exemplified by the Christ. Jesus of Nazareth didn't start life as the Christ. He was conceived by the usual sex act between two not terribly exceptional human beings. Like you and me, he was human, a soul occupying a primate body. . . ."

An image appeared in Corkery's mind, of the parish priest of his childhood, and he almost laughed aloud. *Wouldn't Father Malachy love to hear that!* he thought.

"For some thirty years, Jesus continued to be a human being, a messenger of extraordinary wisdom, compassion and enlightenment, with significant paranormal powers—but a human being. A few weeks before the crucifixion, the soul of Jesus left the body to join the . . . angels, so to speak. That is, he returned to the astral plane."

Corkery's eyebrows raised. *Astral plane? Bald-faced New Age-ism,* he told himself.

"At that point the Infinite Soul assumed the body of Jesus, and became the Christ. Or in Hindu terminology, an avatar, an incarnation of God."

The tall black figure paused behind the pulpit and leaned his forearms on it. In the congregation, more hands thrust upward. Straightening, he pointed. "The man in the plaid jacket."

Corkery's thumb found the trigger and pressed it.

Nothing happened. He pressed again. Still nothing. He resisted the impulse to take the detonator out and look at it. This would never do! Could the batteries be bad? He'd put them in this morning, fresh from the package, and tested the device with the apparatus the Iraqi had provided.

"Are you implying that there's been more than one messiah?" the man asked.

Aran stepped around beside the pulpit again. "On Earth, Jesus was the fourth. At last count we have twice that many living claimants or third-party appointees right now. You'll have to wait and see whether any of them are genuine."

Tentative laughter rippled through the congregation.

"But there *will* be another avatar," Aran went on. "In the near future. It is time."

He paused, then pointed again. "The young lady with red hair."

"What will this avatar teach that Jesus didn't?"

"The man Jesus was born to Galilean peasants, and of course was raised a Jew. And it was the Jews of his time that he taught, speaking in terms and images they understood. At the end, however, Christ, the manifestation of the Infinite Soul, did not teach very much, except to instruct his disciples. He simply manifested by his presence the love and power of God—which is beyond words, deeper and more powerful than any teaching. In that era it was more than many people could deal with, but it was needed."

Several listeners had gotten to their feet, apparently unhappy with their speaker, and pushed their way out through the crowd standing in the rear. Corkery pressed the trigger one more time, to no avail. Exasperated, he too got up, following them out of the church and into the winter sunlight.

With the taste of bile in his mouth, Corkery walked toward the bus stop two blocks away. To clear his mind and senses, he looked at the world about him. Winter-naked trees, gray shovel piles of old snow, and large, faded, nineteenth-century houses.

His eyes stopped on one of them, a rundown place with a ROOM TO LET sign in the yard. They paused on a second-story window, holding there briefly. Someone was peering through the pane. He almost stopped, then thought better of it. Security perhaps? He looked again and saw nothing. Either he'd been mistaken before, or the watcher had moved back from the glass.

Thomas, he told himself, *don't get delusional just because a hit's misfired.*

35

LUTHER KOSKELA HAD CLEANED the window the day before, in order to see through it clearly. It was not a time of year to leave it open longer than need be, and for simply watching, clean glass was good enough. Now, wearing a stained, down-filled parka, he sat on the only chair in his room, watching through binoculars. It was 214 yards to the top step of the Bentham Avenue Unitarian Church. He'd measured the distance the day before with his laser rangefinder, and had set the 4X sniper scope accordingly.

The breeze was negligible. Given his marksmanship, and his single-shot Thompson/Center Contender, he could put a bullet through the center of the man's chest—or his forehead. But the chest was a larger target, and less apt to move out of the way as he touched the hair trigger. The soft-point slug would take care of the rest.

The church's front doors opened. Quickly Koskela stood, set aside his binoculars and opened the window, then knelt behind the gun rest he'd prepared, rather than use the window sill. It was best to have the muzzle completely inside the room, where it couldn't be seen. And even with the silencer, there'd be sound. Better it be inside too, the landlady being hard of hearing.

He watched through the scope now, instead of the binocs. It was ill-suited for watching—the field of view was small—but it was best to squeeze the shot off as soon as the guru showed himself, before he started down the steps. Parishioners began filing out, but the preacher hadn't appeared yet. He was probably doing his goodbyes and handshaking in the vestibule, Koskela decided, where it was warmer, which was unfortunate, because delivering his goodbyes in the doorway would have slowed the flow, providing a better shot.

People moved down the steps and along the walk to the parking lot next door. For one moment he thought he had his target. The color was right, and the height, but the man was older, and walked with a cane. Finally the flow thinned, then stopped. Someone came out, released the doorstops and closed the doors. *Maybe,* Koskela thought, *they're going to feed the sonofabitch before he leaves.* But he didn't really believe it.

He left the window open, but put down the rifle and picked up the binocs again. Feeling edgy. When the guru did leave, with no crowd, no last-minute words, no hands reaching to be shaken, his people would hustle him down the steps and into—

The car! Damn! If they'd been going to use the front exit, they'd have brought the car to the front curb to load their passenger! While he'd sat squinting through the scope, the target could have left by a rear door and be well on his way to Logan Airport! Obviously the guru had a professional security team; if he didn't, he'd be dead by now. They would analyze, foresee risks, and take steps to reduce them.

Or—he still might be inside having coffee and cake with his hosts. They wouldn't bring the car to the curb until he was ready to leave. The car would be the signal. When it stopped, he'd pick up the rifle again.

Luther waited thirty minutes more, then stood and closed the window. The room was cold now, and he felt sure the dove had flown. Still he sat and watched for another quarter hour without the binocs.

Finally he grunted, picked up the rifle and stroked its stock. "Sorry, buddy," he murmured. "No action today. Whoever his security chief is, he knows his job.

"But we'll get him, you and me. It's just a matter of time." *I'll have to watch the money, though,* he told himself. *You can go through a lot of it fast, chasing someone around the country.*

He'd rent a few minutes of computer time, call up Ngunda's tour schedule, select another promising town, go there and find a place to live. Maybe get a job of some kind—the government was opening public works projects—and set things up again. Once more he patted the stock, murmuring, "It's you and me, buddy." Then he broke the rifle down, put it in his suitcase, and began to pack his few clothes.

❖   ❖   ❖

"Millard," Florence Metzger said to the man in her phone screen, "I was just informed you've filed criminal charges against Millennium. What's that about?"

The voice on the other end spoke patiently. "I'm sorry, Madam President, I presumed you'd read my summary report. When their security people found the device, they should have informed us immediately, per the Anti-Terrorism Act. Notified our Boston office. Which in turn would have notified the local police, and a team from each would have gone to the site, to disarm the device and investigate."

"And that's it? That's the sum total of your complaint?"

There was a silence of several seconds.

"Hello, Millard? Are you all right?"

"Yes, I am, Madam President. I don't know what you want me to say."

"A simple yes or no would help. I did read your summary report, but it seemed to me there had to be something more behind it."

She took a deep breath and let it out. "Look, I'm neither a law enforcement veteran nor a lawyer. Not being a lawyer probably helped get me elected. But I wish to hell you'd used some common sense, or talked to someone who does, before filing charges.

"Your report described the bomb as requiring a remote firing device. So then what? When Millennium's security people found it, they'd naturally disarm it on the spot. Right? And right after that they phoned the Boston police, who notified your local office. So suppose they hadn't disarmed the bomb. It would have been half an hour before your people got there. The goddamn thing could have been detonated by then. Did you think of that?"

Again she didn't wait for a response. "And when the Boston police notified your office, what did they say? Were they upset? Not the way I heard it, and I just talked to the police commissioner there. He agreed. Disarming it at once was quote: 'a timely and necessary precaution,' end quote.

"So. What would have happened if Millennium had called, and then waited for your people to arrive? There'd have been a fleet of police cars racing through the streets with sirens yowling, at an hour when people were driving to church. And when the police got there, they'd have cordoned off the building, stirred up the whole neighborhood, and cancelled the church service."

"There *is* the law," the man answered stiffly.

She ignored him. "Furthermore, I asked the commissioner about the qualifications of the Millennium man who'd disarmed it. The name didn't mean doodly to me, but he said the man is one of the foremost bomb experts in the world, for chrissake! Did you know that?"

There was no answer.

"I also asked the commissioner if the crime site had been compromised. He said not by Millennium's security team. The place had been tracked through by others before the bomb was found—it was a hallway, after all—but Millennium's people had kept subsequent disturbance to a minimum. He said the whole thing had been handled very professionally."

She eyed Forsberg with more curiosity than irritation now. "Have you ever heard of the evaluation of importances, Millard?" When he didn't answer, she continued. "Since you haven't seen fit to respond intelligently to my questions, when you answered at all, I've concluded you don't take professional criticism well. So I'm going to dictate a job report on you, expressing my serious reservations about your competence and your judgement. Because frankly, Millard, you acted like a damned robot, instead of a sentient human being. Meanwhile you'll be receiving an order from the Attorney General to withdraw your charges."

She glared at the screen. The face looking back was stiff with indignation and suppressed anger, and she cut the connection, thinking she'd overreacted again. "Hell," she said aloud, "he'll resign and go straight to the Senate with it. But what else could I do with someone like that?"

"I'm sure you'll handle it." Willem Enrico Groenveldt was smiling wryly at her from a chair. She'd forgotten he was there.

"I read the summary report too," he said. "Before you did, while your back was being worked on. It didn't say how Millennium found the bomb. Considering where it was, it's remarkable it was found at all. I'd think dogs would have trouble smelling something situated like that."

The President frowned. "I never thought to wonder," she said, and looked at him appreciatively. "Hank, you're a lawyer, and you also think. How'd you like to be Acting Director of the FBI?"

He laughed. "I'm utterly unqualified. Besides, I already have a job. I'm the personal aide of the President of the United States." He paused. "I do have another question though. Is there any particular reason you decided to intervene in this? Besides the fact that Forsberg went off half-cocked."

Her look turned thoughtful. "Three of them," she said. "First, no harm came of what Millennium did. And secondly, the FBI has worked hard to upgrade their public reputation. This would filthy it up again, especially since Millennium's Ladder and Hand and Bailout projects have earned so many points with the public."

"That sounds to me like two reasons, Madam President. What's the third?"

She sighed. "The third is one of the major financiers of Millennium. I've known him since college; in fact he once asked me to marry him. Biggest mistake I ever made was to turn him down, but my girlish taste ran to hunks. Large hunks!"

Her gaze was direct, calm. "And I trust him implicitly, as I do you. He wouldn't be pumping millions into Millennium unless he was damned sure it was straight, from top to bottom."

She paused, examining her nails. "I wonder if Bill Foley would take the job? Because whether or not Millard Forsberg resigns, I'm going to replace him."

"Who is Bill Foley?"

"The Boston police commissioner. But he's probably got too much sense to work for me."

The phone rang. Thomas Corkery set aside his book and answered, knowing by the caller ID who was on the other end. He touched a key, and a picture popped onto the small screen.

"You're ill-advised," Corkery said, "to be calling me like this."

"What happened? Ngunda Aran should be dead! You were paid a total of $12,000 to get the job done. My money sources are going to demand either performance or their money back!"

"Jack, Jack! I'm surprised at you. After all these years in the murdering business, you still haven't grasped how easily these things go askew. You're too impatient with other men's work, Jack. Impatient! Your trouble is, you've always been a sender. Ye've done precious little wetwork yourself. If any."

"Are you calling me a coward, Corkery?"

"I'm calling you impatient and inexperienced." Corkery grinned into the visual pickup. "And touchy. There's that, too."

He paused, but Russell was too upset to take advantage of it, and the hit man went on. "By the by, you're obviously back from Rome, and I've heard nothing of the Holy Father's demise. How long do you suppose they can keep it quiet?"

Russell glared.

"Ah well. No doubt something happened, something unforeseen, and you had to cancel. No need to apologize; such things happen. The next try may work. Or the third. The third's the charm, you know."

Corkery hung up, chuckling.

36

CNN Weekly Summary
Atlanta, GA, Jan. 11

In December, unemployment increased again, to 23 percent, and wages and prices continued downward. Taking advantage of her new emergency powers, on Thursday President Metzger declared a limited moratorium on home and farm mortgage foreclosures. Utility companies were ordered to continue service until April 15, to those unable to pay their bills.

The federal government has increased purchases of surplus beans, cereal grains, potatoes, cabbage, cheese, and powdered milk, for distribution to the unemployed.

During the week, mortar attacks were made on upscale enclaves in several metropolitan areas. The more serious were near Santa Barbara and Pacific Palisades in California, and near Arlington, Virginia. At both Santa Barbara and Pacific Palisades, more than twenty rounds landed. At Arlington, some thirty fell. Altogether, eight persons have been reported killed, and forty injured. Property damage was extensive.

The fire damage from last week's rent riots in Oakland, California, has been assessed at $130 million. An estimated 1,400 people were left homeless. Over 300 of them occupy emergency quarters in a warehouse provided by a Mr. Ragheeb Lincoln. Mr. Lincoln is a distributor of home appliances, and office and institutional furniture. He made the space available by moving merchandise to warehouses he owns in Fresno, California, 180 miles away, and in Medford, Oregon, 360 miles away. He declined to tell us the cost of the transfers.

The Red Cross provided the cots, mattresses, and other basic furnishings. Mr. Lincoln provided amenities such as televisions.

Ragheeb Lincoln is a lifelong resident of Oakland. Members of his own family were burned out of their homes by the 1991 Oakland firestorm.

Last night, temperatures near or below zero in the Midwest, as far south as Jackson, Mississippi, and Dallas, Texas, caused untold suffering. More than one hundred deaths were reported among the homeless. Thousands were given shelter in churches, schools, and private homes.

———

Journal of Religious Philosophy, January
"Reply to the November article
by Dr. Emmons Hoglin"

Mr. Aran receives both undeserved scorn and undeserved credit for his teachings. Of course, most who attack him would do so regardless of whatever truth or virtue there might be in what he says and writes. And if he actually were a messiah, as some claim, many would hate him even more, because a messiah would not say and do what they would have him say and do.

As for credit—most of what Mr. Aran teaches is derivative. It is rooted in various earlier teachings, most notably in Chelsea Quinn Yarbro's *Michael* books, as Professor Hoglin pointed out. But much of it is also found in such ancient scriptures as the Vedic *Upanishads* and the Buddhist *Sutras,* which are much less known to American readers.

Mr. Aran's primary contribution is the exposure he provides those concepts, exposure increased by the claims others have made that he is a new messiah. While the people he angers were angry already, and in these volatile and angry times, he may actually be a calming influence. Meanwhile his teachings touch far more people than those who write outraged letters to newspapers, and fume or thunder on the Web, or on right-wing radio and television.

Far less sensational than Mr. Aran's theology, and his powerful if low-key charisma, are the accessibility and promotion he has provided two other creations not primarily his own: the Abilities Release procedures developed by Dr. Peter Verbeek, and the so-called Millennium Procedures which are outgrowths of them. They too are basically Verbeek's, with Mr. Aran contributing to their development. Verbeek, a practicing psychiatrist and eclectic, had in his turn borrowed, modified, and expanded on ideas from sources as diverse as Carl Jung and Edgar Cayce.

This is not to belittle Verbeek's work, or Aran's contributions to it. Virtually all useful developments in anything have roots in the research and experience of earlier workers.

In the long run, Mr. Aran's promotion of these demonstrably valuable therapies may prove to be his most important contribution to our tomorrows.

Dr. G.S.M. Venkatanarayana
Associate Professor of Philosophy
Oberlin College
Oberlin, Ohio

Headline News
Atlanta, GA, Jan. 12

Widespread looting of homes occurred last night and this morning, particularly in Pennsylvania. Forecasts of subzero temperatures as far east and south as Baltimore and Nashville drove thousands from homes without fuel oil, and looters took advantage of their absence. There are reports of shootouts between looters on one hand, and family members or neighbors on the other, acting to protect vacant property. Pennsylvania Governor Norris Furnell mobilized National Guard units to stop the looting, and to transport fuel oil from military stocks made available by the White House. Other eastern and midwestern governors are expected to follow suit.

Looters set numerous fires. Other fires resulted from families burning refuse and furniture in their homes, for warmth. Fire departments had trouble with frozen hydrants.

Figures on deaths are not yet available.

Water and sewer lines have frozen and burst in hundreds of thousands, probably millions of unheated homes as far south as the Gulf Coast.

It has been unofficially reported that President Metzger will declare martial law later today, to facilitate emergency activities throughout the country, and to control looting.

37

LUTHER KOSKELA FELT ILL at ease in Denver's McNichols Sports Arena. He'd been more comfortable snooping the Ranch, 170 miles south. But he needed a feel for arenas and crowds as an operating environment.

A pregame hockey or basketball crowd, he told himself, *would be louder.* Presumably most of the waiting 15,000 or so believed in Ngunda, and were there to hear him in person. The simply interested or curious could watch and listen from their living rooms. Given the hard times, the admission wasn't all that low—two dollars for the cheap seats, and three where he sat in the second tier. Those at floor level were $10 each; $25 for the five front rows. Presumably they paid for the proximity to the speaker; he did not doubt he'd hear perfectly well from where he sat. And he had a better overall view of the arena, which gave him a better idea of how events like this were managed.

He hadn't tried to bring a gun in. He was simply scouting. The Arena Authority had manned security screening gates at the entrances, and if he'd brought a gun inside earlier in the week, it would have had to survive the inevitable pre-event shakedown, complete with dogs. And the odds of getting off an aimed shot, then getting out alive and uncaptured . . . Uh-uh!

Lute's continued interest in killing Ngunda wasn't driven by professional pride, and certainly not by religious obsession. It was guilt that drove him now, guilt for escaping the fates of his teammates. The feeling surfaced only now and then, but somewhere beneath that surface it was continuously operative. Actually it was Sarge he felt guilty about; Sarge, who'd kept his mouth shut. Sarge in Leavenworth Penitentiary, under the Anti-Terrorism Act.

Lute rationalized that being free, he could still gun down Ngunda and complete the mission, which would make things right.

He'd already learned some things. Ngunda Aran didn't use a ClearScreen, which to Koskela meant he was either reckless or trying for martyrdom. He also used a slender lectern, instead of the broad variety with veneer over steel plate, popular with politicians in these times. And Ngunda had just two bodyguards with him, walking a stride behind and to the sides. Neither sat close to him on the speakers' platform. The only people physically near him were dignitaries, identified on the program as the mayor, the lieutenant governor, a professor of ethics from Denver University, and the woman who'd sing the national anthem.

When the scoreboard clock showed 8:00 P.M., the mayor stepped to the microphone and greeted the crowd, then introduced the singer. The crowd stood, Koskela included. The organist played some introductory chords, then the singer began and the flag was raised.

Luther stood with hand over heart, thinking about neither country nor anthem. His lips moved—he might even have sung if he'd had any kind of singing voice— but his thoughts were on more important matters. *At an outdoor event,* he told himself, the *hit should be more doable. Not easy, but doable.* But there'd be no outdoor speeches till deep spring. Maybe March or April in places like Florida or the desert southwest. But sometime along the line, a spring and summer speaking schedule would be published. Then he could make specific plans.

Meanwhile he was getting a good sense of the density, positioning, and movements of ushers. They didn't carry guns, but there were radios and cans of whatever on their belts. There were also uniformed armed guards of two kinds: police and armed security people hired by the Arena Authority.

Those things would vary from city to city, but probably not by much. He wondered if there might not be police snipers at vantages in the arena, maybe in the press boxes, watching for reaction vortices in the crowd, that might signify the drawing of a smuggled gun or grenade. Snipers ready to swing their telescopic sights to any disturbance. There'd be serious drawbacks to police snipers though. *If just one of them's a nut who wants to shoot the guru . . .*

Luther didn't notice the grotesque irony in the thought.

After the crowd was seated again, the mayor introduced the other dignitaries. But only when Ngunda Aran stepped to the microphone did Lute pay much attention. Even then, for the first minute or so, the words didn't really register. It was when the guru began to talk about the messiah to come that Koskela paid serious attention.

"Among Christians," Ngunda said, "the thought that the Infinite Soul will incarnate again has been around since not long after the death of Christ, nearly two thousand years ago. In the first decades after the crucifixion, most Christians expected it to happen in their lifetime. When it didn't, the anticipation cooled. It heated up markedly near the end of the first millennium, more than a thousand years ago, and again it cooled when nothing happened.

"There was much less expectation in the last decade of the second millennium, but it heated up several years into the third. Beginning with the nuclear destruction of six Middle Eastern cities during the One-Day War—a war which some Christians considered the beginning of Armageddon—and the nuclear fallout that its initiators had failed to allow for adequately.

"Now we have almost enough proclaimed messiahs to play a basketball game, though not all of them are Christian. One need not be familiar with New Testament prophecy to feel that the time is ripe for the Tao to 'intervene.'

"But what is the nature of this messiah so many hope for . . . ?"

It seemed to Luther Koskela that he could answer that one, though it wasn't an answer most of these people wanted to hear. They wanted God to send a messiah to save them, so they could go on being a pack of idiots. He'd seen a TV rerun once, of *Jesus Christ Superstar,* and it seemed to him the Jesus character had said it about right: "Save yourselves!" Then the poor sucker turned right around and got himself crucified.

Duke Cochran sat much nearer the speaker than Luther Koskela did, and his interest was different. He was quite familiar with Ngunda events now, and with Ngunda's philosophy. What impressed him most was that so many people, some of them very intelligent, took it seriously. Between tours he monitored the Web for reviews and comments. Every talk the man gave, of course, was on Millennium's website, along with favorable commentaries. And there were plenty of sites where he was trashed. Political cartoonists had a ball with him. Independent commentaries ranged from thoughtful, through skeptical and cynical, to acutely hostile. Most of the latter were fundamentalists and conspiracy theorists.

He wondered if some writers weren't actually just a *little* worried that maybe, just maybe, Ngunda was for real. That someday, with a long memory, he'd sit on a pink cloud and send his more serious attackers to eternal hellfire for sticking it to him too hard. Others, without believing in him as a messiah or a prophet, hoped that what the man taught would have a good effect on the world. At least two he'd read had said as much in writing.

The coming incarnation of the Infinite Soul! Now that Christmas was past, Ngunda's comments on a new messiah couldn't be explained away as the season.

Interest had jumped when he'd first mentioned it, and it seemed obvious to Cochran that before long the guru would stake his claim. He'd have to. More and more, others were speculating about when, and his coyness would backfire if he didn't grasp the torch. Besides, any major payoff required it.

Now, on the speakers' platform, Ngunda stepped to the microphone, and Cochran gave him his attention. The subject, Ngunda stated, was the coming "next incarnation of the Infinite Soul." That was his big pitch now. Still, to Cochran, the first minute or so was prosaic, not the sort of thing to excite the guru's audience.

Then he became more specific. "This new incarnation," he said, "what some refer to as 'the Second Coming,' is very close at hand. The physical human being, the receptacle the Infinite Soul will occupy and use, is already teaching among you. Soon the Infinite Soul will descend onto that body, and the human soul which had occupied it will ascend, so to speak, to what is commonly referred to as 'heaven.'

"When that happens, that body will largely cease to preach. For the Logos—the ultimate truth as it applies to the physical plane—cannot be expressed in words, or in paintings or images or abstracts or mathematical equations, or in anything created by humans. Words cannot come close. Occasionally, great music, and the greatest figure skating and dance performances, can give a sense of it. But such transcendental performances are uncommon. Perhaps the strongest sense of it readily available to us over the centuries is experienced by watching a major display of the aurora, the northern or southern lights.

"But that will change when the Infinite Soul travels among you in a human body. Simply *showing* itself to you will demonstrate its incredible power and love. Then you will perceive and *know* more than you can grasp with your intellects, though there are those who will reject it."

Jesus Christ! thought Cochran. *Talk about going out on a limb! He'll have to step up and claim it soon, and make a damned good show of it, or he'll lose all credibility.*

"And at the end of the Infinite Soul's time among you . . ." Ngunda paused, to strengthen their attention, then repeated himself. "At the end of the Infinite Soul's time among you, the Tao will also manifest itself in a geophysical event that no one—*no one!*—will ignore or deny: a geophysical event that began a long time ago, and is only now approaching fruition. For people to whom only physical phenomena are valid, especially painful physical phenomena, that geophysical event will carry conviction.

"But the spiritual manifestation will express itself in the physical form of a human being. Not as Jesus of Nazareth. Jesus was of and for an earlier time. But as someone of and for our time."

He's not leaving himself much wiggle room! Cochran thought. *And now he's pissed off all the people who believe the real messiah has to be Jesus returned.*

It occurred to Duke that Ngunda might believe what he was saying. In that case he might not be influenced by whether people liked it or not. But what about the people pumping money into Millennium: the board of directors of the Millennium Foundation? All were presidents, or board chairmen, or CEOs of wealthy corporations. Estimates of personal, pre-Depression worth ranged from $130 million to $3.7 billion. What were they thinking now, sitting in their mansions listening to this speech? Was this part of their plans? Or were they shocked? Maybe thinking *Oh boy! There goes the farm! How do we cover this?*

It was then Cochran had a major realization: *When Ngunda claims to be the messiah, he'll have to die shortly afterward.* Because no one—not Ngunda Aran, not anyone—could act the role of messiah the way he'd described it. With some good special effects, he might get away with faking it for a few days. But no way in hell could he string it out longer than a week or two. He'd have to die, whether he wanted to or not.

When the time came for the ethicist from Denver University to question Ngunda, the professor blew his opportunity to press him with what Cochran thought of as telling questions. Instead he asked, "What might we realistically hope for as a result of such a remarkable event?"

Ngunda smiled. "The Infinite Soul will not incarnate to 'save' humankind, nor transform it into saints. Combined with the geophysical event, he will help you see more deeply into yourselves—your lives, your motives, your values. And to do so more honestly than you had before. The result will be a substantial shift in the orientation of human society as a whole, from materialism and its idols of comfort and wealth, power and security—toward tolerance and compassion." He paused and repeated. "Tolerance and compassion.

"Note that I said 'orientation.' Many will truly strive

to be compassionate, many more than now. While far fewer than now will simply give it lip service, and fewer yet will scorn it.

"For the ineffable love radiating from the Infinite Soul will have a powerful effect on humankind. Even those who experience it only via television will feel it strongly. It will even touch those few isolated persons *who fail even to hear of it*. This, coupled with the geophysical event, will leave relatively few denying the nature of either phenomenon. Each event—the geophysical and the divine—will certify the other.

"You will still live in the physical universe, with all the problems that go with it. Greed, cruelty and pain, hatred and insanity—all will still exist. So will despair, irresponsiblity, finger pointing, and rationalization. But they will be less than we see around us now. And their expression will become less extreme, because society will change."

Cochran stared at Ngunda. Then the professor spoke again, hesitantly. "What is the nature of this, uh, 'geophysical event'?"

"The long-talked-about asteroid impact. It will not be 'the big one,' but it will be memorable."

"You said these things will happen soon. What do you mean by soon?"

"Within this year, professor, this calendar year."

When the event was over, Luther Koskela walked across the broad parking lot to his car, feeling weird. *It's the guru's bullshit*, he thought. And shook it off, putting his attention on what he should do next. Go to San Diego, he decided. There'd be jobs there, for

someone with his professional skills, who spoke halfway
decent Spanish and wasn't too squeamish.

As he started his car, he wondered if, just possibly,
Carl or Axel, or both, had watched and listened to
the speech on television in their prison cells. Unlikely.
But if they had, Carl for sure would have had a con-
niption, maybe even a stroke.

Because Ngunda had come damned close to nam-
ing himself as the new messiah. When the professor
had asked what good would come of a messiah, the
guru had talked about "you": *You* will do this. *You*
will feel that. He'd never once said *we*. Because he
expected to *be* the messiah. The poor sonofabitch was
crazier than Carl.

And it was all supposed to happen before the year
was out. "Somebody *better* kill him," Lute murmured
to himself, "to save him dying of embarrassment next
January first."

38

> On the reservations, most of the drug and alcohol addiction, and the violence and crime, results from futility. And more and more, Ladder is helping us replace that futility with positive action.
>
> Willard Makes-A-Place-For-Them
> Testimony before the Senate Committee
> on Native American Affairs

LEE COULDN'T TELL if the parking lot was paved or not. Like the roof of the high school and everything else in Lodge Grass, Montana, it was covered with new dry snow, except where the wind had blown it off. Ten or twelve inches had fallen. On a street below the school, a snowplow passed with flashing blue lights and a steady beeping noise.

Lee got out of the pickup and started for the gym's entrance, conducted by Willard Makes-A-Place-For-Them. "Call me Bill," he'd said. She did, but she thought of him as Mr. M.

The line moved steadily through the door. Inside was a hubbub of enthusiastic voices. A gray-haired man with large brown fingers took their money, and a burly youth, perhaps a high school senior, stamped their hands with ink. The stands were already mostly full. Mr. M guided her to a small section of seats reserved for tribal elders and their guests.

The two teams were already warming up. The Lodge Grass Indians wore white warmups with fringes on sleeves and pants, and the team logo on the front: the stylized head of a large-beaked bird that didn't resemble a crow at all. Lee hadn't watched basketball since college, hadn't played it since phys. ed. But the Indians seemed really good, their passing sharp, their dribbling clever, and most of the shots went through the rim.

Except for the visiting team, the Hill City Broncs, Lee saw few Caucasians. There was a small section of seats, with a mixture of Caucasians, which she guessed was for teachers. Another had only Caucasians, and Lee pointed. "Is that the visitors' section?" she asked. "There aren't very many of them."

"It looks like about forty," Mr. M answered. "That's quite a lot, with the driving so bad. Hill City is one hundred and fifteen miles from here, and it's not very big. About the same as Lodge Grass—maybe eight hundred people."

"Is their team good?"

"We beat them sixty-three to forty the last time we

played them. We were kind of embarrassed. We don't like to run up the score that much, but they had a bad second half and our reserves played really good. We play a lot of basketball on the reservation. Everybody or their neighbor has a backboard and basket. Our kids start when they're little, and even guys my age play. Even I do." He patted his considerable abdomen.

The officials came onto the court, two of them Caucasians. The teams went to their benches, the starters stripping off their warmups. The Broncs got the tip, but one of the Indians snatched the ball and drove for a layup, to a roar of cheering.

At halftime the score was 38 to 17. Lee hadn't eaten since she'd had a sandwich at the airport in Billings; there hadn't been time. So Mr. M took her down the street to a cafe, almost empty except for the cook and a waitress. Lee, who ordinarily avoided fatty foods, ordered a burger and french fries.

"Do you have chocolate peanut-butter pie?" M asked.

"We have two slices left," the waitress said.

"I'll take one." He looked at Lee. "You better take the other one. Calories don't count when you're traveling."

She laughed. "I can gain weight just looking at chocolate peanut-butter pie, so I might as well eat it."

The cook brought their coffee and left them to themselves. "I don't know much about the reservation," Lee said. "I asked before I left, and they said I'd do better without a lot of preconceived ideas. So I didn't even look it up in the WebWorld. Just the atlas. It's almost as big as Connecticut, the state I lived in a year ago, but obviously it has a lot fewer people."

"Thirteen thousand," said Mr. M.

"They sent me to get a feel for the people, they said, and to learn what effects *Iiúoo* has had. What effects *has* it had?"

"The real effect," he said, "is on individuals. The effect on the tribe, the Crow people, grows out of that." He paused, considering. "I suppose you know something about the history of the native people since Anglos came here," he went on. "In the old days the Crow people had no money, no houses—nothing like that. But we were rich in horses, and had lodges—tepees—that we took with us when we moved. And we had the use of the land, and the buffalo. We knew how to live with them. No one suffered from hunger very often, but when one did, everyone did. The people felt good about themselves. The downside was, we fought with other tribes a lot."

It struck Lee that when he spoke, he didn't gesture. It gave him a sense of dignity and personal power—power that went well beyond his big shoulders and thick hands.

"Then white people came. They killed the buffalo— *all* the buffalo around here—and the people were often hungry. Sometimes they starved. The government had drawn lines on a map, and called it the Apsáalooke Country. It was to be ours forever. But prospectors came, and ranchers, and homesteaders, and the government took back more than ninety percent of it and gave it to them. Or just kept it. The people felt robbed, betrayed, bitter, but we had no power to do anything about it. It was a little like Kosovo, not so many years ago, but worse. There was no honor in what was done to the people, but it was inevitable."

His calm amazed Lee. He'd said what he'd said with no evidence of anger or bitterness. At the same time she noticed a long scar above one eye, others on cheekbone and upper lip, and his nose had been broken.

"After they took the land," he continued, "and the people were starving, the government and the churches decided they'd better turn the Crows into white people. But they didn't know how to do it, and neither did we. They tried to shame us into being white. They took our children away and tried to force them to be white. None of it worked. We remained Crows, Crows with broken wings. Some of us became kind of white, but even for them it didn't work very well.

"But we couldn't be like our ancestors again, because the world had changed too much. It was impossible. And we couldn't find a new way that worked. The best we could do was to walk an in-between path, and survive any way we could.

"That's what we were doing when Ngunda Aran came here. At first we didn't trust him. His skin wasn't white, but he was, or that's how it seemed to us. And white people had come here before, wanting to help. Honest people. But they didn't know how. They only thought they did. Mostly they depressed the spirit."

The cook brought their orders, and they began to eat, slowly, Mr. M talking between bites.

"The difference between Ngunda Aran and other people who'd come to help, is that Ngunda knew how to do it. He already knew the Ladder worked for people of other races. For rich people who lived in the suburbs; poor people, black and white, in the cities—even convicts in prison. So he tried it here.

"He didn't try to force anyone to do anything. He didn't try to make anyone ashamed. He helped one person at a time, people who were willing, and when he was done, they were still Crows.

"But they had changed. Some others, when they saw that, thought it looked pretty good. They'd like some of that. And before long quite a few people had climbed the same Ladder, changing in ways that helped everyone. So we adopted him, and call him Akbaalía. Then he sent Crow people, volunteers, to learn to do what he did, so we could continue on our own. When someone felt pretty bad, or was coming off a big drunk, or beat up his wife, someone might say to him, or her, 'You might go and see Dan at the clinic. Or Fawn, or Archy. Maybe they can help you.'"

Mr. M's calm eyes found Lee's, their touch mild. A rush passed over her that she couldn't explain.

"Ten years ago, at basketball games, by half time quite a few people would have left. Someone would have a bottle in their pickup or car, and they'd go out and start to drink. Some would be drunk even before the game.

"Liquor was a curse to us, but in a way it was also a blessing. Believe me, I know. It dulled the feeling of futility—temporarily. At the same time it made everything more difficult. A child would be smart in school, but when they got old enough to start drinking with their friends, they didn't study anymore. They got in fights. Some got pregnant. Some committed suicide. Most didn't finish high school."

Lee listened soberly. It reminded her of the black ghettos in Connecticut. "What did they do then?"

"Most lived at home with their parents, for a while at least. From time to time they'd work—mostly day labor. A few sold drugs.

"Some would get a steady job off the reservation. But lots of times they'd lose it because they got drunk and skipped work. Or got in a fight, and were put in jail. Or because they didn't like the job, or the people they worked with, and quit. There was quite a lot of prejudice, more than now.

"Iiúoo made big changes. It's the ladder people have used to climb into the fresh air and sunshine again. Now most of our children finish high school, mostly with good grades. There's a scholarship fund, and quite a few go to college.

"The reservation doesn't have any more resources than before, but we aren't so poor anymore. There isn't much drunkenness now, especially among young people. There aren't many fist fights. Hardly anyone gets cut with a knife. The tribe has a new industry, up at Crow Agency, that makes components for computers. About two hundred people work there, only part time now because of the Depression. All of them, even the managers, are Apsáalooke, Crows. Tomorrow I'll take you around so you can see, and talk to people.

"On the Ladder, some of the things we experience change what we believe. Some people don't like that, some of the traditionals. The Baptist minister isn't happy with it either, or Father Schweiger. But no one I know wants to go back to the way things were ten years ago. We are still the Children of the Crow. We still have our own ways."

Mr. M looked at his watch. "We should go back to the gym," he said, "so we can watch the end of the game." Then he called something in Crow. A woman came from the kitchen, and Mr. M paid her.

They watched most of the last quarter. For the Indians, only the bench played in the second half. The final score was Lodge Grass, 56; Hill City, 52.

39

LEE WAS GLAD to be home. She'd almost never spent the night away from her daughters before. Bar Stool delivered her at her door in midafternoon sunshine, with the temperature 42 degrees Fahrenheit—shirtsleeve weather. Instead of going to the office after unpacking, she phoned Ben, telling him she was home, then drew the drapes, set an alarm clock, and napped on the sofa.

Previously she'd had her project tugging at her. It had been interesting and challenging. Often it had taken an act of will to leave work at the end of the day. But the project was finished, including the procedures for adjusting activities to the new chart. All that was left was any fine-tuning that might prove necessary. Lor Lu had understood it thoroughly, and been enthusiastic when she'd gone over the completed product with him. Minutes later Ngunda had knocked, asking to see it, and he too had left praising her.

She was proud of it, but its completion had left a vacuum in her life. It hadn't, however, left her unemployed, for which she found herself grateful. She was to be Millennium's organizational troubleshooter. Her first assignment was to get more intimately acquainted with people at the ground level and in the field, so on this afternoon it was easy to laze around for a few hours.

It was she who fixed supper that evening. She actually cooked quite well, when she took the time. Here they didn't eat to television as they had at Bridgeport. Lee wanted as much communication with the girls as possible.

"What was it like on the reservation, Mom?" Becca asked.

"Cold."

"Come on, Mom," Raquel said, "she didn't mean the weather. What was it like on an Indian reservation?"

"I've only seen one," Lee said, "and it was cold."

"Mo-om!"

"It was minus twenty-nine degrees the first morning at breakfast, and minus fourteen degrees at lunchtime. And windy! They'd had a snowstorm, and the snowplows were going all the time. Mr. Makes-A-Place-For-Them . . ."

"Mr. who?" Raquel asked.

"Willard Makes-A-Place-For-Them. That was his name in English. I didn't learn to say it in the Crow language, but that's what it means. He told me to call him Bill. I thought of him as Mr. M. It was he who took me around and showed me things. He said the snow never melts there. It just wears out, blowing around."

Ben grinned. Becca laughed. Raquel broke up. "It really melts though, I'll bet," Raquel said when she'd regained her composure.

"Of course," Becca told her. "I looked up the climatic data for Billings, close to the reservation. The thirty-year average temperature for January is twenty-one degrees, so lucky Mom got to see a cold spell, an 'Alberta Clipper.' It can get really cold, and then warm up big league when a chinook wind blows. It can be way below zero one day and way above freezing the next."

Raquel gestured toward her sister. "An old scholar in observation mode," she said, "with a goal of trivia."

Becca began a retort, about old sages in idiot mode, with a goal of obnoxious, but their dad was frowning, so instead she turned back to her mother. "What was it like besides cold and snowy?" she asked.

"Well, the reservation is almost as big as Connecticut. But Lodge Grass, where I was, is about a quarter as big as Walsenburg. I went to a high school basketball game the first night, and was really impressed! They play so well! Their coach had set scoring records at the University of Montana, when he was a student there, and their school has won the Montana state high school championship several times, for schools its size. One of its graduates won the national best cowboy award in college rodeo last year, too."

She couldn't think of anything else that might interest the girls about her trip.

"What about Ladder?" Ben asked.

Lee frowned thoughtfully. "Its services are available

to all children ten and older," she said, "free through
Life Healing." Her voice stiffened. "Although"—her
gesture indicated the girls—"I can't see what good
it does perfectly healthy children."

Becca and Raquel gave serious attention to their
food. Life healing was another sensitive issue.

"If it helps reduce alcoholism . . ." Ben said.

Lee nodded. "It has, a lot. Mr. M showed me the
legal and medical statistics. They're quite open about
the problems they had for so long—their land and
livelihood taken from them, their culture and beliefs
denigrated and forbidden, their children taken from
them in the old days, and brainwashed for years
before being allowed to go home. The Crow Tribe
came through better than lots, but even so . . ." She
turned to Becca. "They call themselves the *Apsáalooke*,
the 'Children of the Large-Beaked Bird.' I made a
special effort to learn to say it in Crow. It seemed
like something you'd like to know."

Becca got from her chair, went around the table,
and wrapping her arms around her mother's neck,
kissed her cheek. Raquel was there before Becca had
finished, and added her own hug and kiss. "We're glad
you're home, Mom," Becca said.

"Yeah," Raquel added. "We missed you. Are you
going to have to be gone very much now?"

"From time to time. But I'm not worried. You'll
take good care of your dad, I know."

"He didn't cook as well while you were gone."
Raquel was back in her chair again, talking between
bites. "He gave us limburger cheese and anchovy pizza
for supper last night . . ."

Lee's eyebrows raised.

"And the night before that, balut and stuffed dog!" She broke into giggles.

"He didn't either," Becca said to her mother, then turned to Raquel. "You don't even know what limburger cheese is."

"I do so! It's a kind of cheese that really stinks!"

"Honey," Lee said, "I'd rather you didn't say 'stinks' at the table." She looked at Ben. "What did you feed them?"

He grinned. "For supper? I didn't. We ate at staff. For breakfast they got the usual: eggs, toast, cereal, and juice."

"What did you get, Mom?" Raquel asked.

"Café food. I ate in the café next to the motel." She turned to Raquel. "What were those other foods you named? Or did you make them up?"

"No, they're real. Domingo Morgan spent last summer with his Filipino grandparents on Luzon, and he told us about it in human geography. I better not tell you what they are at the table though." She made a face, then laughed. "Worse than limburger cheese and anchovies. He ate some before he knew what they were, and they tasted pretty good, he said. But if he'd known what balut was, he'd never have eaten it."

"If you don't eat your mashed potatoes and gravy," her dad told her, "they'll be cold."

"I'll just put them in the microwave."

"Eat!"

She did then, finishing soon after the others.

"May I leave the table, Mom?" Becca asked.

"Before dessert?"

"Dad made cherry pie for you, and I don't like cherry pie that much."

"Ice cream goes with it," her stepfather told her, "or by itself if you'd rather."

"No thanks. I'm already full anyway. May I?"

Raquel passed on dessert too, and both of them left. It was her turn to be first on the computer, while Becca lay on the living room floor with a book. Lee and Ben remained in the breakfast nook over coffee.

"When's your next trip?" Ben asked, speaking quietly, as they often did for privacy.

"In two weeks. To the Seattle office. I'll fly up one afternoon, spend two days there, and fly back the next. It's supposed to be pretty representative of the U.S. branches. Then I might be sent to Europe for a few days, to Rotterdam and Copenhagen." She examined the coffee in her cup. "Did you miss me?"

Ben smiled. "You were only gone two days. Be gone four and I'll miss you."

She frowned as if examining his words, or her feelings about them.

"Do you believe in souls?" he asked.

She looked up at him. "Yes," she said. Then added, "I think so."

"Then let me tell you how it seems to me, about us. Lots of times, two people get married on the basis of physical attraction, two primates, two Homo sapiens who look good to each other. Or maybe they get married for convenience, or because they both like the same things, or it seems to them they'd better do it now, before it's too late. Or for whatever reasons.

"But sometimes two people, before or after they marry, touch soul to soul. And when that happens, a different kind of bond forms between them. They may or may not recognize consciously what happened, but they do realize, at least briefly, that it was something special. And if they validate it and build on it, the relationship can be very very good.

"That's what happened between you and me. At least that's what I think." He lowered his voice a bit more. "The physical is nice, believe me. But it seems to me we have more than that going for us. Something stronger. So for me, it's fine for you to be gone a few days. Weeks if necessary. I'm comfortable with that because I'm comfortable with us."

It had been more answer than she'd bargained for, been ready for, or knew how to handle. She didn't meet his eyes. "Do you ever look at other women?" she murmured.

"Hey, sweetheart, part of me's a healthy, forty-year-old male primate. Of course I look at other women, but looking's as far as it goes."

"You don't—think about them in a sexual way?"

"I respond to them physically, but I don't fantasize about them. If you were gone long enough I might fantasize, but I can't imagine making a pass at one."

Now she did meet his eyes. "You're a nice man, Ben Shoreff. A very nice man. I can't imagine what I did to deserve you."

"Hmm. Well," he growled softly, "try imagining what you're going to do to deserve me when we go to bed tonight."

"Oh! You!" She cocked her coffee cup, then set it back on its saucer, and lowered her voice almost to a whisper. "What's the earliest we can put the girls to bed?"

"Steady, sweetheart. Their usual bedtime, nine. That's about the earliest we can get away with."

40

AFTER RETURNING FROM Montana, Lee had spent two days on her new duties. She knew Millennium's worldwide operations thoroughly, from her work on the operations chart. Now she was discovering the problems of training and installing a large number of new counselors and supervisors at field locations, integrating them, and providing suitable facilities, at minimal cost, and without disrupting ongoing counseling and training.

One thing in particular troubled her, and she'd arrived at the office that morning intending to speak with Lor Lu before he could leave on another tour. It was a nuisance having him gone so much. When he was away, Anne Whistler could answer almost any of her questions, but no one could fill Lor Lu's shoes.

She touched a key on her pad, and waited a second.

"This is Lor Lu. What can I do for you, Lee?"

"Give me a few minutes of your time."

"How would right now be?"

"I'll be right there."

Standing, she grabbed her stenographic recorder and left at once. Lor Lu's office was near the other end of the third-floor corridor. She was there in less than a minute, and began without preliminaries.

"As of last Friday you had a total of 370 Life Healing counselors in training or internships in the U.S.," she said. "About 160 are expected to be certified over the next three months. We have 316 training abroad. Add the 83 advanced counseling trainees, 48 counseling supervisor trainees, and 74 training supervisors . . ." She trailed off, looking meaningfully at the small Asian.

"We'd train more if we had more training supervisors in place," he said. "But I feel quite pleased with our progress."

He grinned. Usually she found that reassuring; just now it troubled her. "So," she said, "where is the business going to come from to keep them productive? It's costing Millennium money to train and house and feed them, and pay their weekly stipends. And when they graduate, there'll be salaries to pay."

Lor Lu's mobile eyebrows had raised questioningly. "True," he said.

"Our business projections only extend for three months. And while the trend has been steadily upward, it's not steep. And if anything, the Depression seems to be getting worse. If we're going to install hundreds of new staff, rent or buy facilities for them, and pay them actual salaries, we need to bring in a lot of new customers. And except for speaking tours, we have about the tamest, least imaginative promotion conceivable. With no plans to increase it, so far as I can see. Is there something I haven't been told? Or what?"

"Not at all. If I may use a cliché, what you see is what you get. We have no plans for expanded promotion. That doesn't mean we won't expand it, but we have no plans to." His eyes were bright but inscrutable. "I'm confident the demand will be there as the counselors are available. Or shortly afterward. The physical universe does not often provide perfect timing, but the people will come to us."

Frowning, she stared at him. "And that's it?"

He laughed, the sound light in the winter sunshine slanting through his windows. "I have faith," he said. "I recommend it to you. The Tao will provide."

She snorted. "Famous last words."

"True again. Nonetheless, act on it as a working assumption: the demand will be there."

His grin had eased off to an easy smile. Deliberately to fit her mood, she had no doubt.

She returned to her office not greatly eased, to find a message on her phone. Duke Cochran wanted to talk to her "for a few minutes, at your earliest convenience."

Well hell, she thought, *why not?* She could use some distraction before returning to what she'd been doing. It wasn't easy to focus when she had serious misgivings about basic assumptions. Reaching, she dialed Duke's number. He answered on the first buzz.

"Mr. Cochran," she said, "this is Lee Shoreff. What did you want to talk about? I really can't see the time for an interview this week." Her tone, she realized, was brusque, an effect of her unsatisfactory talk with Lor Lu.

"Another interview wasn't what I called about," Cochran answered. "Though when you find an opportunity, I very much want to get together with you on that. No, this won't take more than five or ten minutes. I'd like to talk with you about something more specific. In your office, this morning if possible."

She frowned. "The best time would be right now. Before I get reimmersed in what I'm working on."

"Great!" he said. "I'll be right over."

He hung up immediately, leaving her wondering what he might want to know about her work that she could possibly tell him. Minutes later he knocked. When he came in, he was breathing deeply, as if he'd run. "Hi," he said. "How was your trip to Montana?"

He must have asked for her while she was away, and Marge had told him where she'd gone. "Interesting. Is that what you wanted to talk about?"

"Not primarily. But I do want to talk about it sometime soon. I want to visit it myself, when spring arrives."

"So what do you want to talk about *now?*" she asked pointedly.

"I need some information, and I'm not sure you have it. Or whether you can give it to me if you do. Let me tell you what brought it up. I did a WebWorld search on Millennium's financing, and its board of trustees. Aside from providing money, they seem mainly advisory. Actually they could be just window dressing, wealthy supporters who lend their names to help bring in more support. Seemingly—that's seemingly—they don't involve themselves in management. But they do make up the big gap between Millennium's earned income and its expenses, as estimated by people who know how to figure those things. And—"

Lee interrupted. "If you're looking for actual figures, I'm afraid I can't help you." She said it crisply, decisively, leaving no room for discussion.

"No, no! That's not it. But they're very much in a position to insist their advice be taken, if they choose to. And it would be surprising if they didn't, from time to time.

"Also I've come up with someone—a financier—who's not on the board. Another investigator, a lot better qualified than I am to find these things out, has listed all the people who provide major financial support. And when I compare them to the board of trustees, I find a perfect match. With one exception.

"It's that exception that's troubling me. Why wouldn't he be on the board of trustees? His name is David Hunter. Major General David Hunter, U.S. Air Force retired. He's a scion of the 'old money' Hunter family, whose wealth came originally from Green Mountain Distilleries, founded in 1828. His great-great-grandfather predicted Prohibition, and built a distillery in Alberton, Ontario. When his forecast came true, he profited big time, from smuggling.

"As an Air Force officer, David Hunter's postings were more administrative and political than military. His career took off—no pun intended—after he was assigned to Air Force Intelligence. And he took an early and unpublicized retirement less than two weeks after the One-Day War, which occurred only three weeks after an unpublicized working trip to Damascus." Cochran paused.

"So?" Lee prompted.

"I realize none of that is incriminating in any way. But it does tell me something about his family and the way it does business. And it suggests a personality given to manipulation and intrigue. A personality who might be attracted to covert activities to get its way.

"And again, why would he decline to be a member of Millennium's board? I doubt very much that the members have to carry out any actual board duties, unless they want to. Memberships on the boards of foundations are often more honorary than anything else."

"What does this ex-general do now?" Lee asked. "Since he left the Air Force."

"He's a high-priced consultant, a fixer of 'broken companies.' He bails out once successful corporations that have fallen on hard times, often acquiring temporary executive authority to do it with. He's supposed to be very good at what he does. He certainly charges enough."

Lee was interested in spite of herself; interested yet resistive. "So what are you trying to tell me?" she asked. "I was skeptical of Millennium's purposes myself once. But I've been more thoroughly immersed in its operations than an investigative reporter could possibly be, and seen nothing the least bit suspicious. And there's an obvious explanation for the general to keep his Millennium connection quiet. He doesn't have a buffered permanent position; he sells his services. And prospective clients might be uncomfortable with his Millennium connections. Cultish, you know."

She paused. "Why did you come to me with this . . . ?"

"Partly because you don't seem to have the emotional investment in Millennium that the others here do, and partly because you're brighter than hell. And you know Millennium's inside workings and still respect it, which is the kind of commendation for it that money can't buy."

Cochran had said that to make points with her; now it occurred to him that it was true.

"You and I both know that Millennium and Ngunda Aran have done a lot for the country," he went on, "especially through Hand and Ladder and Bailout. But what are Hunter's objectives? His credentials as a philanthropist? I haven't found any except his support of Millennium. On the other hand, he's been instrumental in takeovers of several corporations. Perhaps even engineered them. And you and I both know that Millennium spends a lot more than it earns. Taking all this together makes me wonder what plans Hunter might have for Millennium."

She gnawed her lip thoughtfully. She couldn't imagine someone putting anything over on Lor Lu, but . . . "So you want me to do—what?" she asked.

"Besides completing our interview, I'd like you to see if you can find anything about David Hunter in the dim dark recesses of Millennium's mainframe. By and large, concealment technology is ahead of snooping technology these days, but with your insider knowledge, and your access . . ."

"I'll see what I can find out," Lee told him. "That

doesn't mean I'll make a research project out of it. I can't imagine I could get away with one. Or that there's anything ominous going on. But I'll make a cursory search, and if I find anything suggestive, I'll let you know."

They shook hands on it. His was firm, dry, and warm. And his touch . . . She was reminded of her first impression. This was someone she really shouldn't have much to do with.

When Cochran had left, she sat down at her desk. Prior to her Montana trip, her loyalty to Millennium had been professional. But since her trip, she realized, she felt an emotional loyalty, because Millennium really had done—was doing—good works. Nonetheless, her talk with Lor Lu had disturbed her, and what Duke had said was troubling, even if far from demonstrating anything. And if she uncovered something, she wouldn't have to tell him unless it seemed like the right thing to do.

Turning her chair to her keyboard, she wrote in an instruction, and after a moment another. She kept pulling strings for nearly half an hour, going deeper and further than she'd intended. And learned nothing of consequence. Finally she keyed in a call.

"This is Duke."

"Duke, this is Lee. I didn't learn a thing. If you want to talk about my Montana trip, let's get together for coffee at 10:30, for 15 minutes. In the coffee room or my office, either one."

"Great. Your office at 10:30."

When they hung up, Cochran's mind went to other possible sources for information on David Hunter.

Maybe Nidringham would spring for a private investigator, one who specialized in money people. A fishing expedition, for general information on associations, and anything suggestive of illegal activities.

41

We have further news regarding this morning's failed terrorist attempt on the life of Pope John XXIV. There were three gunmen, and all of them were killed. One has been identified as Jack Russell, once a captain in the terrorist wing of the Irish Republican Army. Dressed as priests, and with several fully automatic pistols concealed beneath their robes, they attempted to kill the pontiff at a papal appearance in the Vatican's Piazza San Pietro. Unable to get nearer to the pope than about fifty feet, they began shooting into the crowd, apparently hoping that people would get out of their way. Seven were killed, including all three gunmen. Eighteen others were wounded. The seventy-seven-year-old pontiff was slightly

injured when thrown to the ground by a Swiss
guard, who then fell on him to protect him.
Headline News
Atlanta, GA, Jan. 17

SCANNING THE ARTICLE, Thomas Corkery's
expression was wry but not distressed. Russell had
fucked it up. They should have had grenades.

Corkery was not surprised. But meanwhile it left
him with no major income source, and his minor
sources had dried up with the Hard Times.

Fortunately the Catholic Soldiers remained, such
as they were, and those who financed them. "So,
Thomas," he told himself in Gaelic, "it's off to Montreal
with you." He had no doubt he'd find the necessary
contacts there within a day or so of arriving, and his
school French would finally serve some purpose. He'd
regret leaving this South Boston Irish neighborhood,
but perhaps there was one like it in Montreal.

42

IN SOUTHERN CALIFORNIA, the year's rainy
season had begun late but with gusto, reminding Rafi
Glickman of winter in Israel. The tires buzzed on the
wet freeway pavement, and the delivery van's wipers
slashed furiously back and forth. Its cargo was not
the bread suggested by the name "Romeo's Bakery"
painted on the sides. The disguise was only skin-deep.
There hadn't been room for even a facade of loaves,
to satisfy a quick look through the door. There was
barely room for the cargo and technician.

"Slow down," Rafi said in Hebrew. "The exit's just
ahead."

Despite the exceedingly sparse 2 A.M. traffic, the
driver had not been speeding. It wouldn't do to be
stopped by the Highway Patrol. It was bad enough
having to leave on an exit whose road would take
them into the mountains. A bread truck driving into

the Cleveland National Forest at two in the morning? If that wasn't suspicious! But the tall step-van would itself seem odd on such a road, so Ben David had ordered something misleading painted on its side.

Rafi was mildly troubled by not knowing how the test worked. He wondered if even the technician knew. He didn't know the technician, not even his name; names were not divulged unnecessarily, and one never asked. Only Ben David knew them all, kept in a memory as remarkable as Rafi's own. Somewhere, presumably, they were written, otherwise the loss of the gray and silent Yeshua Ben David would cripple the organization. Perhaps the names were in a safe deposit box somewhere. If he could find out . . . but he couldn't imagine being so lucky.

He saw the exit sign, and looked at the offside rearview mirror for following headlights. The only pair in sight were a half mile back; judging by the running lights, a semi. Elena moved onto the off-ramp. She was part of the disguise, not only female, but Hispanic-looking and speaking—a Mexican Jew whose Hebrew was limited. Her English was quite good though, with an accent she could thicken as needed.

Lights on dim, they drove a narrow blacktopped road that wound upward through chapparal foothills. It steepened, the winding became a series of switchbacks, and soon they entered forest—pine, eventually with a mixture of fir. With its heavy burden, the van's engine labored on the grades. When they arrived at the crest, Elena pulled off on a short side road leading to an overlook. By day there might have been scenery, but now, all Rafi saw was the sodden sky. At this elevation, he told himself, they were lucky the rain wasn't snow.

Wearing a slicker, he got out to guide Elena with hand signals. She parked with the rear doors facing east, with plenty of room between them and the overlook's waist-high stone safety wall. Then she set the parking brake, leaving the motor running to keep the battery charged. Even though they wouldn't actually launch the bird, the test program required unloading it and "going through the motions." It was a nuisance, but the hardware for monitoring was built into the bird, and only functioned in operating mode.

Elena stayed in the cab, out of the rain, which was better than all right with Rafi. That way she wouldn't see and wonder about some of the things he planned to do.

After opening the rear doors, he took out a pair of chocks and blocked the rear wheels. Inside, he could see the nameless technician at his keyboard, doing what, Rafi had no idea. They were to test the bird's guidance program, that was all he knew. He himself stayed outside in the weather, watching the heavy-duty telescoping ramp extrude from the cargo section, driven by a powerful electric motor. It extruded straight for two meters, supported by folding legs with wheels, till the first hinged joint was clear. Then legs and ramp began to fold, while the extrusion continued.

It seemed to Rafi that the ramp, with its tracks, must have cost $30,000 or more, built and installed, even at current prices. And it had to be compatible with the bird's launch computer. The vehicle's original struts, or whatever it had had, and its brakes, must have been replaced with something stronger. The motor probably had, too, and the van's electrical system must have been augmented. While the cost of the missile

itself had surely been several times that of all the rest.
A lot of money for the times. Obviously Ben David
had very major resources.

When Baran had first mentioned having the bird,
Rafi had researched the available, non-confidential
information on it, including testing procedures. In
military situations, the purpose of monitoring a Ninja
Junior was to support ESAK installations—electronic
seek and kill—reporting any hostile discovery events
and interception attempts detected by the bird's
sensors, and finally reporting its arrival on target.
The reason for this test, however, could hardly be
ESAK.

And from something Baran himself had said, Rafi
had guessed that the bird, as delivered, lacked the
military guidance software. So someone had had to
write a program for one. Thus it seemed to Rafi
that this would be a virtual flight—what the military
termed a planetary matrix exploration—to test that
program.

It was dangerous information for Rafi to have. His
function was simply to see certain actions carried out,
without knowing what they meant.

After a minute, extrusion was complete, the ramp
in three segments, one within the truck, one slanting down to the ground, and the outermost forming
a launch base. But the electric motor still hummed
loudly, and the bird itself began to emerge, its sleek
nose followed by an uptilted body with stubby wings.
It rode a meter-and-a-half carriage, that on the ramp's
sloping mid-section, adjusted itself to the bird's center
of gravity.

When the carriage reached the end, the motor shut

off. Now Rafi could hear a much smaller, whisperlike hum from inside the Ninja Junior. The sound, he supposed, of its onboard computer booting up.

Hitching up his left sleeve, he touched the light switch on his wristwatch, and waited. Heard a tiny beep within the missile, and read the time to the second. Then he clambered into the rear of the van to watch the computer screen, peering intently over the technician's shoulder.

It was a long wait, the bird still crouching on its carriage while an electronic duplicate moved across an unlabeled grid on the computer screen, an icon crossing cyberspace at a virtual 0.8 Mach.

The grid's edges were labelled with latitude and longitude, in ten-minute intervals. What Rafi waited for was something that would tell him what the target was—if anything did. Otherwise he'd figure it out, using his watch, a map, and the terminal phase speed of 0.8 Mach. That ought to do it.

Forty minutes, sixty . . . He'd tensed with watching, and realizing it, relaxed as best he could. He could hear Elena snoring in the driver's seat, but dared not doze himself. He had not taken benzedrine; he would not risk its effects on judgement. He'd stay on his feet, and if necessary fight off sleep using techniques he'd learned in the true Mossad. The old Mossad, the one he'd been proud to be part of.

Finally the icon burst in a virtual explosion. Numbers appeared, held for a long moment and were gone. A moment long enough that his odd and valuable memory had imaged and retained them. Glancing at his watch, Rafi imaged it, too.

Had the actual bird been fired, using the actual

military targeting program, its 500-pound payload would supposedly have been delivered within three meters of its intended target. Theoretically. Three meters! Rafi was skeptical, even with the computer using the planetary gravitic matrix.

"Is that it?" he asked. Pretending he didn't know.

The technician nodded in the dim light of his tiny workstation. "Yes," he said.

"Good. Get ready to leave."

He didn't watch the emergence and extrusion processes reverse themselves. Instead he awakened Elena, rousting her muttering from the cab to walk about a little in the rain, which now was mixed with large snowflakes. He ran in place himself, and did pushups on the cold wet pavement.

When the truck was ready, they drove away. Now the precipitation was all snow, filling the headlight beams with onrushing white, and rattling Elena, who'd never driven in snow before. But by the time they reached the interstate, they were out of it, in rain again.

They arrived at the warehouse in a faint and sodden dawn. There a man they both knew took custody of the delivery van, and Rafi left in his Honda. *Its dirt washed off by God,* he told himself.

In his apartment, he spread a twenty-two-inch map printout of the Southwestern United States, from San Diego eastward to longitude 103 degrees. Then he put a tack at the location approximating the longitude and latitude he'd imaged mentally from the computer screen. It was a little west of Raton, New Mexico. The name meant nothing to him. He couldn't imagine anything there that the Wrath would invest their Ninja Junior on. Perhaps there'd been a programming error.

With pocket calculator and map scale, he estimated how many map inches the bird should have flown, given its stated terminal phase velocity, and fudging a bit for the average 0.65 Mach prior to reaching terminal phase. It was the best he could do. Then he tied a string to a soft pencil, knotted the string to mark the estimated flight length, taped the knot to the approximate location where they'd parked, and pressed a push tack through tape and knot. Finally he used the pencil to describe an arc on the map. It passed through "the impact site," curving northward. Eighty miles north, it passed a few miles west of Lauenbruck, Colorado. On his computer, he accessed the *Absolute Geographical Atlas*, magnified Colorado, then Huerfano County. Fifteen map miles west of Lauenbruck was a dot labelled Henrys Hat. Henrys Hat!

With a toneless whistle he straightened. A Ninja Junior for such a target? It made Ben David and Baran seem more insane than he'd thought. Ben David's cold stare would no doubt inspire his programmer to correct whatever had been wrong. Rafi was glad it wasn't himself.

His small project completed, he swigged orange juice, then poured a large bowl of cereal and put milk and sugar on it. That was quicker than almost any other meal. After eating it, he took a hot shower, and crawled into bed without setting his alarm.

43

From "Ngunda's Room" in
New Age Wonks' Clubhouse

Zen Wannabe: You've said meditation isn't for everyone. Why not? To me that sounds elitest and repressive.

Dove: Different souls have lived different numbers of lives. In general, those who've lived fewer than eighty or ninety lives haven't accrued the lessons necessary to meditate to much avail. As far as that's concerned, in western cultures very few of them are likely even to try. Today's Buddhist and yogic adepts are old souls, all beyond the hundred life-time mark. Back at seventy lifetimes they were still busy

with the lessons of young souls, not those of
old souls.

In fact, most souls complete all the lessons of
the physical plane without ever having meditated.
Although those with certain life tasks find them
facilitated by meditation.

Reality's Child: I'm basically a skeptic.
Hopeful but a skeptic. How do you know all
that stuff?

Dove: Call it *intuition*. True intuition. The word
is also applied to false intuitions growing out of
fear, hatred, prejudice and pride. In that sense,
Adolf Hitler was highly intuitive, but his "intuitions"
grew out of festering hatreds.

As for my own intuitions: like more than a few
people, I've visited the astral plane in out-of-body
experiences. The first was at age eleven, when
I drowned, and before I was resuscitated. On
each successive visit—not trauma-induced like the
first—on each successive visit, my connection was
upgraded. My "modem to heaven," so to speak.

Thus my intuitions are more reliable and
precise than intuitions generally are. But I cannot
prove that to you, and it's quite appropriate
to doubt me. In fact it's natural, especially at
first, if you are "wired" as a skeptic. Nor is
there an objective way of sorting intuitions from
false intuitions. Intuitions nudge us toward our
true goals, completing lessons and fulfilling
agreements, all of which tend to differ at different
soul ages.

In any instance of intuition, different people evaluating its validity will tend to draw different conclusions. One person might regard me as inspired by the Tao, and someone else as a messenger of Satan. Or as a con artist intent on gathering money and power. The decision is up to the individual. I do not expect to convince everyone, nor do I try. Some are ready, some are not. Even the Infinite Soul, when it next manifests, will not convince everyone on Earth. To do that, it would have to preempt their power of choice.

And regardless of what many Christian and Islamic teachers tell you, it is all right to be mistaken. The Tao is neither disappointed nor surprised at mistakes, and does not condemn us for them.

Satan, incidentally, is a myth. Humans can perform the grossest atrocities without satanic inspiration.

Headline News
Atlanta, GA, Jan. 27

After years of increasing contention, "the Republic of Eastern Siberia" yesterday declared its independence from the Russian Federated Republic. The first real secession in nearly a decade, it is also the largest. It involves a remarkable alliance between citizens of

Slavic racial stocks on the one hand, and on the other, a number of native minorities, notably the Yakuts.

Moscow has refused to comment on what its response may be. The White House too is declining to comment until more is known.

A worsening epidemic of virulent, so-called "Polish Flu," reported from Poland earlier this week, has spread eastward to Moscow, and westward past the Rhine River. What appears to be the same strain has also been reported from Japan, China, and Southeast Asia. Poland reported over 1,500 fatalities as of yesterday.

This year's flu vaccine has been ineffective against it.

Headline News
Atlanta, GA, Jan. 28

Deutsche Welle last night reported a claim by two leaders of the environmentalist party, *die Grünen,* that the Polish Flu was engineered by a virologist within their organization to combat what they termed "the disaster of world overpopulation." They predicted that flu deaths would exceed two billion by the end of February. Authorities have closed all German offices of the organization, taken twenty-three persons into custody for questioning, and taken custody of all records.

Yesterday brought the first reports of Polish Flu in the United States, with cases in Boston, New York, New Orleans, Houston, Chicago, Denver and Seattle. This distribution of cases, and the suddenness of their appearance, suggest artificial introduction. The World

Health Organization reports fatalities of more than 7,500, mostly in central Europe.

Headline News
Atlanta, GA, Jan. 29

Concern about the Polish Flu has closed schools in all 50 states, Canada, and Mexico. The disease, which acts quite rapidly, has already claimed its first victims here. Preliminary WHO statistics show more than 100,000 dead worldwide.

Rioters destroyed *die Grünen* offices in several German, Austrian, and Swiss cities. Known members have been found murdered. Police have taken others into protective custody.

Headline News
Atlanta, GA, Jan. 31

The "Green Flu," previously known as "Polish Flu," has been reported in 46 states. The U.S. Public Health Service reports 10,211 known flu deaths here as of 10 P.M. yesterday. The WHO estimates as many as 10 million dead worldwide.

European health officials state that the fatality rate there is falling, though many new deaths continue to be reported. In Poland, 28,000 reportedly died yesterday, compared to 53,000 the day before. The strain does not appear to be as deadly as claimed by *die Grünen*,

but it is the deadliest known since the Spanish Flu
of 1918.

Headline News
Atlanta, GA, Feb. 6

The Green Flu death rate is definitely on the
downswing here. Only 14,612 new deaths were reported
in the United States yesterday, bringing the total here
to just short of 1,600,000. Worldwide, the official death
tally has reached 75 million, with China hardest hit.
Upward of 1½ billion are thought to have had the
illness. Few new cases are being reported.

The historic Greenpeace ship, *Rainbow Warrior II*,
was gutted by fire last night at its mooring, at San
Francisco's Maritime Museum. A caller claimed it had
been burned to avenge the Green Flu victims.

Headline News
Atlanta, GA, Feb. 12

Sometime last night, a Russian Parachute brigade
dropped on Yakutsk, the capital of the breakaway
Republic of Eastern Siberia. The population of Yakutsk
had reportedly been decimated by the flu, and there
is said to have been no resistance. It is not clear
whether groups elsewhere will continue the independence
movement.

44

Journal of Religious Philosophy
March Letters Section

I agree with Dr. Venkatanarayana's comments in the January issue, regarding Ngunda Aran's teachings, and Aran's support and expansion of Dr. Verbeek's mental-spiritual therapies. But I would stress more strongly the value of Mr. Aran's remarkable charisma in stimulating the interest of people normally uninterested in matters spiritual.

We are in a period of dangerous disorders and violence, and we need all the truly spiritual leadership available.

In this regard, it will be interesting to see what Pope John XXIV's Vatican Council comes

up with. I find its title, "Transition to a New Era
of Human Spirituality," very encouraging.
                              Dr. Cloris Stuart Wiesenthal
                              Institute for Human Development

---

A CNN Special Newscast
Atlanta, GA, Mar. 4

"We switch away now from 'Talk Back Live,' to
the Vatican, and CNN's Vatican reporter, Warren
Ohlmann. Because of the extreme number of news
agencies present to carry the pope's address, the papal
Office of Public Information is providing the camera
coverage itself. Thus we will not see Mr. Ohlmann,
but we will hear him. Here he is now."

[The picture changes to a very large, gently sloping auditorium with a broad stage. The seats are full
of people facing the front. The lower rows are filled
with Vatican officials. The men in the first rows wear
the red cloaks and caps of cardinals of the Church.
There is no one on the rostrum except two tall Swiss
guards at the sides, splendid in their broad vertical
stripes: black, gold, and red.]

[We can hear Ohlmann murmuring quietly into a
directional microphone.]

"I'm waiting with several hundred other journalists
in the press rooms in the rear of the Pius VI Audience Hall. Pope John is expected to appear at any
moment. You will notice . . ."

[Ohlmann pauses. Several clerics are issuing from
a door to one side of the stage.] "I believe the Holy

Father is about to enter the room . . . Yes, there he is . . . The seventy-seven-year-old pontiff is crossing to the stage . . . He is climbing the steps . . . Now he crosses to the rostrum."

[The camera zooms on the pontiff, a somewhat heavy-set man. He reaches the microphone, looks out at the crowd, and begins to speak in Irish-flavored English. "May God's blessing be upon you all, and upon His Holy Church and all humankind." [He makes the sign of the cross, then gazes out at the assembled crowd.]

"As an official of the Church, it was my privilege to have been sent by the two most recent popes, as their emissary to one country and another throughout the world. In that role, I witnessed much poverty and hardship, much cruelty and greed, much anger and hatefulness. And received much food for thought, some of it sour in my mouth.

"Also, as a pastor and theologian, it has been my lifelong duty and privilege to study and meditate on many matters pertaining to God and his flock—which is *all* of humankind—and to Church law, precedent, and tradition. On various occasions it was my privilege and honor to be called into the presence of the Holy Father, to confer with him, answer his questions, and advise him to the best of my knowledge and understanding, on a number of matters important to the Church and humankind.

"I have witnessed each of those noble and holy men as they pondered and meditated on the matters we discussed. Often I was called back for additional consultation and examination, for in such matters, none of them acted without careful deliberation.

They felt their responsibilities deeply, and treated them accordingly.

"But when they decided, they acted firmly, without fear, as God's emissary on Earth.

"Recently it became my time to carry that responsibility, and heavy though it is, I bear it gladly, for what a privilege it is to serve God in this role!

"Humankind and the Holy Church exist together as inseparable spiritual entities on a physical Earth. And humankind is unquestionably changing, evolving in mind and spirit—evolving toward a *freedom* of the spirit. And like many adolescent boys and adolescent girls discovering freedom of action, far too many have not discovered responsibility, restraint, and humility.

"Look about you. What do you see when you examine our billions of fellow humans? An evolution toward goodness? Toward the love and compassion of God? Or toward chaos, darkness, death? And who is to guide them? For in this instance we are not talking just about children. Parents, grandparents, officials, rulers, all need guidance.

"Look about you, I say! It is the function and duty of the Holy Church to lead people in right ways for God's sake and their own. *Lead* them! Not force them! Not threaten them! It's not coercion that's needed! Coercion leads not to understanding and compassion, but to hardening of the spirit. Threats lead not to love, but to fearful obedience—and hidden rebellion. We must—*lead* them . . . *teach* them . . . by our deeds and compassion as well as by our words!"

[The pope pauses, scans his audience.]

"We have not been doing our job adequately. Can you not see it? Look at history! And more importantly, *look at the world of today!* 'We're trying!' you say? Of course we are. But in these times, for every step forward, we're sliding one back, and the slope grows more slippery.

"It is a time for change. A change in ourselves, in our attitudes. A change in our ministry. It's a time to change from following our own arrogant preferences, and try instead the way of Jesus Christ our Lord and Saviour. Not a convenient time: Events do not wait on our convenience! It is change—or see long centuries of earnest dedication and work founder and sink in a growing sea of greed, violence and hatred.

"There have been other times when change was urgently needed, and the Church responded. Most recent was the Second Vatican Council. In July a Third Vatican Council will be convened, to address important—vital!—areas of needed change. And we will not fail to act effectively!

"One aspect of the Church most urgently needing change is our attitude toward world population. *Do not delude yourself! It is still a problem!* On this matter, there are difficult questions to be debated and decided on. We will examine it in earnest, debate and meditate on it, and finally define what we will do about it.

"I have conferred with advisors on the entire subjects of sex, birth, and population. I have meditated long on it, supported by the Holy Spirit. And I here and now pronounce and decree a new policy of the Holy Church. And it is, that family planning—including artificial contraception!—may henceforth be discussed with parishioners by any pastor of the Church. The word is *discussed*. Parishioners are free to use artificial contraception *without* endangering their immortal soul. I repeat: without endangering their immortal soul! This far I am willing to go without further discussion. And this policy is not subject to the judgement of any bishop or priest."

[The pope once more pauses.]

"With that I leave you to your thoughts and prayers. You, I—we are all children of God. God is in *you* as well as in heaven. Pray to him for guidance and wisdom, and when he touches you, whispers to you, *heed him!* All of us, ordained and lay, have been part of the problem. Begin now—if you have not already—begin now to be part of the solution."

[He once more makes the sign of the cross.]

"May the love and wisdom of God settle upon you, guide you, and give you peace."

45

COLD RAIN WAS FALLING when Lee Shoreff arrived at SeaTac airport, south of Seattle. An employee of Millennium's Seattle Center drove her through rush-hour freeway traffic to the city's near north side, and her hotel. The director had planned to pick her up himself, the man said, but his daughter had taken sick, and he'd gone home.

Lee asked if it always rained in Seattle. Only from October through March, he answered laughing. During the rest of the year they sometimes even glimpsed the sun. Actually, he corrected, July and August were sunny, and it didn't rain much at all. In fact, Seattle was an easy place to like: friendly, lushly green, and seldom hot. And never very cold; certainly not to him, who'd grown up in Pittsburgh.

After she checked in, he carried her two bags to her 15th-floor room, and asked if there was anything she needed. When she assured him there wasn't, he left.

Opening her drapes, Lee peered eastward through her rain-battered, room-width window, across a cityscape rich in fir trees and vague with rain. Not far away was a lake the color of lead, extending for miles. Somewhere out there, she supposed, were mountains. On the Ranch she'd gotten used to sunny days, and mountains sharply seen.

She decided she didn't care for Seattle, at least not today, and reclosed her drapes. The digital display on her TV wall screen read 4:43 P.M. She activated the set, then opened her two bags and began to hang up clothes. At the periphery of her attention, a male voice accompanied the viewing menu, sounding totally inane. Finally she took off her shoes, racked herself back on a recliner with the remote in her hand, and paged through the menu with the sound turned off: sports, with submenus for college and professional, and sub-submenus for basketball and hockey. Other menus covered movies; politics; news. . . . None of it attracted her. Finally she called up a book, a romance, something she rarely read. It wasn't bad, actually, though steamier than she needed.

At 6:30 she tabbed the page and turned off the screen. Her stomach had informed her it was hungry. She changed her clothes and renewed her makeup, then left the room, following wall arrows to the elevator bay. The elevator shaft was a glass-walled semicylinder. It was past sundown, and the afternoon's gloomy daylight had faded nearly to night. Rain still fell, though thinly now.

By contrast, the hotel restaurant was bright, diners'

conversations light and lively around her, the hostess cheery. "One?" the young woman asked.

"Yes, please."

There were not a lot of diners. The Hard Times. As she followed the woman among tables, she realized she hadn't brought a book to read while waiting. Ever since college she'd made a practice of carrying one in her purse when she traveled, for restaurant and airport waits, but had taken it out while looking for something else.

"Lee!"

She stopped at the call, looked around, and saw Duke Cochran gesturing an invitation from a window table. She put a hand on the hostess's arm. "I see a friend over there," she said.

"Good. I'll send a waitress."

He was on his feet as she approached, grinning with pleasure. "Am I glad to see you!" he said, and held her chair for her. "Until now, this evening threatened to be deadly dull. What are you doing in Seattle?"

He knew what she was doing there. He knew about her trip, and had planned one to coincide with it. Both had been delayed when Millennium postponed all unessential trips because of the epidemic.

"I'm here to familiarize myself with local conditions and personnel at the center," she said. "What brings you here?"

He laughed. "Somewhat the same thing, actually. I'm familiarizing myself with the staff. Interviewing, and asking questions." He paused, taking her in with his eyes. "Well! This is a treat!"

A waitress arrived with a menu for Lee, and Duke

declined to order till she was ready. Meanwhile they both ordered cocktails, and talked. He'd been in Chicago for three days, just before the flu, to handle some things with his editor. They'd been having a brutal winter there. He'd seen a show and a Bulls game . . . "Oh, and I learned some things about David Hunter, the retired general. Nothing sinister, but very interesting: He's not a graduate of the Air Force Academy. He went to school at Cornell, majored in operations management, and took four years of Air Force ROTC. And . . ." Cochran paused, grinning. "He used to date—Florence Metzger!"

Lee frowned, puzzled.

"Our president, back when she was an Olympic swimmer. They were an item, apparently. What do you think of that?"

"I'm not sure. Is it significant?"

"Possibly, but I've wracked my brain and haven't come up with anything. A tantalizing bit of information though."

The waitress returned, took their orders, and again they waited. Their talk turned to the current turmoil in the Catholic Church, which had polarized over the agenda for Vatican Three, and not only birth control. From the Church, the conversation moved to sports. It was, she realized, a treat to sit talking with a mature adult whose views on many things were unknown to her. By the time their meal arrived, she'd started on her third drink almost without noticing. The baked salmon was excellent—she did notice that—and so was the rest of the food. Not till they'd finished eating did she glance out the window.

"It's stopped raining!" she said.

"Good! I noticed a dance club across the street. Shall we check it out?"

"I'll get my rain coat," she answered, "just in case."

She met him in the lobby—he'd gotten his too—and they left. The city smelled clean, rainwashed. As they walked chatting and laughing to the corner, an occasional small drop ticked her face. She hadn't felt so young since she was a student at Syracuse, on a date with a special boyfriend. There were more people in the club than Lee had expected. She supposed they were celebrating the end of the flu, those who could afford to. The band was good. Seventies disco was in style again, both the old numbers, and new ones in the seventies style. They danced and laughed through more than an hour and two more drinks, sweating a little with exertion, eyes meeting playfully. It wasn't until a slow dance was played, and they danced cheek to cheek, that she realized how late it was.

"I think we'd better get back to the hotel," she said. "Merlin will be picking me up at eight tomorrow."

"Right. I'd forgotten all about the time."

They left without finishing their drinks. It was raining more briskly again, and they ran to the corner and across the street. Then they walked, holding hands, Lee breathless and laughing. The lobby, and rotunda, rich in ferns, seemed warm and friendly, and they held hands again while waiting for an elevator.

"What floor are you on?" Duke asked.

"Fifteen. Room 1547."

"I'm in 1643. We're almost neighbors."

He got off with her and walked her to her door. When they got there, she turned to him, and he took her hands. "It was a wonderful evening," Duke said, looking into her eyes. "I can't remember the last time I enjoyed one so much. It's—hard to say goodnight."

"Yes, it is," she said quietly.

"Especially in a strange city, where you're alone and don't know anyone. In weather like this."

She nodded, and they looked at each other for a long wordless moment. "I'd better go in now," she said at last.

"Will you have supper with me again tomorrow?"

"I— Probably. Unless the center has something planned for me."

He nodded. "Well then . . ." He backed away, just half a step, mouth smiling, but gaze heavy with desire. After a long moment, he threw her the same small salute he'd used when he'd walked her home after interviewing her. "Maybe we can continue that interview tomorrow evening. After supper, or after whatever the center has for you."

"That would be good," she said quietly, then turning, unlocked her door and stepped inside. There she paused, turned and looked back at him for another long and pregnant moment, opened her mouth as if to say something—then didn't. He stood motionless, still watching. Her eyes withdrew, and slowly she closed the door.

He went to his room disappointed but encouraged. She'd almost, almost, almost asked him in. For a moment he imagined what they'd be doing at that moment if she had. He'd have her in his arms, kissing her, telling her how he'd fallen in love with her that first evening. And how many times he'd thought about her.

Tomorrow, he told himself. *Tomorrow's the night. I'll interview her in her room, and bring a pint in my briefcase.* His interest, he realized, went beyond both sex and her possible cooperation in an exposé. He'd loved eating with her, talking with her, dancing with her. He could imagine being with her on a long-term, perhaps permanent basis. Especially if she was as good in bed as he was sure she'd be. She could divorce Ben, who could take the girls.

Meanwhile he felt horny as hell, and considered calling an escort service, but decided against it. Lee had wanted him, too. She might call, tell him she was lonely. So instead he ordered a book onto his screen, to settle him down: *Lee's Lieutenants.* It had been years since he'd read it.

Lee took a hot shower, and afterward looked at herself in the mirrored bathroom door. *You still look good,* she told herself. *Good genes.* For years she'd exercised rather religiously, though she'd pretty much lost the habit at the Cote. She promised herself to start again when she got home.

She threw back her bedspread and covers, and imagined having sex with Duke Cochran, watching themselves in the pair of mirrors that constituted the sliding closet doors. The images thickened her breath almost chokingly. She wished she had another drink, and reached for the phone to call room service.

Or Duke. Would he? She chuckled thickly. Does it rain in Seattle?

But it was room service she called, and ordered a

pint of peach brandy. When it had been delivered, she poured a drink, sipped, then phoned Ben, waking him. She wished he was there, she told him, alone with her. It was raining, she was lonely, and the sliding closet doors were mirrors. They talked and laughed for thirty minutes while she sipped.

The next morning at the Millennium center, she met the director, who apologized for not meeting her at the airport. He'd intended to take her home for supper, and an evening with his family, but their daughter had been troubled with one of the "flu echoes" going around, sometimes with complications. By the time he'd gotten home at 3 o'clock, she'd had a temperature of 103 degrees. By breakfast she'd been "all right"—languid but hungry—and he hoped Lee would be their guest for supper.

She ran into Duke that morning at coffee break, and postponed the interview.

The next day she made an appointment with Duke for that evening, suggesting they continue till they were done. He'd agreed that would simplify things. The only drawback, he said, was not having an excuse to see her again afterward.

But at 4:15, when he'd completed another interview, there was a message for him at reception. Lee had gotten a call from home; a family emergency. She'd gotten her airline reservation changed to that evening, and Merlin had taken her to the hotel to get her things. By now she'd be on her way to SeaTac.

46

THE MONROE COUNTY District Court in New York had sent a registered fax to the Cote, ordering Lee to appear on Friday. Millennium's lawyers were onto it, but meanwhile she needed to be ready.

It was dark when Ben met her at the airport in Pueblo, and drove her home in a company car. The girls knew nothing about what was going on, only that he'd be picking up their mom. They were spending the night with the Klein twins.

Lee was upset and worried. When they got home, they had a drink of brandy and Ben took her to bed. It was quite a while before they went to sleep.

Not surprisingly she dreamed of her daughters. In a disjointed sequence in which they were taken from her by Mark, by her parents, by Dove, by strangers . . . And *not* taken from her, or rescued, or . . . She'd wakened yelling and fighting from the first

version, then she and Ben had had a large brandy
each, to late night television, and gone back to bed.
Where she'd reentered the dream sequence, barely
wakening from time to time. Near the end she kept
adjusting the dream script whenever necessary, and
she awoke in something close to glee.

The next day, Lor Lu got a fax from Conroy, Morgenstern, and Blasingame. He took it promptly to Lee's
office; they'd gotten another delay. Their lawyers had
no doubt they could beat this thing. Her ex-husband
was persistent and had resources, but not a compelling
case. Mrs. Shoreff had no cause for alarm.

Later, Ngunda stopped at her office.

"Lor Lu told me your ex-husband persists in troubling you. Perhaps I can help further." He smiled.
"Congressman Ron Craine, of New York's 28th District, is a personal friend, and a friend of Millennium.
And of course is well connected in the 28th District,
particularly within the legal profession. I've just talked
with him. He knows Judge Falcaro well, and will
speak with him. Which does not guarantee anything,
nor should it. But Ron will give him his viewpoint on
Millennium, and at any rate it cannot hurt to have a
congressman visibly in our corner."

Again his visit left Lee feeling much better. *He
really is a good person,* she thought, *even if he does
have some strange ideas.*

47

From "Ngunda's Room" in New Age Wonks' Clubhouse

Christian Seeker: We're already well into the new millennium, so I suppose the New Messiah has already been born. What is there about the passage of 2,000 years that made it happen?

Dove: The passage of 2,000 years did not and will not cause either the birth of the child nor the assumption by the Infinite Soul. Rather, the events mark the convergence of certain processes and trends. Neither the birth, the assumption, nor the death, was or will be exactly 2,000 years after equivalent events in the time of Jesus. And the receptacle of the new avatar is already fully adult.

Christian Seeker: What important happenings of the Second Coming will match events prophesied in the Apocalypse of John?

Dove: None of them, except coincidently and *very* loosely.

Christian Seeker: Then how will we know whether a claimed second coming is the real thing?

Dove: You will know. By the acts and impacts of the avatar itself, and by a very major geophysical event which will coincide with the avatar's death.

Don Samuelson: I hope you know your predictions are at odds with everybody else's. Why should we believe you?

Dove: Why indeed? It's not required that you believe. You will not be damned for disbelieving, or for anything else.

Don Samuelson: That sounds to me like a helluva wimpy religion.

Dove: It is not a religion at all, though you may think of it as one. Religions are a product of human beings, typically with a main goal of control, escape, or vindication, rather than enlightenment. And you are, of course, entitled to choose whatever religion you prefer, or whatever spiritual orientation. Including none at all. And to change your mind whenever you choose.

Skeptical in Muskogee: If each of us lives a whole string of lives, which of those bodies do we resurrect in?

Dove: In none of them. At the end of each life, that physical body ceases to be relevant. And when finally you graduate from the physical plane, you no longer use any body at all. Unless of course you choose to be a *bodhisatva*, in which case you'll have one last body, in which to undertake one final, specific task on Earth. But that is highly unusual.

Ananda: Some spiritual teachers say that whatever you believe with absolute certainty will come to pass. So if you believe without any uncertainty at all that you'll be resurrected, won't you be resurrected?

Dove: On the physical plane, there are universal realities, world realities, and personal realities. At the solo level, the individual level, your beliefs determine your personal reality, *within* the limits of world and universal realities. Limits which are broader than many would have you believe. While the shared beliefs of multiple humans influence world realities within the limits of universal reality. Notably through social and political forces that include religion, government, science, and technology. As for universal reality, it is a direct manifestation of the Tao.

And while each of us contains the Tao, and is part of it, the relationship is not one of identity. If you fill a bottle with ocean water, then seal it tightly and throw it into the ocean, it is of the ocean, and contains ocean, but it is not the ocean. Within the bottle there are no tides or storms, fishes or whales. But the bottle moves with the ocean, shares its motions, and has its own life-forms.

Let me elaborate on those "bottles." When we agreed to take part in the Earth School—our particular venue in the physical plane—we agreed to certain limitations that are hardwired into the "game."

Up Yours: That is the biggest heap of metaphysical, sophistic bullshit I ever heard.

Dove: What I said is metaphor. When the Infinite Soul manifests, it will not teach, because language, including metaphor, is not adequate to the subject. Through the manifestation, human beings will *experience* the Infinite Soul to one degree or another, and be changed by it.

Up Yours: That is still the biggest pile of bullshit I ever heard.

48

COLONEL ROBERT GORMAN sat down in the velvet recliner. Without, of course, racking it back. He and Millard Forsberg knew each other, but they'd never been actual friends. He doubted that Forsberg had any, or cared to. The man was a stick; hadn't even offered him a drink.

He couldn't imagine why the FBI's "retired" ex-director had invited him to his Arlington condo. All they had in common were some aspects of political and social philosophy, uncovered years earlier. Forsberg had been in charge of the FBI's Denver Office then, and Gorman had been the Army ROTC commander at the University of Denver. Forsberg had carried out a successful investigation of the vandalization of ROTC offices by student activists.

Meanwhile they'd discovered they both liked cross-country skiing, and several times had skied together in the Front Range above Nederland. On breaks, they'd talked beside a warming fire, while drinking hot cocoa out of battery-heated Thermoflasks.

Even there they'd had differences, which had bothered Forsberg far more than they had Gorman. The colonel had spiked his cocoa with brandy. Forsberg, consistent with the rest of his personality, was a teetotaler, and visibly disapproved of those who weren't. To Gorman, Forsberg was an interesting duck, with way more than his share of foibles.

Both had been transferred to the District not long afterward, and had run into each other occasionally at social affairs of one sort and another. Forsberg was definitely not a social animal, but first as deputy director, then director of the FBI, there'd been more or less obligatory events to attend. He was a confirmed bachelor, and a misogynist whom Gorman suspected of incipient, or perhaps repressed, homosexuality.

Not that it made any difference to Gorman. People were entitled to their peculiarities, as long as they didn't include what he called aggressive liberalism. He could tolerate liberals, could like them in fact, if (1) their liberalism wasn't militant, and (2) they didn't carry on about it.

Forsberg had invited him to sit, but hadn't yet sat down himself. "Um, would you care for coffee?" he asked.

"Yeah, I could stand some coffee."

The man disappeared from the living room, to reappear a minute later with an empty cup and saucer. Bemusedly, Gorman watched him put them down on the coffee table beside him, then retreat into the kitchen again, to reappear once more with a thermal coffee pitcher. Seemingly Forsberg wasn't having any himself. He probably considered caffeine sinful. He poured, then disappeared into the kitchen again, reappearing empty-handed to sit down opposite his guest.

Apparently, Gorman decided, *he's not going to offer me cream and sugar.* Not that it mattered. More often than not he took it straight anyway. But to see what would happen, he said, "D'you have cream?"

Blinking, Forsberg stiffened in his chair. "No," he said, "I have skim milk."

"That'll do."

Forsberg stood and again left the room, returning a moment later with a quart milk carton. He poured, and returned to the kitchen. *The poor dork can wear out a rug just serving a cup of coffee,* Gorman thought. He heard the refrigerator door close, and bemusedly watched his host come back and sit down again. He was tempted to ask for sugar, just for the hell of it. *The sad sonofabitch is more hopeless as a host than as a guest,* he told himself. But professionally Forsberg was decisive and reasonably smart. And no doubt organized as hell.

Gorman was an inveterate reader of the news—newsfacs, newspapers and zines, and Web journals. And having worked with Forsberg on the vandalism case, whenever Forsberg's name caught Gorman's eye, he read the article—which was rather often after Forsberg became director. So he knew about the man's retirement, and the speculations connected with it. Maybe he'd learn a little more about it this evening.

"So," he said, "what inspired this invitation?"

"We had some good talks in Colorado, on the ski

trails," Forsberg said. "I remember them fondly." He paused, then continued more stiffly. "What do you think of our country today?"

"With regard to what?"

"Morals. Government. Religion."

"Morals? About as good as we could expect. Government? About as good as we deserve. Hard to say whether we're dragging it down with us, or it's dragging us down with it. What the country needs is someone to take it by the scruff and knock the illusions and liberality out of it. Bring it back into the real world again. The new pope's a good example of what's wrong with all three: morals, government, and religion."

An eyebrow and one corner of his mouth quirked. "That about cover it?"

Forsberg's mouth worked as if chewing something bitter. "Yes, I would say so. And what about the false messiah? Ngunda Aran."

"Ah! That's what's bugging you. He's a good thing for the country."

Forsberg stared, startled.

"He's bringing things to a head," Gorman continued. "He'll split the country in two. On one side will be the socialists, daydreamers, do-gooders, greens, and New Agers. On the other side, the rest of us. About even in numbers. Then there'll be a war of sorts, and when it's over, there'll be no more illusions. No more functional infrastructure. No more softness. People will have to claw to live."

Forsberg was leaning forward now, partly mesmerized, partly shocked. "And what side will the military be on?" he asked.

"In terms of sentiments, more on our side, no

question. Though you might be surprised at how many will be on the other. But operationally? Operationally it'll be on whichever side holds the government . . . until things have unraveled so badly, there's no government left. Then the military will be a power unto itself, and a new government will form out of it. Probably regional governments, kicking ass and shaping things up. They'll talk to one another, maybe fight a little, and end up making some kind of joint agreement. Then a real church will grow out of the rubble, and between a real church and an ass-kicking government, morals will be reestablished."

Gorman had answered only half seriously. Now he eyed Forsberg's face. The man looked as if he'd been sandbagged. "That's what you get for asking, Millard. That's the face of the future. The next few decades, anyway. What do you think of it?"

There was a long lag. "It involves more disorder and destruction than I care for. Tell me: Do you think some advance planning and organization might minimize them?"

They talked awhile longer. Gorman wasn't interested in organization. He'd had a bellyful of it for thirty years. But he agreed to give advice from time to time, when Forsberg asked, and if he had something worthwhile to say.

49

ON THE MORNING AFTER Lee left Seattle, Duke Cochran got a call from his editor. His Millennium articles, Nidringham told him, had gone stale. "We're starting to get complaints from subscribers and shareholders. Have you found significant evidence of anything discreditable about the cult? Something you can run with? . . . No? Then I want you back in Chicago, prepared to do other assignments. Mainly on government. You can submit occasional Millennium pieces, but they'll need stronger elements of contention."

This might, Cochran told himself, *be a break in disguise.* It would give him resources, and more reason to investigate the relationship between the president and the ex-general. Something might turn up there yet. And he could see Adrielle again.

Cochran returned to the Cote that same day, and on the next, left for Chicago.

A few days later, a new "writer" arrived at the Cote, and was given a three-week permit to stay in the visitors' lodge. He carried papers, including a passport, identifying him as Father Thomas Edward Glynn, S.J., of Tralee, Ireland. He was currently a doctoral candidate in comparative religion at Xavier University in Cincinnati, supposedly working on his dissertation. Millennium's church liaison office—one person, having other duties—had not checked Father Glynn's background or status, either with his order or with the university. His embossed clerical and student credentials seemed entirely in order.

Actually they were fictitious. And while there was in fact a Jesuit Father Thomas Edward Glynn from Tralee, he was still in Ireland. It was Thomas Corkery who'd landed at Pueblo, taken a bus to Walsenburg, and arrived at the Cote in the Mescalero. He was a cheerful, chatty man, wearing a clerical collar, an attractive brogue, and neatly trimmed red beard, recently grown.

He'd brought no weapon with him. To do so, it seemed to him, would be more dangerous to himself than to Ngunda Aran. Corkery had taken risks from time to time; even extreme risks. If asked, he'd have said it was surprising he was still alive. But his risk-taking required a reasonable prospect of success; either that or the need to counter a compelling threat to his own life.

Corkery's approach to life and to challenges was different than most. Though he could be remarkably patient, he was basically *im*patient, inclined to audacity and shortcuts. But he could also be very indirect, seeming to address a situation aimlessly. In fact he never acted aimlessly. But the course he plotted could be a series of steps, each contingent upon the steps before, with its own purpose and goal. And always with an end result in mind: in this case the death of Ngunda Aran.

Twice in his past, Corkery had risked his own life gravely, in missions where the odds of success seemed poor. Risked it without anxiety. God would provide or not, as He saw fit. Thomas Corkery had no doubt at all in the reality of God, but his God was not vengeful. It was somewhat of an actuarial God, whose inscrutable ways were beyond any theological calculus.

At the Cote, Corkery was given access to Millennium's open archives on the ministry of Ngunda Elija Aran. This allowed easy review of videocubes, audiocubes, transcripts, etc. He was not the first to be allowed that access since the destruction of the International Computerized Library. And no one would pay much attention to him while he used them.

Actually he found the archives interesting, though he saw no connection between their content and himself.

During his three weeks at the Cote, he comported himself as a student and a Jesuit. (He'd been both, before being defrocked for terrorist connections.) And when the three weeks were over, he left with notebooks of actual notes, along with a list of sources. Carelessly compiled, it's true, but they'd do. His purpose, after all, was not a doctoral dissertation.

Now he was prepared for the next step. He even knew what that next step would be, because Millennium had released Ngunda Aran's May-June tour schedule.

50

In June, Ngunda Aran will tour the Inland Northwest, with engagements in several second and third echelon cities: Billings and Missoula in Montana, Spokane and Richland in Washington, Boise in Idaho. In a rather thinly populated region, cities of 50,000 to 300,000 are much more important than they would be in populous regions.

Originally Calgary, Alberta, was to be included. The Canadian government, however, refused entrance to Millennium speakers on grounds that their appearance might cause public disturbances. This in spite of Millennium centers operating legally in five Canadian cities. And whatever you might think of Millennium and its guru, they are the opposite of inflammatory. Last autumn's tour of eastern

Canada—Winnipeg, Ottawa, Toronto, Montreal and Halifax—resulted in nothing more disturbing than sign-bearing pickets and a scuffle or two. In a country whose national sport is ice hockey, and whose history and politics are commendably democratic, this ruling is hard to fathom—even given Canada's religious history, which is somewhat rockier than our own.

I recently spent six months living in the Dove Cote, accompanying Dove Tours, and visiting Millennium field centers, expecting to find evidence of dishonesty and cynicism. I was allowed to interview almost anyone I wanted to. I habitually look at the world with skeptical, investigative eyes, and I keep track of what my peers learn and say about Millennium and Ngunda. And I have yet to come across anything convincingly discreditable about either of them—anything more dignified than rumors.

That doesn't mean there isn't anything, but it makes me wonder about the government in Ottawa. It also helps me better appreciate the government of Florence Elaine Metzger.

American Scene Magazine
"Millennium, the Dove, and Ottawa,"
Duke Cochran

LUTE KOSKELA HAD SOLD the aging pickup he'd been driving, along with the camper shell in which he'd bedded down so often in his recent ramblings.

He'd traded with an old acquaintance for a seven-year-old Chevy sedan and $1,000, the whole transaction as legal as his fictitious identity allowed.

A thousand dollars went a long way in the Hard Times.

He too had seen the Ngunda tour schedule, and chosen where he'd make his next attempt. He had an unmarried aunt in Spokane, Washington—a divorcee, actually—from whom he hoped to get room and board at a reasonable cost. She'd disapproved of his youthful escapades and the company he'd kept, but that had been years earlier, and she'd taken in boarders since the '90s. Computer time rented in Omaha had shown her address unchanged. He knew it as an old barn of a 10-room house in a long-declining neighborhood.

It was nearing noon when he pulled up in front. The yard was as shaggy as he remembered it, with the same old locust trees more decrepit than ever with dieback, dropping branches on the yard. The lawn was thin and weedy, occasionally mowed but otherwise uncared for. Though now, with the early spring warmth that followed winter's snows and rains, it looked halfway decent to his uncritical eyes.

He got out of the car and slammed its door—the locks didn't work—strode up the frost-heaved front walk to the porch, pressed the doorbell and heard it ring. A minute later his aunt opened it and paused, staring.

"Luther! What the hell are you doing here? I'd thought you were in jail somewhere, like those two crazy uncles of yours."

He grinned. "Aunt Sing, you sure know how to

hurt a guy. I've never been in jail in my life. Well, maybe a couple times on charges, but those were misunderstandings. They let me out without even a trial." He spread his hands on his chest. "Innocent as a baby."

She snorted. "You've gotten by a lot more on luck than innocence, Luther Koskela. And you still haven't told me what you're doing here. Not selling Bibles I don't suppose."

He laughed. "I might, if I could make a living at it. I'm looking for a place to board, and a job. I figured you might be able to provide the first; I've got cash for the first month." He patted his hip pocket. "I'm a reformed man," he added. "Disconnected from old friends that might tempt me to get in trouble. Even quit the mercenary profession. Lost my taste for that kind of thing." He laughed. "A guy could get his ass shot off."

She eyed him suspiciously. "I don't suppose Carl and Axel's going to Leavenworth had anything to do with it."

"Actually it did. With my reputation and their conviction, I wouldn't blame the feds if they had me under suspicion. That's why I changed my name. To Karlson, with a *K*. Same initials."

She nodded, suspicions verified. "Well, get your butt in off the porch." Stepping aside, she let him pass. "Nobody here just now but you and me, so you can talk. How in hell do you expect to get a job with a false name? You'll need a Social Security number, which'll go into that big government computer, and if anything's strange about it, the FBI'll be coming around to talk to you."

Koskela shook his head. "There are ways."

She fixed him with a hard eye. "There are ways to get your butt in a sling, too." She eased off then. "My rate is $60 a month for a room, and $150 for meals—breakfast and supper. I put makings out for you to pack your own lunch. And there's a $40 security deposit. Pay at the start of the month. I refund half if you leave before the tenth; no refund if you leave later. You get a room to yourself, with a cable connection for TV. No women visitors allowed. No loud TV or radio, no ruckuses. Otherwise out you go. My roomers don't need hassles. Just a decent orderly place to live."

"Sounds like just what I want, Aunt Sing. Believe me, things I've seen, all I want is to live down the past. And if I hadn't changed already, what happened to Carl and Axel would have done it for me. You know, Axel wasn't ever much for trouble, but crippled like he was, he depended on Carl." Lute shook his head, not entirely insincere. "Carl was the troublemaker, and even he wasn't bad at heart. Just had some screwy ideas."

Signe Johnson grunted. "How do you figure to get a job these days? An honest job."

"I hoped you could help me. I'd take anything, seasonal or whatever. Something where there's turnover, and job openings come up, like roofing, cutting scrap, working on hazardous waste cleanup . . . But what I'd like best is security work. With the papers I've got, I'm eligible."

Her expression had gone beyond skeptical, to scowling.

"I'm not asking you to *find* me work," he went on.

"Only give me a recommendation if I need one. You know: 'Seems like a cleancut young man. Quiet, pays his rent on time . . .'"

She nodded curtly. "I'll go that far, but that's all. Let's see your money. You're family, so I'll skip the security deposit."

Taking out his wallet, he slid out several bills. Signe examined them front and back, nodded again and put them in an apron pocket. Taking a book of receipts from a drawer, she filled one out and gave it to him. "I hope to hell you're telling me the truth, Luther. I really do. I dearly loved your mom. She was my favorite cousin and best friend. Goddamn cigarettes! And you were a cute little boy. That's what got you so damned spoiled. I even liked your dad. His getting shot to death should have taught you something." She sighed. "Don't disappoint me, Luther."

He reached and took her hand, genuinely touched by her words. "Sing, I surely don't plan to. I really do want to keep straight. And I guarantee not to get mixed up with bad company. That's for sure. For me, they're like booze to an alcoholic."

She'd looked away as if not wanting to risk seeing insincerity in his eyes. Now she gestured. "If you want coffee, there's some in the urn from breakfast. You eat yet today?"

"A hamburger in Lewiston."

"How'll pan-scrambled eggs do? You can toast your own bread." She gestured at the large breadbox. "Margarine's in the fridge."

They ate together, neither saying much. Afterward he spent a few minutes with the telephone directory, printing out some addresses. After that he left. He didn't even look at the want ads.

Lute had withheld his real plans. He knew just where he wanted to work, and his optimism was not unreasonable. The documents he'd had made identified him as Martin Luther Karlson. He was stuck with Luther; Signe would never have used a calling name different than his own. He added Martin for the religious impression. The pro had made the documents to match his personal resources—people in positions to enter false but official records into the Web. He took pride in his work. It had cost Lute more than he liked to think about.

Among other things, there was an army discharge stating he'd been an MP. He'd found and downloaded a copy of the military police handbook, and crammed it to prepare himself for possible quizzing. Now he drove to Avista Stadium, home of the AAA Spokane Indians.

He'd been right. The season may have been only six home games old, but as scarce as jobs were, there'd already been no-shows and alcohol-related discharges among the employees. Thirty minutes after arriving at the stadium office, "Martin Luther Karlson" was hired as game security. After the game, he'd work as a swamper, cleaning up the stadium. It wasn't full time—the team was on the road half the time—but there could be other events, and if an opening developed, he'd be considered for full-time security.

He wasn't surprised at how nicely things had come together. He was used to that. The failed Colorado and Boston missions were aberrations.

51

CNN Malik Morris Takes Calls
From the transcript of
"Rappin' with the Dove"

Caller: Dove, how come you ain't gone to Africa?

Dove: I did go to Africa, twenty months ago. To Kenya, Zambia, Malawi and South Africa. But language problems, and in many places, primitive transportation and communication, limit the effectiveness of personal tours there. Too few people heard me, and still fewer understood me. So we made free videos tailored for Africa—shot them in Kenya—with written translations and subtitles in all the major African languages.

Caller: My question's for Dove too. Dove,

what you got to say about government and taxes?

Dove: Taxes are the way the broad public buys certain things you can't buy in stores. Things considered necessities: streets, police protection, schools, public assistance—things like that. Government's job is to arrange supply and delivery.

In the process, government operates about as well, overall, as most big business does. Given the missions assigned them, they're about as efficient or inefficient. And generally as honest; often more. And like businesses, some governments are better than others.

Without government, the more aggressive, ruthless, and power-hungry among us would fight to rule. The disorder, destruction and suffering would make today seem like paradise. If we were *very* lucky, the warlord that won would try to rule well. But the problems of keeping power in a world like that would still result in oppression way beyond anything this country knows.

I realize that sometimes minorities find the police disinterested in their protection—and may find it hard to accept the fact that oppression could be much worse than what they're already familiar with. But imperfect as it is, our democratic system—democratic with a small *d*—our democratic system and its notably imperfect laws give us substantial protection. They also limit and channel the energies and efforts of those aggressive people who make up so many of our businessfolk and politicians. The ballot lets us vote on who governs, and helps channel some public energies and resources to aid the poor, the oppressed, and the disabled.

Our government *is* flawed—because we the people are flawed. The real way to improve government is to improve ourselves.

Malik: You talk about police protection. A lot of people our color need protection *from* the police.

Dove: A hundred years ago, industrialists hired private police, called goons, and arranged with public police forces, to put down labor strikes, and prevent workers from organizing. Their brutality was far worse than that of modern police forces, and often with less provocation. Read the history of the labor movement. Your local librarian can help you get started.

The Japanese cherry trees had bloomed and blown before the "marchers" began arriving, marching almost entirely on wheels. In a single day, West Potomac Park, the Mall—almost all the grassy areas between Constitution and Independence Avenues—had filled with tents, tepees, and pickups with camper shells. The pickups had driven over curbs and across lawns, but security had orders to overlook that. Latecomers squatted on the Polo Grounds, Capitol Plaza, Franklin Square . . . More than a few were strolling near the White House and the

Capitol Building, or snacking and smoking in the sun on the broad steps of the Lincoln Memorial. Marines had kept them away from the fences around Lafayette Park and the Ellipse, and out of government office buildings.

The marchers came from fifty-one states, and many interest groups and constituencies. There were thousands upon thousands of the unemployed, thousands of veterans, of mortgage defaulters, of the elderly, the disabled; single mothers with their children . . . and of course the agitators, who'd come to foment trouble— preferably violence.

People arrived in cars, trucks, and old buses. They growled up on motorcycles. Most arrived unkempt, after a day or two or three of riding, and taking turns driving and sleeping. Of those few who might have arrived nicely-dressed—who'd driven late model cars, and slept in motels en route—most parked outside the beltway and rode the tube in. It wasn't politic to drive up in a late-model SUV or Audi.

Their timing was no accident: The mid-April weather had determined the when, while the Web and the broadcast media had wittingly and unwittingly choreographed their arrivals.

The government, of course, had known they were coming, and when the vanguards entered the city, the chemical toilets, trash containers, hoses and hydrants had already been set up. As had units of marines and infantry well briefed and drilled on crowd management.

Surprisingly, at the start there were no serious disorders. Among the marchers, responsible leaders appeared or arose, notably among the military veterans.

Early efforts by agitators to mount strike forces were squelched before the troops needed to do anything.

Television teams, of course, were everywhere. Demonstrators with loud-hailers orated and ranted, rousing their listeners to chant with them: "Bring out Big Mama!" The tens of thousands of voices carried well in the bright spring day.

Senators, congressmen, chiefs of bureaus, assistant cabinet secretaries arrived from various government buildings, accompanied by sound trucks, or by aides carrying loud-hailers. They invited questions, explained their positions, spoke sympathetically, and in general tried to distract the marchers from actually marching.

Thousands did march, of course, chanting, waving placards and American flags, but not in the single great mass the organizers had in mind. This was not a youth movement with a common passion, focused on a common theme, and there were few onlookers to impress. Instead there were several separate marches; labor's was the largest, and veterans' next.

In early afternoon on the second day, clouds began moving in, and some time later, distant thunder rumbled. The crowd grew restless. About 3 P.M. the temperature plummeted, and the breeze picked up. Minutes later the storm hit, large hard drops of icy rain that quickly became a deluge, accompanied by the first strokes of nearby lightning, and great bangs of thunder.

The crowd broke for cover. They crammed into tents, crowded the Lincoln Memorial, packed the Sylvan Theater, and pushed dripping past entry guards into the museums along Madison and Jefferson Drives. In the first mad rush, some had fallen and been trampled. Almost all were soaked. The troops hadn't been drilled for a rainstorm, but their officers had the good sense to let the crowd run.

In twenty minutes the downpour was over, replaced by lighter rain, steady and cold. When the troops tried to steer people back to their bivouacs, some resisted. In the confusion, some agitators avoided the troops, moving by groups into side streets, carrying with them other able-bodied people. They began smashing windows, stabbing tires. Cars were overturned and set on fire. A gas tank exploded in a fireball. Sirens ululated through the streets, and some who realized now what they were getting into, headed back for the bivouacs. Someone produced Molotov cocktails, which were thrown at police cars and through shop windows.

The rioting, however, did not become widespread. The violence was localized, involving perhaps two hundred vandals, but it triggered something else. Local gangs moved in to loot, and set their own fires.

When the troops had gotten most of the marchers corralled on the vast lawns again, the camps were a shambles. Tents had been knocked down by people trying to crowd into them, out of the rain. In the confusion, agitators had slashed and stabbed the waterhoses, producing geysers, cutting pressure, and adding to the storm floods that formed ponds on the lawns, and flowed into tents. Chemical toilets had been sabotaged, some by pocket bombs. Their contents leaked and stank.

Many of the marchers, disgusted, began to lug their belongings back to their vehicles, preparing to leave.

❖   ❖   ❖

On the first day, the arrival day, Florence Metzger had several times stood at a White House window and looked out—out across the Rose Garden and South Lawn, and over the Ellipse, at the growing tent camp in the park. *Something like this was almost inevitable,* she told herself. She had no doubt the troops would handle the situation properly, and probably no serious harm would come of it. But it was a damned nuisance, and all it would accomplish was distraction from the tasks at hand—hers and everyone else's.

Showers had been forecast for the evening of the second day. *Perhaps,* she thought, *rain will shrink and shorten the demonstrations.*

On the second morning, the marchers were still arriving, but at nothing like the rate of the day before. Near noon the Weather Service warned of a squall line approaching, but no one seemed to realize what it might mean; certainly no one in the White House. When the storm hit, the President was in the Oval Office, having just finished talking on the phone with the secretary of commerce. Hearing the first great thunderclap, she hurried upstairs to the living quarters to watch from a window. The violence of the initial downpour hid the stampede from her, but when the rain thinned a little, she could see well enough to recognize the potential for serious problems.

When reports of vandalism and looting began coming in, she turned grim, and called in a standby marine battalion. They would, she was assured, be on site within an hour.

Before nightfall, gangs of looters ranged in earnest and in force, and she ordered the marines and rangers to clear the streets of them. What they succeeded in doing was dispersing the rioters into peripheral neighborhoods, where they filtered among buildings in clusters too small for choppers to keep track of. There was sporadic gunfire, some by automatic weapons. Around 1 A.M., eight mortar rounds landed in bivouac areas. Remarkably they didn't kill anyone, but military ambulances hauled away more than fifty wounded.

It was the veterans who prevented panic, grizzled old men from the Vietnam War, middle-aged vets of Middle Eastern conflicts and the Balkans, and younger vets who'd served during the Troubles. They surprised both themselves and the troops on duty.

In the morning, Florence Metzger addressed the nation on television, reading statistics from sheets, but mostly speaking off the cuff. She'd scared the hell out of her staff with her determination to do it that way, and after she'd finished, she was sure she'd blown it. She couldn't remember anything she'd said, and afterward feared to watch and hear it on the cube—though she did of course, when at last she found time.

But everyone around her, journalists and staff, told her it was as good as any speech she'd made. Not polished, but rational and compelling. She shouldn't have been surprised. She'd lived with the problems since before her election, been crammed with information, briefed daily by experts, semi-experts, and quasi-experts.

She'd begun with numbers—the known casualties and arrests, mostly of rioters, looters, and vandals.

Then she went on to the Depression, its roots, its consequences, and what needed to be done by the government, the public, business . . .

The rest of the day and the evening were spent conferring with joint operations command, the mayor and police commissioner of D.C., the FBI, and various cabinet members, who were told to unlimber emergency plans for serious work projects. And she spoke with the heads of various interest groups, who promised to call back as many as they could of their marchers.

She wasn't sure what she'd accomplished with all that, but hopefully something. *Better to charge into it*, she told herself, *than wring my hands*.

At 2:30 A.M. she finally lay back in her Flex-Bed with half a glass of brandy, and began watching *True Grit*. Before 3 o'clock she was asleep.

52

FATHER THOMAS EDWARD GLYNN—or a facsimile thereof—settled into a room in Jesuit House, at Gonzaga University in Spokane, in the state of Washington. He was there on the same pretense he'd used at the Cote—research in comparative religion.

Over the coming weeks, Corkery/Glynn would spend some time in the stacks and at a computer in the Foley Library. To his fellow residents at Jesuit House, Glynn seemed a taciturn man, preoccupied (actually cautious), talking almost not at all to his fellow Jesuits, in the dining room or elsewhere. Dressed in civvies, he took walks along the river. No one paid enough attention to seriously wonder about him.

What he was really doing, of course, was killing time. Waiting. Once he attended a baseball game at Avista Stadium, not something you'd expect of some-one not long in the country from Ireland—someone to whom the game must surely be a total mystery. But it was necessary.

It wasn't long before Luther Koskela, alias Martin Luther Karlson, became a full-time security employee at Avista Stadium. Meanwhile, on nights without games, he had time to explore the place thoroughly. The most interesting thing he found was a utility crawl space above a press box, accessible through an entry panel. His master key worked nicely in its lock. It had a plywood floor, and an inconspicuous hatch overhead, easily overlooked. He unbolted the hatch.

Most fortuitous of all, it also had a small panel that when opened, gave a view of the field. Presumably it had once had a purpose; Koskela saw one of his own for it. Chuckling, he shook his head. *Can you say convenient, Koskela?* he asked himself. *You always were a lucky dog, but this takes the prize.*

He closed the panel, then backed out the door.

Ngunda Aran's intercom chirped, and he turned from his computer screen to touch a flashing button. "What is it, Norman?"

"Mr. Knowles would like to talk to you."

"Send him in."

In appearance, Art Knowles was the stereotypical security director: middle-aged, stocky, serious, and seemingly fit.

Ngunda gestured toward his beverage station. "Coffee?" he asked. "Tea? Cocoa?"

Knowles shook his head. "I've had some," he answered, and sat down uninvited.

Ngunda had swiveled his own chair to face him. "What can I do for you?" He grinned. "For you who do so much for me."

"I'm worried about your Inland Northwest trip."

"Ah."

"I have no information about unusual risks. It's simply a feeling. And despite its reputation, region-wide there isn't even an unusual percentage of people hostile to blacks or new ideas or liberals. In fact, the Centrists got an overall majority there in the last two elections. But I'm still worried about your safety there."

Ngunda smiled. "Of course. As the world has learned, a single, unknown dedicated enemy can be highly dangerous. And you are highly sensitive to dangers. I will discuss your concerns with Lor Lu. Is there anything else you'd like me to do?"

Knowles shook his head. *I wish there were,* he thought. *Something concrete.* "Just be careful," he said. "Be especially careful."

"If you think of something, let me know. Or let Lor Lu know. You're aware of his perceptiveness to danger."

"I know he can sniff out bombs better than any dog."

Ngunda smiled and stood, and when Knowles followed suit, put his hands on the security chief's thick shoulders. "Arthur," he said, "let me suggest that with your help I will come through the tour safely. I have no doubt of it." He smiled as if inwardly amused by something. "It is too soon for my death," he added.

For a moment, Art Knowles looked uncertainly at him, then nodded. He believed, but he would leave nothing to chance. "Thank you," he said. "I'll try my best to make an accurate prophet of you."

Ngunda laughed. "And I thank you." He laughed again. "You have my sincere best wishes for your success."

53

From "Ngunda's Room" in
New Age Wonks' Clubhouse

Bertie from Blighty: On occasion you refer to younger souls and older souls, and I have read Ms. Yarbro's interesting books. I would appreciate your elaborating on what *you* mean by younger and older souls, and on what you consider to be the significance of soul age in one's life.

Dove: The first time you were born into the Earth School, you were totally inexperienced in it. So you incarnated into a simple, homogeneous society for the purpose of "breaking in," so to speak. To reduce uncertainty as much as possible.

Life by life you gained experience, but even so, the wealth of choices—of actions and associates—was daunting. A soul lives numerous lives before graduating from *infant* soul to being what I like to call a *fledgling* soul.

At that point you began to reach in life. But that reach was conservative. You interpreted the world narrowly and cautiously. You felt threatened by people who acted or spoke outside the rules you learned from your parents, and on occasion you responded brutally. (Many inquisitors and witch burners have been fledgling souls.) Not that most fledgling souls are brutal: The kindly but dogmatic policeman or teacher is often a fledgling soul. Fledgling souls can be devoted parents and considerate neighbors, but they'll insist strongly on behavior that fits their views of right and wrong. Live and let live is most definitely *not* their motto.

After a number of lives at the fledgling level, you graduated to being what might be called a *young* soul. You'd gained confidence, and planned more ambitious lives, aiming for a higher level of success. Spirituality seldom plays an important role in the thinking of a young soul, though religion often does. Most of the material advances of the physical plane are developed and produced by young souls. Most politicans and big-league athletes are young souls. A great majority of tycoons are. Although far more often than not, the young soul does not succeed in making it big. In any case, important lessons are learned.

The young soul motto is "do it my way," but young soul motives tend to be different than those of fledgling souls.

When you completed your cycle of youth soul lives, you graduated again, becoming a *mature* soul. At that point you knew, deeply and fundamentally, that there is more to life than material success. Mature souls are inclined to "soul searching," and to agonizing over issues of justice. They may be inclined toward social reform.

Eventually we graduate to the *old* cycle. As an old soul, you may be interested in reform, but you're less likely to be *driven* by that interest. You are much more willing to "live and let live," and you're even less likely to be focused on material success. And when we complete the *old* cycle, we graduate from what the Hindus think of as the wheel of rebirth.

At this point I must make a disclaimer. Prior to the midlife crisis, a person, even an old soul, will be more or less under the influence of false personality, accrued in childhood under the pressures of the environment—notably family and society. A personality more or less at odds with the "true" personality, which we select for the life before being born into it. But even in children, the experienced viewer can commonly recognize the true soul age on brief acquaintance.

Tilly the Toiler: Jesus taught in brief parables, and Buddha sometimes taught without words. But you're pretty gabby.

Dove: [☺] True on all counts. Jesus the man taught mostly simple, unsophisticated people, in terms meaningful to them. Later, as the Christ, an incarnation of the Infinite Soul, he scarcely taught at all, excepting his disciples. However, he powerfully changed many others by his presence, his *vibrations*. The term "good vibes" is more than slang, and an avatar's vibes are far better than good.

I am a human being, teaching humans of much greater sophistication than Jesus did. The viewpoints and attitudes of today's humans have been influenced through cultural osmosis. They are the beneficiaries of centuries of human strivings and experience. Their inner worlds have been penetrated and transformed by seepage from quantum mechanics, chaos theory, molecular biology and so forth. Even though most have only a vague sense of those subjects.

Thus today's people benefit most from a different teaching style than that of Jesus. His teachings are not obsolete, but in important respects, humankind has changed.

And of course, what Jesus taught has been distorted by the cultures and agendas of those who reported it, and again and again by those who passed it on, and interpreted it.

Up Yours: You feed us this bullshit without any proof or data. Why should we pay any damn attention to it?

Dove: Why indeed? Attention is not required.

When the time comes—when the Infinite Soul manifests itself—then most will pay attention. And they will remember what I've said—I and other teachers. But even then there will be some who disbelieve—notably those who have lessons to learn that require disbelief. And their disbelief will hold lessons not only for themselves, but for everyone else.

54

LEE KNEW SHE HAD a problem, had suspected it at supper. The girls had been less spontaneous than usual. Then, after dessert, they'd sat a few feet apart on the sofa—sat upright!—reading. Raquel, whose evening it was to be first, had not gone to the computer, and Becca hadn't asked if *she* could.

Which made it difficult to concentrate on the *News Hour*. The Mexican government had collapsed that day, and the Mexican army had taken over. General Montoya was talking good intentions. One might hope. The fighting in Yucatan and Chiapas, and up north in Chihuahua and Sonora, had slackened, but it was unclear whether the rebels were interested in negotiations, or were simply shifting gears.

Ben came from the kitchen after cleaning up, and plopped down in his recliner. Then Becca, as if she'd been waiting, got up soberly from the sofa and walked over to her mother.

"Mom?"

Lee hardened inwardly. It seemed to her she knew what was coming. "Yes?" Her voice was hard.

"I've got a question."

"What is it, dear?" She said it stiffly.

"Well, Dad has finished the Millennium Procedures and started on the Advanced Spectrum. And Raquel and I . . ."

"No!"

Becca continued evenly, but there was hurt and resentment in her eyes. "I am the only child in sixth grade who hasn't done Life Healing."

"We went over this last fall. I will not . . ."

Lee stopped herself short of saying "allow you to be brainwashed by this cult." *I am the only child . . .* Not *all the other kids.* Not even *the only kid. I am the only child.*

Somehow that choice of words hit Lee. And Ben had done Life Healing before she'd met him. Now he'd done far more. And his only fault was, he handled situations smoothly and considerately, though occasionally that irritated her when she thought he should be angry. And there was Mr. M, and the Crow nation, and everyone here including Susan Klein, whom she liked more than any other woman she'd ever known.

She bit her lip and looked at Ben, who pretended to be intent on the *News Hour,* leaving her on her own.

"The only child," she echoed.

Becca nodded soberly, and from the sofa came another voice. "I'm the only one who hasn't in the fifth grade, too, who's old enough. But that's all right for a little while. Becca can start first, and when you see it isn't hurting her, you won't feel as bad when I ask to."

Lee looked at her husband, his gaze still on the television. "Oh Ben!" she said, half irked, half plaintive.

He looked at her, smiling slightly. "Why don't you and I talk about it in private. You can ask questions and I'll answer them. Maybe it'll seem less threatening."

"Or maybe it won't."

"True, but you'll have a clearer sense of what it is you're—um—protecting them from."

She wondered what he would have said if the "um" hadn't saved him. Or her. "Becca, Raquel," she said tightly, "your father and I are going in the breakfast nook to talk. You will go to your room. Or to the computer room. Do not interrupt us. And *don't* get your hopes up!"

"Yes, Mom." Solemnly.

"We won't, Mom." Also solemnly.

Lee led the way into the kitchen area and slid the door closed behind them. Then they sat down across from each other at the table. "All right," Lee said, "talk."

After a moment he did, for fifteen minutes. "It might help to evaluate the people who find it useful," he finished. "Susan and the other teachers you know, and the people you work with."

She nodded. "And you, most of all. You're good people, all of you, but . . ." She pressed her lips together.

"But it's a cult, right?"

She nodded.

"Define *cult* for me. Your own definition."

"What good would that do?"

"Well then, let me try. A cult is a group that has beliefs falling outside those of the group that calls it a cult."

"Oh cut it out, Ben!" Her voice was sharp, angry. "That's sophistry!" She paused, frowning, the anger suddenly sagging. "You know, I can almost accept the stuff about past lives, even if it's not true. If it works in therapy, as apparently it does—if it helps people—then a person can make some sort of case for it. But the rest of it—*overleaves* and the rest of it—that's *cult* crap!"

His nod was acknowledgement, not agreement. "Nominally my mother was Catholic," he said, "and my dad Jewish, but so far as I could figure out, they were actually somewhere between agnostic and deist. So it's hard for me to really get your point of view. What were you taught in church and Sunday school?"

She took a deep breath, and exhaled through pursed lips. Beneath the surface of her consciousness, memories of lessons flickered. Hell and heaven, loaves and fishes, wine out of water. The Red Sea parting, the pillar of fire . . .

She spoke without looking at him. "I remember the last service I attended in my parents' church," she said quietly, "the church I grew up in. I was home from college, on spring break. After that I always found a reason not to attend—which brought me some lectures from my parents, believe me."

She raised her eyes to Ben's. "The preacher was

new since the last time I'd been there." Her voice was little more than a whisper. "He was an older man named Holst, and he opened the sermon with a story of his first parish. There was a young girl in the town who wanted to go to church, but her father wouldn't let her. She begged him, but he wouldn't change his mind. Then she got leukemia, and he still wouldn't let her go. Finally one day her mother called the preacher. She told him her husband was away, and asked him please to come at once."

Lee's lips twisted. "The way he told it, the girl was dying when he got there, screaming 'My feet are burning! My feet are burning!' He'd gotten there too late."

Eyes blazing with anger now, she continued, almost hissing the words. "That *asshole*! He told us she was descending into hell because her father hadn't let her go to church!"

Lee sagged then, and for a moment said nothing more. When she did, the intensity was gone. "I don't know whether he actually believed it or not. Maybe he did, and couldn't help himself."

She inhaled deeply, and sighed. "Most preachers would probably puke at a story like that. At least I'd like to think they would. But it really *really* got to me."

Ben smiled gently. "I can see it did."

"Huh!" The sound was half chuckle. "You noticed!" She straightened. "I'll admit I never heard anything so repulsive from Reverend Haener when he was there. And our Sunday school teachers never told us anything approaching that. But compared to some of the things they did tell us, overleaves may turn out to be pretty mundane.

"So," she said, "explain overleaves to me."

"Hmm. Overleaves are parts of the basic personality."

"Like . . ." She paused, fishing up a memory—something Raquel had said. "Like 'old sage in passion mode'?"

Ben grinned. "That's part of a set, yes."

"Why are you grinning?"

"I'm thinking of Raquel. It's a perfect fit."

"Why not just say 'personality'? Or 'personality element'? Instead of confusing people with new terms?"

"Because the term *personality* hasn't been functionally defined. It means different things to different people. *That's* confusing. Overleaves are explicitly defined, and come without baggage. And they explain a lot of phenomena."

"Why call them overleaves though?"

"I suppose because they overlie the soul, in a manner of speaking."

Lee frowned. It was time, she decided, to nail this down.

Half an hour later they came out of the kitchen. She was far from sold on overleaves, but at least they weren't alarming anymore. She could even see how observations could lead to the theory. So instead of going to the girls' room, it was the phone she went to. She dialed, waited a moment, then spoke. "Hello, Susan, this is Lee. May I . . . may I come over and talk awhile? Privately? Something's come up. . . . Thanks. I'll be right there."

Ben said nothing, his smile subdued as he watched

his wife put on coat and snow boots. When the door closed behind her, he went to the girls' room. "Mom hasn't decided yet," he said. "She's gone to talk with Mrs. Klein." He held up his right hand, fingers crossed.

"Thanks, Dad." They said it in nearly perfect unison. Then their stepfather returned to the living room and his book.

"I know that may sound strange to you," Lee said, quietly, over the table in the Kleins' breakfast nook. "But I feel driven into a corner by this. Ben is so patient with me—even the girls are, mostly. But I'm really afraid of this—Life Healing. I don't mean to be insulting, but I feel, really feel . . . I don't know. Millennium seems like a cult to me, and . . ."

Susan Klein nodded, and laid her hand atop Lee's. "My mom felt the same way when I told her I was going to do it. And from a certain point of view it is a cult. But I was twenty-eight and a divorcee with kids, so she wasn't in a position to do more than wring her hands.

"Actually I felt a little like she did—afraid, that is—but I'd met Chuck a few months earlier. He'd proposed to me, and I really wanted to say yes. I'd dated quite a few guys, but he was in a class by himself—considerate and mature. The problem was, he'd gotten Life Healing at Denver the summer before, and been so impressed, he planned to go back after graduation. To train as a Millennium facilitator—a counselor! Hoping to practice in a center they planned to open in our home town, St. Louis. Chuck! A man with a shiny future in electronic engineering, switching to counseling!

"And it seemed to me I needed to know, really and personally *know,* what I'd be getting into if I married him." She shrugged, then grinned. "So I did it, and here I am. You might say I'm hooked, but I think of it as convinced."

Lee looked at her searchingly, not sure what she hoped to see.

"One possibility," Susan said, "is to try it yourself before you approve or disapprove the girls taking it."

Lee shook her head, small quick movements, as if trying to ward off gnats. "No," she said. "I need to . . . to keep my own . . . objectivity intact. In case it doesn't work out well."

Susan nodded, her reply cheerful. "Sounds like a workable approach. Evaluate the results on Ben, and maybe the girls, and from there, do whatever makes the most sense."

Lee did not brighten.

"Dear," Susan said, "it may help to keep this in mind. In a few years the girls will overrule you, as I did *my* mom."

Lee looked at that. "What does your mom think now?" she said after a moment.

"She treats us all lovingly when we visit—the girls, me . . . and Chuck. When she met him, she soon adored him. She was always a woman with lots of love. And quite good at compartmentalizing, in that case, the cult member from the man and fiancé."

Lee nodded, still visibly troubled. "Thanks, Susan," she said soberly. "You've helped. You truly have."

She left then, her coffee untouched. Through a window, Susan watched her walk the shortcut home, a path trodden by their daughters through the snow. She hadn't added that her mother had later taken Life Healing herself. It seemed best to leave the subject where she had.

Lee and Ben went to the girls' room. Becca and Raquel sat reading at their desks, and turned as their parents came in. Lee sat down on Becca's bed, facing her daughters.

"Girls," she said, "Dad and I have talked it over. Becca, you have my permission to do—or take or whatever they call it—you have my permission to do Life Healing. She turned to Raquel. "And you can start when she's finished. *If*—if everything goes to my satisfaction."

The response surprised Lee, though on second look it was predictable: It was Raquel who popped off her chair first, bounded to her mother, and threw her arms around her neck. "Oh, Mom, I knew you could do it! I knew you could! You're the best mom in the world!" Both girls kissed her before Raquel said chirpily, "I'll be in the computer room," and skipped off.

Becca still stood by her mother. "Mom, you really won't regret this," she said, then picked up her book and went out to the living room.

Lee sat thoughtfully for a minute, her attention inward, then looked up at her husband. "I'm going in the bedroom for a few minutes," she said. "Nothing's wrong. I just need to be alone for a while."

Ben nodded, and she left. Lying on their bed, she stared toward the ceiling, seeing nothing, reviewing first her talk with Ben, then with Susan. And told herself that whatever Millennium beliefs the girls picked up, they'd be no weirder than the things millions of children were taught in Sunday school each week. At least Life Healing didn't seem to fill them with prejudices and false fears. Whether they'd come away with false expectations was another matter.

But then, she'd graduated from college with false expectations. Brainwashed by society, no less! She'd married Mark with false expectations. Had quit a good job—a good salary at least—and gone into business for herself with false expectations. The only major thing she'd done, she told herself, that had matched her hopes, exceeded them actually, was marry Ben.

And at any rate the damage, if any, had been done. The girls were already full of Millennium ideas, and Life Healing didn't seem likely to harm them. *Looked at honestly,* she told herself, *it's just therapeutic counseling.*

Life Healing. She still couldn't see what good it could do two girls as healthy as hers. *Better adjusted than their mom,* she told herself.

Sighing, she got up and returned to the living room.

A while later, Raquel came out of the computer room. "Mom," she said, "I'm going to brush and get ready for bed."

"What's the matter?"

"Nothing, really."

"You look like something is. Will you tell me?"

"Well . . . Sometimes I wish *I* was the oldest, instead of Becca."

"I understand. Okay. Go brush."

Raquel disappeared into the hall. "Ben," Lee

murmured, "we might as well let both of them start at the same time."

He scowled a mock scowl. "If you say so."

"Snot!"

He laughed, then turned to their eldest. "Twenty minutes, Becca," he said.

"Yes Dad."

Gentle Ben, Lee thought. *The strongest in the family.*

The oven timer buzzed. Curious, she went into the kitchen and peered through the oven door. There was a cherry pie inside. She turned the buzzer off, turned on the exhaust fan, and opened the oven door. Ben, she realized, had put it in while she was in the bedroom.

"Thanks, hon," he said. He'd followed her in.

"One more question," she said.

"Yes?"

"Becca said something about the 'astral zone.' What's the astral zone? That really sounds New Agey."

"It is New Agey, like heaven without the harps and angelic choirs and pink clouds and alabaster pillars, or whatever. I think of it as a sort of graduate school for souls, without the bureaucracy and pressures, the campus and occasional desperation. But I suspect that's a pretty inadequate description." Again he grinned. "Actually I've never thought much about it. I'll just wait till I get there."

My pragmatic spiritualist, she thought. *My tender, patient, loving man.* "Have I told you lately that I'm the world's smartest woman?" she asked.

His eyebrows rose. "No, I don't believe you have."

"And I suppose you didn't notice for yourself." She moved to him, stood inches from him. He leaned backward in mock concern. "Well I am," she growled. "Because I married you."

"Oh. Well. Of course."

"In a minute I'm going to put your pie in the window cooler." She sounded more than a little like Lauren Bacall in an old Bogart movie. "An hour and a half from now, you and I will polish it off, and after that we'll polish off each other. The girls will be asleep by then."

They did. Afterward, lying side by side, Lee said, "I did it again. After I get upset, I always need you to make love to me."

He chuckled. "You know what they say."

"What do they say?"

"Every cloud has a silver lining."

She sat up and hit him with her pillow, not hard enough to start a pillow fight, then lay back down. "For about the thousandth time," she said, "I find myself awed by my daughters. *Our* daughters. They're an incredible mixture of the best aspects of children with the best aspects of adults."

"Yup."

"And my husband isn't so bad either."

"Yup."

She looked at him lying on his back with his eyes closed, a half smile on his face. "Remember what I said in the kitchen?" she asked.

"About polishing each other off?"

"No! About being the world's smartest woman. I take it back."

"You do?"

"I do. I'm the world's luckiest woman."

His eyes opened, and raising himself on an elbow, he kissed her. "Remind me to thank you properly some time. In half an hour or so."

She kissed him back, and this time did another impression. "Any time, pilgrim, any time."

Ben lay bemused. Lee could be playful on occasion, but this evening . . . First a recognizable Bacall, and now what had surely been John Wayne!

Mentally he grinned. *The most inspired thing I ever did,* he told himself, *was to marry her. And I got her daughters in the bargain.*

It was midnight when Lee went to sleep. She awoke in the morning aware of having dreamt, but not of what. Only that the dream had been long and rambling. She was also aware that she was comfortable with her decision of the night before.

55

Headline News
Atlanta, GA, May 6

April economic figures are mildly encouraging. For the second month in a row, unemployment has held at 24 percent. The May level is expected to be down, as new public works projects get under way. The number of businesses failing decreased again. Economists are generally in agreement that the more susceptible businesses had already failed.

Meanwhile, people continue to make adjustments. The number of families living with relatives or friends reached 40 percent, 2 percent higher than in March. The number of rental vacancies was up again. Meanwhile, the federal moratorium on home mortgage foreclosures by lending institutions has kept many other families in their homes.

This just in. A light plane made an emergency landing this morning near Hartsburg, Ohio. It carried a footlocker loaded with explosives and fitted with a detonator. When the pilot refused to dive into the federal building, his passenger shot him, then shot himself. After radioing authorities, the pilot managed to land on a country road. He has been hospitalized in serious condition. His passenger was pronounced dead on arrival at the Hart County hospital.

THE NEW MOSSAD had moved its headquarters to another Riverside warehouse. There the Wrath had called in six of its soldiers, including Rafi Glickman. He didn't want to go. The old Mossad had been vital to the morale and survival of Israel. The new was a malignancy, a festering abscess of psychosis. Two members no longer attended. Rafi assumed the Wrath had had them killed.

He'd suggested to his "true" organization that he be pulled out of the Mossad. Turn in the Wrath to the FBI, and the outlying groups would wither. But they wanted him to stay, hopefully to learn who supported it financially, and see them bagged, too. The FBI, they believed, could never get the information out of the Wrath, and it was doubtful they'd get anything out of the Wrath's computer. Probing would cause a system meltdown.

At any rate, there he sat. Reports and assignments were made. Aside from skinheads, most of their victims now were Jews—both refugees and American. Jews, two as distant as London, with whom the Wrath was angry. They were easy targets, and their deaths were intended to intimidate other Jews.

The phone rang. It was Moishe Baran who answered. "Yes?" he said, then listened intently. "Good!" Smiling, he disconnected, and looked at the other two of the Wrath. "The bird has flown," he announced.

The statement jerked Rafi, though he sat as motionless as before. He felt sure it referred to the Ninja Junior. He'd heard nothing more of the cruise missile since the dry run on that soggy winter night, but that needn't mean the Wrath had given up on it. Personnel were often switched at different stages of a project. His greater uncertainty was whether Ngunda Aran was still the target, though that too seemed probable.

The meeting returned to business. After a minute, Rafi stood. "Excuse me," he said. "I need to use the restroom. A touch of the flu."

A potent word, "flu." Yeshua Ben David scowled. He had a phobia of germs, sufficient that the Wrath had ceased to meet not only during the Green Flu, but for two weeks afterward. "Go," said Ben David. "Then go home."

Rafi stood, nodded, and left. He had not even hoped for that last command. What he planned to do would soon be attributed to him. He would go home, throw things into a suitcase, then make his own call to the FBI's informant line, and leave. Leave Riverside; leave California.

He did go first to the restroom, however, stayed there for two or three minutes, flushed, then left. The door guard held him up for a few seconds while checking with Baran on the intercom, then saluted Rafi through.

As he crossed the cindered parking lot, Rafi was struck with a sudden determination. He would not sneak away like a sick cur. After starting his car, he switched on its phone and called up the directory assistance menu. A minute later he dialed the Cote.

The night receptionist there connected him promptly with Security. He reported what he knew, even telling them he was a mole in the New Mossad. Gave his apartment address, and the address from which he was calling, to convince them that this was no prank.

Finished, he replaced the receiver. As he reached for his stick shift, he looked through the windshield and saw Baran running toward him not thirty meters away, an Uzi in his hands. Others followed. Slamming the shift into low and hitting the accelerator, Rafi jerked the car forward, aiming it at Baran. But the elderly car was not a drag racer. Baran jumped aside and fired a burst. The Honda careened into a large forklift, Rafi unconscious with three gunshot wounds, one of them through the brain.

In the absence of quick medical help, that one would have killed him soon enough. But Baran was not satisfied. Pulling open the driver's door, he fired another burst into Rafi's head.

❖   ❖   ❖

Every phone in the Cote rang simultaneously. Almost as quickly, the company's security van began quartering the village streets, red light flashing on its roof, bullhorn bellowing instructions. In less than ten minutes everyone was outside, hastily dressed, bundled against the freezing spring night. Most staff families had cars. Those who didn't, climbed in with others. Millennium vans and buses loaded guests, there for processes or training. A truck cruised to pick up possible stragglers. In less than twenty minutes, everyone except certain Security personnel sat or stood waiting half a mile north of the Cote. The fire truck and ambulance kept their motors idling.

A little more than forty minutes after the warning call, they saw the incoming missile, then the blast, the brief fireball, followed quickly by the roar. And stared.

The Wrath's debugged guidance program, coded to the planetary matrix, had worked perfectly. The missile had gone through Ngunda's roof and blown the house apart. The explosion blew out hundreds of windows in the Cote, and glaziers were promptly contacted in Pueblo, Walsenburg, Trinidad, even Colorado Springs, to replace them. Ngunda was installed in an unoccupied staff cottage.

Before leaving the Cote, Art Knowles had burped the recording of Rafi Glickman's message to the Riverside office of the FBI. Agents reached Rafi's apartment before the New Mossad got there, and their search came up with the solo debriefs Rafi had recorded from time to time as backups.

Ben David was found two days later, dead of a coronary thrombosis. One of the female soldiers betrayed Moishe Baran, who would be killed in a shootout with federal marshals. The least of the Wrath, Chaim Plotkin, was wounded in the same shoot-out, and shortly afterward told all he knew. It was enough.

Within a week, the National Security Agency had provided the Mid-American and West Coast surveillance satellites with new programs. Among other things, they would specifically report intrusions onto the Ranch. The agency's director wondered who had the necessary influence with the White House.

Two days after the missile strike, the staff was mustered in the cold and drafty auditorium, its large windows not yet replaced. There Lor Lu assured them that further missile dangers were essentially nonexistent. They took his word for it. He repeated his reassurance in the school auditorium, and the kids cheered. The guests were reassured by Ngunda himself. Art Knowles, who was paid to "worry," knew the steps the government had taken, and even he felt assured. In his business you didn't think in terms of absolute safety; there was no such thing. But this felt as safe as he could hope for.

56

From the beginning, some readers objected to my series on Millennium. But like it or not, Millennium is very much a part of the American scene. And electronic hits on our website increased substantially, indicating that many people were interested.

After a while, people tired of the series, so we've cut back to occasional articles, of which this is one. Let us know how you feel about it.

In the past, the attitude of Millennium's staff was that although their guru's life was at risk while on tour, at home he was safe. The attempt by infiltrators was considered an aberration unlikely to recur. Then his house was blown up, reportedly by a cruise missile.

Now he's on tour again. Perhaps he'll be

safer there, for this is a different kind of tour. He has spoken to full or almost full houses in places like San Francisco's DiBartolo Dome, the Joe Louis Arena in Detroit, and Yankee Stadium. In all of them he drew crowds of every ethnicity, crowds of up to 50,000 plus.

His present tour will take him to much smaller cities, and publics of a very specific ethnicity. He will speak at the Alaskan Federation of Native Peoples Convention at the Egan Center in Anchorage; the Navajo's Diné College at Tsaile, Arizona; the high school football field at South Dakota's Pine Ridge Reservation; and the Native American Cultural Center at Tecumseh, Oklahoma. The trip will take 10 days, and the total number of people who attend may be less than attended his appearance at the Rose Garden Arena in Portland, Oregon.

As I've written before, admission fees at his usual engagements are only enough to hire the stadium or arena. On this Native American tour, no fees at all will be charged. It is conceivable that Ngunda Aran has ill intentions, but those who accuse him of getting rich on the gullible need to come up with evidence.

I don't expect them to.

> *American Scene Magazine*
> "The Dove and Scam Allegations"
> by Duke Cochran

COCHRAN SCANNED HIS SCREEN. While writing, the words had flowed swiftly from his fingers, and he had not evaluated them. Now, reading and polishing, they surprised him; they read almost as if he'd become a believer. He pursed his lips, then clicked on "send," zapping the file to the editor's desk. He had no doubt he preferred Ngunda Aran to most of the man's detractors.

But he did need a different viewpoint on him. He thought about something Nidringham had suggested: that he sign up for Life Healing, pretend to take it seriously. Go through the motions, and afterward write it up. He could do it without leaving Chicago.

57

The Medical Channel, *Panel on Miracles*
St. Louis, MO, May 3

" . . . Dr. Hahn is the physician of Margaret Colletti, the young woman healed last fall by Ngunda Aran at the Pueblo, Colorado, airport. Dr. Hahn, what is Ms. Colletti's current condition?"

"If I didn't know her, I'd wonder if it was real. Six months ago, I'd have assured you she'd never walk again—never stand again. Her knee joints had degenerated almost to undifferentiated tissue, and her hip joints weren't much better. They'd no longer even begin to bear her weight.

"The most remarkable thing about the healing is that structurally it was instantaneous. When she came into my office the next day, I was astonished to find the joint structure fully reconstituted and functional, and the muscles somewhat recovered.

"Today she leads a class in aerobic dancing. If that doesn't qualify as a miracle, then nothing does."

AFTER HIS NATIVE AMERICAN tour, and two weeks before his Northwest tour began, Ngunda held the usual preliminary planning session with his tour staff. They were experienced with tour operations and problems, so his remarks were brief. Since that memorable day at the Pueblo Airport, when he'd healed Margaret Colletti, there'd been healings following almost every tour event, and a couple of times things had gotten out of hand from a security standpoint. On the Northwest tour, he said, *group* healings would be featured—the tour announcements would invite them—and this created security challenges they hadn't dealt with before.

He turned the meeting over to Art Knowles then, and sat down with the others. As a group they'd decide how to handle things. Ngunda's part in it was to make sure that procedures would not hamper his contact and relationship with the audience.

Art Knowles was used to that, too, though less than comfortable with it.

When they'd finished, Lor Lu and his secretary walked to Lor Lu's office. "Dove's been changing lately," the secretary commented. "Don't you think?"

"Oh yes." Lor Lu grinned. "He's definitely changing. But wait a few more weeks."

He said nothing more. He didn't need to; his secretary knew exactly what he meant. She'd realized it for herself, and been fishing for confirmation.

And group healing! That was something to contemplate. The time was coming! She felt no misgivings at all, only excitement.

Wearing clerical black, Thomas Corkery entered the Spokane mayor's office, his white collar like a flag at his throat. The receptionist looked up at him. "Can I help you?" she asked.

"I'm Father Thomas Glynn," he said, his Irish accent conspicuous. "I have a ten o'clock appointment with his honor."

Her fingers moved quickly on her keyboard. "Mayor Barnes is on an important call just now. It'll be about ten minutes, I expect."

"Fine. I'll wait."

He picked up a copy of *Newsweek* and settled onto a chair. Almost exactly ten minutes had passed when the receptionist spoke again. "Father Glynn, the mayor will see you now."

When Corkery stepped inside, Mayor Ted Barnes was on his feet waiting. "Good morning, Father," Barnes said. "You wanted to talk about the Ngunda appearance next week. Exactly what did you have in mind? I had the impression the Church was not actively opposed to him."

"Indeed it's not. Certainly the Holy Father isn't.

He feels that Mr. Aran does far more good than harm." Corkery chuckled. "And of course, there is Mr. Aran's Irish surname. My interest, besides wanting to hear him speak in person, is a dissertation I'm preparing on him, part of my doctoral program at Xavier of Ohio. It has his holiness's personal approval, incidentally. It's nothing he needed to approve, but it was mentioned to him by Archbishop Hannery, and his holiness said he'd be interested in seeing it when it's finished."

He'd said the latter with a note of pride. "And what I'd like is to be part of the Spokane group who will meet Mr. Aran and share the speakers' platform with him. Hopefully there'll be an opportunity to actually talk with him."

The mayor looked thoughtfully at the man seated across from him. He seemed all right; certainly he was personable enough.

Corkery held up his attaché case. "Would you care to see my work to date? It's not fully organized yet, but . . ."

The mayor waved the offer off. "That's not necessary. But I expect the Sheriff's Department won't want you to carry that briefcase in with you."

"I certainly understand that. I've read of the bomb threats, and armed men infiltrating in the night. And that terrible thing a few weeks ago—the missile that destroyed Mr. Aran's home." He patted the case. "No, I'll leave this at Jesuit House."

The mayor felt somehow uncomfortable with the request, but saw no reason other than his general concern for security. "Just a moment." He buzzed his receptionist. "Marie, I'm adding Father Glynn's name to the list of dignitaries for the Ngunda event. Pull a form and have him fill it out . . . Fine. I'll send him right out."

He stood in dismissal, reaching to shake Corkery's hand. "Millennium's security chief asked that the party not number more than eight," he said. "So I invited eight, but I'm afraid three of them turned me down, and another is waffling. I'm sure you understand how that might be. In spite of the public enthusiasm for Mr. Aran, there are a lot of people who find him offensive, and bring pressure to bear.

"Millennium has authority to reject anyone they don't like, and I'll have to fax them a copy of your form, but I don't suppose there'll be any difficulty there."

"I wouldn't think so," Corkery replied. "I visited them on the Ranch before I knew they'd be here. They let me use their library—view cubes and read transcripts. I did everything but meet himself." He chuckled. "I may be the one person on your list they already know."

In filling out the form, Corkery mentioned under comments his stay at the Cote. Then he left, feeling positively high—although he hadn't expected any difficulty. Things generally worked out for him. Besides, who'd suspect a garrulous priest?

58

I've made the point before, but it bears repeating: When the Infinite Soul manifests in human form, it is not to "save" anyone. It is to provide a new platform from which to continue our spiritual and social evolution, individually and together. The Infinite Soul will not whisk any of us away from our responsibilities, or from the need to complete the lessons of life on the physical plane.

Devotions will not exempt you. That is wishful thinking. Nor will the Infinite Soul make your choices for you. You make them for yourselves.

In that regard I've been asked, what about when your Essence, your inmost being, "speaks" to you? Or a "guardian angel?" But they do not command you, and far more often than not, you, as your personality, ignore them. And when you accept and act on their promptings, it is usual to rationalize, come up with a "reason"—in order to protect your paradigm of the physical universe.

Occasionally, in emergencies, you experience a sudden powerful impulse to comply, but even that is not coercion. It is timing and presentation. The choice remains yours, whether or not there is time for preliminary reflection.

Rather often when this happens, the person, the chooser, is changed by it. Not often transfigured, but nonetheless changed for what you might think of as "the better."

From *The Collected Public Lectures*
of Ngunda Aran

THOMAS CORKERY WAS SURPRISED to find a stretch limo in Spokane. It didn't seemed to him a stretch limo sort of city. The town was large enough, but not sufficiently conceited. *Still,* he reflected, *to transport the featured speaker, three bodyguards and five guests, with a policeman in front ... And they'd hardly ask the man to ride in a van.*

He wondered what would happen if he made his try now, in the crowded vehicle. Nothing good, it seemed to him. Assassination was more difficult than most people realized, certainly when the target had professional protection. And this operation was undoubtedly his most dangerous ever. It had started well. The entourage hadn't been checked with a metal detector before getting into the limousine. It would have been an insult to the host city, and terrible PR. But the greatest danger, should he get that far, would be when he drew and fired. Truly he did not expect to survive the evening.

He would, of course, have just one chance. And there was the bloody damned headrest in the way—steel beneath the padding.

Besides himself, it seemed to him the bodyguards were the only watchful people in the limo. One of them was seated on his right. Could he draw, point his weapon, and put a lethal bullet through the brain of the guru in front of him, before he was shot himself, or his gun arm grasped and broken? The bodyguards would have quick reflexes, and they'd have been drilled in situations like this. Also, he had no doubt they wore body armor. Even the guru might, though he didn't appear to. Some models were unnoticeable beneath jackets.

His mulling, he told himself, was nerves, nothing more. His best script for success assumed that the entourage wouldn't be checked at the stadium. The guards and police escort, of course, would all carry guns. And if that many armed men passed through all at once, the detection equipment would melt down from shock.

But if they *were* checked, it would be off to some American prison for him. Then Ngunda Aran might die of old age for all he could do about it. As for himself—given his British record, he'd doubtless get the maximum punishment allowed under the American Anti-Terrorism Act. The amnesty granted by the Dublin Agreement wouldn't cover this. And the police would be authorized to kill, if they deemed it necessary to protect the guru or themselves. Or anyone else for that matter.

The parking lot was nearly full. There were no lines at the ticket windows, but people were still moving through the two entrance gates, showing their tickets and passing through detection. The limo drove past them, turning heads, and let its passengers off at another gate, private and somewhat removed, manned by police.

It was there they encountered a metal detector. Corkery's guts knotted, the breath locking in his chest. If need be, he was prepared to draw and make his try then, first at Ngunda, then at shooting his way out. But they went through the detector without anything happening. Apparently it was turned off. He was relieved, but not surprised, with so many armed guards around the guru.

They entered a tunnel, well-lit and painted white. To Corkery's now hypersensitive senses, their shoes sounded harsh on the concrete. They passed doors and side corridors, then emerged into evening again. Being early June, the sun had not yet set. The sky was cloudless, the playing field vividly green. Beyond the outfield fence were high ridges dark with pine forest. There was a murmur of crowd voices, swelling as people became aware of Ngunda's entrance. Scattered cheers spread, becoming general but not rowdy. The stands were brightly mottled with the red, blue, yellow and green of jackets, for out of the sun, the evening was cool.

Corkery saw and heard it all, but dismissed it. It was meaningless to his mission.

They'd entered from the third base side, bypassing the diamond itself. The grass was thick and yielding beneath Corkery's sturdy black oxfords. Not far behind second base, they climbed the steps to the temporary speakers' platform. There, with uniformed police standing by, they were met by ushers wearing blazers, who led each guest to a designated folding chair, then left the stand.

The guests and bodyguards sat in a single crescent facing the lectern. Not a straight line. That was deliberate, he was sure, for bodyguards sat at the ends, from where they could see all those on the platform. And on the grass, at each of the platform's front corners, stood a policeman, armed and watchful.

The time is at hand, Corkery told himself, and felt the focused calm that normally settled on him with the moment of truth imminent.

He was next to the bodyguard on the crescent's left end, not ten feet from the target. A squeeze of the trigger, then shove the barrel into the bodyguard's waist for the second round, and—possibly, if he was very fast and very lucky— *Don't think about that,* he told himself. *Hope of survival weakens a man. Leave it in the hands of God.*

The mayor was first at the lectern. Corkery had wondered how the introductions would be handled. Would everyone on the stand be introduced? And the men whose money had sent him—were they watching from Montreal, Toronto, New York? Might they see him stand, recognize him and feel a rush of fulfillment?

It was the briefest of thoughts, then Corkery's attention was on the mayor again, taking the microphone from its stand. "Ladies and gentleman," the mayor said, "please stand while Bruce Chilgren sings the national anthem."

Corkery's eyes gleamed. This was the time he'd planned for since that first ballgame, when the crowd had stood for the anthem. He watched the mayor turn and hand the microphone to the husky young man who'd stepped forward.

Then Chilgren turned full around to face left center field, where the flag would be raised. All the others on the stand followed his example, eyes toward the flagpole. Now the crescent was inverted, himself at one tail, a bit behind Ngunda to the guru's right. Corkery took a deep breath, let it out.

Most of the men in the stands, and all of them on the platform, had their right hand on their chest. Corkery's slipped inside his jacket, unsnapping the holster's safety strap. His eyes were on Ngunda, not directly but obliquely. His fingers closed on the pistol butt, his index finger entered the trigger guard, his thumb found the safety. The organist played the opening chords, and Chilgren started to sing. Corkery began his draw.

Wearing his security uniform, Luther Koskela lay in the crawl space on a narrow foam mat, peering through the panel. He'd been there since just before the gates had opened to the public.

Most of the outfield was rich with sunlight, and people continued to flow up the aisles to upper seats, the only seats left. The shadow of the grandstand roof was invading the speakers' platform.

He was ready, surgeon's gloves snug on his hands.

His trusty Thompson/Center was beside him on the plywood decking, silencer in place, the laser rangefinder beside it. He'd smuggled them in five nights earlier, along with the foam pad. The team had been on a road trip, and Luther hadn't known when Millennium Security and the Sheriff's department would install special procedures. So far as he knew, Stadium Security hadn't been party to their plans; certainly peasants like himself hadn't.

The shadow would soon capture the speakers' platform. The stadium seats were nearly full, and people were still coming in. There had to be more than ten thousand already.

The crowd sound grew, swelled to cheering, and he felt his own surge of energy. There they were, a short file of people marching past third base toward the platform, convoyed by deputies. From the panel he watched through, it was 247 feet—82 yards—to what Luther thought of as the pulpit, with its microphone. He'd already set the range on his scope. From where he was, he could detect no breeze. The target wouldn't be in direct sunlight, but ordinary skylight would be more than adequate. Or the field lights if it came to that.

He could easily have shot Ngunda then, but it might not be fatal. He'd wait till the man was standing still, with the crowd looking out at the flagpole. And the organ playing, covering the muffled sound of his "silenced" rifle.

There were ten people on the platform, one a priest, Luther realized. Somehow the man raised Luther's hackles. A heavy-set man stepped out to the microphone and announced the singing of the national

anthem, then handed the mike to the singer. All of
them turned toward the outfield. Luther positioned
his rifle, heard the first organ notes, put his eye to
the scope, moved the muzzle toward Ngunda—

And in passing saw the priest's hand holding a gun,
as if newly drawn from his jacket! Without thinking,
Luther paused the cross hairs on the priest's head and
squeezed the trigger, felt the recoil against his shoulder,
saw the priest fall. And felt a surge of exultation! The
sharp gunshot Luther heard was not his own.

On the platform, people scrambled, some jumping
from it onto the outfield grass. There were screams
from the crowd, though the organist kept playing.
Someone had thrown Ngunda down and was lying
on him, but whether either had been shot, Luther
had no idea. He watched for only a moment. Then
leaving rifle, rangefinder and pad in the crawl space,
he slipped out through the overhead access, took
off his snug plastic gloves, put them in his pocket,
lowered himself to the walkway behind the press box,
and hurried down the short stairway to an aisle. In
his security uniform, no one thought anything of it,
if indeed anyone noticed him at all.

Thomas Corkery never knew another thing in his
life, simply collapsed onto the platform. The bullet
from his pistol slammed into the right buttock of the
man to his left. The bodyguard on his right ignored
the splatter of Corkery's brains on his own face and
neck. Charging over the corpse and brushing the
wounded man aside, he rode the unwounded Ngunda
to the deck, shielding him. His partner and the sheriff's
people would handle anything else.

✧   ✧   ✧

After the stadium had been cleared, Art Knowles met with Sheriff Edwards. The very preliminary assessment was that the "priest" had been a would-be assassin, and judging by the angle of his wound, had been shot by someone on the grandstand roof. By someone with tour security, the sheriff was sure, though Art Knowles insisted he'd had no one up there. The sheriff pointed out that his own snipers had not been equipped with silencers, yet the shot had not been heard. And none of his own snipers admitted having seen the priest draw his weapon, or firing their own. It seemed to him Millennium's security chief was lying.

Meanwhile, Edwards needed to account for the killing. It would be a damned legal nuisance, and cost the county money, but there was no way around it, even though the priest had almost surely intended to kill Ngunda Aran. But on the other hand, whoever the murderer was, he'd saved Spokane a lot of terrible publicity.

Edwards did some serious figuring that night. Afterward, getting to sleep had taken two jolts of bourbon, an hour more of lying awake, then more bourbon. But he had a decision of sorts: he'd voice no speculation till the autopsy report was in. He'd simply tell the press that the unknown gunman had apparently fired from the stadium roof. They'd speculate like crazy, but he could live with that.

Two days earlier, Luther had told friends, including his supervisor, two other guards, one of the boarders and Signe, that he'd had a phone call from a friend in

Oakland. There was a job for him there if he wanted it, with the Port Authority. A job less agreeable, but paying somewhat more.

After the shooting, he completed his shift, then drove home to his aunt's. Before going to bed, he packed most of his things in his large, scuffed leatherette suitcase. When he did go to bed, he slept like a baby.

As usual he slept till nine, then went to the kitchen and rustled up his own breakfast. Signe had almost nothing to say to him—avoided looking at him, as if she wondered. That shook him. Driving to Avista, he went to Security wearing civvies, and turned in his uniform. It seemed to him they looked at him speculatively. He said he'd send an address when he had one, so they could mail his final paycheck. After that he sat around in the coffee room for a few minutes, joking with a couple of guys.

Afterward he drove back to Signe's. To his relief, she was out on errands.

After stowing his suitcase and sleeping bag in his trunk, he drove east, not south or west. That afternoon he located an old buddy in Lolo, Montana. After supper they drove into the Bitterroot Mountains, where Lute picked his careful way up a primitive road, his friend following in a pickup. At the edge of a rugged wooded canyon, he stopped and removed his license plates. Then the two men pushed the car over the edge, watching and listening to it bounce and smash its way almost to the bottom. Someone would find it eventually, of course—some hunter or forester—but by then . . .

Next his buddy drove him to Missoula, where he bought a bus ticket to Salt Lake—for cover. He buried the ticket in a pocket, and his friend drove him all the way to Great Falls, where he jumped a freight train.

Ever since he'd left the crawl space, he'd known it was time to get honest—as honest as possible without turning himself in. He'd find a job of whatever sort, hope his past didn't catch up with him, and start a new life.

Two days later he was in Duluth, where he got an under-the-table job in a scrap iron yard. No formal employment, no papers, no questions. Just show up for work, do his job, and be paid in cash. It would take quite awhile to accumulate money for new counterfeit papers.

Meanwhile he had no further interest in Ngunda Aran, and didn't wonder about it.

He'd acted none too soon. The evening after the shooting, Spokanites heard on the six o'clock news that the unknown gunman had apparently fired from the stadium roof, behind the third base line. And that police snipers there denied having fired, or seeing anyone else fire.

An electrician heard the newscast. It was he who'd wired the new press box, when the ball club went triple-A, and remembering the crawl space, phoned the sheriff's office. By eight o'clock, the rifle and rangefinder were in the sheriff's evidence room. Then stadium security reported Karlson's fortuitous departure. No prints were found, but questioning Signe brought out that Karlson's real name was Koskela. That he was an ex-Ranger and mercenary, who obviously carried false ID. He became the lead suspect.

Meanwhile an Interpol check of the dead man's fingerprints uncovered his actual identity as an ex-IRA terrorist. This shifted the investigation to the FBI, and the sheriff's office was glad to be rid of it. The FBI, in turn, theorized that someone with an old grudge against Corkery had caught up with him: someone Irish or English.

It was hardly compelling—a theory of convenience. But the bureau was swamped with cases, and no one was clamoring for an arrest on this one. They gave it a low priority, and it faded from sight.

59

Charles Milton, discussion
PBS, May 24

Milton: . . . When I read the letters pages, I can hardly believe the rancor and intolerance in some of them. But some others show a lot of tolerance, even wisdom. It's as if there are two different tendencies in the world at the same time. The latter toward growth, the evolution of humankind, and the former digging in its heels to prevent it.

Dove: That is a perceptive statement. But the coming manifestations—the Infinite Soul incarnate, accompanied by a violent geophysical manifestation—will greatly strengthen the movement toward spiritual growth. Even while triggering a brief explosion of violence. Let me repeat that: even while triggering a brief explosion of violence. It will pass.

But the Infinite Soul is not coming to "rescue" humankind. It will only facilitate and strengthen our own efforts. Or to rephrase that: "God" will not "save" humankind. That's up to us. God will help, but the responsibility is ours.

Milton: You've been asked this question before, and you've never really answered it. Now, yes or no: Do you believe you are the person who will receive the Infinite Soul or whatever you call it, and be the next avatar? The Second Coming?

Dove: You will answer that for yourself when the time comes.

It was only the third all-staff briefing since Lee had been with Millennium. The first had been to announce reductions in pay. The second had followed the missile attack. She no longer fretted about RIFs, but she did wonder what this one was for.

It was Art Knowles who stepped before them in the small auditorium. "Good morning," he said. "This will be short. Dove wants me to update you on the Spokane affair.

"The man who was shot to death was a defrocked Jesuit priest and ex-IRA terrorist named Thomas Corkery. He'd been indicted in both England and Ireland for several shootings and bombings, and was one of the IRA people covered by the amnesty that made the Dublin Agreement possible.

"He has since been tied to the Montreal-based 'Catholic Soldiers in America,' the organization responsible for the assassination attempt on Pope John XXIV. Lor Lu is confident that Corkery was also the man who planted the bomb in the Unitarian Church in Boston.

"More recently, Corkery had been posing as a Father Thomas Glynn. It won't comfort you to know that he spent twenty days here this spring as our guest, supposedly doing research on Dove's theology." He paused, allowing time for the information to sink in. "His motive for the assassination attempt is anyone's guess. Meanwhile, Dove has agreed to new clearance procedures, to avoid anything like it happening again."

Once more Knowles paused. "The upside of the situation is that while Corkery had twice gained proximity to Dove, Dove is still alive and well, while the late Mr. Corkery is no doubt reviewing his most recent life even as I speak."

Again Knowles paused. Lee's eyes were round. *That man was here!* she thought. The realization shook her. She'd seen him herself, she was sure, a short man with thin red hair and a clerical collar.

"The lead suspect in Corkery's murder is even more of an enigma," Knowles went on. "The evidence on him is considerable, but apparently not conclusive. His name is Luther Koskela, an ex-Ranger and mercenary, one of those who trained Stephen Ogunsanwo's Nigerian guard. Lor Lu is confident that Koskela is also the missing 'fifth man' of the mercenary group that tried to reach the Cote last fall. The recruiter of the infiltrators, one John Sullivan, known as 'Sarge,' was a veteran of the Lagos Rescue, and like Koskela, had trained Ogunsanwo's guard. They must have known one another well.

"Also, Koskela has two uncles in federal prison for criminal conspiracy, and for financing terrorist acts. That much we have from federal authorities. Lor Lu tells me that Koskela had been at the ballpark to assassinate Dove, but saw Corkery draw his pistol, and shot him instead. He states unequivocally that Koskela has no further designs on Dove's life.

"There are, we know, numerous people who'd like to see Dove dead, but Lor Lu insists that at present, the threat is less severe than it has been. At any rate, my job does not include taking things for granted. I'll continue to take such precautions as I can get Dove to agree to."

That ended the briefing. Lee left not at all reassured, though most of the staff seemed cheerful about it.

It was over dessert that evening that Lee brought up the subject with Ben, while the girls listened. "It frightens me," she finished. "With so many lunatics wanting him killed, I'm really afraid for him."

It was Raquel who answered. "Everyone dies sometime, Mom, but no one will kill Dove till he's ready. The Tao won't let them."

Ben cocked an eyebrow at her. "Whatever became of choice? The assassin's choice, I mean."

Raquel shook her head, while Lee stared at her husband. "People can choose to *try*," Raquel said, "but something goes wrong. Because someone else chooses to stop them."

"Sure, Dad," Becca added nonchalantly. "It's the

usual between-lives agreement thing, but with more backups, and stronger commitments. It's not all right for a messiah to be killed before his time."

Ben shook his head. "You guys are making too much of between-lives agreements. They're important all right, but a lot *more* things are done without between-lives agreements. And as often as not, between-lives agreements get abrogated by the people involved anyway. This-world choices get in the way."

"Just a minute!" Lee said. "Is this something from school? Something you discussed in class?"

"No, Mom," Becca answered. "It just follows from the Michael teaching, the books. Even our disagreeing, because Dad's right, but so am I. And so is Raquel. There are lots of possibilities, and this just isn't a very predictable world."

The exchange shook Lee, enough that she totally overlooked Becca's improbable maturity. She'd known her husband and daughters had strange ideas, but this? She waited for the girls to leave the table, then led Ben into the kitchen, closing the door behind them. They sat down at the dinette table.

"Ben, I— It spooks me that you—the girls and you—have such strange ideas. I mean, 'between-lives agreements'? And some 'Tao' protects Ngunda from assassins?"

"Those ideas aren't so strange, hon. You've been exposed to them all your life, just differently phrased. You've heard 'it was meant to be'; or 'a match made in heaven.'" He gestured the quotation marks. "That sort of thing. They're just oblique ways of talking about between-lives agreements. And if we call the Tao 'God,' then Christians have believed for two thousand years that the Tao can protect people. The amount of time spent praying, the tons of candles burned . . ."

"All right. I admit that. But it makes no sense!"

"Lots of things don't, sweetheart. Your parents said it made no sense for you to marry me. Your mother told me flat out that you should have stuck it out with Mark—whose dad, she pointed out, is a multimillionaire." He paused. "To her that was the last word, the decisive factor. It made perfect sense."

Lee took a quavering breath. Mark the Asshole. Comparing him with Ben was ludicrous. What would the girls be like if she hadn't left him?

"And Lor Lu—what he said about the man who was shot and the man who shot him . . . How does he know those things? Or was he speculating from the evidence?"

"You'd have to ask him about that."

She didn't say anything more for half a minute, remembering what Dove had told her about *bodhisatvas.* "Ben," she said quietly, "talk to me more about Millennium's beliefs. Between-life agreements and *bodhisatvas*—things like that. Maybe I'd feel better about them if I knew more."

"Sure, sweetheart," he said quietly, and began.

At the end of her hour with the computer, Raquel came into the living room. "Your turn," she said to her sister, then gesturing toward the kitchen, lowered her voice. "Are they still talking in there?"

Becca closed her book. "Yep."

"What about?"

"Dad's making Mom feel better. About what we

talked about at dinner: between-life agreements and stuff like that."

"Did you eavesdrop?"

"Of course not."

"How do you know then?"

"I know Mom, and I know Dad. She's coming along all right." Becca paused. "You know what? If the judge makes us go live with Mark, you and I should make his life hell. And his wife's, if she's like him. He'll be glad to send us back here."

Raquel's eyes widened. "Do you think he will? The judge? Make us live with Mark?"

Becca grinned. "It might be kind of fun. I mean, we'd run rings around him, he's so fixated and stupid. I remember him better than you do. You were barely four. But no, we won't have to. I feel sure of it."

PART THREE

THE
MANIFESTATIONS

60
Evening Meeting

LEE WAS SCHEDULED for a trip to Helsinki, with Mike Schuster of Legal and Jim Pendleton of Properties. There they'd meet with Finnish supporters interested in establishing a Helsinki center. From Finland they'd fly to Istanbul, to examine a proposal by the Turkish mental health movement for the first Millennium center in Islam.

Unrelated to the trip, a meeting set up on short notice was to be held in the admin building on the evening before she left. She knew about it, but attendance was not required, so she decided to stay home, have a brandy and go early to bed. At dawn, Bar Stool would fly Schuster, Pendleton and herself to Pueblo, to catch the 7:05 commuter flight to Denver International.

✧   ✧   ✧

By Millennium standards, the tall west wall of the third-floor conference room was an extravagance, a floor-to-ceiling plate of thermal TuffGlass. It had withstood the blast of the Ninja Junior only 250 feet away on the opposite side of the building.

The drapes were opened, exposing the night sky; the conference tables had been removed, and chairs were lined out in rows. The attendees included the directors of the level one Millennium centers in North America, and the division and department heads at the Cote. About all the place could hold. And Bar Stool, whom Lor Lu had brought with him for no stated reason.

Dove stood before the window, watching them enter. Through sunglasses, as if something was wrong with his eyes. At his nod, the lights were slowly dimmed till they were out, and while they dimmed, he removed the sunglasses. Finally the room was lit solely by a slender moon. The tiny red lights of elevated camcorders glinted in the upper rear corners.

He glows in the dark, Bar Stool thought, *like he's got a colored mist of light around him.* He'd seen Dove before in the near dark, but never seen him glow.

"Good evening," Ngunda said. "I have important news to share with you. My ministry is over. I have done my part, prepared the way, and my departure is very near. Though it looks essentially the same, my body has been changing. You may be able to see its energy field now. It has been preparing itself to receive the Infinite Soul, at which point it will need to accommodate new spiritual and biological energies.

"That's why I've been so reclusive these past several

days." He laughed. "In the process I've caught and surpassed even Lor Lu, our resident *bodhisatva*, in psychic perceptiveness.

"When the Assumption occurs, I myself will vacate, and move to the astral plane. And I wanted to see you, say goodbye to you, while I am still wearing this body, this good friend of mine and yours."

His gaze took in his audience. "All of you are dear to me," he told them, "and have important roles to play after mine is over—roles you are well prepared for. The things I'll tell you here will not surprise you. You've heard or read them before, or known them intuitively. But repeating them under these circumstances will make them more powerful. As I am now more powerful."

He paused. "I do not fully know what it will be like for you, when this body is occupied by the Infinite Soul. But you will feel a potent difference. You will know it is not me. It may or may not take some getting used to, but the avatar will be the personification of love. In fact, it will have a greater impact on you than on most others."

He saw his audience clearly, despite the darkness and the tears. The tears he felt and saw were not of grief or loss, but joy, an emotion not always respected in the world of humans.

"Many people," he said, "will consciously accept the avatar for what it is. Others will first know, then reject what they know; to them, only the physical is real. They will fully accept only after a powerful and traumatic physical event, a concurrence that can hardly be explained as coincidental. For the Tao will also manifest as a major geophysical event at the time of the avatar's death, or immediately afterward.

"For this body standing before you *will* die. It will be murdered, and the manner of its death will make the reality more dramatic, more compelling."

Ngunda chuckled. "When I've been asked if I am the Messiah-to-be, I have neither admitted nor denied it. Perhaps the avatar itself will not, but it will be apparent. At some level, conscious or subliminal, it will be clear to even the most resistive.

"Even then a percentage will deny it, because they will be deeply frightened. And the backwash of that fear will manifest as violence. A violence mostly brief, but you will need to protect yourselves for a while. Some of you know the preparations made for that.

"And now about your task to come." Again he paused, literally feeling their attention. "After the geophysical event, new religious sects will arise. Some will hew rather closely to my teachings, and to those of other deeply inspired sources whose teachings are, or will be, basically consistent with my own. Other sects, particularly religions already established, will deviate to substantial degrees, or will preach doctrines resembling my teachings only superficially."

He paused for several seconds, to underline what would follow.

"It is important . . . important . . . important—to realize that each of those teachings will have its own validity. *Each will have its own validity for its adherents.* There are still hundreds of millions of infant and fledgling souls literally *unable* to grasp or accept what I have taught. But they will *believe.* They will believe in the visitation—the avatar, messiah, mahdi, Maitreya . . . whatever they term it. They will believe more fervently than many young souls—and create or accept doctrines quite foreign to my teaching. *And . . .*"

Once more he paused for emphasis. "*And at their level of evolution, they will benefit from those doctrines.*

"Young souls will also create their own doctrines, from which they will benefit, and these will be more or less accepted by billions. While the doctrines created and accepted by the billions of mature souls, and the many millions of old souls, will differ from my teachings in diverse but relatively minor ways. All this is inevitable, in accordance with the Tao."

Again Ngunda paused.

"Now about you. When the Infinite Soul assumes this body, you will find yourselves more powerful than ever. Spiritually powerful. You will know with a fullness of knowing rare among humans. Yet even your knowing will be limited, as mine is, and that is not a flaw, nor a thing to regret, for it will be more than enough. You will retain your humanity, yet excel in spiritual love, honesty, and wisdom. You will have the power to heal bodies, minds, and souls. In some respects, you will be more powerful than I have been.

"And your role will be to teach what I have taught— to do what you have learned to do—without creating a church or orthodoxy. *Without creating a church or orthodoxy.* Do not, do not, *do not* criticize the doctrines others will propagate. Simply teach, heal, and be spiritual examples."

Watching, listening, Bar Stool became aware that he was no longer inside his body, nor outside it as he'd occasionally been. Rather he *contained* his body, instead of the other way around. He felt himself expanding, contacting and interacting with the souls of those around him. He felt their feelings with his own, in a chorale of love. Heard Ngunda Aran's words, and beyond the words, felt the concepts flow into him, into all of them.

When Dove was done, they stood silent and motionless for an uncertain period—seconds or minutes—while the feeling, the spell, the powerful, indescribable sense of spiritual oneness faded. Never to be forgotten. Leaving not a sense of loss, but a rich residue of strength, love, and unity.

Again Ngunda chuckled. "I suggest you all go to bed now, and get a good night's sleep. What you've experienced here this evening is marvelous for souls, but it needs to be assimilated quietly." Again he chuckled. "In dreamland."

He was answered by grins and chuckles. Someone opened the door, and the attendees began to flow out into the corridor, leaving Dove behind. It was Lor Lu who stood at the door smiling and nodding to them as they departed. When Bar Stool came to him, they shook hands, then embraced. "That was quite a goodbye," Bar Stool said. He was grinning broadly.

Lor Lu laughed aloud. "Yes, it was, and it's not over yet. Go to bed. You'll have dreams like none you've ever had before."

61
Night Dreams

LEE POPPED OUT OF SLEEP and sat up in bed. She'd been dreaming—a dream that had both thrilled and frightened her, then slipped away at the moment of wakening. Briefly she tried to get it back, examine it, but it was gone, like air squeezed in a fist.

She looked around. Ben was not in bed, and it was still dark. The clock read 01:03. Sitting up, she swung her feet out, and with them located her slippers. She found Ben in the kitchen; he'd turned on the beverage machine. He grinned at her, a bright-eyed grin, but her attention hadn't regained focus.

"You're up early," he said.

"So are you."

He laughed. "Yep." Placing his cup beneath the

decaf spout, he pressed the button. The black liquid flowed till he took his finger away.

"What got you up?" Lee asked.

"I woke up and decided I was done sleeping for a while. How about you?"

"I—" She shrugged. "A dream woke me. I don't remember what it was about."

His grin widened. "How did it feel? The dream."

She looked puzzled. "It was—a dream." She gestured toward the decaf he held. "Do you plan to stay up?"

"Might as well. I'm wide awake. I'll read for an hour and see what happens."

Lee frowned. Ordinarily Ben slept like a baby until the alarm woke him. "I'm going back to bed before I get any more awake than I am," she said.

He put down his cup, took her shoulders in his hands, and softly kissed her. "Go do it. I'll be fine."

As she left the kitchen, she heard what could only be the girls' slippers. What in the world were they doing up? She felt a brief impulse to check, but shuffled back to bed instead, hoping to fall quickly asleep again.

She did. She had more dreaming to do.

The girls had started for the kitchen, then heard their parents talking, and stopped in the hall. When the voices stopped, they hurried back into their room and to bed, in case their mother looked in on them.

Several minutes later they got up again, and went to the kitchen. They found their stepfather drinking decaf, and reading. He looked at them and grinned. "Dreams?" he asked.

Becca nodded. "I'll bet yours woke you up too. What did you dream?"

Ben looked at them. He was still grinning. "You tell me," he suggested.

"Dove went to the astral plane tonight, didn't he?" Raquel piped.

Ben put a finger to his lips. "Ssh! We don't want mom to hear. She'd be upset. But yes, I think he did. I think he was telling us all goodbye, this time from the astral plane."

"Then the Infinite Soul is being Dove now. Right, Dad?" Becca asked.

"I expect so."

"What do we call him?" Raquel asked. "Still Dove?"

"I would think so, yes."

"Can we have some hot chocolate?"

"That sounds like a good idea. You two and I have something to talk about."

The girls got their thermal mugs from their hooks and drew hot chocolates. "We already know not to tell Mom," Becca said.

"Right. You realize we're not the easiest people for her to live with these days."

"Easier than Mark," Raquel sniffed. "He liked to make Mom feel like dog-doo. Even I remember that."

"I used to want her to hit him with something," Becca put in. "A baseball bat."

Ben was impressed. Ordinarily Becca was calm and even-tempered. "So we're not going to mention any of this at home," he said. "Okay?"

"Of course we won't," Raquel answered.

"She's going to find out anyway," Becca pointed out.

"Sooner or later. But let's not have it be here at home."

Becca cocked an eye, frowning, looking as if she was examining the statement. "It would be a lot easier for her if she'd just read some of Dove's talks. She'd have an explanation then, even if she didn't believe it."

"I've suggested that to her. She says she doesn't have time. 'Maybe later.'" He set quotation marks with his fingers.

Becca shrugged. "I'm glad I didn't grow up with her parents. It had to be tough, being a late-cycle mature warrior, growing up with a fledgling warrior mother and a fledgling priest father. No common reality, just orders and lectures! I suppose it was something she had to experience for the lessons, but she's my mom, and I hate to see her go through stuff like she does."

Raquel went to Ben and hugged his neck. "I'm glad she's married to you now," she said.

"Why, thank you, Miss Shoreff. I'm glad too."

Legally the girls still wore Mark's name, but they'd have been offended if he'd used it. They were even registered in school as Shoreff.

The three of them finished their drinks quietly, as if thinking. Even Raquel said nothing more till they were nearly done. It was Ben who broke the quiet.

"It'd be a good idea for you two to go back to bed now. There's school tomorrow."

"Are you going back to bed too?" Raquel asked.

"Yes, I think I will. I thought I'd sit up and read awhile, but I guess what I really wanted was to talk to you guys."

They all went back to bed then, and before long even the girls were asleep.

62
Phone Calls

EACH MORNING, Florence Metzger read the news clippings excerpted for her by her computer. She'd given it a number of key topics, which it used to glean articles from a large array of newsfax, papers, telecasts and zines. One of those topics was Millennium, another Ngunda. Anyone who'd taken the interest of the public so strongly, and drew such crowds worldwide—who'd created such a following and such fierce hostility, from Kabul to Dubuque, from Melbourne to Reykjavik—anyone like that was important. And if some nut case succeeded in killing him . . .

The man preached hope, a hope tied in with

self-responsibility. His murder would be a public wound, and the public was already overwounded.

Besides, David was involved with him, admired him, and almost surely helped finance him. The *Post* said he did, listing him with more than a dozen others, all of them sponsors of Hand and Ladder and Bailout, as well.

Now, according to the clippings, Ngunda was going to tour the South and Midwest in a bus, of all things. She couldn't imagine anything that would present more security problems for him, or more opportunities for the people who wanted him dead.

Reaching, she tapped out David's confidential access. It took a minute, and twice her quick fingers had to tap out further instructions; he'd augmented his firewall since the Black Plague.

Finally she had him. When he saw who it was, he activated his own camera, so she could see too.

"Good morning, Madam President. It's nice to see your worried face this morning. Can I do something for you?"

"You can advise me. I see by the fax that Ngunda has a bus tour scheduled for the Midwest and South—which scares the bejasus out of me. I don't want to see him killed; it would be bad for the country at a time like this. But I have the impression from the media that he pays little attention to risks, so I intend to dog his tour with federal marshals, and try to get him through it alive. And it will help if he's cooperative. Can you influence him?"

David Hunter looked at her long and thoughtfully. "No, Florence, I can't. I could try, but it would be fruitless. He has to follow his own advisor."

"I didn't know he had one."

"He doesn't, in this world."

She stared, rattled for the moment. This *was* David, after all.

"I hope I didn't turn you off with that. I'd hate to think you wouldn't phone me anymore. But I wasn't joking; his advisor really isn't of this world. And Flo, more than that: messiahs have to die. And they pick their time, or try to."

She still stared. *Messiahs?* After a moment she made the mental adjustment, and shifted gears. "You're asking me to let be? Let whatever happens happen?"

"That's what I'm asking."

She exhaled audibly. "That's hard advice to take, David."

"It's hard to give."

She looked blankly past the camera at an undefined space in the upper left area of the room, then pulled her gaze back to his. "If you say so, that's what I'll do."

He nodded. "Thank you, Flo. Is there anything else I can do for you?"

"One thing. Laurel's been dead for two years now. And as for me, I don't intend to run again. Remember what you asked me, that evening thirty-three years ago?"

He smiled. "Yes, I do."

"Ask me again sometime. I'm not a good-looking female athlete anymore, but give it a thought."

His mouth curved up just a bit. "I'll stay in touch."

The ringing jerked Colonel Robert Gorman, U.S. Army, retired, out of his book. The caller ID meant nothing to him. He poked a button. "Gorman," he answered.

"Robert, this is Millard. I—wondered if you'd care for a game of chess this afternoon."

The colonel almost said he didn't know Forsberg played, but thought better of it. Chess was not what the man had in mind.

"Huh! It's too rainy for golf. Yeah, I'll beat you a game or two of chess. At my place. You know how to find it?"

"I have your address."

"Good. When'll you get here?"

"In an hour."

"Okay. That'll give me time to run the girls out."

There was silence.

"Only kidding, Millard. I never bring girls in. I meet them somewhere else."

Forsberg decided to ignore it. "Have you read the *Post* today?" he asked.

"Always. I can't start the day without the funnies."

"In an hour, Robert. And thank you." The ex-FBI director hung up.

Thank you? That was out of character. Gorman cradled his phone, chuckling. Reading the funnies would be as unreal to Millard Forsberg as having girls in for sex. He had no doubt what Forsberg wanted to talk about. They'd talked ten days earlier, after Rod Beauchamp's funeral. Forsberg had decided the president had had Beauchamp murdered. Gorman was no fan of Florence Metzger, but he still wasn't buying that theory, and had said so, plainly.

Forsberg hadn't argued, or even acted resentful.

Instead he'd shifted the conversation to what was really bothering him. On his Northwest tour, in June, Ngunda Aran had done group healings. Small groups, to be sure, but talk of his being the Messiah had flourished like mushrooms on horseshit. The guru himself, though, had dropped out of the news for a while. Then, this morning, the papers had announced a big Dove bus tour in the Midwest and South, another Mississippi Valley tour, but different. He'd do group healings all along the way. It was to start at La Crosse, Wisconsin, and "wander" its way south to New Orleans. The route and stops would be announced on radio and television a day in advance.

The ex-director had become agitated just talking about it. Gorman had no doubt that Forsberg wanted Ngunda assassinated during the tour, and was looking for help. He already, of course, knew people in the FBI who were safe to approach. Now what he no doubt wanted was a line on some military people he could rope in on it.

What Gorman didn't know was whether he himself was willing to be involved even peripherally. If they got caught, their asses would be in the hottest part of the fire. But on the other hand, if people in government—other people—could be shown to have killed Ngunda, it might well spark an explosion serious enough to result in a military takeover. Not likely, but possibly, and a consummation devoutly to be wished.

63
Preparations

DOVE NO LONGER appeared in the dining room at noon. Lee, when she returned from Istanbul, scarcely noticed, and the rest of staff took it for granted. She'd heard nothing of Ngunda's farewell. She almost never took coffee breaks—had her coffee in her office—and worked alone most of the time.

On the day after Ngunda's goodbye, Lor Lu had video cubes of it distributed to all staff families. Ben and the girls had watched together, as most families had. Lee had been in Helsinki by then, or somewhere over Europe, and when she'd returned from Istanbul, people's attentions were on other matters.

And Ben and the girls deliberately avoided mentioning it.

Thus the transformation of Dove never really came

up in her presence. She had, of course, been exposed to comments a few times, but hadn't paid enough attention to wonder what they meant.

Lor Lu had told Ben that Dove wanted her along on the bus tour. And that he himself preferred she not know yet, either about Dove, or about going on tour. It would distract her from what she was doing. He would, he said, wait till shortly before the tour. He trusted her operating style and attitude to protect her from learning accidently.

To Ben they seemed like odd decisions, but he trusted them.

It was twelve days after the farewell meeting when Lor Lu stopped at her office with a surprise. "Lee," he said, "Dove has listed you to be on the bus tour."

"*Me?*"

"Right."

The order stunned her. For it was an order, not an invitation or suggestion; that was clear from Lor Lu's wording and tone of voice. And the tour group would leave in only five days. "Why me?" she asked.

"Why don't you ask Dove?"

"I— But . . ." She frowned. "What about the girls?"

"They'll be in school. And Ben will be here; they'll be fine."

"How long will it be?"

"It's planned for three weeks, but it may be shorter."

She sat as if dropped there, her mind blank. "You won't be able to take much," Lor Lu went on. "A large suitcase that will ride in luggage, and a small one overhead. The bus is a deluxe sleeper. The seats recline way back, and there are pillows. We'll stay in motels or hotels every third night or so, to shower and do laundry."

The word "we" brought her out of it. "You'll be there too?"

Grinning, he nodded. "I'm very good at playing by ear, dealing with things off the cuff. That will be important on so unstructured a tour."

"I won't be the only woman, will I?"

"One of five."

For several long seconds she thought, then looked earnestly at Lor Lu. "I *really* don't want to go," she said. "I really really don't."

Beneath Lor Lu's mild, steady gaze, her eyes lowered. She thought of the extras and privileges she'd been granted: the deluxe office, and the high-powered legal help against Mark's threat to the girls.

But she still didn't want to go. The thought somehow frightened her. "It is necessary that you go," Lor Lu said abruptly, and turning, left.

She'd never seen Lor Lu abrupt before, and wondered if he was angry at her. Giving him time to reach his office, she dialed him. He wasn't back yet, so she got herself a cup of tea, added sugar and milk, then tried again.

"This is Lor Lu." He sounded as cheerful as ever.

"Lor Lu, it's Lee." Embarrassingly she giggled.

For an instant on the screen his eyebrows rose, then he grinned. "The alliteration," he said.

She nodded, serious again, wondering what had come over her. "I called to tell you I'll go on the tour. I mean—of course I will."

The grin changed to a warm smile. "Good. See Norman for a briefing sheet and instructions. Do it now. Put aside whatever you've been working on, even if you're in the middle of a sentence. From this point until told otherwise, you are assigned solely to tour duties."

She watched the picture click off the screen. Four days. Could she learn her tour duties in four days? And what in the world could they be?

It turned out she had no readily definable tour duties. She would, Norman told her, be Lor Lu's assistant, expediting various tasks as they came up, and "soaking up the experience."

Anger swelled. She recognized flunky work when her nose was pushed in it. "For that he pulled me off my regular job?"

"My impression is that Dove and Lor Lu have a future role in mind for you, and this will help prepare you for it."

"A future role? What future role?" The words spilled out rapidly. "I need to know more about this! Why are other people told these things, but not me?"

"I don't know what role, Lee," Norman said patiently. "I simply put two and two together. Ask Lor Lu. He'll know."

She left glowering, the slim packet of briefing sheets in an envelope, along with general instructions. *Ask Lor Lu! Huh! He'd say ask Dove.*

By the time she'd finished reading the briefing and policy, she'd semi-cooled down. Calling Lor Lu, she asked what to do next. "I've finished reading the stuff

Norman gave me, and it's not even noon. Should I go back to what I was working on before? Or what?"

"I've pulled Ben off Accounting for now," Lor Lu answered. "He'll work with you on what comes next." He paused. "I'm afraid you're ill-prepared for this, but don't worry, you'll do just fine."

He disconnected then. *Ill prepared?* she thought angrily. *Don't worry? And Ben will work with me? He's an accountant, for god's sake! What in hell is going on? Why is this happening to me?*

At noon the family met in the dining hall, as usual. But Lee insisted that she and Ben eat at home, leaving the girls at the dining hall without supervision. She was upset, angry, feared she'd lose control, and didn't want to make a spectacle of herself. Ben of course was agreeable, and they walked home through a lovely summer day at 7,800 feet elevation, the sun bright, the sky a vaulting, vivid, high-country blue, the temperature 74 degrees. Behind them, as they walked, the high peaks of the Sangre de Cristo, twenty miles west, formed an array of dark stone and bright snowfields. She noticed none of it.

"What are you supposed to work with me on?" she demanded. "You're not in Tours. Lucky you! And what's so goddamned ill-prepared about me? Even I know I'm ill-prepared! That's the one goddamned thing I do know! I didn't need some goddamned Asian 'holy man extraordinary' to tell me that! If he knew you were in the goddamned basement doing the goddamned laundry, why didn't he know how goddamned ill-prepared I am?"

Ben walked faster. "I'm going to put a Mexican

pizza in the oven," he said. "You can help me eat it, or you can fix something else. You don't have a clue how ill-prepared you are, and it's mainly my fault. Now shut up before you piss me off!"

His response stunned her, jolted her out of her tizzy. Ben had *never* spoken to her like that before. She said nothing more all the way home. There he opened the door, held it for her, and when he'd closed it behind them, grabbed her and kissed her, hard. Then he held her at arms length, looking at her seriously.

"I love you, Lee," he said, "even though I got exasperated just now. I love you dearly. And the girls do, too, so we've been trying to spare you upsets and confusion."

Her mouth was slightly open in surprise, and he let her go, striding into the kitchen while she stood watching. She heard the oven controls beeping; the freezer lid open, then close; heard the oven door. Shaking herself free of astonishment, she followed Ben into the kitchen and went to the beverage station.

"Seven-Up?" she asked. "Pepsi?"

He turned. His grin was back. "How about rue? Some bitter rue would be about right." Laughing he added, "This time I'll try root beer. The girls prefer it with pizza. I ought to give it a try."

The words echoed in Lee's mind: *"The girls prefer it. . . . I ought to give it a try."* There was a double meaning there, deliberate or otherwise.

He turned the breakfast nook TV on, to tennis, making it easier not to talk until they'd finished the pizza. When it was gone, they looked at each other. "Let's go in the living room," Ben said, and turned off the game. "I'm going to put a cube in the player, the first step in your preparation. We'll watch it together. It's a talk Dove gave in Sacramento. Then we'll watch one he gave in Denver, and another in Boston." He paused long. "And then an especially important one he gave here two weeks ago. After that we'll talk, but until then we'll just listen. By that time you'll understand what the tour's about. And what Dove's about. I don't know what you'll think of them, but at least you'll know."

She watched without arguing. The first three videos Lee found interesting enough, even thought-provoking, and of course informative on Dove's theology, or philosophy—whatever they called it. But they were hardly compelling; not for her. Ngunda's short farewell video, on the other hand, made her skin crawl. Not with fright, but it was definitely a strange sensation. When they'd watched it through to the end, she was quietly sober.

"Any questions?" Ben asked.

"No, I don't think so."

"Fine. Anything that especially struck you?"

She shook her head. "Nothing in particular. The last one did seem—spooky. And it made me remember the dreams I had that night. I think it was the same night."

"Yeah, that was the night." Apparently, he decided, she hadn't perceived Dove's aura on video. *Interesting*.

"There's something I would like to know, though," she went on. "What this new *role* is I might have after the tour."

"I honest to God don't know," Ben said. "Apparently Lor Lu wants to tell you himself. Lor Lu or Dove."

"And I have three more days after today for preparations. What will they be? More videos?"

"No, sweetheart. We'll watch another after supper." He paused. "And tomorrow you'll begin Life Healing. A start."

She didn't argue, just looked very very sober.

On her way to the scheduling director next morning, she felt—not bad, actually. Not eager by any means, but not fearful. Resigned, strangely relieved—and remarkably enough, curious.

They were ready for her; she'd already been fitted into the schedule. Her facilitator was female, her face familiar from the dining hall—young, pleasant-seeming . . . not sinister-looking at all. The woman got to her feet. "Good morning, Lee," she said, "my name is Jenny Buckels. Please have a seat." She gestured at a chair in front of her small worktable.

Lee glanced around as she sat. The room was pleasant enough. There were framed nature photos on the walls, fresh flowers on a stand and on the facilitator's table. The flowers, she supposed, were from the greenhouse out back, like the flowers in the dining room. "I thought there'd be an aura analyzer," she said.

"Some of us read auras clearly enough without equipment. Are you comfortable?"

Read auras without equipment? My god! Lee thought. "As comfortable as I'm likely to be."

"Good." Jenny smiled. "Were you hoping for an analyzer?"

"Well, yes. I hoped I could get you to sit in front of it, and let me look. So I could see what an aura looks like."

The facilitator laughed. "You're not the first person that's told me that. We'll borrow one afterward. Good enough?"

Lee's smile was mostly politeness. "Afterward's fine."

Jenny's fingers hovered relaxedly over a keyboard. The monitor stood between them, just below Jenny's line of sight.

"Good. Have you had an adequate breakfast?"

"Yes."

"A decent night's sleep?"

"Yes I have."

"All right, we're ready then. I'll read from a list of words and phrases, and note your aural reaction to each of them. You don't need to say anything, but you may if you wish. After that you'll have a short break while I set up what comes next."

Her fingers were poised over a keyboard. "Okay," she said, "start of procedure," and began to read the list.

By noon, Lee had wept and laughed. Twice she almost fell from her chair, with a desperate grogginess that left as inexplicably as it had struck. She ate lunch with Ben and the girls, and said very little, while they made small talk. It wasn't that she was depressed or preoccupied. Spaced-out was the word.

After lunch she got three more hours of it, in two installments. Then she was offered a choice of snacks—she chose a bowl of French vanilla ice cream topped with butterscotch and chocolate—and was provided with a cot in a quiet cubicle, for a half-hour's nap. She slept almost at once.

She left cheerful, and not at all introverted. Actually it didn't seem like that big a deal. She was certainly no cultist convert, she felt sure of that. But it had been interesting and powerful, and she felt good about it. And it was, after all, only therapy. Lots of people had therapy.

She hadn't, she decided, been as ill-prepared as she'd feared. The girls had been preparing her for months: the girls and Ben—without any of them knowing it. She wondered what the next two days would be like.

You'll know, she told herself, *in forty-eight hours*.

64
Opening Day

WEARING SHAMROCK-GREEN blazers, the tour crew had taken off early in the Mescalero, to Pueblo. From there they'd left on a chartered turboprop, on a three-hour flight to LaCrosse, Wisconsin.

From the air, LaCrosse was a pleasant-seeming city built along the Mississippi, its residential areas green with trees. Their chartered bus met them at the airport, bearing neither signs nor banners, only the logo "Celebrity Tours," in large gold cursive letters on its blue and white sides. It even had separate men's and women's restrooms, and two tiny shower facilities just large enough to change clothes, stand in the spray and wield the soap. Though its new passengers didn't know it, on its last trip it had hauled a major rock group and its technical crew.

It took them to the parking lot of a large Lutheran church. Lee peered from her window. They parked at a reserved length of curb. The lot itself was crowded with people spilling onto the sidewalk, plugging the opening of an adjacent alley, standing on the concrete parking barriers along the perimeter. Television trucks stood by, with cameramen on cherry pickers. Small children and some not so small sat on grownup shoulders in order to see, perhaps someday to say they'd been there. People stood on adjacent porches; older children perched on porch and garage roofs. Faces peered from windows.

As crowds go, it was quiet. City police in white shirts and blue trousers stood about relaxed.

Dove stepped from the bus, surrounded by a golden aura that no one could miss. The crowd quieted, then began to buzz, not loudly, but differently. Dove seemed taller than usual. Wearing a short-sleeved, open-throated white shirt, dark blue slacks and the aura, he strode to the crowd's edge, a policeman beside him. Art Knowles and one of his security men followed a stride behind. Somehow an aisle opened for them, and when they'd passed through it, it closed, like the Red Sea, supposedly, for Moses.

They homed on an American flag in the center of the lot. It stood on a small, thirty-inch stand. To one side of it were gathered those to be healed—thirty or forty of them—along with a worried-looking pastor in clerical garb. Dove reached the platform, mounted it, faced them, and raised his hands, palms outward. Watching from the bus, it seemed to Lee his aura flared upward then, and when he spoke, his deep strong voice was easily heard to the street, though to those in the front row it seemed not especially loud.

"By your trust in coming here," he said, "and through the loving power of God, you . . . are . . . healed."

There was a silence that lasted two or three seconds, then a graying woman struggled from her wheelchair, raised her arms and screamed, "Praise God! Praise God!" A young man took off thick dark glasses and, laughing, threw them as far as he could, before turning and hugging the woman beside him. There were cries and sobbing embedded in a growing babble. Someone shouted, "I can breathe! I can breathe again!" People dropped to their knees, not only the healed, but numerous bystanders, praying, thanking God.

Lee stared through her window, her skin gooseflesh. She'd known and accepted that this was a healing tour, but what she saw was somehow unexpected. Beside the stand, the pastor stood with arms skyward, his mouth moving. Though Lee couldn't see it from where she sat, tears flowed down the man's cheeks.

With no further words, Dove stepped glowing from the platform, the aisle opened again, and with right hand raised in blessing, he started back to the bus. The brief babble had faded, softened by awe. The most conspicuous emotional reaction was tears. As he passed, hands reached out, touching his aura. Several people fainted. Then he climbed aboard the bus. Bar Stool revved up the diesel, the police moved some people out of the way, and it left.

It was as simple and brief as that. As the bus pulled from the curb, Lee could hear people in the crowd begin to sing "A Mighty Fortress," led perhaps by the pastor.

❖   ❖   ❖

The TV cameras had recorded it all, from the ground as well as from the cherry pickers. Even after the bus had left, the production managers sat intent at their monitors. Reporters and camera operators began to work their way through the crowd, to talk with the healed, if indeed that's what they were.

The tour crew had watched and listened from the bus, partly through the windows, partly on television. They hadn't fully known what to expect, and when it was over, it took awhile for the experience to sink in. The primary reaction was sobriety, rather than exultation.

Dove sat in back, calm and serene, looking almost as if he were alone.

By arrangement with the bus company, Bar Stool was their actual driver. The company's driver served as his relief. Dove had specifically wanted Bar Stool for the tour, and Personnel had hired a temporary replacement to fly and maintain the Mescalero. A long-time friend of Bar Stool's, he'd flown a chopper for Special Ops in Afghanistan, and afterward for a westwide charter service on spray jobs, rescues, forest fire suppression and the like.

The bus rolled out of LaCrosse heading south, tailed by TV trucks. There was no interstate; they took a state highway. Duke Cochran was aboard, again representing *American Scene*. He did not approach Lee, nor she him.

Twice the bus stopped, once at a truckstop for lunch, and once for a prearranged healing in a small park at the edge of Prairie du Chien. A couple of dozen sick and disabled waited there, along with three or four hundred spectators. Lee wondered how many of the healed would remain healed in the morning. Twenty percent? A hundred percent? She could almost believe a hundred, but twenty would be remarkable enough.

From Prairie du Chien, the bus crossed the Mississippi into Iowa. Even driving south from LaCrosse there'd been clusters of people here and there along the road, waving or just watching. Lee didn't pay a lot of attention to the people or the scenery—the broad Mississippi, high bluffs, country towns. She had other things on her mind. When she'd re-viewed the brief "farewell" video, after her abbreviated Life Healing, she'd wondered if Dove's aura was produced by some electrical device or by Dove himself. It had been deep blue then, with sparkles of gold and rose. Now it was golden, as in pictures she'd seen of Christ, and she did not doubt it was genuine.

The tour itinerary, flexible though it was, had been widely publicized by the media. At the front of the bus, above the aisle, a TV faced rearward. The suppertime TV newscasts showed numerous shots of the healings in LaCrosse, shots of the crowd, and brief interviews with some of the healed. One psychiatrist interviewed on CNN's *The World Today* pooh-poohed them as "hysterical healing," which he termed a mental disorder. To the delight of millions, anchor Michael Sandow's response left the doctor confused and upset. "If you were to treat some of the healed for their mental disorder," Sandow said, "and they became ill or crippled again, would you feel you'd helped them?" When the doctor failed to answer, he asked, "Well then, would it give you a feeling of satisfaction?"

At that the poor man stood abruptly, pulled off the microphone clipped to his shirt front, and stalked, stiff and red-faced, from the set.

Brief interviews with bystanders found them as impressed with Dove as with the healings. None of the cameras failed to show his vivid golden aura, and none of the interviewed failed to comment on it.

The crowd at Dubuque, Iowa, that evening jammed the intramural soccer field at the university. Parked cars and pickups almost plugged the streets. It was several times the size of the LaCrosse crowd; people had seen or heard about what had happened there. The bus pulled into a laundromat driveway a block and a half away; that was as close as it could get. Dove, with only Knowles, one other security man and two officers, walked through the crowd. It was louder than the LaCrosse crowd—some people were even boisterous—but an aisle opened. Again the rest of the tour group stayed on the bus.

And again before he left, people had gotten out of wheelchairs and off of pallets, had thrown away crutches, walkers, white canes . . .

The number of people healed there was not explicitly known—estimates varied from a hundred to two hundred and fifty; the crowd was estimated at from three to five thousand. In ten minutes, Dove, Knowles, and the others were back on board, but it took twenty minutes for the bus to work its way to the highway. While it rolled southward on US 61, Lor Lu

spent considerable time on the phone with city and
county authorities, particularly regarding healing sites
convenient to highways, where crowds were less
likely to cause traffic jams. He also called network
and local television stations, giving them information
and suggestions for the public, to reduce crowd
problems.

So far the tour crew had had little to do. Lee was
the exception. She rode next to Lor Lu, in the seat
across from the driver. She'd finally been thoroughly
briefed back at the Cote, Lor Lu reviewing with
her the things she'd be doing on her communications laptop. It was loaded with a huge number of
broadcast stations, shopping mall managers, motels,
restaurants . . . and every law enforcement agency, large
and small, in fourteen states. Rather quickly, she was
handling the more routine logistical and liaison work.
Lor Lu handled major decisions, overall integration,
and emergencies.

After Dubuque, instead of stopping at a motel
or rest area, they drove through the early evening
to Maquoketa. There a substantial crowd waited in
a theater parking lot, and several dozen more were
healed. Then the 69-year-old Bar Stool turned east
toward the Mississippi again, and drove to another
theater parking lot at Clinton, Iowa. There perhaps
a thousand waited to see Dove, with a hundred to
be healed. When the bus left Clinton, Bar Stool's
backup was at the wheel.

Bar Stool and Lee weren't the only non-Tours staff
pulled from their jobs for the tour. There were also
seven case facilitators, selected and prepared by Dove

as healers. One of them was Jenny Buckels. Beginning at Dubuque, these support healers had moved around the back fringes of the crowds, healing such things as astigmatism, bad backs, arthritic fingers—whatever presented itself. An enterprising citizen with a camcorder had followed one of these secondary healers as she did her work, and when the bus left, interviewed several of the healed. One of them claimed that before his healing, he'd been unable to bend far enough to touch his knees. Now, beaming, he demonstrated that by bending his knees just a little, he could touch his feet. "My wife," he said, "won't have to put my socks and shoes on for me anymore."

He hadn't joined what he referred to as "the sick and wounded" up front, because "that's for people in worse trouble than me. All I had was some pain and inconvenience. With no more wrong than that, I didn't want to trouble the messiah."

The amateur video cubeage was sold to Davenport's NBC affiliate, and broadcast nationwide on the news. It showed the backup healer's aura, which photographed as mostly pale blue mistiness, with areas of pink and green.

Meanwhile the bus had driven on to Davenport, where a midnight healing was held in a mall parking lot. Most of the sick and disabled there hadn't seen the Clinton healings; they'd already been gathering hopefully for their own. But they'd seen the LaCrosse and Dubuque healings.

It was the largest crowd yet, despite the late hour. Police had cleared a place near the entrance for those who'd come for healing, but the crowd was so large that many onlookers could hardly hope even to glimpse Dove.

He handled this by having the ill and disabled brought to the curb. Then, upright and calm, he levitated, *floated* a dozen feet above the crowd, and healed from there, appearing in the darkness like a great golden torch. The levitation affected the crowd like nothing else. There was a sound like a great "ah-h-h," punctuated by scattered screams.

Art Knowles winced at such exposure. It occurred to him that Dove might actually be safer than anyone else there, but he was taking nothing for granted.

During the healing process, cameramen in their cherry pickers recorded visible auras scattered throughout the crowd, like soft round bunsen burner flames, as if of people caught up spiritually by the experience. This was the most dramatic stop yet; joy made a bedlam of it.

When it was over, the bus moved on to the fenced and guarded sheriff's department parking lot near the courthouse. There it stayed the rest of the night, curtains drawn, most of its travelers sleeping.

Despite the hour, Lor Lu sat using his laptop and its phone, arranging things ahead. Lee sat next to him, her tasks somewhat similar, working from a list he'd printed out for her. When she was done, she wanted to talk to someone, but Lor Lu was still busy, and almost everyone else asleep. Each person had a double seat to themselves. The auras visible earlier had faded from her perception, except for Dove's and Lor Lu's, which still were strong. Dove sat upright, in back again, smiling, glowing, calm—engaged in what contemplations, Lee couldn't imagine. She doubted that even Lor Lu knew.

Duke Cochran also sat awake, writing on his laptop, and Lee went over to him. "Is it all right to interrupt?" she murmured. "I need someone to talk to."

Duke grinned. His eyes were bright, he seemed pumped, but his voice was a murmur. "Sure," he said. She sat down by him. "What did you think of it?" he asked.

Her voice was as quiet as his. "It was incredible. Inspiring! It's hard to believe this is really happening, and that I'm part of it. Here, in our time."

"And the levitation," he said. "That killed any doubt."

"Did you have any?" Lee asked. "Before that?"

Duke nodded. "Oh, yes. Even if he wasn't an avatar, it seemed to me that some people would truly be healed, with all that energy out there. But now . . ." His expression turned thoughtful. "Maybe Dove turns on some latent energy that all of us have. He does say they heal themselves."

Wearing his Tours blazer, Duke had climbed on top of the bus to watch, and had seen the auras manifesting among the crowd. Some reading he'd done stated that an aura was simply an energy field, and that everyone had one, all the time. But apparently they could intensify. He supposed they'd been energized by Dove's presence.

"I'd assumed you'd reject even the possibility," Lee said. "I know I did, till recently."

"Me too." He grinned again. "Even after I had personal proof that Life Healing is for real, whatever *real* is."

"Personal proof?"

"I tried it out. I wouldn't say it qualifies as a miracle, but it definitely demonstrates effective therapy." He laughed softly. "It took me totally by surprise. Got rid of old regrets, fears, resentments . . ." Again he laughed softly. "And fixations. Things like that." Then added, "When did you do it?"

"Just before we left. I'd been resisting it for months."

A minute later, Lee excused herself. Duke watched her move forward up the aisle. He still found her sexually attractive, but no longer lusted for her. Then he returned his attention to his laptop, and the article he was writing: "Inside the Healing Tour." It could serve later as a chapter in the book he intended.

Lee walked past her "sleeping seat," and sat down again beside Lor Lu. She had a question for him, and intended to watch for a gap in his activities. He was talking into his phone, but all she heard was a murmur, as if he had a "cone of silence," like Maxwell Smart in the farcical secret agent series she'd enjoyed as reruns as a child.

It was Lor Lu who spoke first. "You have something to say," he said.

"Yes," she answered quietly. "Dove levitated. He really is the Infinite Soul, isn't he."

It was a statement, not a question.

"The Infinite Soul incarnate. Yes."

"I could never have imagined the things I've seen," she said, then paused. "Auras! I didn't even believe there were such things. Then the night before we left the Cote, Ben and I watched the 'goodbye cube' again. It showed Dove with a sort of turquoise aura, flecked with rose and gold." She chuckled. "The first time I watched it, I didn't even notice, as if it wasn't there. But now . . ." She gestured toward Dove. "Now it's pure gold. What makes the difference?"

His smile softened. "Part of the aura shown on the cube was that of a human soul, Ngunda Aran. Another layer was the body's aura, and still another was the personality. But now there is simply the aura of the Infinite Soul, and of the body fully adapted to it."

Lee stared at the Hmong for a long moment, thinking how young he looked and how—ageless he sounded. Nodding, she got up and started toward the rear. A glance showed Dove still upright, unmoving and seemingly unchanged. For just a moment their eyes met, and a wave of unexpected *rapture!* flowed through her, leaving an afterglow of exaltation, expansion. She reached her seat beaming, took her pillow from the overheard compartment, let the seat back all the way and reclined on it. Almost at once she slept, without thought, without question.

65
The Tour Unfolds

LEE AWOKE TO LOR LU'S hand on her arm. "You may want to freshen up," he told her, then walked forward to his "office."

The bus was moving down a city street. She looked at her watch—7:08 A.M., Central Time. The town, she supposed, was still Davenport. Getting up, she started back toward the women's restroom. Dove sat upright in the back seat, as before, and she wondered if he'd slept at all—or moved at all—during the night.

She washed, tidied her hair and fixed her face, skipping the shower. The water pressure was too weak to enjoy, and the space a bit tight for dressing and undressing. She might, she thought, try it out when she had more time and greater need.

At an interstate exchange they pulled into a

restaurant parking lot. It wasn't a publicized stop, and there was no crowd. The phoned-in orders were waiting—mostly assorted omelets, ranging from spicy Mexican to American cheese, with buttered toast and half-pint cartons of juices and milk. The bus had its own hot drink and cold drink stations.

The tour crew's service team went in to pick them up, and Lee went with them to handle the charges. The bus stayed in the lot for nearly thirty minutes, long enough for the TV crews to get their orders, then they all pulled out together. By that time a number of people had come outside to stare at the bus.

Their first healing stop of the day was at a mall parking lot on the fringe of Galesburg, Illinois. West of Galesburg they left the four-lane, and by noon had made scheduled stops at a truckstop outside Monmouth, the village park in Roseville, and outside the high school at Macomb. Here and there along the way, people stood at country crossroads, or on the roadside in front of farmhouses. Once, one of the watchers sat waiting in a wheelchair. On another occasion, one watched propped on wrist crutches. In each instance, Bar Stool had stopped. Dove had gotten out, walked back and healed the person. The network cameras captured all of it.

During that day and the next three, they wove their intermittent way generally southward. They meandered as far west as Hannibal and Bowling Green, in Missouri, then eastward again, headed for Springfield, Illinois, then southward, with what to Lee was a blur of stops. Meanwhile they'd acquired an ever-lengthening train of companion vehicles that began with the TV trucks. And of course there were the highway patrol escorts, their identity changing with the jurisdiction. More and more other vehicles attached themselves: cars, vans, pickups, retired school buses, a truck with a canvas cover . . . vehicles filled with passengers who wanted to "be in the presence," as one had said to a TV news anchor.

Now and then, one of the tour group would sit next to Dove and they'd talk, briefly and quietly. Mostly, though, he sat alone, erect but relaxed, smiling. Lor Lu told Lee that what Dove was doing was restful; physically equivalent to meditation. Bodies were subject to physical limitations, he said, even when the occupant was the Infinite Soul, and the energy flows involved in mass healings and levitation were hard on Dove's body.

Lee herself felt remarkably good—strong—despite not having slept in a proper bed. As Lor Lu's assistant, she dealt with a lot of details, and was pleased at how well things worked out. She depended almost entirely on people she didn't know, and would never meet except on the Web or the phone, asking them to improvise. Her past experience had been that in situations requiring constructive improvisation, people were likely to screw up—bog down or self-destruct or drop the ball. You had to work out the details for them, break things down into easy steps. Here there was limited opportunity for that, but mostly things went well anyway.

Shortly after leaving McLeansboro, Illinois, the tour crew was eating carry-out lunches while watching CNN's *NewsStand*. Clips of the healings at East St.

Louis and Mt. Vernon were shown. At both, Dove had healed while levitating. After the clips, a physicist from Penn State University was questioned about Dove's levitations. "They're faked," he said, "the result of technology, not holiness. During the last year," he went on, "two different research projects have been closing in on a practical anti-gravity device. And one of Millennium's supporters is Harlan Springer, president and CEO of Leading Echelon, one of the world's major high-tech development firms."

"How do you explain the auras?"

The professor snorted. "That one's easy. They're wearing generators."

"Can these generators be bought in stores or on the Web?"

The professor paused, looking confused. "On the Web, possibly," he said at last. "You can find anything on the Web. Or Springer could provide them."

On the Web possibly? He's not a very good liar, Lee told herself. *Now if he'd said Motorola's model 6X-B at $84.95—something like that—he might have been believable.*

"What about the people in the crowd who show auras?"

"Shills. People Millennium inserted in the crowd to add to the effect."

It surprised Lee that she didn't feel angry at the professor. The realization was spooky. Looking around, the most evident emotion on the bus seemed to be amusement. Dove himself was chuckling.

She had slack time now and then, and spent some of it reading a book of Ngunda's dialogues. A month earlier she couldn't have imagined doing something like that.

One of the service team was Jenny Buckels, who'd guided Lee through Life Healing. The procedure had involved communication at a level Lee had never consciously experienced before; thus Lee had bonded to her strongly. Riding through the rural Illinois night, after the long second day, Lee sat down beside Jenny, and they talked quietly for half an hour. As her facilitator, Jenny had learned a lot about Lee's past. Now Lee began to learn something of Jenny's. She left impressed; this was a strong young woman.

The truck stop was an oasis of lights in the night blackness of rural Posey County, Indiana. A large Rent & Haul truck was parked in the dimness near a back corner of the lot. The only other vehicles within two hundred feet were semis parked for sleeping. A delivery van drew up only yards from the rental truck, behind it and to one side. It bore the name of a major restaurant supply company. The driver of the van got out, followed by two others.

Matthew Shaughnessy got out from the cab of the rental truck and met them in the darkness, peering closely at the driver's face, making sure of his identity. "Any problems?" Shaughnessy asked. "Anything suspicious?"

"No. Surprised?"

Shaughnessy didn't answer. Instead he said, "You've heard Unit Three's report."

The man nodded. His van had a security band radio with descrambler. His was a highly demanding and unforgiving business, with clients that included

African warlords, foreign drug lords. . . . "The local yokels aren't on top of it at all," he said. "Sounds like a gimme."

Shaughnessy's lips moved a couple of times before anything came out, as if he was talking to himself. "Any of your people coming down with second thoughts?"

"You've got to be kidding."

"I'm following protocol. Are there?"

The man half-laughed his answer. "Hell no!"

"Let's get on with it then," Shaughnessy said. He stepped to his truck's rear door, unlocked it, raised the latch and lifted. The door slid up almost soundlessly on its tracks. There were men inside. They handed out two large canvas bags. Two of the van driver's men took them, and the driver signed Shaughnessy's receipt book. When the transfer was complete, he offered his hand to Shaughnessy. "Wish us luck," he said.

Shaughnessy looked at the hand but did not take it. He did say "good luck" however, as if it hurt, then turned away and climbed into the rental truck's cab.

The van's driver got into his own vehicle. *Feeb asshole,* he thought, and laughed. He'd neither wanted nor expected a handshake—in his profession he was used to assholes—he'd simply wanted to see if he'd get one. The guy had struck him as a rogue Feeb, and for him, the refusal to shake hands confirmed it. Starting the motor, he swung the van past the rental truck, then drove to the I-64 on-ramp and out of sight.

At the edge of Evansville, the parking lot of the "Cornbelt Super Multiplex" was a mob scene. The sheriff's department estimated the crowd at 12,000—some from at least as far as Cincinnati—and for the umpteenth time, Dove had levitated to do his healing.

It was the first place they'd been exposed to open hostility—an angry man waving a pistol, shouting obscenities about the antichrist. But he hadn't fired. People around him had disarmed him—taken him down and held him for the police. To Lee, watching from a window, it was a sobering sight. If someone shot Dove, would he heal himself? Christ had died, and so had Buddha.

More sobering to Art Knowles had been a report from the Vanderburgh County Sheriff's Department. A State Patrol cruiser had stopped a delivery van, and been struck by a storm of automatic weapons fire that killed both officers. An unmarked backup car, two hundred feet away, had seen it happen, and reported by radio. Before the van could leave the scene, a patrolman jumped out of the backup cruiser and hit the van with an antiarmor rocket. The rocket, and the brief firefight that followed, killed four of the six occupants and critically wounded the other two. Only the driver carried identification, probably false.

Knowles suggested to Lor Lu they discontinue the tour. It had been a huge success already. He wasn't surprised, though, when Lor Lu said they'd continue. He even thought he knew why.

On the road to Louisville, the farthest east they'd go, Dove called Lee over to sit by him. "Your duties here are demanding," he said, "and you do them well."

"Thank you."

"You will do more, before you have finished. The vectors are unequivocal on that. And if any further evidence were needed, you are the mother of your daughters." He paused. "Tell me what attracted you to Ben."

She supposed he knew, and wanted her to look at it. But she missed what he was after, so he led her. "What body type had always attracted you?"

She looked at that. Not dark-complexioned men, nor tall gangly men. She'd favored football types, particularly blonds. But when she'd met Ben, she'd never even thought about that. He was the one. Dove nodded as if he read her mind. "Remarkable, isn't it. Despite your parents and their pressures, and the acculturation of your adolescent coterie, you recognized Ben when you saw him. Your purpose and your agreement were strong. Congratulations!"

When her goose flesh had settled down, she thanked him and left.

After Mount Vernon, Illinois, they traveled divided highways almost exclusively. The train of vehicles following them formed an unacceptable traffic problem on lesser roads. Even on the interstates, from time to time the police stopped the entire train except the TV trucks, holding them until the bus was miles ahead. But the train soon reconstituted itself from those who caught up again, plus newcomers.

On a number of occasions the "messiah followers" had informed the police of vehicles whose occupants were behaving "suspiciously." Mostly the drivers proved to be high, but on three occasions the passengers had been armed with sniper rifles or automatic weapons, and there'd been another shoot-out, with casualties. Art Knowles and Lor Lu were kept informed, and Lor Lu told the crew.

Lee had arranged with a national supermarket chain to meet the cavalcade at prearranged points with "deli trucks," providing a considerable selection of sandwiches, salads, hot soup, pizza. . . . Before arranging a meeting with one of them, she'd ask the police escort how long the train was. Then she'd inform the supermarket chain headquarters. For the most part, the police let her know in advance of plans to chop the train off.

Every healing stop had become more or less like the one at Evansville: a huge mass of cars and people, with hundreds waiting to be healed. And the whole country witnessed it. Seldom had so many people followed an event so closely, in America and internationally.

Matthew Shaughnessy had two strike teams of his own. The problem was positioning them. In the cab of his headquarters truck, he could monitor Millennium's "Tour News" on the WebWorld, and generally knew when the bus was scheduled to be somewhere. But those somewheres were always loaded with cruisers and police, while a hit attempt along the highway was high risk. Any vehicle waiting beside the road was quickly investigated, and there was always at least one police chopper overhead, with more standing by, ready to act.

He was also monitoring the police channels, but

there was so damned much radio traffic on them, a lot of it pulse traffic that had to be descrambled. And for the most part he never knew which call units were which, and which were important. He felt like a blind man groping through a heap of chocolates, hunting for the raspberry creme centers. Finally he'd settled on command channels, which greatly reduced the radio traffic to sort through, but mostly lacked needed details.

Obviously Forsberg hadn't foreseen the amount of police resources the states and counties would invest in protecting these Millennium sonsofbitches. And one thing about Forsberg you could rely on: he was a tightwad, never willing to assign adequate backup units for contingencies.

Now, of course, Forsberg didn't have anything remotely like the resources he'd had as director, not in quantity and sure as hell not in quality. And he'd failed to realize that mercenaries lacked the brains and discipline for a mission like this. If that strike force in Indiana had been driving within eight miles per hour of the speed limit, they wouldn't have been stopped. And if they'd been paying attention, they'd have seen the backup cruiser, for crissake, and taken it out when they took out the first one.

He'd have to rely on his own wits, and improvise. It was what he did best. Probably, he told himself, that's why Forsberg had sought him out. That and his perseverence.

On the twelfth evening, the tour bus pulled up to a small motel on I-40, at the east edge of Memphis. Lor Lu had reserved it for Millennium and its media entourage. National guardsmen had kept the parking lot clear, and people well away. Their pitch was, "Stay back, folks. Even messiahs have to get their rest." It seemed to work.

Lee had showered and was getting ready for bed when someone knocked. "Who is it?" she asked.

"Security, Miz Shoreff."

Security? It wasn't a voice she knew. Motel security, she decided.

"Just a minute," she said. "I just got out of the shower." After wrapping herself in her bathrobe, she set the safety chain on the door, and opened it a few inches. Through the gap she saw a uniformed man with a star on his shirt. "You Miz Shoreff?" he asked.

"Yes, I am."

He handed her a folded paper. "Sorry, ma'am," he said, and waited while she unfolded it, scanned it, then braced herself on the doorpost. The Shelby County Sheriff's sergeant repeated himself. "I really am sorry, ma'am," he said quietly, then turned and left.

The words she'd read, the operative words, filled her mind, blocking out everything else. *Monroe County District Court—appear on July 16—*in three days!—*to give reason why your daughters, Rebecca and Raquel Kramer, should not be remanded to the court for disposition to their father.*

After closing the door, she sat down heavily on a chair, and for a moment stared at nothing. Then she straightened. "You have resources, Lee," she muttered. "Use them." She'd gotten up and started for the phone, when it rang. She answered.

"Lee, this is Art. Something urgent has come up.

Everyone needs to be on the bus, with their bags, by eleven. Not a minute later, because that's when we leave."

She hung up frowning, then moving quickly, began to dress and pack. She'd talk to Lor Lu on the bus.

66
Prime Time

OUTSIDE THE BUS, people were stowing luggage. Bar Stool sat in the driver's seat with the motor idling. Across from him, Lor Lu was in his usual seat, his office. He'd lowered the hinged worktable in front of him, and his laptop sat open on it, with a map on its screen. At the moment, though, his attention was elsewhere. Taking the summons from her purse, Lee held it out to him. "Excuse me, Lor Lu."

For a long moment he seemed unaware of either the summons or of her, which was very unlike him; she half withdrew it. Then, glancing sideways, he took it, read it with raised eyebrows, and smiled wryly up at her. "It seems," he said, "the artillery I called in was not adequate. I will notify the strategic air

command." His sudden laugh startled her. Getting
up, he left the bus.

To make a call in private? she wondered.

He'd just returned when Art Knowles came aboard.
It was Knowles who explained the situation to the tour
crew. The plan had been to enter Arkansas tomorrow
after breakfast, but Arkansas's Governor Cook had just
declared martial law, to take effect at midnight. And
word had leaked that he'd deny them entry. Lor Lu
had notified Mike Shuster, at Legal, who had called
Conroy, Morgenstern, and Blasingame. The firm had
personnel on night standby to cover emergencies.

"They should get us at least an abeyance based on
the First Amendment," Knowles finished. "Meanwhile,
Dove's stealing a march on the governor. We'll cross the
river before midnight."

Duke Cochran frowned. *This was Dove's decision?*
He'd have expected patience. Why would Dove antago-
nize the governor? Marius Cook was well known to
journalists as a far-right Christian activist, full of bona
fide zeal, not simply a politician posturing for support
from the Religious Right.

Cook had been part of the conservative backlash
that led to the GOP split, and the formation of the
America Party. But at crunch time he hadn't joined the
Americists; his conservatism had too strong a populist
streak, which had helped him unseat Ted Jamison
as governor. By and large, the media liked Marius
Cook—he was neither pompous nor abrasive—but
when it came to religion, he had a short fuse, so
Cochran felt uneasy.

Bar Stool pulled out of the motel lot and turned

onto the interstate approach. They were on their way, but the TV trucks were not. Obviously Lor Lu hadn't notified them, and it was no oversight, Cochran felt sure. Moments later they turned south on the Memphis beltway, and Duke, who'd called up a map on his laptop, wondered if Bar Stool had made a mistake. It seemed to him they'd have taken Summer Avenue, or perhaps I-40. But a quarter hour later, when they hit the westward jog of I-55, it struck him: they were going to cross the state line on the I-55 bridge. Perhaps Cook had the Arkansas Highway Patrol watching the I-40 bridge but not the I-55, and Lor Lu or Knowles had learned of it.

A few minutes later they crossed the Mississippi into Arkansas, without incident or a cavalcade of followers. Within minutes, I-55 joined I-40. Near the junction was a visitors' center, but the bus tooled on past it. No pursuit developed, and Cochran relaxed. The roadblock was either at the foot of the bridge or not yet in place. Or maybe the report had been a false alarm.

Cochran closed his laptop. It was 130 miles to Little Rock. They could be there in a couple of hours; time enough for needed sleep. Though if the governor didn't want them there, it seemed likely the highway patrol would intercept them somewhere along the way.

"All right, folks, let's get it loaded! We got a hundred forty miles to Little Rock, and the sooner we get there, the sooner y'all can shower down and get to bed!"

The midsummer tour of Donnie Jamison's Christian Singers had drawn poorly, very poorly. Because whether or not Ngunda Aran was for real—something Donnie rejected as a matter of Christian principle—the "Dove Tour" had totally attached the public's attention. So money was tight, morale was low, and Donnie Jamison was worried about meeting his expenses. Usually he did a pretty good job of trusting in God, but his credit was tighter'n a mosquito's ass stretched over a rain barrel. He'd arranged in advance to park in the YMCA lot, and the night watchman was to let them in to use the gymnasium shower rooms. They'd have to sleep on the bus though, with seats that tipped back only eight or ten inches. A few might spring for a room out of their own pockets—he wouldn't blame them—but he'd sleep in the bus with the others.

After tomorrow night's performance, they'd leave Little Rock and drive home to Knoxville, some 600 miles. They'd have to overnight somewhere along the way, at some motel for the driver, but he couldn't afford to put his own folks up.

Celebrity Tours! The outfit that hauled Rhonda McCrory and groups like hers, but not in a bus like this one. Only the logo was the same.

With the instruments, equipment and bags stowed, Jamison and the others who'd helped with the stowing, boarded the bus and settled into their seats. A minute later it pulled out of Memphis State University's auditorium parking lot, found its way onto Poplar Avenue, and headed west.

Donnie tried closing his eyes, but there wasn't any sign at all that he was going to fall asleep, so after a couple of minutes he opened them again. It was past midnight, and there wasn't a lot of traffic. Pretty soon he saw the river. They'd started across the bridge, *when something slammed the bus and exploded. There were screams, smoke, a stink of explosive. Donnie found himself on the floor, in the aisle, the bus rocking back and forth as the dying driver tried to steer. It hit something, and careened along the rail. Metal tore, screeching, and the bus jerked to a stop.*

Some of the screams became articulated. "My God!" someone cried, "help me!" And "Billy! Billy! Don't be dead, Billy."

But that was brief, cut short by a series of explosions that started from the rear and worked to the front. After that, there were no more screams, not even moans. Just the reek of burning diesel fuel.

By night, the flat, midnight-shrouded farmlands of eastern Arkansas offered little of visual interest to the casual traveler. Lee soon drew her window curtain and lay back to sleep. When she awoke, they'd left the interstate; the road was rough, and the bus moved slowly. *Construction,* she thought, *a detour,* and slept again. The next time she awoke, her watch read 2:05, and they had parked. *A truck-stop parking lot,* she thought sleepily. She wobbled back to the ladies' room, then returned to her seat and to sleep, without opening her curtain to peer outside.

It was daylight when next she awoke. They were moving again, slowly, and she opened her curtain. They were on a dirt truck trail along the edge of a floodplain woods. It occurred to her they'd hidden out for the final hours of the night.

Minutes later they were on a blacktopped county road. Half a mile ahead she could see the interstate. The summons from the Monroe County court popped into her consciousness, along with an expletive, not quite voiced. She didn't allow herself to dwell on the situation though. Lor Lu would handle it.

Lor Lu waited till they were back on I-40 before phoning Little Rock's network affiliates and the *Democrat-Gazette*. They'd done well not to be spotted the night before. Or, more accurately, Dove had done well. But now it was time. A roadside sign announced a restaurant at the next exit. He noted the exit name and number, and got back on the phone again.

For the first time, Dove went into a restaurant with them. His aura brought immediate recognition. People stared. The hostess told Lor Lu to seat themselves however he pleased, and a couple of minutes later came to Dove's table with menus and a coffee pot. She seemed unawed by him, and after she'd poured, spoke to Dove, her voice brassy and cheerful. "You're Mr. Aran, ain't you?"

"I am. And you are Mrs. Wallace."

Surprised, she looked down at her name plate. *Edith* was all it said. She laughed. "That's pretty good. If you're not the McCoy, you're close enough. I'll bet you eat though. Jesus even sweated. Did you know that?"

He beamed. "Oh yes."

"Were you him?"

"No I wasn't. A person is chosen who was born and raised in the time. Jesus' parents were Mary and Joseph. Mine were Maryam and Howard."

"Well that's interesting! Maryam and Howard! I'll tell my grandkids that, when I have some. I'll tell them you told me yourself." She spoke more quietly then. "Amy's supposed to be your waitress. She's nice, but when she saw who you were, she almost peed her pants. No way would she come over here. So I'll be your waitress."

She left them to decide their orders. When she'd gone, a fiftyish woman came hesitantly to his table. "Excuse me, uh, sir. Mr. Aran. I hate to bother you at your mealtime, but my husband's got prostate cancer." She gestured toward a booth. "The doctors want to operate, but he won't let them, and—can you . . . ?"

"Bring him to me," Dove said, and a minute later she returned with her husband.

"Do you want to be healed?"

"Yessir."

"Do you believe you can be healed?"

The man eyed the golden-auraed Dove worriedly. "Uh, I sure do hope so. Seems to me you might could."

"Well then—" Dove grinned, a grin brighter than even Ngunda Aran's had been. His aura flared to enwrap those around him, and it was not frightening at all. "By your trust in coming to me," he said, "and through the loving power of God, you are healed."

The man's eyes widened, then he stood, seemingly dazed, before starting back to his booth, his wife murmuring to him that he hadn't thanked the man. He seemed not to hear. Dove smiled after them before turning his attention to his coffee. Lee noticed that when Dove's aura had flared, so had Lor Lu's, and the others had strengthened enough that she could see them too. Even Duke wore one around his head and

upper torso. She looked down at her arms, wondering
if people could see hers.

Duke Cochran wasn't paying attention to auras. His
mind was examining a question: After taking the I-55
bridge, and hiding by the woods part of the night,
why were they sitting in this restaurant for breakfast?
It was bound to take the better part of an hour, and
their bus could be seen from the highway.

Edith Wallace returned shortly, took their orders
and left. Several tables away, Jenny Buckels had given
her order too, and was sipping her coffee when a
voice called her name. She knew at once who it was:
Steven! She'd gotten to her feet before she saw her
father a few feet behind him; he seemed shrunken
and hesitant.

Beaming, Steven strode to her, their father following. "It's too good to believe," he said. "I'd left the
freeway to get breakfast before I noticed the bus." He
glanced over his shoulder at their father, who hung
back; Jenny sensed his grief.

"Mom died," Steven said, "and Dad's had second
thoughts. He asked if I could find you, and I learned
from the, uh, Ranch that you were with the tour.
We started too late to catch—Mr. Aran's Tennessee
appearances, but I thought if we got to Little Rock
in time . . ."

He straightened and looked around, his eyes moving
to Dove and Lor Lu, with their conspicuous auras. "I
never imagined," he said.

Edmund Buckels did not look around. His discomfort was palpable.

"Why don't you and Dad get a table or booth," Jenny said, "and I'll join you there." She glanced at Dove; he was smiling broadly at her.

"Of course," Steven said. "Come on, Dad."

She watched them go. Her father's eyes still avoided Dove. He'd never been against civil rights for blacks, though his tolerance for "pushiness" was limited. He'd made a point of "befriending" the first black family to move into the fringe of Loblolly's white community. It never grew into actual friendship—they were never comfortable with the Johnsons—but the Johnsons were Baptists, and Willis Johnson a pharmacist like both Edmund and his father. And associating with them was the Christian thing to do.

"Lee, tell the waitress where I've gone," Jenny said. Carrying her coffee, she followed her brother and father. They'd chosen a booth, and seated themselves side by side. She slid in across from them. "Hello, Dad," she said. "I'm glad to see you. And glad you wanted to see me." She'd realized his grief had more to do with her than with her mother's death, but she hadn't anticipated the silent tears that overflowed his eyes when she spoke to him. Reaching, she patted his hand. "Mom's watching us," she said, "and she's glad we're together here." Edmund nodded, unable to speak.

She turned to Steven. "Who's filling your pulpit while you're gone?"

"Esther Ruth Maddox," Steven answered. Then gestured with his head toward Dove. "Is he—who he seems to be?"

"I have no doubt. None at all."

Steven nodded. "It seems that way to me, too. And

to Dad. Either the Second Coming, or he who comes before, to prepare the way. In either case..." He shook his head. "It's hard. He doesn't say the things we expected. But then, Jesus didn't say the things they expected him to, either."

Lee watched them from across the room. She too had sensed Edmund Buckel's emotion, been touched by it. Then her waitress brought her breakfast, and took Jenny's to the booth. Lee was finishing her waffle when the police arrived. The captain in command eyed the auras, then gathering himself, approached Dove and spoke to him calmly and professionally, addressing him as Mr. Aran. Dove's people, he said, could finish breakfast, but afterward he'd need to talk to them outside. He'd barely said it when the man who'd asked for healing came from the restroom. "It worked!" he shouted. "I'm healed! Thank you, God, he healed me!" He looked around at the startled faces. "I just had my first really good pee in years!"

For a moment, silence reigned, followed by applause and friendly laughter, breaking the tension of a moment before. The police captain stared, then retreated to the vestibule, shaking his head.

After Lee had signed the receipt, the captain led the tour crew out into the sunshine. Overhead were two police choppers. Some distance off, a TV chopper circled slowly. Eight or ten police cruisers blocked the entryways and approach road. The captain led Dove to one of the police cars, while a sergeant and several other officers gathered the tour crew. Art Knowles remonstrated with the sergeant in charge.

He was Dove's security chief, he said, and should be allowed to go with him. Politely but firmly the sergeant refused. "Sir," he said, "nobody's going to do him any harm. He'll be just fine."

Several people had followed them out of the restaurant, and one of them shouted to the captain. "I hope to hell you know what you're doing, officer."

The captain turned and called back. "I hope so too, sir, I surely do." He got into the cruiser beside Dove and closed the door. Then the car pulled out onto the frontage road, and accelerated sharply as it headed for the on-ramp, followed by other patrol cars.

The senior sergeant and three other highway patrolmen herded the rest of the party toward the bus. Lor Lu confronted the sergeant. "Sergeant, I am Lor Lu, Mr. Aran's administrative assistant. In his absence I'm responsible for these people. What exactly is this all about?"

"Mr. Lu, martial law has been declared in Arkansas. You folks are in danger of your lives, and Governor Cook isn't about to let Mr. Aran get killed here. Or any of the rest of you folks. Last night about midnight, a whole busload of folks got all shot up—Donnie Jamison and his Christian Singers. They were in another Celebrity Tours bus, on the I-40 bridge out of Memphis. Seems likely someone mistook it for yours. Slammed a bunch of rockets into it. Killed everyone on board. So when nobody knew where you were last night, Governor Cook was worried to death about y'all. Now you're under protective custody, and one of my men is going to drive. He knows where we're going, and there's no need for any of you to worry."

Good God! Lee thought, *a whole busload killed!*

That's terrible! She wondered if the police had anything to do with it.

Steven Buckels introduced himself to the sergeant, and explained that he and his father weren't part of the tour crew. "But my sister is," he said, indicating Jenny. "We drove out from North Carolina to see her. We'll follow you."

"I'm afraid that won't work, Reverend Buckels. Your sister needs to come along with the rest of Mr. Aran's folks, and the escort isn't to let anyone follow." The sergeant frowned. "Now my orders don't say anything about—guests of the tour. So if Mr. Lu is willing to call you that, and if you're willing to leave your car here . . ."

Steven hesitated for perhaps a second, then—"I'll be right back, sergeant," he said. His eyes found Lor Lu, who was ushering the last few crew members aboard the bus; Jenny was the last of them. Steven strode over to them, and briefly they talked. Two minutes later, Steven and Edmund Buckels were aboard with the tour crew, carrying only a small bag each.

The sergeant took a seat halfway back in the bus, and sent the remaining two of his men farther to the rear. The trooper-driver seemed familiar with buses. After warming it up briefly, he drove from the lot, preceded by a patrol car and followed by others.

The TV hadn't been turned back on, so Duke Cochran booted up his laptop. *Protective custody,* he said to himself. *And the pope is Presbyterian.* He wondered where they were taking Dove, and if they'd be stupid enough to do anything to him. Jail him perhaps.

It occurred to him that might be what Dove intended; they might be playing into his hands. Although what possible purpose that could serve . . . He'd already rejected the idea that the state patrol might have shot up the other bus. He was no lawyer, but it seemed to him the FBI would assert its jurisdiction over murders aboard an interstate commercial carrier. And if the state police were guilty of the killings, the feds would stick it to them ruthlessly.

His thoughts were interrupted by a patrolman collecting laptops and cell phones. Without them, Cochran felt naked.

Lor Lu turned on the television, which as usual was set to CNN. The picture gave them an aerial viewpoint. The TV chopper had accompanied the captain's cruiser, keeping the prescribed distance, but telephoto shots showed Dove visible through a window. A radar readout showed the cruiser's speed—87 miles per hour. The pilot increased his speed, moving to a position perhaps a half mile ahead of the cruiser. The bus was not in sight. From a seat next to the pilot, a newswoman provided commentary.

Abruptly the shot changed to show one of the police choppers moving toward the camera. Via a radio-camera hookup, the viewers could hear the police chopper ordering the TV chopper back to Little Rock. They could also see a gun of some sort, seemingly an assault rifle, being used to gesture from the door. The view swung away westward as the TV chopper started for home, shepherded by one of the other police aircraft.

❖   ❖   ❖

Race played little or no part in Governor Marius Cook's hostility toward Dove. He'd grown up in his parents' church, an Ozark Baptist congregation with an old antislavery tradition. They may not have considered blacks as good as whites, but even then they'd regarded them as human beings, God's children, not to be bought or sold.

Today he sat in his office with his aide and his pastor, watching the wall screen intently. "Everett," the governor said to his aide, "what is that stupid sonofabitch doing, waving that gun out the helicopter door like that for the whole world to see? I explicitly ordered that everything was supposed to look cool!"

It seemed to Everett Miller the answer was obvious: in an operation involving that many people, some were likely to screw up. He did not, however, point this out. He was worried, wondering if Marius Cook hadn't bitten off more than he could chew. For two weeks, Everett had been keeping up with the TV highlights of what the newspeople were calling "the Messianic Procession," and he couldn't help wondering if Dove wasn't what so many people now claimed he was. Or hoped he was.

Everett didn't mention that either. He'd learned not to disagree openly with Marius on anything to do with religion. In other matters, he could and did level with the governor—selectively. He and Marius Cook had been boyhood friends, himself the elder. Later they'd overlapped for two years at the U. of A., from which Everett Miller had graduated in public management with honors, and a minor in political science. Marius had squeaked through in law, and by dint of hard work—he'd always been good at that—had passed the bar exam on his third try, which was respectable.

They'd worked together politically beginning with Marius's first run for the legislature. Everett Miller had always known that his friend had flaws of character, not all of them trivial, but they'd been friends since second grade, and Everett Miller stood by his friends. Especially he stood by Marius Cook. And politically, if Marius said he'd do something, he at least gave it an honest try. That made up for a lot.

The flaw that had gotten him into this situation— Everett Miller was confident it was a situation—was that Marius could not abide what he considered heresy.

And Marius had become somewhat erratic after an attempt on his life that spring. He'd have been killed if it weren't for a misfire—that and the pistol in his desk drawer. He'd gotten it out and fired back, while the would-be assassin was trying to unjam his weapon. Afterward Marius had given the credit to the Lord, "who has a purpose in mind for me," he'd said, "a task for me to fulfill."

Still, "in these lawless times with their Godless men," Marius had not left it *all* in God's hands. Not only had he added additional security personnel to the mansion staff, he'd acquired "a real Uzi"—actually an Iraqi-made copy—which he kept in a capacious lower desk drawer, loaded. He'd even practiced with it several times, early on, on the capitol police's underground firing range.

More recently he'd pretty much forgotten about it, which didn't surprise his old friend. Marius had always tended to enthusiasms, and to getting over them in a week or a month. The "Church of the Divine Exhortation" was the most conspicuous exception to that.

Senior Sergeant Carl Lavender knelt on the bus's rear seat, looking out the back window. They'd left the interstate, exiting unnoticed onto a county road. Unnoticed because road blocks had prevented interstate entry both ahead and behind, to keep the media from knowing where the bus was. Going up front again, he sat next to Lor Lu, diagonally across from the trooper driving. A mile and a half farther on, they turned off the narrow blacktop into a county road department equipment yard. It wasn't much—a large semi-cylindrical Butler shed where equipment was worked on, and a yard with a couple of dump trucks, a grader, bulldozer, front-end loader, semitractor with flatbed trailer, a big pile of crushed rock, and a bigger pile of gravel. All of it surrounded on three sides by thick-trunked cottonwoods, and on all four sides by a high chain-link fence topped with razor wire. It was Saturday, and no one was there except them.

"Pull in behind the shed, Loy," Lavender told the driver, "so's we can't be seen from the road. But under the trees; otherwise we'll have to keep the motor running so's the sun don't cook us." He turned to his captive passengers. "All right, folks, you can get out five at a time and stretch your legs if you want. Just stay close. I definitely don't want to handcuff anyone, but if I need to, I will."

"Excuse me, Sergeant," Art Knowles said, "but we haven't been shown any warrant for our arrest."

"That's right sir. You're not under arrest. Like I said before, you're in protective custody. Though I suppose it doesn't make that much difference just now, from your point of view. Just keep in mind that martial law's been in effect since midnight. Y'all been drawing awfully big crowds with not much security, and the amount of traffic following you . . . Yesterday you had more than a hundred vehicles chasing along behind. The Tennessee Highway Patrol called it the worst traffic situation they'd seen since their big ice storm of '94."

Those who got out used a chemical toilet near the shed, to spare the ones on the bus, which otherwise would soon need to be pumped out. But mostly the crew stayed on board, watching TV.

Local television, including the network affiliates, were skirting the subject of Dove's seizure and the disappearance of the bus—mentioning it but not speculating. Duke Cochran supposed they'd been constrained by martial law provisions.

CNN, of course, was giving major time to both description and speculation, and to demands by the U.S. Attorney General's office for an explanation. Constitutional law experts speculated that if Governor Cook wasn't quickly forthcoming, he'd find U.S. marshals on his doorstep with a warrant for his arrest.

Sergeant Lavender watched along with the tour crew, saying nothing, but looking increasingly unhappy. After a few minutes, a highway cruiser arrived with two more troopers. Lavender had them pull in behind the shed, too.

Steven and Edmund Buckels had taken a seat together in the bus. After a bit Jenny went to them and looked at Steven. "Hello, big brother," she said. "Trade you seats. It's my turn to sit by Daddy."

Steven smiled at her and moved across the aisle, while she sat down beside their father, putting her hand on his forearm. "I'm glad you came, Dad. You've made me very happy."

Again silent tears overflowed his eyes. She squeezed his hand gently, saying nothing more till she sensed he could speak without breaking. Then she asked what kind of summer they'd had back home. "About right," he said. "Not too hot, and God has sent rain when needed. The farmers are happy with it, and it's to them that weather means the most." He looked searchingly at his daughter. "Jenny," he began, paused, then continued. "I've come to ask your forgiveness."

Leaning, she kissed his cheek, then chuckled. "I'll forgive you if you'll forgive me."

He smiled wanly. "I believe we have already. But— the greater fault was mine." Once more he paused. "Do you truly believe Mr. Aran is the messiah?"

"I do, Father. I'm a healer now; he taught me. His love and compassion are beyond my comprehension. I've been blessed to know him." She gestured. "We all have."

He examined his hands. "I fear I cannot let go my doubts. He is—beyond anything I'd thought to see, but I have not been able to swear a belief in him. I have been warned too often of the antichrist."

Her voice softened. "That's all right, Father. The Infinite Soul doesn't demand. It simply loves. It *is* love. There is no punishment for doubting."

Once such heresy would have triggered anger.

Now he simply nodded, not convinced perhaps, but receptive.

Noon came and went, and Sergeant Lavender's stomach began to complain. He had no doubt everyone else's had too. He began to look at ways to get food delivered, sufficient for his detainees and his men, without tipping anyone as to whom it was for.

Then he heard a chopper in the distance, and left the bus to look. It came nearer, to hover directly over the shed at about two hundred feet. It had neither police nor national guard markings, nor the logo of any TV station.

CNN in a charter job, sure as can be. He shook his head. It was probably just as well. It would put pressure on old Marius, and maybe the damn fool would realize the trouble he was making for himself.

He became aware of Art Knowles standing a few feet behind him. Knowles spoke quietly: "I guess the fat's in the fire now, eh, Sergeant?"

"I wouldn't be a bit surprised, Mr. Knowles, not a bit."

But he didn't send anyone for food until the telltale video shots of the bus were shown on CNN, and the location announced. Then he had lunch orders compiled for his prisoners and troopers—the state would pay—and called Bell Creek, placing orders for pizza, tacos, burgers, and fried chicken.

Before the food was delivered, the first rubberneckers and believers had parked along the road and were looking through the fence. Minutes after the food arrived, so did the first wheelchair case.

❖   ❖   ❖

It was 3 P.M. when a police van pulled up in front of the governor's mansion in Little Rock. The street had been blocked off most of the day, and the sidewalk and grounds were also out of bounds, patrolled by capitol police. Thus, as Dove was taken from the van and hustled inside, no spectators stood by. Only two video cameras, and inside the entrance two more, one following, the other backing ahead of him, across the foyer and along a corridor.

In his office, the governor watched Dove's progress on the wall screen. This was to be Marius Cook's finest hour: the public interrogation of Ngunda Aran, and his exposure as counterfeit. So far as possible, Marius intended to undo the damage brought about by the antichrist's false teachings, which meant it had to be on national TV, preferably on prime time. So he'd had "the guru" quietly kept in a holding cell at the Highway Patrol substation outside Lonoke.

He'd had to jump the gun though, move it up to midafternoon. The public detention of the guru, followed by the discovery of the tour bus and its passengers by CNN, had brought a demand from "Babylon on the Potomac" for an explanation, and he didn't want the FBI pounding on his door. So he'd promised to explain everything at 3 P.M., on network television. On Saturdays, afternoon was as prime as evening anyway, in the U.S.A. and Canada. And CNN would get him coverage throughout the rest of the world.

Standing, he watched Ngunda Aran being marched down the corridor to his office, and noticed with satisfaction that the man was handcuffed. Captain Swingel had protested the order, but obeyed it. He should have removed the man's aura machine, too, stripped him if need be. It wasn't seemly that a false messiah wear a halo to his interrogation. Good God! He looked like some kind of big yellow torch! Now they were at the door, and Captain Swingel was reaching, knocking. As Marius Cook turned his attention from screen to door, he found his guts in one titanic knot. There were three sharp raps. One of the governor's bodyguards opened to them, and Ngunda Aran entered.

Somehow the guru seemed taller, more imposing in person than on the screen, his aura more *alive*. Two troopers had entered with him, one holding each arm. When they stopped in front of his desk, the governor was tight as a fiddle string. Licking dry lips, Marius gathered himself.

"Are you the man known as Ngunda Aran?"

"I am called that, yes."

"Is it true that you have also called yourself God? Or a new Messiah?"

"When the Infinite Soul manifests itself in human form, it is each person's choice to recognize it or not."

The brief exchange had strengthened Marius Cook, but still he was tense, a spring wound near its limit. "Are you familiar with the Holy Bible, that it is the Word of God?"

"I know the Bible more thoroughly than you do. It is the word of men, some inspired, some not."

Cook's jaws clenched, and he began to redden. *Oh God*, thought Everett Miller, *here we go. Marius is going to make a fool of himself on national television.*

The governor's voice displayed an edge now. "You think you're pretty smart, don't you, Antichrist!"

Dove didn't answer, simply gazed calmly at the governor.

"Answer when I speak to you, you spawn of Satan!" Cook spit the words.

"Your question was rhetorical, not requiring an answer."

Marius Cook's jaw muscles were large and powerful, developed by a lifelong habit of grinding his teeth. Now they bunched like golf balls, and he jabbed the air with his finger. "When you land on God's doorstep, it's Him you'll answer to."

He paused, gathering himself again. He'd had this man brought here for interrogation, not to squabble with him. "Tell me, Ngunda Aran, what must a man do to be saved?"

"There is no need to be saved. The body dies whatever one does. And the soul is immortal; it cannot be threatened. Nor is there a hell, unless one insists on experiencing it."

Cook turned to one of the cameras. "Note that! He says a man need not be saved!" Then he turned back to Dove. "What about where Jesus said, 'Except a man be born again, he cannot see the kingdom of God'?"

The calm face smiled. "You have been and will be born again and again, in the usual manner. Eventually you will be gathered with the rest, into the Tao. You may wish to think of it as into the loving arms of God."

Marius Cook no longer felt the slightest apprehension. He was a warrior now—a soldier of God. He no longer even saw the vivid golden aura. This devil was damning himself with his answers. "And what have you got to say about false messiahs? False Christs?"

"The man Jesus has been quoted as saying, 'By their fruits shall ye know them.'" Dove paused. "Marius, Marius, you are full of fear and hatred. You claim to love God, but no one truly loves God unless he loves his fellow humans—all of them, including those who hate and despise him, who persecute and kill him. If you loved me, you would not have brought me here chained."

It seemed to Marius Cook that his prisoner had suddenly grown, a head taller. The apparency shook him, and he felt his fear as itself, not disguised now as anger or scorn. Meanwhile his prisoner spoke on.

"To love others, Marius, you must first love yourself. And to love yourself, it will help to examine yourself, as honestly as you can, without rationalizing, without excuses. And without withholding. The wrongs you've done, you cannot hide from the Tao." The voice softened. "Yet the Tao loves you as it loves the most innocent child.

"Take responsibility for your acts, starting with what you did to the children Julia and Benjamin, and Millie-Rose." Marius Cook's eyes bulged in sudden shock. *What? How could this be?* "And to the wife of Harmon, and the wife of Bobby John . . ." The governer's jaw fell slack. " . . . And the widow Frankie Mae, who trusted you with her property . . ." Marius dropped into a crouch, an idiotic "wa wa wa" issuing from his mouth. Jerking his lower right-hand desk drawer entirely from the desk, he scrabbled within it, and came up with the Uzi. " . . . and your old mentor and law partner Earl, when he began to be senile, and your . . ."

Rising, Marius fired a short burst into Dove's mid-section, the slugs erupting through the erect body, one striking a highway patrolman behind him. The officer fell, but Dove merely stopped listing the governor's hidden sins.

"Ah, Bird," he said. His voice was strong and clear, speaking the love name Cook's mother had used. "You cannot kill the Tao's love for you. It is impossible, however unworthy you think yourself."

"Wa wa wa!" Cook's finger convulsed, this time emptying the magazine in a long burst, the weapon climbing with recoil, stitching Dove from belly to forehead, blood gushing from a torn throat. Fragments of skull and brain splattered behind him, and plaster fell from the wall. Most in the room had dropped to the floor, even Everett Miller, who hadn't known his old friend as well as he'd thought.

Everyone dropped in fact but Dove and the governor. And those behind the cameras, who transmitted it all and got it on cube, though they wouldn't remember doing it.

For a long moment Dove remained upright, his smile and aura bright almost beyond bearing. With a nasal cry, Marius Cook threw the empty Uzi at him, the weapon striking him in the chest. Dove began to slump, folding at knees and hips, falling forward to the blood-pooled floor. The governor screamed, opened an upper drawer, this time bringing forth a .38-caliber pistol, shoving its barrel into his own mouth so hurriedly he broke teeth with it, as if he couldn't do it fast enough. And pulled the trigger.

The cameramen got that, too.

67
Aftershocks

AT THE EQUIPMENT YARD, the crowd outside the fence had grown slowly at first, then after one o'clock more rapidly, despite the baking sun. As always, some were ill or crippled: arthritis, cancer, emphysema, Parkinson's, multiple sclerosis . . . The healers with the bus left none of them unhealed, while Jenny Buckels' father and brother watched from the shade of a dump truck.

At two o'clock, Sergeant Lavender called head-quarters and asked for reinforcements. His small force numbered eight now, including himself, but there were, he reported, about three hundred people along the fence, both sides of the road, and in the road itself. Most were well-behaved, but Lavender was worried about "militia." "And martial law or not," he said, "I'm not about to start shooting. Too many folks to get hurt."

After a time, three more cruisers pulled up in front, each with two officers.

The healers, including Lor Lu, hung out with the police, one of whom got a toothache healed, and another a groin muscle he'd pulled sliding into third in a police and firemen's league softball game. But the rest of the tour group sat in the bus watching television. They'd all wondered what had become of Dove, so when CNN switched to the front yard of the executive mansion, Art Knowles went outside and informed the others. Most reached the set in time to watch Dove enter the governor's office . . .

. . . And watch the interrogation.

At the climax there was one scream, Lee's. Carl Lavender was at the fence when he heard it, and hurried to the bus to find out what was wrong. It was Lor Lu who told him. "The governor has murdered Dove," he said. Said it through tears, his smile beatific.

Thunderstruck, Lavender strode back to where he could see, then looked horrified at the others, all with tears running down their faces. Hurrying out to one of the patrol cars parked behind the shed, he called department headquarters in Little Rock. A male officer took the call.

Lavender identified himself. "I've got a busload of Millennium folks here, and I need to know what's going on. Can you . . ."

He'd intended to ask whether his orders had changed, but his phrasing opened a floodgate. "Going on?" The officer completely forgot the department's rules of radio etiquette. "Marius went totally bonkers; shot old

En-gunda full of holes! Jesus Christ, everyone here saw it! And the guru just stood there, smiling and talking and bleeding. Looked like he was on fire, the way that halo of his flared up. So Marius emptied the whole goddamn magazine into him! Jesus Christ! And he just stood there smiling"—the man's voice broke—"while the blood pumped out of him!" He paused, struggling for control. "Told old Marius God loved him anyway! Jesus Christ, I never saw anything like it!" Tears were running down the man's face, and again his voice broke, but he continued. "He must have had fifteen, twenty holes in him . . . blood all over the place! Then Marius took out another gun, put the barrel in his mouth and pulled the trigger! Oh, God, it was terrible!"

"You mean put it in his own mouth? The governor is dead?"

"Hell yes, the fucker's dead! Jesus Christ! Splashed his brains all over the place! He killed Christ, for God's sake! He *should* have shot himself!"

The man broke down entirely then. Lavender waited. Someone else got on the line and called the shift commander for him. "Captain," Lavender said, "what do I do with these Millennium folks I got here? And their bus?"

"Just keep them there till we get instructions. Pete MacIlvaine's governor now, but he don't know it yet. He's supposed to have gone fishing today, somewhere on the Upper White. We're trying to get in touch with his wife, to find out just where. Everything okay there now? You got enough men?"

"Boy, I hope so. I surely do. Oh my! This feels bad to me, Captain. If you can send me some more people, I'll surely be grateful to you."

Then the sergeant had his men get the heavier weapons from their cruisers—a 12-gauge pump shotgun and an M-16 assault rifle from each. Somehow it seemed like the thing to do.

By that time, the crowd had learned of the killing from radios in cars, and on car and cell phones. A few cars drove away, but most people stayed. There was some wailing and sobbing, but most of the weeping was quiet, wet faces peering through the fence. Others stood dry-eyed but solemn, some talking in undertones.

About 3:40 P.M., three men got out of a newly arrived pickup, assault rifles in their hands, and pushed their way roughly through the crowd. After sizing up the situation through the chain-link fence, they turned and left, apparently not liking the look of the shotguns and M-16s.

Lavender got back on the radio to Little Rock. "Captain," he said, "three militia types just sized us up. They carried assault rifles. When they saw my folks carrying M-16s and shotguns, they left, but they could just as well come back with friends. And all the bystanders along the fence would be like shields . . . which means we can't defend the people we're holding. Or ourselves. 'Cause there's no way in hell I'll have my people shoot into a crowd.

"What I need here is a National Guard infantry platoon. If there's not one available, then martial law isn't worth a hill of shit. Anyway I need a lot more backup, either that or authority to take these Millennium people somewheres else."

The captain said he'd see what he could come up with. Lavender posted one of his troopers on the radio, then reexamined the situation. More of the crowd was leaving, apparently because of the militia visit, but two new vans had just arrived, bringing people to be healed. That made Lavender uneasy too. No telling what someone in a wheelchair might be carrying under their blanket. But he wasn't willing to refuse people healing, not yet anyway. So he gritted his teeth, and hoped for quick action from Little Rock.

The President of the United States sat at her computer, looking at an array of rectangles on her wall screen, each showing the face of one of the persons she was on a conference call with: the attorney general; her newly confirmed director of the FBI; the secretary of Homeland Security; and General Alvarez of the army's Continental Command. Her White House chief of staff stood beside her.

"Those of you who haven't seen or heard what happened in Little Rock this afternoon," she said, "will tune to CNN as soon as this call is over. Telling can't do it justice. The governor of Arkansas not only arrested Ngunda Aran today, he had him brought to his office, and at about three P.M., murdered him with an automatic weapon, on televison. Then he committed suicide. The whole damn country—the whole damn world!—has either seen it or soon will.

"We can expect all kinds of weird crap to follow this, and we need a plan, with specifics. That's what I've called you for. We're going to hammer one out right now, within the hour. We can adjust it as necessary, as we go, but we need a basic plan to start with.

"Anderson, we'll start with you. Give us your considerations."

They hadn't gotten very far when something came up that changed the situation drastically.

Lee's scream had been followed by tears and shock. Now she sat watching TV again. She hadn't seen the militia types, but Art Knowles had, and warned them to be ready to hit the floor.

Then CNN's announcement of a special report snatched their attention.

"Minutes ago, at 4:43 P.M. Eastern Time, an astronomical monitoring satellite reported a rogue asteroid on a course intersect with Earth. The predicted time of impact is 5:52 P.M. Eastern Time—that's 22:52 Greenwich Mean Time and 2:52 P.M. Pacific Time—almost exactly one hour from now." Michael Sandow's black face was as calm as usual. "It is not the doomsday collision that's been speculated on for some unknown date in the future—the sort of cosmic collision that wrote finish to the dinosaurs, sixty-seven million years ago. But it will be a major astrogeological event, far greater than anything in the previous history of humankind. It is almost certain to cause great losses of life—how great will depend on where it strikes—and will severely disrupt worldwide weather.

"The mass of the roughly potato-shaped asteroid, which is about a thousand feet long, is estimated at thirty *million* tons. It was presumably knocked out of its orbit in the asteroid belt by a collision with another asteroid, and may have been further diverted and accelerated by a close flyby of Mars. It is now approaching at some 21,000 miles per hour, some ten times the speed of a deer rifle bullet.

"It might have been detected months ago, but

last year's solar storms damaged surveillance satellites, and severe cuts in NASA's budget have delayed their replacement.

"The odds of all this happening were minuscule, but happening it is, and scientists with the Skywatch Project say there is virtually no chance it will miss us.

"Some of you are wondering if this impending event is in any way connected with the murder of Ngunda Aran earlier this afternoon, by Arkansas' late Governor Marius Cook. Our CNN staff has called up excerpts from speeches by Mr. Aran, in which he predicted that exactly such an event would take place, this year, immediately following the death of a new incarnation of the Infinite Soul." [Sandow looks away from the camera.] "I believe we're ready."

The tour crew knew the approximate content, but watched anyway. The man on the screen was the pre-Assumption Ngunda Aran: kind, wise, and entirely human. They could tell the difference instantly.

Carl Lavender hadn't before heard of the guru's asteroid prediction. It sobered him even more than the collision forecast. When it was over, he went outside to tell the crowd to turn on their car radios to KLRN, or CNN Radio, where surely the meteor report would be playing. But even as he stepped out, he heard someone shouting the news from their car door: "Turn on your radios, folks! To KLRN! God's sending down his revenge! A big old meteor's coming down to hit Little Rock at 4:52 P.M.!"

There was a general exodus from the fence to the vehicles parked along both shoulders. They did not at once drive away though. Instead they turned on radios to hear for themselves. *Most*, Lavender told himself, *would listen, then head home to be with their families*.

But the crazies around the country? God only knew what they'd do. *Bad things,* he told himself, *bad things*. As he turned to reenter the bus, he hoped headquarters got those reinforcements to him quickly.

Lee had gotten out of the bus, Duke Cochran with her. Parked where it was, all they'd been able to see through its windows was the machine shed on one side and cottonwood trunks on the other.

What was left of the crowd stood around the parked cars and pickups, or sat in them, listening.

"How long do you suppose we'll be held here?" Lee asked.

"I doubt if even the sergeant knows," Duke answered, then shrugged. "The world's going to be a different place, that much I'll bet on." *Five fifty-two Eastern Time,* he thought. *That's 4:52 here.* He looked at his watch. Less than an hour. He wondered if it *would* impact Little Rock, then dismissed the notion. But if it did, would the shock wave reach them here, dozens of miles away? *Probably,* he thought.

Wherever it hit, a lot of people would die, and what kind of world would the casualties be reborn into? Better in some ways, if Dove's forecasts were right, but there'd be heavy adjustments to make. People would have to abandon a lot of long-held must-haves and must-dos and can'ts—a process the Depression and the Green Flu had begun, and the asteroid would accelerate big-time.

If it hit in the Atlantic, the tsunami would probably take out Boston, New York City, and Florida. Funnel up Chesapeake Bay, the Potomac, the Saint Lawrence, and take out Baltimore, D.C., Montreal. And the Netherlands, Belgium, Denmark . . . ! And up the Thames through London! Good God! The population of those places totalled scores of millions.

It would be a *very* different world.

Lee's interests and education hadn't given her a sense of planetary dynamics; her focus was her family. Turning, she reboarded the bus, planning to bug the sergeant and Lor Lu for action on leaving, getting back to the Ranch. And there in his usual front seat was Lor Lu, with the sergeant sitting beside him in conversation. Instead of interrupting, she listened.

" . . . was he really the Messiah? A new Messiah?"

Lor Lu's eyes were steady on the sergeant's. "That is each person's decision to make for themselves. Whenever someone asked Dove that question, he answered them as Jesus of Nazareth had: 'By his fruits shall you know him.'" He paused. "What do you think?"

"I hope he was. We sure could use one. People don't pay much attention to the original anymore, even most that claim to. I've been reading old En-gunda in the newspaper for the better part of a year now. He was interesting, but I didn't pay all that much attention till the last week or so." He paused thoughtfully. "I'm a lot more at home with the Bible—the New Testament anyway—than with what he wrote. Been reading it all my life. But if anyone's a new Messiah . . . I'll tell you, with that aura and all the healings, and how he died—it seems to me he must have been." He gestured toward the sky. "And now this. Is he going to rise from the dead?"

"Not physically. A physical resurrection was useful two thousand years ago. Now it would be counterproductive, and the asteroid will certify his reality. Nor did he intend that people look to him or his death for salvation. The teaching of Ngunda Aran, followed by the visit of the Infinite Soul, were simply to enlighten us—to provide new understanding, and inspire us. Which they're doing. And the process will be greatly strengthened by the meteor impact."

Pete MacIlvaine sat in the Marion County Sheriff's Department cruiser, beside the deputy who'd found him. It was parked in the shade of a black oak, doors open to the breeze. The reservoir was some sixty yards away.

"I'm the *what*?" MacIlvaine said into the radio. "What happened to Marius?" His face fell. "Good gawd! I'll be right down." He shook his head. "And killed himself too. Huh! Probably just as well. It lessens the outrage. . . . Yeah, I'll head south right away. . . . Can you what? Everett, if it's all that urgent, do what you think best. I'll back you on it."

He disconnected. "Deputy," he said, "call your sheriff and tell him I want you to escort me till we meet a state cruiser. Past the county line if need be. Sounds as if I'm needed in Little Rock right now."

Simeon Narezhny put aside his wrench and wiped his hands on a piece of shirt. The mayor of Yakovskij Zaliv was not a paid official. He derived his living from a fishing boat he owned, and operated with his son and a nephew. The problems of the village he addressed according to their urgency and the available time. And resources, which in small Kamchatka fishing villages were mostly the ingenuity, strength, and patience of their people.

This morning he'd needed to change the head gasket on the diesel-powered generator that provided the village's electricity. To economize on fuel, it operated only at certain hours, varying with the season, mainly in the evening, and at noon so people could hear the midday news from Petropavlovsk.

He was reaching for the starter—and facing the open door—when a sleeting flash of light and heat seared him. He raised his forearm as if to shield his eyes.

War! was his first thought. But who would waste a nuclear bomb on this part of the world?

The glare died quickly, and he stepped outside. Even damaged, his eyes, looking eastward over the Pacific, saw a vast wall of something—steam, water—climbing into the sky. A miles-long mushroom cloud! At the institute he'd najored in fisheries science, but had been required to take courses in the Earth sciences as well, and he'd always read. So it seemed to him that he knew what this was, what it had to be, Not a bomb, not any kind of bomb.

Warn the village, he thought, then realized how badly damaged he was. Start the generator! The radio station in Petropavlovsk will warn them! He moved to step back inside, and fell. So he crawled, intent on finding the starter. Nausea seized him, and he vomited violently, as if to expel breakfast; stomach; gullet. When he'd finished, time seemed suspended, his sense of urgency alive but paralyzed. Finally he moved again. He couldn't see at all now, so as he crawled he groped. Outside, he told himself. His hands found the wall, then a doorjamb, and

*with great and desparate effort, he pulled himself to
his feet. His body felt on fire, but the pain was muted,
separate from him. Staggering onto the stoop, he fell
again, hard, to sprawl stunned in the dirt.*

"Simeon! Simeon!"

*Who was calling him? The voice wakened him again
to his responsibilities, and he made it back onto his
hands and knees. "Tsunami!" His intended bellow was
a croak. "Tsunami!" He lay gasping like a beached fish.
How many minutes did they have? "Tsunamiii!" he
rasped again, sure now his skin was peeling off.*

*Miraculously the pain stopped. Surprised he looked
around, able to see again, and recognized his own
body lying in the dirt. There were no flames on it.
He saw his cousin Natalya sitting on her stoop like a
puppet with the strings cut, leaning against the wall,
staring seaward. Dear Natalya, he thought fondly,
everyone's friend.*

*Then the wave hit. Not the tsunami. The shock wave.
He saw his body thrown twenty yards, and all eighteen
of Yakovskij Zaliv's frame houses knocked flat.*

Unknown to Carl Lavender, something more serious
than the three departed "militia types" was coming down
a tree-lined county road nearby—a truck with the logo
of a rental company. Michael Shaughnessy sat beside
its driver. He'd decided to lead this strike himself, to
be sure it was done right. He hadn't been listening to
commercial radio, and didn't know about Dove's death
or the meteor. The man who'd been directing him via
a security band hadn't kept him up with events. He'd
simply given directions, guiding Shaughnessy along
rural roads. He'd also shown him the equipment yard,

an early view from the CNN aerial camera, revealing the bus behind the machine shed.

"It should be the next crossroad," Shaughnessy told the driver. "If there's a sign, it should say Bell Creek Road."

There was, and it did. The driver turned south. A half-mile ahead, some dozen cars were still parked along the road. Shaughnessy raised a microphone to his mouth, talking to the men in the rear of the truck. "We'll arrive in about a minute. When I stop, pile out ready for action. Kill anyone in your way. The local yokels are highway police, with shotguns and automatic rifles. They may take positions behind gravel piles. Finish them off immediately; handling surrenders is too dangerous. Then hang one of the blanket charges on the fence, blow it, get through the opening and take out the bus. Don't leave anyone from Millennium alive. Some of them may hide in the machine shed, so check it out."

He'd gone through the instructions before, en route, giving the men time to get used to them. If they didn't have it now, they never would.

Luther Koskela sat with the others in back. The truck carried more than a stock of weapons. If anyone looked in the rear door, all they'd see were wardrobe boxes and furniture. Behind the facade, sixteen mercenaries had made themselves as comfortable as they could, on sofas, easy chairs and mattresses. Now they got up, quiet, alert and ready. And disgruntled. None of them were happy with the "no prisoners" order. It went seriously against the principles of the mercenary brotherhood. But it was too late to back out.

They were even less informed than Shaughnessy, not even knowing that Dove had been arrested.

Luther had slipped into a dark and dangerous mood. From the beginning he'd hadn't liked this job, but the scrap yard had RIF'd him. Needing work, he'd gone to Minneapolis, where he'd looked up an old buddy from their Nigerian days, and one thing had led to another . . . In a minute or so, there'd be shooting, with civilians in the way—Americans, bystanders who had no part in this, no fault. Nor did he have anything against police.

A crock of shit, he thought, angry with himself for getting into this.

The truck had slowed. Now it stopped. Masterson, their command sergeant, threw the door lever and lifted. The door slid up and the men piled out, Luther the last of them, M-16s ready. There were cars along both sides of the road, people standing by them. Some of them looked toward the newcomers, shock beginning to register. Luther followed Masterson and the others, for one of the few times in his life reluctant. There was a vicious sputtering of automatic rifles, the boom of a shotgun. A grenade exploded . . .

The Arkansas National Guard Jicarilla was approaching fast from the northwest when its pilot saw the moving van pull up outside the equipment yard. Saw armed men emerge, saw the firefight begin. He carried a squad of riflemen in back, but knew at once he'd have no time to set them down. Instead he accelerated and aimed the helicoper, slanting downward. Saw startled faces turn upward toward him, and fired the multi-barreled 7.62 Thrashers, side-mounted on sponsons. Small-arms fire rattled on his armor, spalled his armor-glass windshield, and ended. He veered off, only then informing the troops of the situation. He would examine his results before putting them down.

He wasn't sure how ready these weekend soldiers were for a firefight, and neither were they, most of them.

Shaughnessy had jumped from the cab as soon as the truck stopped. Focused as he was on the police, he hadn't expected intervention. He heard his men fire. The police in the open were cut down almost before they knew anything was wrong. Others had returned fire. A grenade took out two of them. One of Shaughnessy's men threw the blanket charge on the fence and activated it, but before he could run, rifle fire from behind a bulldozer knocked him down.

Only then did the chopper's beating vanes register on Shaughnessy's hearing. He glanced toward the sound, saw and dove, taking cover beneath the motor block. Fire from the chopper's multibarrelled guns chewed dirt, then men, then ripped into the truck. As the aircraft veered off, the charge on the fence blew.

The gunfire had stopped. Shaughnessy crawled from beneath the cab, then became aware of someone who'd come around the rear of the truck. Turning, he recognized the face.

"Goddamn you, Koskela!" he shouted, and gestured with his pistol. "You're supposed to . . ."

He didn't even have time to be surprised; Luther fired half a magazine into him. Shaughnessy's return shot was purely reflex, the spasm of a dead man. It took Luther through the forehead. Had there been an actual hell, they'd have arrived in a dead heat.

Florence Metzger sat in the Oval Office with Heinie Brock, Willem Enrico Groenveldt, and Andrea Jackson. They were sharing home-made Mexican pizza from the White House kitchen, and watching CNN. The hour and minute had arrived; they were waiting to hear about the geophysical manifestation.

Again it was Michael Sandow who reported. "This just in. The giant meteor has impacted in the Pacific Ocean thirty-four miles east of Siberia's Kamchatka Peninsula, in about four thousand feet of water. It has sent a pillar of steam and water some twenty miles in diameter more than four miles into the sky, and is still climbing. That is twenty-plus *miles* in diameter. Hundreds of cubic miles—that's *cubic miles*—of water have been displaced. We'll bring you more as we get it."

"My God," Heinie breathed. "My God!" Intellectually, he'd realized the enormity of what was going to happen, but only now was it real to him.

The President's phone warbled. For a moment she ignored it, then took it on her handset, for privacy. "Put him through," she said. Then, "David, what can I do for you?" She listened. "I'll be delighted to. I'd sound more enthusiastic, but the rogue asteroid just hit in the North Pacific. It's not just a warning any longer . . .

"You hadn't heard? The warning was on radio and TV an hour ago. Turn your set on, to CNN. And David, the answer is 'yes.' If you're willing to be married to the President of the United States in times like these, I'll be glad to have your shoulder to cry on now and then. When I have time. And let's not put it off. Given the world as it is . . .

"Wednesday? To tell you the truth, I don't know what the legal requirements are in the District. I'd have to check on . . . You already did. I should have known . . . What about right here in the Oval Office? The White House chaplain can take care of it . . . How about just you and me and a few close friends? A dozen or so: half yours and half mine . . . Look, I'll call you back. I've got a major league emergency."

Every eye in the room was on her when she hung up. Mentally she shook herself. "Heinie," she said, "call FEMA and get me in touch with Colonel Cosetta. I want to know the major features of their evacuation plans as soon as she can fax them, complete with time tables. I'm no geophysicist, but there's going to be a tidal wave like nothing ever seen by human eyes."

68
Wrap-Up

A TEAM FROM THE SHERIFF'S department arrived at the equipment yard just before the ambulances from the county hospital. Two highway patrolmen and six terrorists were dead. Four patrolmen and seven terrorists were wounded, all seriously or critically except the driver of the truck. The bystanders had hit the ditches at the first sign of armed intruders; only one had been killed and one wounded. Two apparently unwounded gunmen had fled across a field. The healers helped the wounded—police, bystanders, and gunmen. (Later, identification of Shaughnessy's and Masterson's corpses would give a new starting place and direction to the investigation.) The unwounded bystanders who hadn't already left were held as material witnesses.

No tour people had been hurt. They were, however,

emotionally drained. The only one of the tour group whose aura was still visible to Lee was Lor Lu, and even his was not as large or strong as it had been.

Sergeant Lavender had been in the bus when he'd first heard the chopper, and had just gotten out when the shooting started. By the time he'd run around the end of the machine shed, pistol in hand, most of it was over. Now he sat in a patrol car, its police radio on.

Another Highway Patrol car pulled in. Lavender was told by radio to work with a team from the Arkansas Bureau of Investigation, who were on their way by helicopter. The newly arrived Sergeant Hood would take charge of the Millennium people.

While they waited for the ABI, Lavender briefed Hood on the Millennium group and their situation, as he saw it. Lor Lu sat in. Shortly after the ABI arrived, the acting governor called via Highway Patrol radio, asking for whoever was in charge.

"This is Sergeant Elrod Hood. . . . Yes, sir, I just took command from Sergeant Lavender. He's been with these Millennium people since they were taken into custody, but he's working with the ABI folks now. The Millennium folks would like to leave, head back home to Colorado. . . . No, sir, they don't appear to. According to Sergeant Lavender, didn't any of them actually see the firefight. They were in their bus, watching the news on television, about the meteor . . . No, sir. The bus was parked behind a big old Butler shed . . . That's a big metal machine shed, sir. All the shooting was on the other side of it . . . Yes, sir. I'll send for him right now."

A week earlier, Sergeant Hood had been hostile

toward Millennium, and the healings hadn't conspicuously changed that. They had, however, undermined it at a subliminal level. What had made the crucial difference was what he'd seen and heard on TV at the substation: the guru's enumeration of the governor's felonies, Marius Cook's deadly psychotic break, and finally the asteroid. Now he sent a patrolman to bring the ABI lieutenant over.

The governor spoke briefly with the lieutenant, then asked for Hood again. "Sergeant," he said, "is Mr. Lu with you?"

"Yes, sir."

"Good. Mr. Lu, as soon as the medical examiner releases it, the State will turn Mr. Aran's remains over to whomever you designate.

"Meanwhile I'm going to let you folks go, with your own driver. Sergeant Hood and one of his officers will ride with you, and two patrol cars will escort you. The only direction I want you to go is west on I-40. Stop and fuel up at the next truck stop. The sergeant will know where it is. You'll stay there till National Guard helicopters meet you. They'll escort you on west, on the interstate.

"Now I-40 passes through North Little Rock. Do not stop there. Drive right on through. This city has gone totally bonkers. We've got riots, shooting, arson fires . . . Just now it's the insanity capital of the known universe, and it's not a whole lot better in any other large town in the state. I suppose because Arkansas is where Mr. Aran got shot. Anyway, I want you to keep on rolling till you hit Oklahoma. I'll see if I can't arrange with Governor Eagle to provide you with another escort at the state line.

"Sergeant, you-all will need to stop and eat. I'll leave it to your discretion where. When you decide, phone the nearest substation. They'll provide you with extra cover while you're stopped. I sure as hell—pardon my French, Mr. Lu—I don't want these folks to go through any more trauma."

Drained though they were, the Millennium people did not nap. As they rode, they watched CNN. Michael Sandow had several geophysicists on a conference call, talking about actual and probable results of the asteroid impact.

A record tsunami, well beyond anything in recorded history, was forecast for the entire Pacific and associated waters. Evacuation of coastal areas had already begun, an evacuation far larger than any in history. Seismographs worldwide had gone off-scale from the impact. Earthquakes had been triggered around the Pacific Rim and elsewhere. Most of the volcanoes on Kamchatka and the Aleutians were erupting. Hokkaido had been shaken by destructive quakes, and the volcanoes in the central part of the island were in active, though not explosive, eruption.

Sandow replayed the Dove predictions, and asked the experts whether it was reasonable to draw conclusions from them. One answered that he was qualified to discuss only the geophysical aspects. He said, "Considering the impossibility of predicting the impact location, a twelve-hour warning would have been of little more use than the one-hour warning."

Another said that the only rational conclusion was that Ngunda Aran had been connected with a better informed source than anyone else on Earth.

And that the odds of the prediction having been fulfilled by chance were small beyond reckoning.

A third said, "Whether or not the two events are parallel manifestations of an intelligent deity, billions of people on Earth will believe they are. Which may be the only good to come out of this."

A police cruiser had taken Steven Buckels and his father back to Steven's car. Steven was anxious to get home to Dorothy and the children. Meanwhile he'd sent them a message via the Southeast Law Enforcement Network.

Lee had sat down beside Jenny, whom she thought might want someone to talk to. But Jenny seemed composed, even tranquil. She'd been reconciled with her father, and felt very good about it. And Dove had completed his mission on Earth as intended. "Now," Jenny added, "we have to follow through without his physical presence. Or Ngunda's. But I don't expect major difficulties, do you?"

Lee shook her head. "I'm really—too new a Milli to have much of an opinion yet."

Jenny laughed. "Too new a what?"

"A—Milli. Actually I'm not sure I like the term. It just popped out. It doesn't reflect what we are or what we do, and even Lor Lu probably isn't that irreverent."

Jenny laughed again. "I wouldn't bet on it," she said. Then added, "So far as I know, we've never had a nickname, which is surprising now that I think of it. Maybe Lor Lu can ask for candidates." She grinned. "'Millis' could head the list."

They talked briefly about the Millennium Procedures.

It seemed to Lee she needed to do them. But soon Jenny began to sag, and Lee went to her own seat.

While the bus refueled, its personnel received a large assorted take-out order from the truck-stop restaurant. Lee had set it up. Then they rolled westward again toward Little Rock. Meanwhile, Lor Lu had been busy at his laptop, and on the Web and the phone. After a bit he called the governor's office and got authorization to transfer the tour crew to a chartered plane at Fort Smith.

Most of the crew napped, but Lee wasn't sleepy yet. She sat alone, at times paying attention to the television, and at times immersed in thought. It was dusk when they passed through North Little Rock. The air was rank with smoke, and they could see flames, but the fires were isolated. As they continued north and west, Lor Lu seemed unoccupied, so she went to him.

"May I sit by you?" she asked.

"Of course." Smiling, he moved his laptop from the empty seat beside him, and gestured. "I'd hoped you would."

She sat. "What do we do now? Will things continue to be dangerous for us?"

"Not particularly. And things will settle down. Meanwhile, a ranger platoon is being flown to the Ranch to stay temporarily in the visitors' lodge—under the Anti-Terrorism Act. In a day or two . . . we'll see. Many older vectors have been erased by events, while many new ones are not yet adequately defined. Meanwhile, we have another location prepared—more remote than the Ranch, but less convenient. I doubt we'll need it."

"What about the court summons?"

He laughed. "We have put a series of obstacles in the way of your ex-husband's legal team, repeatedly escalating the level of influence we've used. We were prepared to continue until either Mark or his father decided to drop out. After today's events, however, Judge Falcaro will throw the case out of court." He grinned at Lee, and patted his laptop. "That is one of the things I checked on this afternoon, after our equipment was returned. As of today, Millennium no longer qualifies as a cult."

Above their heads, a voice from the television caught their attention, and they moved back in the bus to see. It was still set on CNN. Reconnaissance planes, flying beneath the clouds, had reached the vicinity of the meteor impact, and were sending back pictures. By the clock it was still day there, but the scene was darkened by a great pall of ash and smoke. The Kamchatka Peninsula is a 700-mile-long range of volcanoes, and to north and south, as far as the cameras could show, its slopes were lit by lava flows and forest fires. While from above, satellite cubeage showed dense clouds of mixed ash, smoke, and water droplets, glowing from beneath with ruddy volcanic light, and pulsing with internal lightnings.

Again CNN had called on experts, this time climatologists, who agreed unequivocally that a season of unprecedentedly bad weather would result. There would be weeks of rains over much of the world, causing extreme flooding and mud slides. Severe crop losses were assured. One voiced concern that methane clathrates might be released from the ocean floor. "If that happens," she said, "the resulting greenhouse warming is likely to prove much more drastic than anything so far predicted. But probably not until after a period of cold, resulting from a major increase in albedo."

"Explain albedo for our listeners."

"Earth's albedo is the reflection of the sun's rays back into space. In this case from the layer of volcanic ash in the stratosphere, and from clouds from the trillions of tons of water converted to steam by the impact—clouds that will spread worldwide."

It was dark in Arkansas when the TV announced that the sound wave from the asteroid impact had reached Seattle, 3,500 miles from point zero. Reached there like thunder, 4 hours and 49 minutes after the asteroid impact.

The media were calling it "the Fist of God" now.

Lor Lu laughed ruefully. "One of our jobs will be to reestablish that the Tao is love," he said to Lee. "That the asteroid was not a punishment but a sign." He said it loudly enough for all to hear.

"Not a punishment?" Lee asked. "It wasn't?"

"The asteroid would have arrived even if Ngunda hadn't. Not 'directed' here by the Tao, but simply arriving as part of it. An expression of that part of the Tao which we term the universe, the physical plane. The rest of the scenario was timed to its arrival."

The entire tour group was paying attention now.

Lee frowned. *Scenario. The rest was timed. Then*— "So it was destiny," she said aloud. "It was all preordained. Governor Cook—all of it."

Lor Lu shook his head. "There is no 'destiny,' in the usual sense. There are causes and effects, and of course, chaos dynamics apply. Looked at a bit differently, there are events, including human choices, from which grow sprays of potential event vectors, some much more likely than others.

"It was an ability to perceive and evaluate such vectors that permitted the human being, Ngunda Aran, to detect and predict, and thus do much of what he did—with my collaboration; we were an effective team. But the Infinite Soul's ability to perceive and evaluate vectors is infinite. Had Marius Cook not chosen to play the role of messiah assassin, someone else would have. And we would have been there instead. There were various suitable candidates.

"The asteroid, now . . . Asteroids and comets are mechanistic; they do not have choice as we perceive it. Thus, given adequate information, they are far easier to predict. But they are not absolutely predictable. The physical plane has laws of operation, one of which is 'uncertainty,' which goes well beyond what is known by statisticians and quantum and chaos physicists.

"So even this afternoon, it wasn't known where, after its long trip, the asteroid would impact. It could have struck anywhere in the Pacific basin north of the tropics, from eastern Asia to western North America.

"Meanwhile the human species, along with all of life, the universe, the Tao, continues to evolve."

Lee sat quietly, staring out a window at the lights of an approaching town. "I think I need to sleep on it," she said.

"Good idea. Dreams knit up not only 'the raveled sleeve of care,' to quote the Bard, but sometimes the diverse threads of understanding."

She reclined her seat and closed her eyes. *The diverse threads of understanding!* Vague memories of dreams moved in softly, dreams she'd seldom remembered for longer than seconds. Then she slept . . .

. . . To awaken groggy and disoriented, when they parked at the Fort Smith airport. Walking to the chartered turboprop, she sorted the dregs of dreams from the reality around her. It was across the aisle from her that Lor Lu chose to sit, and after she tilted her seat back, she spoke quietly to him.

"What are you smiling about?" she murmured.

He countered just as quietly: "You tell me."

"You're smiling because Dove's not dead."

"Not dead? We watched his death on television together."

"He's not dead. He simply vacated his body. I can feel him hanging around."

Lor Lu's smile broadened to a grin. "Really?"

"You're teasing me. You've known it all along. And he's not somewhere 'up there.' He's right here. Heaven . . ." She paused. Not heaven; the word had too much baggage attached. "Wherever he is, it's not 'up there'; it's all around us."

She paused again, then continued thoughtfully. "You know, your old organization chart wasn't very good, but it functioned. My project was useful but not essential, and there are other consultants who could have helped you. Why me? Why fly all the way to Connecticut to recruit Ben and me?"

Lor Lu spoke as softly as she. "You have much to share. You're only beginning to discover how much. And you have been a part of Ngunda Aran's people in other lifetimes, both you and Ben. Also, you had agreed in advance. Thus you were gathered."

She didn't reply, didn't even examine his answer. She simply closed her eyes, and within a minute fell asleep again.

Another dream was waiting.

Acknowledgements

Before I could begin to write this novel, I had to decide on what Ngunda's teachings would be. It was not a serious problem. The teachings in Chelsea Quinn Yarbro's four "Michael books" are the most interesting, coherent, and rereadable I've run into.

I've also been influenced by that remarkable compilation of inspiration, dogma, folklore, history and poetry known as *The Holy Bible*, by volumes of commentary on it, and by decades of absorption via cultural osmosis. And by numerous other books read over the decades, their authors as diverse as (in alphabetical order) Jacques Barzun, Alfred Korzybski, Jerry Simmons, Huston Smith, Jan Christiaan Smuts, D.T. Suzuki, Paramhansa Yogananda, and Gary Zukav. If my memory was better, the list would be longer.

I owe thanks to several author friends for their critiques of my first draft: novelists **Mary Jane Engh,**

Jim Glass, and Jim Burk, and to the late Dr. Jerry Simmons, sociologist and author. The first two in particular really beat me up, and properly so. Sue Jones of Auntie's Bookstore in Spokane read and commented on an early draft from the point of view of an informed and dedicated Protestant Christian. Thanks are also due a Catholic religious historian and a Jesuit brother for their time, tolerance, and comments. (I was assured there'll never be an Irish pope, but I wrote one in anyway, for my Irish-born grandmother. Fifty years ago, who'd have predicted a Polish pope?) And to novelist Patty Briggs, for her extensive comments on a later draft. Kathy Healy, of the Spokane Word Weavers, gave her relentless critical attention to details in two drafts.

Prior to writing this, I'd had no personal contact with Crow Indians, but I'd worked with Indians of other tribes in logging camps, the merchant marine, and the Forest Service. And I had read anthropologist Rodney Frey's enlightening *The World of the Crow Indians* (1987, University of Oklahoma Press). By telephone, I talked about the Native American experience with Lewis Walks-Over-Ice, of Little Bighorn Community College on the Crow Reservation. Later, Lewis read and commented on a preliminary draft of the chapter set on the reservation. Still later, Principal John Small (half Crow, half Cheyenne, ancient antagonists) showed me through the Crow Reservation's Lodge Grass High School, including its fine basketball facility. Another Native American, personal friend Cindy SiJohn, read and commented on part of the manuscript.

❖   ❖   ❖

The Millennium therapies, which play a role in this novel, were inspired by **Dr. Frank "Sarge" Gerbode, M.D.,** and his system of Traumatic Incident Reduction that has proven so helpful to victims of post-traumatic stress disorders—notably rape victims, and combat veterans of the war in southeast Asia.